Abra Cadaver

JAMES TUCKER

A SIGNET BOOK

SIGNET
Published by the Penguin Group
Penguin Putnam Inc., 375 Hudson Street,
New York, New York 10014, U.S.A.
Penguin Books Ltd, 27 Wrights Lane,
London W8 5TZ, England
Penguin Books Australia Ltd, Ringwood,
Victoria, Australia
Penguin Books Canada Ltd, 10 Alcorn Avenue,
Toronto, Ontario, Canada M4V 3B2
Penguin Books (N.Z.) Ltd, 182–190 Wairau Road,
Auckland 10, New Zealand

Penguin Books Ltd, Registered Offices:
Harmondsworth, Middlesex, England

First published by Signet, an imprint of Dutton NAL,
a member of Penguin Putnam Inc.

ISBN 0-7394-0134-3

 REGISTERED TRADEMARK—MARCA REGISTRADA

Printed in the United States of America

PUBLISHER'S NOTE
This is a work of fiction. Names, characters, places, and incidents either are
the product of the author's imagination or are used fictitiously, and any resem-
blance to actual persons, living or dead, events, or locales is entirely
coincidental.

"Don't let yourself think of him as a living, breathing person."

Tory breathed loudly and took several small steps, edging closer until she could see into the body. The air was thick with that peculiar odor and the lights seemed to get much brighter. She was mostly numb and had no idea that Julian had moved to catch her if she fainted. What struck her first, and what she would remember most from the day was the shock of not witnessing any of the unknown red-haired man's agony. No blood. And his frozen expression belied the excruciating pain she had expected to see. It didn't look real. A rigid figure no more lifelike than a latex Halloween mask. It was almost possible to forget that he had once been alive.

"This one's got me baffled," Julian said.

"Why?" Tory asked.

"I know 'what' happened to this man. Anyone can tell you that, and in most cases that's enough to answer all the questions you DAs have. But I can't make any sense of it. There's something missing . . . this body's been embalmed."

"How the hell did that happen?" she wanted to know.

"That's the bugaboo. Bodies don't come out of the river embalmed. . . ."

For Peter, Brad, and Scott

ACKNOWLEDGMENTS

There are many I must thank. Mark Baseman and Bill Steiner led me through a series of legal queries. Steve Strelec helped me with the drugs used during anesthesia. When I needed to understand how the telephone-paging system works in a hospital, the real-life Rayma proved knowledgeable. And the guys at the Allegheny River Arsenal taught me everything I know about handguns.

Jeanne Baseman was the catalyst, while my parents offered never-ending encouragement. Jim McKennan always made himself available for a thoughtful opinion. And Eben Weiss was never too busy to listen.

I am very grateful to my editor, Joe Pittman, who made the book better.

Over the last year I have come to appreciate how important an agent is. Without Jake Elwell, of the Wieser and Wieser agency, this never would have happened.

Finally, I could not have done this without a wonderful and talented family. Peter, who would come up with the perfect name whenever I needed one. Brad, my complicated thinker, was always willing to help me talk through a confusing scene. And Scott, the intrepid optimist, who said to me when I worried that the book would never get published, "Dad, you've got to think positive."

Special thanks, without a doubt, goes to my wife, Kim. She listened to a thousand ideas, left me alone when I needed to think, corrected every sloppy sentence I wrote, and proved to be my toughest critic. When she said it was good, I knew I was done.

Prologue

Whenever Erno and Satch dug a grave the routine was the same.

First Erno drove the panel truck past Pittsburgh International, out on the narrow roads, winding around a farm or two, finally turning onto a dirt road, a path really, and into the woods.

By 10 A.M. Erno could tell it was going to be sticky hot, and turned up the air-conditioning in the panel truck. He dressed the way he thought he was supposed to dress: thin leather jacket, white-on-white shirt, fly-away collar, suit pants too tight in the thighs, thin socks with a design down the sides, and slip-on half-boots with inch-and-a-half heels, a zipper on the side.

Erno had an unctuous presence; he worked on his body language until it oozed intimidation. He was a big man with a barrel chest who could walk into a room—any room—snap his right arm to full extension to straighten his sleeve, and everyone immediately knew he was there. At parties, back when he used to be invited to parties, he was always afforded a wide swath of carpet by the men in the room, while the women secretly met in the bathroom to gossip and gasp at the rumors.

You *knew* when Erno was looking at you. If someone whispered, "He killed a guy with a knife," you'd nod knowingly, never dreaming of questioning it. There was no way you'd want to take the chance that someone might repeat the story with your name attached to it.

His last legitimate pursuit was football in high school. At two hundred twenty pounds he was a mean defensive end and had seven tackles his senior year where he ripped his opponent's helmet clean off his head. Ten years later he considered himself more refined, and after shaking hands with him it could take several washngs to dissipate the linger of his sweet cologne. His hair was long and greased; a tangled mess of curls always sat on his collar in back like a bird's nest perched on a gutter.

With great panache Erno was the quintessential thug.

Satch Pantuzzi, Erno's cousin, never questioned whether Erno was in charge. As hard as it was to imagine, Satch did not have his cousin's people skills. The only reason Satch got into the business was Mrs. Pantuzzi—Erno's mother—made her son vouch for his cousin.

Satch dressed like Erno, but his clothes hung from his bony frame like a scarecrow. People back in the neighborhood used to say he was "mean ugly": pockmarked skin, black eyes set so deep in the sockets he had almost no peripheral vision, hollow cheeks, and dirty blond hair, stringy in back. It was his teeth, though, that really made people remember him. A multicolored array of dentition, in various stages of decay, that looked like he'd shoved an ear of Indian corn in his mouth sideways.

Erno used to say Satch could never get laid without money or a knife.

He was the quintessential wanna-be thug, pushing around kids and women. Yet you wouldn't mess with Satch. He was always one step behind Erno.

Suddenly the dirt path got bumpier and the shovel rattled around in back.

"Can't you shut that thing up?" Erno demanded in a thick voice.

"Ern, we're almost there."

Erno looked over at Satch all hunched forward, skinny

forearms resting on his thighs for support, his head drooping down below his shoulders so his bony shoulder blades poked out the back of his jacket like tiny wings.

"Hey. Sit up fuckin' straight. I can't stand to look at you sit like that," Erno said, irritated.

"Jesus Christ, what difference does it make how I sit?"

"You look weird, like an animal. That's it. You look like one of them birds. What do you call 'em? Vultures. Yeah, a vulture waiting to eat a dead cow or something. That's what you are. A vulture."

"Big deal."

"You know what you need? A nickname."

"Satch is my nickname."

"What's that mean? What's a 'satch' anyway?"

"I don't know. It's what my mother started to call me."

"Vulture. That should be your tag. It means something."

Satch sat up and lit a cigarette. *Vulture.* He smiled. It made him sound cool, someone to reckon with. "I'm gonna open the window. Okay?"

"We're here, forget it." Erno stopped the truck and sat for a couple of minutes, making sure they were alone. Then he got out and waited in the shade of a thick oak. "Get me the shovel. I'll start." He watched as Satch opened the back of the van and pulled out a long garden shovel. "Hey, Vulture, what do they call a Quarter-Pounder with Cheese in France?" Erno asked.

Satch looked down at the ground. He looked pitifully stupid. "What? I don't know. A Big Mac," Satch said, handing off the shovel.

"A Big Mac. A Big Mac, yeah, you can go big time with an answer like that. Didn't you rent *Pulp Fiction* like I told you?"

"I told *you,* Erno, I don't like movies."

"I know what kind of movies you like. You like those exercise videos."

"What?"

"Yeah, the kind that exercise your right hand." Erno pumped his right hand up and down. "All I know is they know how to talk in *Pulp Fiction.* Really know how to talk about things. I mean, they made a movie about those two guys. A fuckin' movie. All we got to talk about is dong jobs and coming out here.''

''What's the big deal I didn't see the movie?''

'' 'Cause I gotta hang out with you. 'Cause I gotta see you every fuckin' day. As a matter of fact, it's a big fuckin' deal, 'cause you don't know nothing. I can't talk to you. I feel like I'm alone. You don't know sports. You don't even read the paper. All you want to talk about is the neighborhood and those stupid skin mags. Why don't you go out and get the real thing. I shoulda teamed up with Einstein. At least he can talk.''

''Einstein's a retard,'' Satch said, annoyed.

''A retard who goes to the movies and can talk.''

Satch walked away and sat on the back of the truck, sulking.

Erno walked over to a grassy spot next to the oak and started digging. The first two or three digs were always easy, but then he hit a stone, and he cursed some before taking off his jacket, carefully draping it over some bushes so it wouldn't get dirty.

Erno dug another couple of minutes, then started to get sweaty.

''Hey, Vulture, quit feeling sorry for yourself. You're on.'' Erno stepped on the shovel with his full weight. It cut into the ground easily, and he left it for Satch, the handle standing straight up in the air as rigid as a fence post. ''You got a TV or what?''

''Nah, I told you it's broke,'' Satch said. He had to work the shovel back and forth before he could loosen the soil. Then he stood on the shovel with both feet, looking like a big kid on a pogo stick.

''How much you got in your pocket, Vulture?''

Satch liked the nickname more and more each time Erno said it. He smiled. ''Whatever you gave me yesterday.''

''Okay, you got what—eight, nine hundred bucks? Go buy a new one. Watch a ballgame or something.''

Erno left Sutch to his chore. There was a log nearby. Before sitting down he pulled a cell phone out of his jacket. Then he looked at his hands and smelled them. Under one of his nails was a line of dirt and he ran it back and forth over the sharp edge of a tooth to clean it. Then he punched a series of numbers into the keypad.

"Hey, operator, page Dr. Antony for me. I'll hold on," Erno said.

There was a pause. "I'm sorry, sir, we don't have a beeper listing for a Dr. Antony. Do you know what department he's in?"

Erno already knew about the fail-safe paging system hospitals employ using both beepers for the medical staff as well as an overhead loudspeaker system. He was annoyed at the routine he had to go through each time he called Dr. Antony. "I know. I know. He's new. Don't have a beeper yet. He told me you should voice page him until he gets his beeper. So do that, will ya?"

Erno waited, half-listening to a recorded message about annual physicals and heart disease.

"Yeah." A voice came on the line in a soft whisper.

"Hey, Doc, you take care of that extra stiff we sent you?"

"That wasn't part of the deal. I mean—"

"Hey. Hey! *Hey!!*" Erno said, raising his voice progressively louder. "Listen to me, asshole. I talk, you listen. You capice? Don't make me break a sweat." Erno's voice was angry. "You take care of things last night?"

There was a pause. Before Erno really got pissed off and started barking into the phone the voice came back on. "Yeah. I took care of things. What choice did I have? I mean, you would've screwed up the inventory. Somebody would've noticed. I put him—"

"Hold it! I don't wanna know. I don't really give a fuck what you did, as long as you did it. Disposal's your problem, Doc. I don't want no loose ends, that's all you got to tell me. No loose ends.''

"Yeah, well it's done.''

"Then so are we.'' Erno hit a button and ended the conversation.

"Hey, Erno, I'm hitting roots,'' Satch complained. "How far down d'we hafta go?''

"Deep. Like I told you, we don't want no hunter smelling anything.''

Satch was hacking away at the root with the end of the shovel. "Then why the hell we have to dig so close to a tree every time?''

"That's why Mr. Bevel has me running things. You'd dig in an open field wouldn't you? Think, Vulture. Think. I don't want somebody to see us digging out here. Keep going. Hack away at the root. Consider yourself lucky.''

"Yeah, right. Lucky to be out here on a hot day, sweating up the inside of my leather.''

"That hole almost had to be twice as big. Think about that. We mighta been putting two in the ground. Quit bitching and keep digging.''

Erno punched another series of numbers on the keypad. He coughed a couple of times to clear his throat. "Hey, Antony, it's me, Erno. How you doing?'' Erno asked, taking on the obsequious tone of a rank-and-file trying to get in good with management. (Pause) "Jus' wanted to let you know everything went real smooth last night. No problems or anything. Me'n Satch'll be hanging out if you need us.'' (Pause) "Heay, how 'bout them Bucs last night?'' (Pause) "Okay, I'll let you go—hey, maybe sometime we take in a ballgame or something together.'' (Pause) "Okay, yeah I know, you gotta go. Bye.''

Erno snapped the phone shut.

"Vulture, I'm going places. Up, mostly. And if you wanna come along, go see that movie.'' Erno studied Satch leaning on the shovel. "Keep digging.''

One

It was early evening when Jack Merlin's yellow beeper went off. He was on his way out of the hospital, too tired to talk to another resident, or the ER, or a nursing station. But he pushed the little black button anyway and heard a female voice say, "Hey, Merlin, if you're not busy we could use a magic trick for your patient Brad. He's got surgery . . ." Merlin wasn't surprised. He often got consults from the various pediatric units for a magic trick to help calm a nervous child.

As he walked up the stairs Merlin fingered a couple of spounge balls in his pocket. Although he was in the fifth year of a surgical residency at Pittsburgh University Medical Center, magic was Merlin's passion. Actually, he adored surgery but insisted on the illusion that he was a magician first, and he was a terrific magician for some of the same reasons he was becoming a fine surgeon: great hands and great timing.

Almost every surgical resident wore the same uniform, and Merlin was no exception: standard issue white pants, a blue short-sleeved scrub shirt, and a short white jacket with a name tag. The omnipresent yellow resident's beeper was clipped to the waist of his pants. Merlin's leash was, like all residents', short.

In a couple of minutes Merlin found fourteen-year-old Brad sitting in a wheelchair near the nursing station, staring out a window.

"B-Man. What's up?" Merlin greeted his patient with a smile.

Brad looked like he wanted to cry. "Oh, nothing."

Merlin pulled out a deck of cards. "All right, Brad," Merlin said, executing a perfect Faro shuffle, then a series of one-handed cuts. "Watch this." Merlin expertly fanned the deck. "Pick a card, any card," Merlin said in a hokey voice out of the side of his mouth.

Brad sniffed to clear his nose and selected a card.

"All right, look at it . . . don't show it to me . . . and put it back in the deck." As Brad slid the card back in the deck Merlin said, "Hey, you know tomorrow's no big deal."

Brad frowned. "Not for you," he said in a low voice, and looked up at Merlin with wet eyes.

"You want to talk about it?" Merlin asked softly, shuffling the cards.

Before Brad could answer Martin Wheeler, a senior resident who always seemed to be campaigning for the job of chief resident, thrust himself between Merlin and young Brad. He ostentatiously avoided the usual surgical garb, opting instead for dress pants and a long white coat. "Merlin, where the hell's your buddy?"

Merlin kept shuffling, winked at Brad, and said to Wheeler, "Beat it kid, you're bothering me," in a good knock-off of W. C. Fields.

"I'm in no mood to fool around," Wheeler said with authority, putting his hand on Merlin's shoulder to get his attention.

This was a magical opportunity that Merlin couldn't resist. The planned routine was abandoned, and Martin Wheeler was to become the unwitting stooge. Merlin smoothly palmed one card from the deck and handed the other fifty-one to Brad. "See if you can find your card."

Then the real magic began. As he turned to face the senior resident, Merlin asked Wheeler if he had met Brad. While Wheeler offered the teenager the briefest of nods,

Merlin's left hand slipped into Wheeler's back pocket—unnoticed—gently removing his leather wallet.

Wheeler, evidently too busy to waste time with mundane pleasantries, turned back toward Merlin and said, sarcastically, "Now can we conduct some hospital business?"

"Just a second," Merlin answered. Innocently Merlin looked at Brad thumbing his way through the deck and said, "Oh that's it, isn't it?" and leaned in to fake a closer look.

Merlin knew there would be an instant when Wheeler's eyes reflexively followed his, and that's when Merlin had a second or two to open the wallet and sneak the seven of hearts among the credit cards. "Which buddy are you talking about, Wheeler?" Merlin asked, replacing the wallet in Wheeler's pants with a practiced touch that aroused no suspicion.

"Your buddy Kevin didn't show up today."

"What?" Merlin questioned, sounding surprised.

"Lover boy skipped out today. Didn't have the common courtesy to call in."

"Lemme call the apartment."

"Forget it. I tried. Jan doesn't even know where he is."

"You'll jump on any excuse to call Jan."

Wheeler frowned; his cheeks turned red. "No, Merlin. It's a good excuse to tell you there's a gallbladder admitted to Four South. Been sitting there all afternoon."

"Shit, where could he be? That's not like him."

"It's exactly like him—or you, for that matter."

Merlin hesitated and decided to avoid a fight. "Look Wheeler, I better head home, see if he's okay."

"Forget it. Go work her up."

"Who?" Merli asked.

"The *gallbladder,* goddamnit."

"Why me?"

"Two reasons. One: You and your roommate are interchangeable, so if he's not here to do the work you might

as well be. And two: I'm running the service you're on.
Simple, isn't it?''

"What's the patient's name?"

"What difference does it make? It's just a gallbladder."

By now Brad had finished his search. "The card's not
here. It was the seven of hearths. Is that the whole trick?"

"I'm gonna find Kevin." Merlin scooped up the cards,
did a quick cut of the deck, and handed them back to Brad.

Before Wheeler let Merlin walk away he demanded,
"When you don't find him at your apartment, get back
here and work the gallbladder up."

"Hey, Dr. Merlin, what about my card?" Brad asked.
He sounded disappointed.

"Check the cards one more time, Brad. Maybe I'll stop
by and teach you the trick a little later, then we can talk
about tomorrow."

Brad found a credit card buried halfway in the deck
before Merlin was very far away. "Hey this isn't the seven
of hearts. It's a credit card. Wait a second, it says—"
There was a pause. "Martin Wheeler."

"What!" Wheeler exclaimed. "Give me that," he said,
grabbing the card and snatching his wallet from his back
pocket. "Goddamn, Merlin." He opened the wallet,
jammed his gold American Express back in, and spotted
the card. "Here's your silly seven of hearts," he said,
flipping the card onto Brad's lap.

"Cool. Thanks, Dr. Merlin."

By now Merlin was waving over his shoulder as he
disappeared into the stairwell.

Two

Julian Plesser, medical examiner of Allegheny County, had been called before midnight about an unidentified man with red hair found in the Allegheny River, just north of Oakmont. He only needed to ask three or four questions before he said, "That'll keep. I'll be in around eight," and hung up the phone. But his curiosity had gotten the better of him, as it usually did, and he'd arrived before seven. In less than an hour Julian, who would turn fifty this year, had rolled him over, inspected the entire body, and removed a plastic six-pack holder from the left ear as well as some river debris from the mouth. Next he'd made the standard Y-incision and widely opened the thorax and abdomen of the still unknown red-haired man, exposing all the colorful organs of the body.

That's when the smell hit him. It was unmistakable. Any first-year medical student could identify it. Julian lowered his head, stuck his nose right into the opened belly, and inhaled deeply, pulling the familiar fragrance in, closing his eyes like a sommelier back to work after a bad cold. *This is gonna be good.* He slowed down and worked with more deliberation than usual.

Karen, his secretary with big hair and short skirts, was buzzed on the intercom and given a series of specific orders that would keep her on the phone for the next hour. Then Julian carefully inspected the neck for almost a minute with a magnifying glass and finally said, "Aha!" Julian smiled.

The medical examiner's autopsy room was located on the second floor of a three-story brick building in downtown Pittsburgh. It was, as every important building seemed to be, less than a ten-minute walk from the Point, where the Allegheny and Monongahela Rivers join and form the Ohio. Pittsburgh was a big enough city that the medical examiner had two assistant medical examiners assigned to him, both part-timers who worked at the University as staff pathologists. But Julian was the franchise player.

He was working alone in the autopsy room, as usual, standing at the middle of three stainless steel tables. Each was set at a subtle tilt, like pinball machines, so that a continuous trickle of water could be directed to run down from the cadaver's head toward its feet, washing away blood or urine or whatever might spill during an autopsy. On that rare occasion when all three tables were in simultaneous use, Julian would be positioned to perform his own autopsy as well as supervise those on the other two tables.

The walls were gray cinder block, painted so many times over the years the mortar joints could barely be seen. A cluttered desk, a scattering of metal bar stools, a small refrigerator, and two empty metal bookcases completed the furnishings. There were no windows, potted plants, or decorations, only a single poster recently added to the back wall. A *Forrest Gump* poster had been slightly modified with black Magic Marker to read "Death is like a box of chocolates." Julian looked at it for inspiration, and murmured, "You said it, Forrest. You never know what you're gonna get."

A microphone hung above each table—operated by a foot pedal—and allowed the pathologist free use of both hands while he droned on incessantly about exit wounds, volumes of bodily fluids, and times of death. Julian wore a white butcher's apron over his white lab coat. A ubiquitous plastic pocket protector, the ultimate nerd boutonniere, stuffed tight with pens and pencils, bulged from his chest. Light blue, size seven-and-one-half latex gloves were donned before touching anything near the autopsy table, and the armpits of his lab coat were discolored with large yellow stains.

Julian started with the abdomen. He always started there for some reason, and after removing the spleen from the upper left side with one deft slice of his scalpel, Julian plopped it on a hanging butcher's scale and waited for a second as the spring-driven needle swayed back and forth before stopping. "The spleen weighs, uh. . . ." Julian squinted, leaned toward the scale, and tipped his head back slightly to view the numbers through his half-glasses. ". . . 675 grams. The surface is intact and has a normal homogeneous reddish-purple appearance."

Retrieving the spleen from the scale, Julian brought it close to his nose and once again inhaled slowly, then scrunched up his face and thought for a moment. The smell. At home and out of place. *What the hell is going on?* He looked at his poster. *I know, I know, I can't see the forest through the trees.* Then he smelled it once again before placing it on the stainless steel autopsy table behind him. Soon there would be a cluster of eviscerated organs, each one a different shape and color, all glistening brightly from the intense overhead lighting.

He went back into the abdomen and gently ran the length of small intestines with his index finger, exploring the last segment of the coiled-up bowel, where it emptied into the large intestines at the cecum. "The absence of the appendix is noted."

Next Julian turned his attention to the liver and examined it as it existed, *in situ,* within the abdominal cavity. Gently caressing the surface Julian commented, "The liver is small and bears the gross stigmata of alcoholic-induced cirrhosis. The liver weighs. . . ." Again Julian stopped talking as he quickly removed the liver from the right side of the abdomen and placed it on the hanging scale. Waiting for the needle to stop moving Julian absently crossed his arms over his chest and tucked his gloved hands into his armpits and enjoyed a brief rest. "The liver weighs one thousand, two hundred, twenty-five—no, scratch that Karen—one-two-*three*-five grams. Cross-sections will be obtained for microscopic examination." A scalpel, fitted with a new number-12 blade, quickly took a chunk of liver, which was slipped into a small glass bottle filled partway with clear preservative.

Just as the "ankle bone is connected to the leg bone," so is a cirrhotic liver linked to several other parts of the body. The liver had become the center of a complicated maze. Julian would now branch out, proceeding in anatomically logical directions, following the disease process.

Knowing that cirrhosis of the liver blocks blood flow through it like a dam to a river, Julian worked his way upstream. The esophageal veins, at times dangerously swollen in this situation, needed to be examined next. Julian jumped his attention to the thorax.

The trachea and main bronchi are the most superficial vital structures in the chest and were removed first. Julian examined them, first with his nose, cocking his head to one side. Then, after placing the Y-shaped structure on the stainless-steel table, he stepped over to the cluttered gray metal desk. As he picked up a Styrofoam cup of coffee and took a quick swig, he pressed the intercom button. "Karen, you out there?" He waited, sipped some more coffee and seemed to relax. A small radio on his desk played one of Bach's Brandenburg Concertos.

"Yes, sir," Karen answered crisply. Karen was new and insisted on formality.

"Karen, I told you, just call me Julian."

"Yes, sir, I mean—"

Julian rolled his eyes. "Got any response from the police?"

"I talked with three departments. Just hung up with the last one. No funeral home has contacted them."

"Hmmm. How far up the river'd you go?"

"Up to Kittanning, like you said. But if you want, I could call—"

"No, no. That's far enough. What about the Medical School?"

"No one there. I left a message on three different voice mail . . . uh . . ." She groped for a word. ". . . *Systems* to fax us something. I'll bring it in as soon as I get it."

"Thanks, Karen."

"Oh, Dr. Plesser . . ."

"What's up?"

"I got a call from the DA's office. District Attorney." There was a rustling of papers in the background. "Mark Peters called. He's on his way."

Julian rolled his eyes again, took another quick swig of coffee, and, without answering Karen, turned back to the cadaver.

"Dr. Plesser. Hello. Did you hear me? Dr. Plesser?"

Refusing to look away from the body, Julian spoke in a carefully modulated voice. "I'm sorry Karen, I did hear you. I think I might have had a small seizure or a stroke."

"Really?" Karen said.

"Ooooh. Do I have my work cut out for me!" Julian said softly.

"What? I couldn't hear you, Dr. Plesser." Karen's voice was suddenly much louder, as if her lips were only inches from her intercom.

"Karen, just send the *assistant* district attorney in when he arrives."

Julian returned to the red-haired man, his eyes glowing with anticipation. There were so many interesting possibilities he momentarily forgot about the esophagus and became fascinated with the lungs, which were visible on both sides of the thorax, ugly grayish-black sponges tucked neatly into the chest.

The easiest way to determine if a body had drowned or was dumped into water after death was to examine the lungs. Breathing underwater, gasping liquid down the trachea, invariably led to wet, spongy lungs. Gentle pressure on the lower lung tissue, just above the diaphragm, revealed exactly what Julian's sensitive fingers expected. The lung tissue was firm, like stale sponge cake—not spongy, and definitely not wet. *That makes sense.* But as his fingers pushed deeper and moved the lung out of the way, he noticed a reddish gelatinous mass that at one time had been a puddle of blood. Julian's pupils widened and the steel blue of his eyes all but disappeared.

Now his brain was clicking faster than his hands could work. Julian immediately went back to the esophagus, the muscular tube responsible for taking food from the mouth to the stomach. His gloved fingertips methodically traced the length of the esophagus, touching lightly, lingering here and there, probing gently, working their way down, stopping just before reaching the stomach.

He found it.

There wasn't much to feel, what with the stiffness of the tissues, but he definitely felt something, a small slit in the wall of the esophagus, running vertically for about an inch. Julian tried to pinch the tissues in a north–south direction, hoping to pucker the esophagus and open the slit, like one of those plastic coin purses kids carry. But he was unsuccessful. Then he steadied the esophagus with his left hand while he gently worked his right index finger up through the rent in the wall of the esophagus. After several seconds of observation and digital exploration, Julian began talking, this time with hurried enthusiasm. ''I'll be damned. Uh, don't transcribe that Karen. Start over. Examination of the distal esophagus reveals a longitudinal, through-and-through laceration of the esophageal wall. The laceration runs approximately three centimeters in length and is consistent with a Mallory–Weiss tear. That's M - A - L - L - O - R - Y dash W - E - I - S - S, Karen.'' Julian smiled. The pieces of the puzzle—God's puzzle, as he sometimes called it—were fitting together.

Before Julian could return to the abdomen and open the stomach to look for blood, the door to the autopsy room burst open. Mark Peters strode in and pointed a finger toward Julian in greeting. "Julian," he said with a clubby tone he might better reserve for the men's sauna after a round of golf. Peters was one of many assistant district attorneys who, Julian thought, epitomized the belief that one tended to rise to his level of incompetence and remain there forever.

"Ahh, the walking Peters Principle," Julian replied with a chuckle.

Mark Peters, who loved being described as "up and coming," was playing in the big leagues, but he still couldn't hit the curve. Not a complete idiot, though, Peters knew he was either being kidded or insulted, but had no idea which. He was baffled, hesitated for a second, ran his options, and finally decided it safer to hope it was a little good-natured kidding and chuckled uncomfortably right along with Julian.

Peters was dressed in a beige Brooks Brothers suit with vest, light blue button-down collar, cotton shirt—"*pinpoint cotton,* I only wear *pinpoint*"—and an orange and black silk rep tie. He had a thick head of curly hair and horn-rimmed glasses.

"That the floater they pulled out of the Allegheny?" Peters asked, as if he had noticed the smell he didn't comment on it.

Julian turned to look at the unknown red-haired man's body and mumbled, just below Peters's auditory threshold, "Harvard boys, Yale men, Princeton assholes," putting a new spin on an old saying.

Peters, with great confidence, took two or three long strides right past Julian, clicked his shoes smartly on the linoleum floor, bent over the cadaver, and peered into the open chest cavity. Peters nodded his head several times and apparently liked what he saw. "Looks good, Julian.

What was it, a boating accident? You get a blood alcohol?"

Julian's jaw dropped. *Holy shit.* Watching Mark Peters's behavior was the most puzzling thing he'd seen—or smelled—all day, and he was about to comment on this peculiar show of bravado when Peters, still leaning over, engrossed with what he saw in the abdomen, said, "Oh, Jules, snap off those gloves and say 'Hi,' to Tory Welch. Just joined us outta Pitt Law. First day."

Julian looked around. The two of them were alone in the room.

"Pleased to meet you, Miss Welch. Peters try to hustle you in bed yet?"

Peters whirled around, saw Tory Welch was not in the room, and immediately marched back toward the heavy frosted glass swinging doors, rolling his eyes for effect. "I'm sorry, Jules. What can I say? Rookies. I guess we all started out—"

"Hey, Peters. Hold on. Hold on just a minute." The assistant district attorney stopped, turning back toward Julian. "You a gambling man?"

"Sure thing—whatcha got in mind?" Peters replied, as he jumped at any crumb of an opportunity to improve their often caustic relationship. He beamed and looked right at Julian, smiling broadly, feeling for a moment like he was fitting in.

Julian flashed a riverboat gambler's smile with some Cheshire cat on the side. "You're sure," Julian said, not so much a question as a statement, pulling Peters in beyond the point of no return.

"Yeah, go for it. Pens. Bucs. Whatever, I'm in."

"Okay, Peters. Five bucks says she's a looker."

"What?" Peters asked, confused, but feeling the heat rise in his cheeks.

"You heard me. Tory Whatshername. The kid you brought with you. *The rookie.* Five bucks says she makes your bishop stand up."

Peters's cheeks flushed red. "I, uh, really hadn't noticed. She's just a kid fresh outta law school." He swallowed hard. "The boss assigned me to orient her. First day." The glare from the lights seemed almost blinding, and he squinted.

"Good. Then we're on. A fin."

Peters stood in front of Julian, rubbing his cheeks, adjusting his glasses, delaying the trip through the doors to retrieve Tory Welch. Julian was quicksand and Peters had stepped right in. Wiggling would only make it worse.

Julian seized the opportunity and kept on talking, "Peters, I see it this way. You're usually real squeamish here. Hell, I usually get a kick outta turning you green, so when I see you strut in here like some peacock and practically do a swan dive into the thorax I say to myself, 'Hmmmm.'

"Then, when I find out you've got a lady friend who you *think* is right behind you when you do your Greg Louganis, I say, 'Hmmmm. Peters is showing off.'

"But the clincher, the *pièce de résistance* . . . ," Julian said, holding his hand out in front of him, thumb and fingers together, pointing up toward the ceiling, like some kind of gourmet discussing a fancy dessert, ". . . is the three-piece. And the tie. Orange and black. The calling card of the horny and shallow. Oh, Peters, you've outdone yourself. I *know* she's a looker." Julian savored a five-second pause.

Peters was starting to sweat, and his mouth had gone dry.

Julian continued, "Tell you what. Make it easy on yourself. Pay me now so I don't have to embarrass you in front of her when I collect."

"You're a clever guy, Julian," Peters chuckled amiably, hiding the hurt, and wasted no time getting out his wallet. He quickly plucked a bill and held it out. This was a conversation he wanted to end. "Look, the smallest I've got is a ten. You know I'm good for it," he said, and started to replace it back in his wallet.

Julian was still wearing his surgical gloves. He took a step forward, snatched the bill from Peters's fingers and slipped it into his lab coat pocket. "Mark, my good man," Julian said, imitating the prep-school tone Peters favored, "I'll keep the ten. Figure the extra five is hush money." Julian laughed, and Peters pushed through the doors.

Mark Peters sighed and thought briefly how well the day had begun.

He had arrived at the courthouse almost an hour before he was supposed to meet Tory. He asked the night receptionist if anything good had come in, and while he flipped through half a dozen cases, mostly misdemeanors and minor felonies, he was told about the unknown red-haired man who had been pulled out of the river. The case was a grabber, the kind of story that made the evening news. It was graphic yet simple, a perfect focal point for their day, and for a few moments he imagined himself dazzling Tory. He grabbed the file and familiarized himself with it while he waited for Tory in the lobby of the county courthouse with a premeditated insouciance.

Tory was already widely known among the mostly male bastion of the district attorney's office. Although she'd only been there for a brief orientation a week earlier, the right combination of shiny hair, shy smile, and what the let's-grab-a-beer-after-work crowd deemed a body hot enough to tent up a judge's robes like the Ringling Brothers Big Top, brought out the real Mark Peters.

The district attorney—the *real* district attorney who didn't have to leave out the word "assistant" when he gave his title, agreed to let Peters orient Tory Welch if only to get the obsequious Mark Peters out of his office.

In anticipation of spending the day with Tory, Peters had laid out his clothes the night before. *The Princeton tie, absolutely.* He'd even slapped some after-shave on his buttocks, a ridiculous ritual from his freshman year in college that he swore brought him luck with the ladies.

"Tory, Mark Peters. We talked on the phone," he said confidently as he shook her hand. "I hear we're both Columbia Law."

Tory looked sleek in a blue linen suit, the skirt cut just at the knees. A single piece of jewelry, a gold bangle with subtle lines that looked like rope, hung loosely from her left wrist. "I'm Tory, but who told you I'm Columbia Law?"

"I thought the boss mentioned something about it."

"No, he must have been mistaken. Did we meet the other day?" Tory seemed confused.

"No. The boss gave me your resume. Picture certainly didn't do you justice. Coulda sworn he said Columbia. Anyway—"

"Well, nice to meet you, Mark."

Peters pulled the several folded papers of the unknown red-haired man out of his breast pocket. "Got a good one for you, a floater pulled out of the Allegheny. I know it may be a bit much, but I thought, what the heck, jump right in."

"A floater. Is this gong to be my case?"

"Oh, no, no," Peters laughed. "This is strictly a senior-level case. I've been here almost seven years. Murders, suicides, organized crime—don't worry about 'em. Not for at least a year. This one should be nice and neat, though, no loose ends. Perfect place to start." Peters started walking to the door leading back to the street. "C'mon, we've got a full day," he said, holding the door.

"Where're we going?" Tory asked when she got outside. The air was thick, but it felt good to get out of the building.

"We're gonna head over to the ME's office. You ever meet him?"

"I don't think so."

"Real cantankerous. Julian Plesser. You won't like him. No one does. Smart sonavabitch, though. You just need to know how to deal with him."

Tory looked at her watch. "We're going there now?"

"No, let's grab a bite. Ease into things. I can go over everything for you. All the politics, everything. You a breakfast person?"

Peters seemed too pushy. "I had a muffin in the car," Tory said matter-of-factly.

"There's a good diner around the corner. Great sausage. They even have steak and eggs."

"I think I'll pass. I'm not much of a meat eater."

Peters kept on going. "They have fabulous blueberry muffins, doughnuts."

"Great," Tory said softly, looking down at a crack in the sidewalk.

He took her to a coffee shop, not a diner, for a lengthy preview of their day. Then they walked the several blocks to visit Julian Plesser, Peters working every interesting case he'd ever had into the conversation. Although he was quite uncomfortable around the medical examiner and the cadavers, this case wasn't intimidating: a nameless derelict who fell, probably drunk, into the river and drowned. Straightforward. Plesser wouldn't insist on showing him any God-knows-what slimy organs. And then, on the way back to the office, they could stop for coffee to discuss what role the DA's office would play in the case.

Now, as Peters stepped out of the autopsy room he found Troy leaning against the wall, head down. Her shoulder-length black hair had shifted forward covering much of her face, so he was looking down a short tunnel to see her nose.

"What's going on?"

"Mark, I don't know if I can handle this." Tory didn't look up. She held a balled up Kleenex in one hand, a small brown leather notebook in the other.

"Sure you can. Nothing to it. This is a nice, tidy little case. The guy was a drunk or something. It's a cinch,"

Peters said in his most soothing tone, then snapped his fingers, showing Tory just how easy it was.

"I've never seen a dead body."

"It's okay. I'll get you through it. You've got to trust me." He wanted to put his arm around her, but settled for a pat on the shoulder.

"I'll be okay. I guess I expected a tour of the office, maybe visit the courtroom. Just give me a minute, will you Mark?" It was not so much a request as a statement. Tory put her hand to her mouth and swallowed deeply.

"Take as long as you want," Peters said, his voice rising subtly in a clumsy effort to speed her up.

Tory wiped her nose with the Kleenex. Her eyes were wet, lips dry. Strands of hair hung down in front of her eyes, and she looked a little green. Tory Whatshername was a mess.

Damn! Peters took a good long look at her and wondered if he paid off his bet too quickly. *I should go back in and press the goddamn bet.* Everything was beginning to come apart. He looked at his watch, then at the doors with the frosted glass leading to the autopsy room. He put his hands in his pockets, pulled them out, then in again and out. *C'mon, goddamnit.* Peters noticed he was getting panicky—it always started in his loins as a tingling he dare not rub—and his voice took on an increasingly demanding tone. *Get control of the situation. Get her inside* before *Plesser comes out.*

"Look, Tory, Jules is the chief medical examiner—"

Tory looked at Peters. "I *know* who he is. And I know you're pissed off, but I'm doing the best I can."

"Then you should know he's also one tough cookie. I really don't think we want to keep him waiting. That's not what I'd call career building."

Tory had an edge to her voice whenever she was pushed too hard. She intensified her look, "Career building? I'm not trying to build a career right now. This is my first day. I'm trying not to get sick!"

Peters rolled his eyes in frustration. He also remembered his own weak stomach when it came to the autopsy room and did not want Julian to end up comforting Tory by recounting his maiden trip there.

Peters summoned his most imperious tone of voice and stated, "Tory, you told me you always wanted to be a district attorney. You've made it. This is one of the toughest jobs in the world, but the rewards are worth it," he said as he nodded to the doors marked "Medical Examiner" in black lettering on the bumpy glass and came to his big finish. "This stuff is a big part of it. Now, let's go in there together."

Satisfied with his rousing pep talk, Peters pushed the door open and tapped his foot several times as Tory wiped her nose and hesitantly walked through. His fate was sealed. Try as he might over the next few weeks to compliment Tory on her first day's performance, he was never to have Tory Welch, who was, despite being a mess—and just as Julian Plesser predicted—a real looker.

Three

Tory was furious with Peters, and that's what gave her the strength to walk through the doors. They were both watching, Plesser in front of her and Peters behind, as she walked several steps into the room quite timidly, like a child walking into the doctor's office to get a shot. The smell was so strong she could almost taste it. Julian stood, hands tucked in opposite armpits, directly in front of the unknown red-haired man. As he sized up the newest member of the district attorney's office, he deliberately blocked Tory's view. Mozart played softly, competing with the tinkling sound of water running through the metal drain of the autopsy table. It helped to fill the void.

That dread, sick, hide-your-eyes feeling grabbed her. There was nowhere to hide. Nowhere to be safe. Not like her grandfather's funeral when her mother's black dress with the crisp black pleats enveloped her, hiding her eyes, while her mother's hand stroked her hair softly. She wanted to pull that black shroud around her now but stood there, clutching her little brown notebook like a Bible, feeling sick. The soft whoosh of the door closing and Peters walking past her, staring at her as if he was waiting for her to throw up, reminded Tory she was on display and couldn't stand there forever. She swallowed hard and took several more measured steps toward the medical examiner. *Don't look at it. Don't look at it.* But it was an effort, almost overwhelming, to keep her eyes from wandering, and she spotted that shock of red hair.

"Dr. Plesser, I'm sorry to hold you up. I'm Tory Welch," she said in mid-swallow, and realized her voice sounded alien, the way it does on a tape recorder. Tory offered to shake hands with Julian but noticed his greasy gloves and, not knowing what to do with her hands, immediately dropped them to her side.

After what seemed like an eternity the three stood together, Tory and Peters in neatly pressed suits, Julian in his stained butcher's apron and pocket protector, eclipsing the body from Tory's view. Change the setting and the two district attorneys could have been a yuppie couple giving directions to the aproned Julian, a painter about to start on their new condo.

Julian took charge and said, "Don't worry about it, Tory, you're gonna do fine. Peters told me a lot about you. I hear you just graduated Pitt Law," Julian said.

Tory shot Peters a glance, one that said, "I didn't tell you I was Pitt Law. I know what you're all about."

Julian continued, "I hope they gave you some time off before starting. There are certain moments in your life that you remember forever. I'm afraid this is going to be one of them." Then the medical examiner, savoring the moment, turned to Peters. "Did Mark tell you about his first trip here? I'm certain you remember your first cadaver, Mark."

Peters smiled lamely. He knew it was coming.

Julian continued, "When Mark here joined me for the first time, he vomited. On me."

Tory smiled, then looked over at Peters. "I can't believe he forgot to mention it. I'm still embarrassed. I guess that's why we went into law."

"No, no, no. Don't be. If you feel faint, just sit down. And if you think you're gong to vomit, just do it on Peters." Tory and Julian shared a genuine laugh.

Tory tried to take in the room, allowing herself only an occasional glance at the body. The poster on the back wall caught her eye. "Is that your credo?"

"More than you can imagine." Julian could see Tory's shoulders relax ever so slightly.

Peters felt left out and wanted to redirect the conversation. "Julian, why don't you tell us about this case?"

"Okay. This is a puzzler. Best case I've had in a couple of years."

"C'mon Julian. You think they're all great cases," Peters said in a friendly tone, kidding his buddy right back, telling Julian to stop joshing him.

"C'mon, nothing. It's the most confusing post I've ever done." Then, looking at Tory with understanding eyes, Julian said, "It won't be as bad as you think. Try to think of what I do as solving a puzzle. Don't let yourself think of him as a living, breathing person." Julian stepped aside. The eclipse was over. "Come a little closer. Let me explain what's going on. I have a feeling you're going to do just fine."

Tory breathed loudly and took several small steps, edging closer until she could see into the body. The air was thick with that peculiar odor and the lights seemed to get much brighter. She was mostly numb and had no idea Julian had moved close enough to catch her if she fainted. What struck her first, and what she would remember most from the day, was the shock of *not* witnessing any of the unknown red-haired man's agony. No blood. And his frozen expression belied none of the excruciating pain she had expected to see. It didn't look real. A lifeless, rigid figure, looking no more lifelike than a latex Halloween mask. It was almost possible to forget he was once alive.

"You okay?"

"I think so. Looks a lot like those cellophane pictures in the *World Book Encyclopedia*."

Julian laughed. "This one's got me baffled," Julian said.

"Why?" Peters asked.

"That's what I don't know. The 'why.' I only know

the 'what.' '' Julian turned toward Tory and ignored Peters. "You know what I mean?"

Tory shook her head.

"I know 'what' happened to this man with the red hair. Anyone can tell you that, and in most cases that's enough to answer all the questions you DAs have. But I can't make any sense of it. I've got all the pieces put together but I can't solve it. The genius of pathology—what every forensic pathologist is in it for—is telling 'why' the 'what' happened in a case like this. There's something missing."

Peters sensed his presence in the room was slipping. He had to jump back into the conversation. "Sort of like 'Who's on first?' '' Peters said with the start of a smile.

"Cute, Peters. I guess it's better than you throwing up on me," Julian said sarcastically. "Anyway," he continued, "this body's been embalmed."

"What?" Peters exclaimed.

"My God. Don't you notice the smell? My eyes've been burning all morning."

"How the hell did that happen?" Peters wanted to know.

"That's the bugaboo. We don't get embalmed bodies at the morgue. Bodies don't come out of the river embalmed. What do you think happened, Mark?"

"A couple of kids found him floating in the river. Figured he drowned."

The swinging doors opened and Karen walked over to her boss and handed him a fax, which he read quickly. Then she hurried from the room without saying a word. Tory noted how careful the woman was not to look at the cadaver.

Julian folded the fax and pushed it in his pocket. "No, this wasn't a drowning. The lungs are dry. In fact, he went into the Allegheny River someplace north of Oakmont *after* he died. And with all the formaldehyde in the tissues. Here, smell this." Plesser offered his gloved hand for Tory to smell.

Tory was intrigued with Julian's vivid description of the case and leaned forward to take a couple of brief sniffs before pulling back. She nodded in agreement. "Smells like biology class."

"Exactly. That's formaldehyde. Formaldehyde is a preservative. He doesn't look like a floater—he's not all bloated up. He looks like something in a wax museum. I can't tell how long he's been dead. Could've been months. Or years. I also can't test for drugs or alcohol."

"Can't you tell anything?" Peters whined, sounding frustrated.

"You're not listening, Peters. I can tell you everything about what happened, but it won't make any sense. The more you know about him the less you understand. This guy was, oh, about sixty—"

"You can look at his wrinkled face and see that," Peters said in a ho-hum tone of voice.

Julian paused. "Be patient. Let me continue. *And* he was a chronic alcoholic, *and* he vomited so hard he bled to death."

"Wow! How can you tell all that?" Tory asked, wide eyed. As soon as the words left her mouth Tory clamped her hand over it to prevent any other stupid thoughts from popping out.

Peters caught her eye and stared at her like a child jumping into an adult conversation. "Troy, please," he said, scolding her.

"I'm sorry—that was amazing, absolutely fantastic."

"I'll take that as a compliment," Julian said as he slipped the ten-dollar bill out of his lab coat pocket and placed it, in full view of Peters, on the autopsy table. Julian tapped it several times to quiet him, reminding him who was boss.

It immediately got Peters's attention; he understood the bill's intent.

Unfortunately Tory misread Julian's message. "All right, guys. Very funny." Looking at Peters she said,

"What is this? My initiation? You two bet I'd say something stupid, right?"

There was a quiet moment. Julian knew Peters would speak first.

"Of course not." Peters was red.

"Of course not," Tory said, mimicking Peters, her inflection exaggerated perfectly. Turning to Julian, she said, "How do you like that? My mentor bet I'd make a fool of myself. Even if *you're* sophomoric, Dr. Plesser, at least you didn't bet against me. I can forgive you. You might as well pay him—you lost."

Julian held out the ten-dollar bill.

"I'm not going to accept that," Peters said.

"Let me clear the air, Tory. Maybe this is all my fault," Julian said, waving the money in front of Peters.

"No, let's drop the whole thing!" Peters said.

"I've got to apologize to you, Tory. What you said wasn't stupid, so I don't want you to think it was. I'm wrong, so I suppose I don't actually owe Peters anything," Julian said and put the ten dollars back in his pocket.

"Forget it," Tory said, and rolled her eyes.

"Wait a second," Peters said to Julian.

"Don't worry about it, Mark. I'm good for it. I'll pay off if you win. I threw in the towel too quickly. The bet's still on. In fact, now that I've met Tory, I'll double the wager if you like."

The situation was obviously delicate and Peters couldn't possibly untangle things without mucking them up. "Forget it. Tory, I'd never make a bet like that. Honestly," Peters said, holding out his hands for emphasis.

"What *would* you make a bet on, Mark?" Tory shot back.

Julian was definitely going to like Tory Welch.

With a gentle tone Julian said to Tory, "See, I told you I had a feeling about you. And call me Julian. C'mon, look at this part of the esophagus."

Julian leaned over the cadaver. His enthusiasm was contagious. Tory hesitated for a second but quickly became fascinated with what she saw. Julian had grasped the lower segment of the esophagus and gently slid his fingers into it. "See that? This is called a Mallory–Weiss tear—I'll explain in a second—now look at the liver."

Julian picked up the liver from the table. Several drops of clear fluid fell to the floor as his finger traced the rounded edge of the organ. "This is what a cirrhotic liver looks like. It's smaller than usual, shrunken, and it feels more dense. Alcohol would be my guess. We'll know for certain after I check it under the microscope. Anyway, alcoholics can get so sick and malnourished they start vomiting. The more they vomit the harder it becomes to stop. They actually retch so hard they can rip a hole in the esophagus and bleed to death. That's what we call a Mallory–Weiss tear. Gruesome, but here's the puzzle. With a shrunken liver and a hole this big in his esophagus, nothing could have saved him."

"In other words, he died of natural causes," Tory said.

"Exactly. He died of natural causes, then he was embalmed and then—and I can't think of any reason for this—he was dumped into the river. That's the 'why' that bugs me."

"Could there be a simple explanation? An accident, maybe?" Tory asked.

"Good thought, but take a look at his back." Julian walked around the table to the right side of the cadaver and reached across to the left arm, paying no attention to his own sleeve rubbing up against the wet tissues. The cadaver's muscles were rigid, and although the red-haired man was partially emptied by many pounds of internal organs and chest wall, he was difficult to pull up onto his side. Julian kept him from sliding across the table toward him with his left hand and, with a small grunt, succeeded in turning him on his side. Tory and Peters now had an excellent view of his back.

"Oh my God," Tory said. "What did that to him?"

All of the skin was badly abraded. Raw muscle, reddish-brown with a sprinkling of black speckles, was exposed at the shoulder blades, fringed here and there with loose strands, like a cowboy jacket. At the base of the skull the scalp was eroded to the bone.

Peters fixed his gaze on the wall behind Julian to keep from getting sick. He did not want to supplant the odor of formaldehyde with that of bacon and eggs. Everyone had a limit and Peters knew he was pushing his.

Julian continued, "He was dragged a long ways. And this is fresh. I'll show you why."

The cadaver was on his right side, balanced enough to allow Julian to steady him with one hand. Reaching around the torso, he gently rubbed the visible muscle at the shoulder blades, and the black speckles rubbed off and fell to the stainless-steel table like hail on a tin roof. "These are cinders. The only way they got here—"

Julian had gotten too graphic for Peters. He was getting dizzy and turning green.

Julian smiled. "Tory, grab a chair."

She raced to the desk, grabbed the chair, and firmly rolled it into Peters's calves, forcing him to sit down clumsily. He was flushed and starting to sweat. Plesser gently lowered the cadaver back on the table, snapped off his rubber gloves, and flipped them next to the body. Then he went to the small refrigerator by his cluttered desk and got a can of Coke, which he popped open before handing it to Peters.

"I think I'm coming down with something. Been feeling flushed all week," Peters said rubbing his eyes.

"Okay if I keep on with the story?" Julian asked, then gave Tory a quick wink.

Peters nodded. "Of course. It's just the flu. I'm fine."

Julian continued, "Anyway, judging by his weight, a single man, or maybe a couple of women, dragged him to the river and dumped him in."

Tory's eyes were full of enthusiasm. "And the wounds

are fresh because if he'd been in the river for any length of time the water would have worked the gravel out.''

"Right. And you mentioned an accident. I thought of that, too, just to be sure. There are only two places you find embalmed bodies. Funeral parlors and medical schools. As soon as I smelled the formaldehyde we checked with the police and the university. Nothing. No bodies missing from any funeral homes, no accidents on any of the bridges that might dump an embalmed body into the river, and the medical school doesn't have any missing bodies.''

"Could someone have poisoned him and used the formaldehyde to cover it up?'' Tory asked.

"Why bother? With that hole in his esophagus he would have been spurting blood like a crimson geyser. He didn't need to be killed.''

"So what's next?'' Peters wanted to know, leaning forward in the chair, staring at the ground.

"One more thing. Embalming's basically easy.'' Julian said. "All you really need is a bathtub and ten gallons of formaldehyde. But this guy was embalmed by a pro.''

"How do you know?'' Tory asked.

"Two reasons. First of all, he wasn't embalmed in a bathtub. Professional embalming is done with an arterial infusion pump that pumps the embalming fluid through the arteries and veins of the deceased. Much quicker and neater. Access to the circulatory system is most conveniently achieved through the neck. He's got the characteristic small puncture mark on the right side of his neck where the catheter went in. You don't need to see it, trust me, okay?'' He waited for a nod from Peters. "Second, take a look at my glove.''

Julian picked up the gloves he had discarded on the autopsy table, and moved them back and forth like a kid showing off a wiggle picture in the schoolyard. "See the shine on the glove? I think the embalming fluid actually is a combination of formaldehyde and glycerin. That's what probably gives the slimy shine. Anyone who has ever taken high school biology knows about formaldehyde. That's what an amateur would use: a simple solution of formaldehyde. This is a more sophisticated mixture."

"So this man died of natural causes, was embalmed professionally, and then was dumped in the river. Doesn't make any sense," Tory said.

"I can't even come up with a farcical explanation," Julian added.

"How about a sick joke, a prank?" Tory wondered.

"The body's got to come from somewhere. Nothing reported stolen."

"I'd love to know how it comes out."

"I'll let you know. It's a real brain teaser. When I finally discover the answer I always say to myself, 'So that's it. I shoulda had it.' " Julian went over to his heavy wooden desk. The largest drawer, one that could hold hanging files, was labeled with a handwritten sign: HALL OF FAME. "The case file will be here," he said, gently kicking the drawer. "Someday we'll get one more piece of information and this case will come alive. Until then you can file your report and call this one unsolved."

Four

September 16, 1996

Jack Merlin loved a captive audience. Maybe that's why he went into medicine.

Today Merlin was performing in a bright solarium off the pediatric post-surgical unit, and almost every member of his small but enthusiastic audience was connected to a cumbersome IV pole. The kids were in various stages of their recovery and had arrived in wheelchairs or hospital beds, but they loved Merlin's tricks and adored his slightly bawdy patter. The audience also had an assortment of pretty nurses who certainly could have found a better way to spend forty-five minutes if the head nurse had not been at a meeting. No one was going anywhere.

The shows Merlin performed had a dual purpose: entertaining the kids and relaxing the magician. Two hours earlier Merlin had been paged by the transplant coordinator and got word that a kidney was being harvested at City General Hospital for a patient whom he had been following. Mrs. Weinstock was a fifty-four-year-old woman with chronic kidney disease who had been in and out of the hospital while waiting for a suitable donor. Merlin had just spent forty-five minutes sitting on Mrs. Weinstock's bed, holding her hand and promising to work closely with her attending surgeon, Dr. Brenner. Mrs. Weinstock had to remind Merlin twice that she never really liked Dr. Brenner and that it was really important to her that Merlin do her surgery. Then, after calling Mrs. Weinstock's daughter for her, Merlin scheduled the magic show to blow off some nervous energy before the surgery, which would last at least four hours.

Smoothly juggling four ("Not three—anyone can juggle three. FOUR!") bags of IV fluids for a minute brought a cheer from his audience and Merlin was ready for his finale. "For my next trick I need a piece of rope." All the props were purloined hospital items: cotton balls, empty syringes, medicine cups, rubber tubing, and anything else Merlin could scrounge.

The kids looked around to be the first to spot some rope. Everyone immediately spotted an orthopedic patient, a shy boy named Matt Klein, who was brought to the show in his bed because of his complicated traction. He had been in an accident and was still in a lot of pain. His right leg was elevated a foot off the bed by a system of ropes and pulleys. The extra rope was coiled up at the end of the bed.

Merlin walked over, shook hands with Matt. "Your name is Matt, right?"

"You know my name is Matt, Dr. Merlin."

"And we've never met before, right?" Merlin winked at Matt. He'd been through this silly charade with each of the kids, all of whom Merlin knew well from bedside rounds.

Matt started to giggle as Merlin unraveled the rope, held it for audience inspection, produced a scalpel, and prepared to cut a three-foot length. "Hmmm, this ought to be fine. Don't worry, Matt, I *think* I know what I'm doing. I should warn all of you, though," Merlin said, turning to the rest of the audience, "this rope is critical to this young man. He needs every inch of the rope you see me holding. If this trick fails we'll have to take poor Matt back to the OR and start over again." Another wink to Matt.

There are dozens of cut-and-restore rope routines. Entire books have been devoted to them, but Merlin favored a very simple version that could be done with no preparation beforehand. Merlin had great hands, but he was a master of patter. For as long as needed he could keep up an effortless verbiage that so distracted his audience he could often get away with illusions other magicians wouldn't dare try. His favorite ruse was to offer a demonstration of how he performed a particular trick, and while his audience thought they were being treated to a trade secret, Merlin would actually be setting up for an even more amazing illusion.

"Now, I'm not certain where I should make this cut," Merlin continued as he looped the rope over his middle finger and slid his hand up and down, looking for the perfect spot to cut. After several seconds of concentrated effort, Merlin appeared to find a spot that suited him and made a separation with a single swipe of the scalpel blade.

As the rope broke into two pieces Merlin's eyes widened and he seemed genuinely distraught. "Oh, no. I think I goofed. I didn't mean to cut all the way through. I'm sorry Matt." Wink.

The audience howled.

Merlin turned to one of his coterie of young nurses, "Kim, please call someone from orthopedics to rescue poor Matt."

Kim knew her role well. "Yes, Dr. Merlin," she said dutifully and left the solarium hurriedly.

"Well, while we're waiting, let me tie the ends together so Matt's leg doesn't fall off." Merlin tied a simple knot and held up the restored length of rope with a large knot in the middle. "You know, I'm really gonna catch hell for messing Matt up. Tell you what. Let's promise we won't tell anyone I did this."

The kids screamed in delight.

"Oh, so you're gonna get me in trouble. Well if there's no evidence to the crime there's no trouble, right?" Merlin grabbed the knot with his right hand and smoothly slid it off the rope to reveal that, in fact, the rope was intact. Merlin tossed the knot to Matt as a memento.

As he got an enthusiastic round of applause, Martin Wheeler, three months into his coveted chief residency in general surgery, walked into the solarium and quieted the room like an outlaw walking into a frontier saloon. "Excuse me, everybody, but I've got to steal Dr. Merlin." Then, turning to the magician, "Now."

Martin Wheeler, although Merlin's boss, was not liked or respected by any of the residents. He was seen as an opportunist who had been chosen for his plum position by socializing with the attending staff. Wheeler was a third-generation Pittsburgh surgeon who was quick to tell anyone who would listen that he fully intended to live in Sewickley, the same prestigious community in which he grew up.

Merlin wiped his nose with the tips of his fingers and gave Wheeler a subtle nod as a signal to wipe his own nose. Wheeler immediately pulled out a handkerchief. "You got it, Martin. Something brown. You must've had a meeting with the chairman."

"I'll see you in the doctor's lounge in three minutes, Merlin." Wheeler turned and bolted from the now-silent room.

"I'm sorry, gang, I've got to go," Merlin said.

As the nurses started to ready their charges for the return trip to their rooms, Merlin couldn't resist one last quip. As a very pretty blonde nurse, whose bouncy breasts caught the older patients' attention, crossed in front of Merlin, he stage whispered, "Too bad I've got to go. My next trick was gonna be to vanish Miss Parker's bra."

The boys hooted and hollered at the thought of a naked woman. Merlin hit himself in the forehead as if he'd just remembered something important. "Oh, wait a second. I already did that trick"—he waited for several seconds,—"last weekend. Ta-daa."

Nurse Parker turned in mock anger. "Merlin."

Merlin gave a little wave as he hurried down the hall. After taking the stairs down half a dozen flights, he entered the surgical suite and knocked on a door marked DOCTOR'S LOUNGE. A muffled voice from within clearly said, "Come in." Merlin knocked again and a muffled voice said, "It's open, goddamnit." Merlin knocked a third time and finally Martin Wheeler opened the door.

"Merlin, what the hell's wrong with you?"

"Your memo: 'Surgical residents and medical students are not permitted in the surgical lounge.' I don't know the password."

Wheeler took a single deep breath. He was dressed in surgical blues and he wore a disposable scrub cap. His yellow beeper was clipped inside the V-neck of his shirt. "I need a meeting with you." Wheeler stood aside and Merlin walked in. The two were alone.

The only true concessions to comfort on the surgical floor could be found here: a sofa, several easy chairs, and a large-screen TV perennially turned to CNN. Several copies of *The Journal of Surgery* were scattered about, and some medical knowledge actually was exchanged here, but most of the talk involved money and nurses, in that order.

"Oh baby! Doughnuts! So that's why you didn't want us in here," Merlin said, crossing the room.

"Jack, will you cool it? Sit down." Wheeler called the meeting and he wanted to run it.

Merlin turned away from the snack table and looked around. "Jack? Who's Jack? No one calls me 'Jack.' This must be serious. It's not kinky, is it, Wheeler?" An overstuffed easy chair sat by the TV, and Merlin flopped down on it with one leg slung over the armrest. As soon as he was settled he began to roll a shiny fifty-cent piece back and forth across his knuckles.

Wheeler remained standing. "I just got off the phone with Dr. Brenner," he said, as if delivering some bad news.

Merlin rolled the coin across his knuckles one final time,

slipped the coin into his fist, blew on it twice, and said, "Penny for your thoughts, Martin." Before Wheeler could say anything Merlin opened his hand and in place of the half-dollar was a shiny penny that Merlin flipped in the air and caught. "Nothing I like better than a standing O."

Wheeler pressed on. "You know I was accepted into the transplant program next year."

"That's not been a guarded secret, Wheeler. I heard it from the salad girl in the cafeteria."

"Well, I've got a problem. I've only done one kidney—"

It hit Merlin at once. He sat bolt upright then sprang out of the chair. "No fucking way, Wheeler. You can do all the kidneys you want during your fellowship. This is my case."

"It still is your case. Dr. Brenner wants you to second-assist me."

Merlin went toe to toe with Wheeler. "Then it's not my case. It's your case, and I get to write the post-op orders."

"No, wait a second." Wheeler realized Merlin wasn't going to acquiesce easily and probably needed to blow off a little steam.

"You really are something, Wheeler. You can second-assist *me* if you want. Maybe pick up some technique."

"Dr. Brenner really wants me to—"

"No he doesn't. He doesn't give a shit who operates so long as he sends out the bill. Or maybe *dad* called him."

"You're out of line, Merlin."

"Okay, Wheeler, fine. That's the way you want it. The case is yours, goddamnit," Merlin said in the same tone of voice he might challenge someone to a fight.

The chief resident nodded one time. *Thank you.*

Merlin continued, "Have you examined her?"

"No. There wasn't time. I reviewed the chart, though."

"Then operate on the chart, you asshole."

"Watch your mouth, Merlin."

"What's her name?"

Wheeler paused and thought. "Clara."

"Clara what?"

"I just reviewed the chart. I didn't memorize it. Weinstein, I think."

"You're gonna operate on her and you don't even know her name. Listen to me, Wheeler. You're practicing country-club medicine and you're still in training. Her name is Weinstock. Mrs. Weinstock. No one in the hospital calls her Clara."

Wheeler walked over to the snack table and poured himself a large Styrofoam cup of steaming coffee. He looked away from Merlin. "I am the chief resident. I do have the right to operate on interesting cases."

Merlin became quieter and more philosophical. "You look at surgery like an auto mechanic looks at a Chevy. Open up the hood and slip in a new kidney. You've really missed something. Someday you'll be making statements like, 'My technique was perfect but we lost the patient.' And you'll never see the irony."

Wheeler's eyes tightened. "Look, Merlin, the chief resident has the prerogative to take any complicated case and I'm exercising my right. Period. I don't need your permission, and I don't really give a fuck what you think. You can either second-assist me or keep the hell away from the OR."

"You're always coming in where you're not wanted." Merlin pointed at Wheeler. "Always grabbing something that doesn't belong to you."

"What the hell does that mean?"

"Think about it. Think about grabbing a couple of 34Bs that didn't belong to you."

"What! You're nuts. You don't know when to stop."

"Jan."

Wheeler paused, a hesitation that lasted several seconds longer than true spontaneity would allow. "Jan?" His voice was half a key higher; he cleared his throat.

"*Oops,* I guess I do know where to stop. I know about Jan. And now you know that I know."

"I don't know what you're talking about." He sounded like a Vienna choir boy.

"Sure you do. Jan, as in 'Kevin and Jan.' " Merlin waited for Wheeler to react.

Wheeler took a breath and thought for several seconds. "I'm surprised you can say 'Kevin' without reaching for a box of Kleenex."

"I read the letters," Merlin shot back, quick to take the offense.

"I'll see you in OR, Merlin." Wheeler walked to the door.

"I made a promise to her," Merlin said quietly.

Wheeler left quickly, not wanting to hear what promises Merlin had made to Jan. When Merlin was alone he said, "And I'm not going to let Mrs. Weinstock down."

The kidney for Clara Weinstock arrived just as the first incision was made and sat, in ice, in a small Playmate cooler on a stainless-steel table. As the anesthesiologist, a slow-moving Texan named Steve, put Mrs. Weinstock to sleep and intubated her, the operating room was filled with activity. The three surgeons, Merlin, Wheeler, and Dr. Brenner, were helped into their sterile gowns by the scrub nurse and waited, in turn, hands held out, chest high, for assistance donning their latex gloves. As soon as the patient was sufficiently asleep, everyone assembled around the narrow operating table as Merlin finished his skin prep with Betadine and proceeded to place disposable sterile drapes, layer after layer, leaving only a small patch of white skin, brightly lit by the manmade sun overhead. This was the Emerald City, light green tiled walls and floors, and the surgical team outfitted in various shades of blue-green tended to blend with one another such that an outsider might have trouble telling the scrub nurse from the senior surgeon.

The transplant team stood shoulder to shoulder around the unconscious patient; Wheeler and Dr. Brenner to the patient's right and Merlin to the left. A male orderly— really a hook holder selected by Wheeler for his strong arms—stood next to Merlin and would be relegated to the unenviable task of holding retractors to give the surgeons a wide operating field. A scrub nurse, female, was also chosen by Wheeler to distribute the myriad instruments used during an organ transplant and because she had marvelous breasts. She stood next to Wheeler.

Almost all kidneys transplanted were placed on the right side of the abdomen because of favorable anatomy. But there was a second reason, one of convenience. Most surgeons were right handed and that approach seemed most natural. Merlin, relegated to the left side of the patient, was offered a great view of the surgery, but would not participate in anything more exciting than tying off bleeders as the layers of skin and muscle were penetrated on the trip into the abdominal cavity.

Merlin smiled beneath his mask. He'd made a quick trip to the pharmacy after his heated discussion with Wheeler and written a script for Lasix, a medicine well known to increase urination. The pharmacist had joked, as he poured the liquid medicine into a calibrated cup, that the amount Merlin requested, 250 milligrams, was enough to make a rhino pee. Merlin smiled and said, "I'm gonna make medical history—I'm gonna make an asshole pee."

Then Merlin found Wheeler sitting at the nurses' station writing pre-op orders, drinking his Styrofoam cup of coffee. Timing is everything. Merlin never hesitated as he walked toward his stooge. In one graceful, fluid motion Merlin slid into the seat next to Wheeler and dumped— with wonderful finesse that went entirely unnoticed—the entire 250 milligrams into the steaming black coffee. "Hey, Wheeler. Sorry I blew up in there. Just wanted to let you know." Merlin patted Wheeler on the back.

Wheeler was taken aback and looked at Merlin with

utter amazement. *He's sorry! I can't believe it.* "Don't worry about it." He picked up his coffee and took a swig.

Merlin's eyes did not betray him. His pupils did not dilate even when Wheeler made a face as he tasted the coffee. Like a good magician he did not dwell on the Styrofoam coffee cup, but questioned the look of pain on Wheeler's face. "You okay?"

"Yeah," Wheeler said looking at the coffee cup. "This swill gets worse all the time. If they switched to battery acid, would anyone notice?"

They shared a laugh.

"Anyway, I'll see you in OR," Merlin said.

"Great. Hey, next one's yours." Wheeler was feeling confident. "I got an idea. Why don't we grab a beer after surgery?"

"I'd love to," Merlin said as he got up to leave, but immediately sat back down. "Oh, shit. I can't. I'm the teaching assistant in anatomy, starting this afternoon. Sorry."

Wheeler drained the remaining coffee, scrunched up his face and threw the Styrofoam cup in the trash. "My condolences. I've heard Olsen is as ornery as ever." Wheeler stood, gave Merlin a very sympathetic pat on the shoulder, and walked off to scrub for Mrs. Weinstock's transplant.

Now, as Wheeler made the diagonal incision from Mrs. Weinstock's right hip toward her groin, Merlin clamped hemostats onto the four bleeding vessels that sprouted from the incision. Dr. Brenner, the senior surgeon, helped in much the way Merlin was helping, but like the captain of a ship, he mostly watched and stood ready to take control at the slightest hint of indecision by Wheeler. The brightly lighted patch of flesh quivered slightly as the incision was completed. Wheeler shot a glance at the anesthesiologist, who was seated at Mrs. Weinstock's head. "Hey, Steve. She's moving. It's not that hard putting a patient to sleep, is it?" Wheeler felt a twinge deep within his pelvis.

The anesthesiologist looked at Wheeler and then at his medication flow sheet. He said nothing.

"I mean, there *are* only two drugs involved, right?" Wheeler said. The oversimplification was intended as a slap in the face, but largely demonstrated Wheeler's lack of sophistication. Anesthesia was misunderstood and underrated by surgeons. Good anesthesia involved a balance between several drugs, sometimes as many as four or five. Minor OR nuisances frustrated Wheeler tremendously, and the anesthesia department had long ago concluded—correctly—that he lacked the confidence of a truly great surgeon and so ranted over peccadilloes a better physician would ignore.

Wheeler continued talking to no one in particular, "What's the rule of thumb? Help me here, Steve. One drug to comfort the patient, one to comfort the surgeon, right?" Wheeler looked at Dr. Brenner for a nod of approval but couldn't catch his eye. It never occurred to Martin Wheeler that someone might want to distance himself from him. The room was quiet except for the rhythmic hissing of the ventilator and the stereo playing the opening strains of Handel's *Water Music*.

The eternal struggle between surgeons, the glory boys with the pulsating egos, and the anesthesiologists, the generously paid but rarely respected servants of the OR, often revolved around the amount of medication used. Good general anesthesia always involved the combination of several drugs. Pentothal, infused intravenously, was used to put the patient to sleep so there would be no memory of the surgery. A narcotic, fentanyl, was added to block the pain of the scalpel. But the drug Wheeler now ranted about, pancuronium bromide, was given to paralyze the muscles to make the work of the surgeon easier. Surgeons wanted their patients absolutely flaccid; anesthesiologists had to worry about side effects of the medications as well as eventually waking the patient up after surgery was completed.

The anesthesiologist picked up a syringe filled with a clear liquid.

"I can't work on a bucking bronco. We'll wait," Wheeler said impatiently and stood watching the anesthesiologist squirt some pancuronium bromide into an IV running into Mrs. Weinstock's arm. Wheeler shifted from his right foot to his left and back again and appeared frustrated with the poky anesthesiologist, but Merlin knew better.

Merlin picked up a second scalpel and made a slicing motion through the air.

"What the hell are you doing?" Wheeler snapped.

"Cutting through the tension, Dr. Wheeler." Merlin's eyes smiled. The female scrub nurse giggled.

"She's a blob of Jell-O, sir," the anesthesiologist said sarcastically.

"That's better," Wheeler said, still sounding irritated. He resumed his incision and fully opened the skin, thereby exposing the bright red striated muscle of the abdominal wall.

Wheeler's bladder had filled steadily since his last gulp of Lasix in the nursing station. It was now tense with urine and probably looked like a kid's water balloon waiting to explode. The urge was overwhelming. The muscular walls of the bladder contracted rhythmically, trying to initiate the emptying process but to no avail. With great willpower Wheeler was able to tighten his muscles at his bladder outlet and avoid—if only temporarily—the inevitable. Wheeler began to sweat, and he suddenly found it difficult to concentrate. He timidly cut into the muscle and made a superficial scratch that oozed blood but didn't open the layer. A second cut was necessary and Merlin again applied hemostats to catch the bleeders.

When Wheeler thought he was about to pop, the bladder became forgiving, and relaxed momentarily before tensing again. The pains were coming in more frequent waves, similar to a pregnant woman about to deliver. Wheeler couldn't stand it any more. "Dr. Brenner, I'm not feeling well. I'll need to excuse myself." Without waiting for permission he stepped away from the table, still holding the scalpel, and headed for the door.

"Okay, Merlin, let's get a move on. It's your case, after all," was all Dr. Brenner said.

Merlin was already walking around the table, arms out, bent at the elbow, to take Wheeler's vacated place at Mrs. Weinstock's right side. Merlin couldn't resist the opportunity. "Nurse. Order a case of Attends for Dr. Wheeler, and if he doesn't wet his pants at all take him to Chuck E. Cheese. Now let's get to work." Merlin was adjusting the retractors while he chatted, then he picked up a small two-inch-by-two-inch piece of gauze, folded it twice, and made a small wad. Taking it in his right hand he appeared to hand it to his left hand, then offered the sponge to the scrub nurse. As she reached her gloved hand to accept the sponge, Merlin opened his left hand to show it empty. He was already using the sponge, still in his right hand, to mop up a small trickle of blood coming from the incision.

Wheeler had heard some of Merlin's comments as he hurried from the room but didn't think about it as he ran down the hallway to the bathroom. It was not until he had relieved himself for almost a minute that he realized what Merlin had said.

In the end, the surgery went, as Merlin had promised Mrs. Weinstock, splendidly.

Five

Dr. Jonathan Olsen was the only physician who held dual appointments within the medical center: chairman of anatomy at the medical school and chairman of pathology at the hospital. The esteemed Dr. Olsen, "Jonathan" to attending-level physicians, weighed in at almost two hundred sixty pounds, sported a bald head, neatly trimmed salt-and-pepper beard, and wore suspenders, which he called 'braces,' in a tone that could only be described as haughty. No one could remember ever seeing him without his white three-quarter-length lab coat, a freshly laundered one each day. And incredibly the correct name tag was always displayed, stating either CHAIRMAN OF ANATOMY or CHAIRMAN OF PATHOLOGY, depending on the local geography, and he switched them as his peripatetic day progressed. This morning his tag read JONATHAN OLSEN, M.D., PH.D., CHAIRMAN DEPT. OF ANATOMY. He held an unlit pipe and a mug of coffee in his left hand, standing there at the walnut lectern, savoring the moment.

The brass plaque above the door to the gross anatomy lab read: *"Mortui Docent Vivos,"* the dead teach the living. Nowhere did it say "Gross Anatomy." In fact, the gross anatomy labs had a distinction of being the only place in the City of Pittsburgh, including the classics department at Pitt, whose sign was written entirely in Latin. The outside wall of the huge room was a series of grand windows overlooking the football stadium. There were twenty-eight stainless-steel dissecting tables arranged in four columns of seven. Each cadaver was covered with a stiff yellow tarp, and only the prominence of the head could be recognized. A metal bucket, lined with a white garbage bag, sat under each table.

On the wall opposite the windows were three heavy wooden doors. The first was the diener's office, the second the embalming room, and the third the cadaver storage room.

This was the first day of gross anatomy, *the* rite of passage for the one hundred twelve first-year medical students who stood nervously, four to a table, waiting for Dr. Olsen to speak. No one dared peek under the yellow tarps, and only the most daring students whispered to one another. The few attempts at humor fell flat.

"Class," Olsen said in full baritone and waited for absolute silence.

The students were dressed casually, no white coats but rather an unimaginative variety of jeans, T-shirts, sweatshirts, and sneakers. Some were holding dissection manuals, and everyone gave Dr. Olsen complete attention. He placed his mug and pipe on the wooden lectern and folded his hands beneath his chin like a priest. The newness of his relationship with the students excited Dr. Olsen, and he prolonged the moment with some philosophy, a bit hackneyed, but a tradition in the department. "I am Dr. Jonathan Olsen, and it is my task to lead you on an incredible odyssey through the human body. The very mystery of life is about to unfold in this room," he said, putting his hands out theatrically. "The greatest minds in medicine have taken this journey—some, I'm proud to say, under my tutelage. You will not be disappointed.

"But, but, listen to me carefully: This is a sacred privilege that has been granted you, and I will not tolerate anything but the utmost respect for the teachers in this room with whom you are about to spend the next six weeks. Mortui . . . decent . . . vivos." Olsen picked up his unlit pipe and placed it to his lips momentarily. Most of the students did not understand Latin and so the message was lost. "We begin each year with the thorax. From there we will do head and neck. The heart and the soul. Anatomy is demanding—a thousand names to master—and I will be a stickler for details. Accordingly, the laboratory will be open twenty-four hours a day. Welcome to Human . . . Gross . . . Anatomy.''

The swinging doors opened and Merlin, hair wet from his post-surgical shower, wearing his usual white pants, blue scrub shirt, and yellow beeper, swept in.

Olsen stopped talking abruptly and looked at his watch. His voice quieted and he talked directly to Merlin, "You're late, magic man."

"I'm sorry, Dr. Olsen. Kidney transplant." Merlin was matter of fact, anything but contrite.

Olsen glared. He had a deserved reputation for showing no respect for any of the patients at the Medical Center until they fell within his domain. After several seconds he turned back to the class. "This is Dr. Jack Merlin, a surgery resident who will be happy to assist you in your quest. Call on Merlin to demonstrate sharp dissection and blunt dissection. He will point out to you the splenic flexure, the anterior descending coronary artery, and the vagal nerve. He will be *my* laboratory assistant this semester. He will be *your* humble servant. Abuse him. Now, class, fold back the yellow tarp and expose only the cadaver's chest."

Amid the rustling of plastic tarps and whispers of nervous excitement, the twenty-eight cadavers were exposed. The air became thick with the odor of formaldehyde and irritated the wide eyes examining death for the first time. Merlin stood near Olsen and enjoyed the reactions of the students as they caught their first glimpse of their cadavers. Many of the students donned gloves. Although not medically necessary after embalming, it made the students feel like doctors and kept them from smelling when they went off to their next class.

The professor waited for relative quiet and said, "Begin your dissection of the thorax with your copy of Olsen opened to page six." Medical texts were rarely, if ever, referred to by title, which in this case was *Manual of Human Dissection,* but rather by their author's name, which was, of course, Dr. Jonathan Olsen. Turning to Merlin, he said, "C'mon, magic man, make like a red cell and circulate."

Merlin rolled his eyes and walked slowly down the second aisle and caught snippets of conversations. A tradition handed down from one medical school class to another was the naming of the cadavers. The obvious names resurfaced every couple of years, and Merlin heard a variety of names bantered about: "Marine Corpse," "Working Stiff," "AbraCadaver," "Boris," "Doornail," and "Dead Last."

Jake Barnhouse was working alone in the embalming room, thinking how much his lower back was still bothering him.

His knowledge of human anatomy was legendary, and his skill with a scalpel was impressive, but he was not a member of the surgical staff. He wasn't even a physician, although he'd toyed with the idea of medical school as a kid watching his father prepare the bodies in the funeral parlor his family had run for two generations. Far removed from a gimpy, hunchback swathed in a black cape, Jake was the diener.

Within the cloistered world of gross anatomy a diener is a man—rarely a woman—who embalms the cadavers and prepares them for dissection and generally oversees the gross anatomy laboratory. With seventeen years' experience Jake was most proud of his proficiency at prosection. Although first-year students are expected to dissect their cadavers independently, many delicate nerves and blood vessels are accidentally ruined by the clumsy misuse of a scalpel. A perfect dissection—or prosection—

displayed in the front of the anatomy lab offered even the most heavyhanded students the opportunity to view the intricacies of human anatomy. Of course, relying only on the prosection was akin to reading *Cliff's Notes* and shelving *Silas Marner,* but hospitals are full of respected physicians, even surgeons, who owe a debt of gratitude to the dieners of the world.

Jake had spent the last two days moving the cadavers from the storage room, where they had been suspended from ceiling-mounted metal tracks by head braces that resembled football helmets with large air vents cut into the side. There were twenty-nine in all, some massively obese. Each was a struggle to get onto the gurney; one for each table, and one for the prosection. His back would hurt for days.

The afternoon moved slowly for Merlin. His beeper kept going off with questions from the recovery room. He was dead tired, and it was painful to watch the students fumble in their attempts to expose the muscles of the chest wall. What was done so easily in the operating room with vital tissues that separated effortlessly was as difficult for these novices as removing an apple skin in one continuous piece. Some of the students cut too deeply, marring the smoothness of the pectoral muscles, while others timidly cut into the superficial epidermis and became mired in the inch or so of greasy fat in the more rotund cadavers. Like opposite ends of a balanced centrifuge, Merlin managed to stay as far away from Dr. Olsen as he possibly could.

Halfway through the class Merlin suddenly stopped, did a double-take, and looked at the third cadaver in the second row, the one called "AbraCadaver." The students' babble continued; Merlin heard it off in the distance. There was a terrible taste in the back of his mouth, and he looked as if he had seen a ghost. A sudden thickness in his throat made it hard to swallow, and he became hot and uncomfortable. AbraCadaver's brown hair was greasily matted to his head and had skin so rubbery that once-sharp facial features took on the rounded appearance of an ice sculpture that had begun to melt. He was as hideously anonymous as the other denizens of the laboratory, yet something was familiar. Merlin stood for several minutes, staring hard at the cadaver, before realizing a student was right in his face, asking a question.

"What?" Merlin asked pulling his eyes from AbraCadaver and focusing his attention on a student who blathered on about some anatomical minutia. The next forty minutes seemed like an eternity. Merlin found himself lingering in the vicinity of AbraCadaver, approaching him from a variety of angles, hoping to see something new. At one point he was almost certain, wanting to shove the students out of the way and ask them what the hell did they think they were doing. A minute later, from a different vantage, he wasn't convinced. The nose looked wrong.

Most gross anatomy classes began with the thorax for one simple reason: It was a relatively easy place to start. Few anatomically important structures existed between the skin and the rib cage, and the more complicated internal organs were protected from even the most sloppy dissection. The students' confidence increased as they successfully exposed all of the pectoral muscles, and Dr. Olsen took great pride, as the session neared its conclusion, that the students were already beginning to relax.

Merlin, on the other hand, was a mess. His mind was numb from a gnawing realization he couldn't allow himself to believe. His antiperspirant wasn't holding him, and he checked his watch too often in anticipation of the class ending.

At five o'clock precisely—Dr. Olsen produced a pocket watch—the cadavers were covered, waste was placed in the trash cans beneath the dissection tables, rubber gloves were discarded, and the students left for showers and clean clothes. In the coming weeks, as the medical students became increasingly comfortable with their cadavers, they would forgo the gloves and even be so bold as to eat while doing dissection. But as the weeks progressed the penetrating odor of formaldehyde would become less and less easily washed away as it seeped into the pores beneath the skin, and several hours after a hot shower the familiar odor could be detected as it oozed back to the surface. It was not unusual for a first-year medical student, at locales far removed from the medical center, to be asked, "Are you a first-year medical student?"

Olsen and Merlin were the last to leave and parted company outside the doors to gross anatomy. The ninth floor of the medical school was one long hallway. The anatomy labs were at one end near the metal fire doors to the hospital. A small alcove set the labs off from the long hallway, making it difficult for someone to see inside even when the doors were open. Olsen turned toward his office and the throng of students waiting at the medical school elevators.

Merlin needed some air. The formaldehyde had gotten to him. Thoughts whirled through his head, and he needed to get outside and think. The express elevator to the outside loading dock, right across the hall from the Anatomy Labs, caught his eye. It was used exclusively to transport cadavers up to the ninth floor and was summoned at both ends by a numerical keypad to keep the ninth floor secure at night. Without the combination the elevator was off limits. Merlin punched 5-7-3-4 on the keypad and the door immediately opened. As Merlin stepped inside he hit the down button and leaned against the wall waiting for the doors to close. Absently he stared across the hall at the doors to gross anatomy.

The elevators doors started to close. Before they shut completely Merlin shot his hand between them, hitting the black safety bar.

His breathing was faster. A patina of sweat shone on his forehead. Merlin walked with long purposeful strides off the elevator and across the hallway. He approached the two swinging doors straight on, pushing one hand firmly against each door, sending them wide open, banging them loudly off the doorstops. Like computer-driven laser sights, Merlin's eyes locked in on the third cadaver in the second row, the one nicknamed AbraCadaver, and walked straight toward it.

Merlin stood facing the left side of AbraCadaver and, like a magician dramatically pulling the sheet from a levitated lady, took his right hand to his extreme left, grabbed the yellow tarp near the feet, and in a single, fluid motion, removed the cover to reveal the naked cadaver. It was hard to look at his chest, relieved of skin. The striated muscle, red like raw beef sitting out too long, wrapped around the ribs. Merlin took a close look at the face for several seconds. It was the worst moment of his life. His eyes were moist and ready to overflow, but he didn't notice the odor of formaldehyde.

The noises from the ventilation system became distorted, and Merlin thought for a second he heard someone crying. For some reason the overhead paging system was mercifully quiet. His hands were shaking and his mouth was dry. Walking around the table to AbraCadaver's right side Merlin stared at the face. When he reached the feet Merlin criss-crossed his arms, right hand grasping the left ankle, left hand grasping the right ankle. He was breathing through his teeth and spittle formed at the corners of his mouth. With a loud grunt, Merlin pulled the right leg up, pushed the left one down, and flipped AbraCadaver over onto his stomach. The table shook with a metallic rumble. When everything stopped moving the cadaver was prone, but horribly askew, so that his head and shoulders were stiffly off one side of the table, and his legs, from the knees down, were projecting off the other.

Merlin leaned in close and examined the right calf. A birthmark, reddish-brown in color, raised only slightly, and looking very much like the characteristic boot shape of Italy, was visible just above the right calf. *Oh, God.* Merlin swallowed. Hesitantly he touched the birthmark for several seconds, gently tracing his fingers over it like a kid exploring the wonders of a raised topographical map for the first time. His hands glistened with embalming fluid, and as he wiped a tear from his right cheek, he smeared the smelly mixture on his face. A stream of emotions collided with each other: confusion, anger and grief. His lips opened wide to show his clenched teeth and he hissed, "Jesus Fucking Christ. *Kevin!!!*" His anger took control of his hands and he turned around, facing the next table, and struck the covered cadaver hard in the chest. The dull thud sounded good and was a catharsis. He did it again and again. Tears streamed down his face and he slowly slumped to the floor and leaned against the leg of the table that his friend and roommate, Kevin Hoover, lay upon. He brought his knees up to his chest, clasped his hands in front of them, and closed his eyes.

He would sit there forever if they let him.

Forever turned out to be about fifteen minutes. Jake opened the door connecting the embalming room to the anatomy lab and wheeled the prosection table to its position in front of the lectern. In the preceding ninety minutes he had dissected and displayed the various muscle groups of the chest, removed the chest wall, exposed the lungs and heart, and made several incisions into the fistlike pump to reveal the four chambers and valves.

Immediately he spotted the third cadaver in the second row, uncovered, prone, and horribly askew. His first thought was that Olsen would walk in and see one of his cadavers uncovered. Jake hurried to the one the students had named AbraCadaver, and as he bent down to pick up the yellow tarp, spotted Merlin sitting on the floor.

"What the hell! You're Jack Merlin, right?"

Merlin didn't look up. Weakly he nodded his head, staring off through the table legs.

"What the hell is going on, goddamnit?" Jake's voice was raised.

"That's Kevin Hoover. My friend. Kevin . . ." Merlin said, but as he spoke his voice trailed off to a whisper. "What are you talking about?" "That's Kevin. The birthmark. It's *his* birthmark." "Who's Kevin?" "Kevin *Hoover*. He's dead. Kevin's dead."

Jake looked at the cadaver, noticed the birthmark on the right calf, then at Merlin still sitting on the floor, nearly catatonic. He clearly didn't know what to do and left the room to find Dr. Olsen, calling over his shoulder, "You wait right there."

A half-hour later AbraCadaver was still in the cockeyed, prone position, and Merlin remained on the floor leaning up against a table leg, while Olsen and Jake stared at the naked body. Olsen had stormed into the anatomy lab, his unbuttoned white coat streaming behind him like a cape. First he stopped to see his cadaver, not even looking for the lab assistant. The sight of AbraCadaver arranged so haphazardly on the table was an affront to Olsen's sense of order. "Where's Merlin?"

Jake motioned with his head toward Merlin. Olsen said, "Merlin, can you explain what's going on?"

Merlin continued to stare straight ahead, through the forest of stainless-steel table legs and said, "No, I can't."

"Dr. Merlin!" Olsen said sharply, trying to snap his lab assistant out of his stupor. While Olsen waited he exhaled loudly. Exasperated, he squatted down, which was uncomfortable for so large a man. As the material of his expensive trousers stretched taut around his massive thighs and his custom-made shirt pulled free of his pants, a large portion of his white coat lay limply on the filthy floor. Olsen asked Merlin, "Jack, what's going on? Why did you do this?"

Their faces were less than eighteen inches apart. Merlin looked at Olsen and spoke quietly, "That's Kevin Hoover. You remember . . ."

Dr. Olsen nodded. "I remember Kevin. Go on."

"I recognized him during class. At least I thought I did."

"How sure are you, Jack?"

"Hundred percent. You've gotta believe me. That's Kevin."

Olsen patted Merlin on the shoulder, but actually used him to steady himself as he stood up. His pants were riding high in his crotch, his underwear wedged beyond the point of no return, and his shirt billowed out around him. "Jake, let's turn him over."

"Yessir." Jake immediately went to work on the shoulders while Dr. Olsen controlled the feet. First they straightened the body so his head and feet were centered on the narrow dissecting table. Then, working under Olsen's clipped verbal commands, the two turned the body on its side and wiggled him back to the center of the table before clumsily letting him drop, with a shudder, to his back.

Olsen and Jake then looked at the cadaver's face closely. Greasy, matted hair, mouth half-open, cheeks pushed up toward the eyes, stretched from the pressure of the head brace. Olsen shook his head. "I don't know. I knew Kevin pretty well. This guy doesn't look familiar at all."

"I have no idea what he looked like. I don't think I even knew—" Jake said before being cut off.

"Jake, why don't you run and get me the paperwork on him." And, as if it were necessary to add, he said, "Now" in a patronizing tone.

As Jake turned, relieved to be dismissed, and walked toward his office, Olsen leaned over AbraCadaver and looked at him intently, studying the face, then worked his eyes down the torso.

Olsen's masseter muscle, responsible for closing the jaw, bulged and pulsated in his cheeks. He could feel moisture collecting in his armpits, and he had a sick feeling the day was going to get worse.

Jake returned with a clipboard stuffed to capacity with typewritten forms, one for each of the cadavers. "Read me the number on the toe tag," Olsen demanded.

Jake turned the tag over and read, "Number 4-1-7."

"Let's see. Four-one-seven is a Robert, then it says "Red" in parentheses, Gardner. Uh, sixty-seven year old. No family. Homeless." Olsen looked at cadaver number 417. "Oh, shit. This body's not sixty seven. I doubt if he's half that age. There's no medical history here. Goddamnit. I don't know who he is but we've got a mess." Olsen thought a moment before continuing. "Okay. Who knows about this, Jake?"

"No one. The three of us."

"Let's keep a lid on this. All right, let's go step by step."

Merlin stood to look at Kevin. "Dr. Olsen, that *is* Kevin Hoover. There is no doubt."

"I agree that this cadaver isn't sixty-seven, but I don't know how—"

Merlin's emotions were brittle. Tears started down his cheeks again and he raised his voice enough to startle Olsen and Jake, *"Jesus Christ, will you listen to me!! This–is–Kevin."* Merlin turned back to the cadaver he had been beating on and pounded some more on his yellow-tarped chest. "What do you want me to do? Tell me and I'll do it!"

Olsen said nothing. He looked at Merlin, then at the cadaver, and finally at Jake. "Jake, you'd better call hospital security."

"What about the medical records? I can send for them if you want, Dr. Olsen. I'd have to check where he came from."

Olsen looked at the record and said, "He came from City General. Good luck finding anything there."

"You want me to try?"

"Absolutely. When I do the post it may be important."

*   *   *

Hospital security arrived in the form of Big John, a six-foot-five black man who wore a Pittsburgh University Medical Center patch on the sleeve of his uniform. He had skin that was almost black and thick sideburns; the rest of his cranium was shaved to a shiny smoothness. Short sleeves were all his thick forearms, with prominent veins that meandered their way up toward his biceps, could fit into. Although physically intimidating, Big John was hugely liked by the female medical, clerical, and nursing staff. Every night, when the evening shift let out at eleven o'clock, he walked a group to the hospital parking garage and hung around until everyone had driven out.

Big John listened intently as Olsen described the events of the previous hour. Not once did Olsen say the cadaver was Kevin Hoover, or that he believed him to be Kevin Hoover. He only recited what he knew to be true, and Merlin glared at Olsen when he dropped his voice and said, "This may be a mistaken identity and some sloppy record keeping on our part."

Big John walked over to the body and looked him over for about a minute before saying, "We've gotta call the police."

"Why?" Olsen wanted to know.

"Look, Doc, the last thing I want to do is call in a bunch of uniforms who'll treat me like I'm dressed up for Halloween. But if Merlin here is right, and this is Kevin, then we've got a big-time investigation. If I'm ever gonna get in the academy I better not screw up. You know what I mean?"

Dr. Olsen stepped close to Big John and spoke quietly. "What about first doing the post mortem . . ." Then, assuming Big John couldn't possibly know what a "post mortem" was, he said, "I mean an autopsy—"

"I know what a post mortem is, Dr. Olsen. I've been doing some studying on the side."

"Good. Then let me do the post before we call the police—"

"We can't do that without first calling the police. We'd be tampering with the evidence if it turns out," Big John quieted his voice so Merlin could not hear him, "this body *is the evidence*. I'm supposed to know better'n to let that happen."

"I understand what you're saying, John. I really do, but I may be able to sidestep what will be a media nightmare if I can do the post and at least determine the cause of death. As soon as the police arrive, even if this is just a mistaken identity, this whole thing takes on the aura of a scandal. The Medical Center can't afford this kind of press. You with me?"

"Let me call this in, Doc. They'll send someone out and you can discuss it with them."

"I don't like this. Not one bit. I don't want a circus down here with the press. You tell 'em we're not certain what's going on, that this may be a big nothing."

Jake showed Big John to his office. The number for the Pittsburgh police station in Squirrel Hill was well known to all the hospital security personnel, and he dialed from memory. Big John immediately got through to a sleepy sergeant who said, "Sergeant Steckman," and chewed his sandwich loudly as he listened to the story. The details had a surreal quality, and Big John felt as if he were being swept up into a dream. He hadn't known Kevin Hoover, but wasn't quite as skeptical as Olsen had been about this being a case of mistaken identity.

The conversation lasted less than three minutes. What the sergeant heard was that a doctor *thought* he recognized one of the cadavers and that it *might* be someone who had disappeared more than a year ago. After hanging up the phone, the sergeant rolled his eyes and scratched his head. *Yeah, right. What a load of bullshit.*

A single phone call, after he finished his sandwich, was all it took to turf the case. The DA's office was anxious to work closely with the police and would occasionally be asked for a favor.

Mark Peters took the call. "Hello, Mark Peters."

"Yeah, Peters, this is Sergeant Paul Steckman, over here Zone Six, Squirrel Hill. We could use a little help."

"What's up?" Peters put his feet up on his desk.

"Just got a call from up the Med Center. Someone *thinks* he recognized one of the cadavers they got up in there for the students to dissect. A really bullshit case, if you ask me. Like something from *Hard Copy.* You know what I mean. But they requested someone go over, you know, calm 'em down. If it's anything, then the cavalry rides in."

"We can help," Peters said unenthusiastically. "You want one of my people to go over? I got a lot of hungry first-years." He laughed, like he and Steckman were working together, dumping the case on some pathetic first-year schmuck.

"I got six officers tied up at a burglary. You got someone who can stop by? You know, look official. I'd appreciate it."

"You bet."

"All right, Peters! Thanks a lot. Hey, lemme get your name. We like to know who the good-guy DAs are. You know what I mean?"

"Mark Peters. Mark with a 'K,' Peters with a P-E-T-E-R-S."

Each time Peters said a letter Steckman repeated it aloud slowly, like he was writing it down, but he was cradling the phone with his shoulder, holding a bottle of grape soda in one hand, a second salami sandwich in the other. "Hey, Peters, thanks a lot. Have 'em talk to Dr. Olsen—I think they said the ninth floor."

Like an adult version of whisper down the lane, each successive person who heard the story gave it an increasingly fictional quality until it almost sounded like a practical joke to Mark Peters, who debated less than the several seconds it took him to crack his knuckles which tight-ass assistant DA would enjoy a trip to the gross anatomy labs at the Medical Center.

Tory Welch stepped off the elevator on the ninth floor of the medical school trailed by the two drivers from the medical examiner's office. Even after a year in the department, mostly sitting in a chair, she still had the sleek, graceful look of an athlete playing dress-up. A long-distance runner at Yale, Tory always wore clothes that fit comfortably regardless of how dressy her outfit was. She tended to look as if she could sprint home without getting rumpled, and the two drivers had to walk double time to keep up. One of the drivers pushed a stretcher with an empty body bag.

Meanwhile Peters had spent the better part of an hour—about the time it took Tory to get to the medical school and meet up with the drivers from the medical examiner—going office to office telling his buddies the big joke. Ever since their first encounter, Tory had refused to have anything to do with him, which embarrassed Peters after the colorful show he had arranged for her first day.

Recently, Tory had been asking for cases more demanding than parking violations, and now, much to the delight of the let's-grab-a-beer-after-work crowd, Peters could send her on what seemed to be a cruel joke. Peters's recollection of their first day together went something like this: Tory's initial problems viewing the body extended through their entire visit to the ME, and that was the reason she had nothing to do with him.

As Peters said, with a toothy laugh, over and over to each comrade who would listen, "She couldn't stand to be in the morgue with *one* dead body—she'll be sportin' brown panties when she walks into a room *full* of dead bodies!"

Mortui Docent Vivos. Tory read the sign twice and wasn't certain she was at the anatomy labs until she meekly pushed one of the doors open. The rows of yellow-tarped cadavers reminded her of Times Square filled with taxis, and Tory immediately spotted the small group huddled around one of the tables. Their backs were toward her and she could not see the body. One of the medical examiner drivers, a veteran who had worked for Julian Plesser for more than a decade, gave Tory a reassuring nod.

The walk across the room seemed to take forever, Tory's heels clicking loudly off the linoleum like a metronome. As she approached the only table with an uncovered body, the group of four stopped talking and turned to watch her. Olsen, shirt tucked in, underwear plucked from his crotch, looked official with his CHAIRMAN OF PATHOLOGY nametag displayed, medical necessity taking precedence over geography. He spoke first. "Are you from the police department?"

"No, I'm Tory Welch from the DA's office."

Dr. Olsen looked at Big John. "Didn't you call the police?"

"Yes, I did—"

"Why don't you just call KDKA?"

"Doc, I did just what you told me—"

Tory cut Big John off, "The police department contacted us and asked if we would investigate. Are you in charge, sir?"

He liked being called sir. "Yes. I'm Dr. Jonathan Olsen. I'm chairman of pathology. One of my lab assistants, Dr. Merlin here"—Olsen pointed toward Merlin with his pipe, which felt reassuring in his hand, like a pacifier in the mouth of a two-month-old—"recognized this cadaver as Kevin Hoover. As you may remember, Kevin Hoover was a resident in general surgery here at the Medical Center who disappeared a little over a year ago."

"What do you mean 'disappeared?' " Tory asked.

"I mean he left the hospital one night after his shift in

the ER and vanished. The police looked into it. It's all well documented.''

Tory took a couple of steps forward and tried to look at the cadaver's face but she couldn't see beyond the exposed chest muscles as her mind wandered to her one and only experience with a dead body. After several seconds Tory turned to Merlin and said, ''How can you be certain? Could this be someone who looks like Kevin Hoover?''

''No. This *is* Kevin. I know for a fact that it is. And I can prove it to you.'' Merlin looked at Jake. ''Jake, help me flip him.'' The two worked as a silent team and quickly flipped the cadaver over onto his belly. The entire group, huddled tightly around the table, watched as Merlin pointed to the unusually shaped birthmark on the right calf. ''See. That birthmark, it's shaped like Italy. We used to kid him about it. That's Kevin's birthmark, same shape, same *exact* location.''

Tory stepped closer and nodded her head at the unusual shape of the brownish mark. Out of the corner of her eye Tory noticed Olsen staring at the back of the cadaver's head. He chewed on the end of his pipe as he bent forward in a frozen pose. ''You said he disappeared a year ago?'' Tory asked Merlin.

''About thirteen months ago. He disappeared one night. No one ever heard from him.''

''Until tonight, if we can believe this is Kevin Hoover,'' Olsen said.

''Print him,'' Merlin said. ''I know the police dusted his room for prints. See what was on his toothbrush; it'll match.''

Tory jotted something in her notebook. ''Dr. Olsen, have you examined this body?''

Olsen scratched his face before he answered. ''No, we waited for you. Politely, I might add, for almost two hours.''

''Is there something about his head that concerns you?''

"Not at all. But I'll have all your answers after I do examine him," Dr. Olsen answered matter-of-factly. "Do you have any paperwork or documentation?"

"My assistant, Jake Barnhouse, is trying to get it faxed from City General. What we've got here describes him as being sixty-seven years old. Look, Miss Welch, with your permission, I'm going to perform the post-mortem tonight. You can watch if you like. I think it would be best if we kept a tight media lid on this thing until after I've finished."

"Dr. Olsen, from what you've just told me, if this is really Kevin Hoover—and it appears we have good reason to believe he is—then a crime has been committed. This is clearly a case for the medical examiner."

"Miss Welch, do you realize the impact this will have on the Medical Center?"

"I certainly do. But there are protocols we must follow."

Olsen stepped closer to Tory. "The only protocol I'm interested in is finding out—"

"Doctor, what were you examining at the back of his head?"

Tory had pressed the button. Lightning coursed through Olsen's veins and he startled everyone with his explosion of anger. Olsen turned crimson; the veins in his neck bulged. "*Mzzzz* Welch," he hissed, and pointed a fat finger at Tory. "Don't you DARE interrupt me! Now, this is how we should handle this case. I will do the post—tonight—and provide you with a complete report. You may stay and watch if you like—"

The chairman of pathology easily intimidated the assistant district attorney. But it was obvious to Tory this was a coroner's case. "I'm sorry, Doctor. And I most certainly apologize if I've upset you. But this isn't our decision where the autopsy takes place. If there is any question that a crime has been committed, I've got to take the body downtown. This is a coroner's case. Period." Tory's voice was shaky.

"Counselor, it is usual and customary for hospitals to deal with, and investigate, the cause of death of patients—"

"I agree with you. But this body wasn't a patient in your hospital, Dr. Olsen. But I'll give you the benefit of the doubt. Let me make a call to the medical examiner and discuss the situation with him—"

"Who, Plesser?" Olsen's voice was louder.

"Yes."

"*Julian* Plesser?" Olsen screamed. "The hell you will. I'll give Jules a call. *You wait here.*" Olsen stormed out of the room. As he disappeared behind the swinging doors Tory let out a sigh.

Although there was a certain comic appeal watching a hugely corpulent person having a tirade, Olsen's anger had a raw edge, and no one thought to giggle. Tory gave a subtle nod to the drivers who stood silently by the stretcher. "You'd better take him quickly before the good doctor gets back."

The drivers beamed and immediately began an efficient transfer and bagging of the body.

Tory looked at Big John for the first time. He smiled and gave her a friendly two-fingered salute, brushing his fingers against his right eyebrow, and turned to leave.

Finally, Tory said to Merlin, "You okay to talk?"

"I don't know. I'm feeling pretty numb, and I've got to call Kevin's dad."

"Just give me a few minutes," Tory said softly.

"He'll want to know. He's been waiting a long time." Merlin looked off at the dark windows.

"Five minutes."

Somehow Tory and Merlin ended up in Jake's office. The door was open and the lights were on, and it seemed natural to walk away from the empty dissection table. But the office was gloomy. Gray everywhere—walls, floor, and desk. The only personal touch was a framed picture of a Doberman on the desk. Several old cardboard boxes were stacked in a corner, and a metal bookcase—gray—sagged under the weight of huge tomes on anatomy.

Tory sat behind the desk and opened her small brown leather notebook. Merlin slid a metal chair close to the desk and sat down. He rubbed his temples.

"M-E-R-L-I-N?" she asked, jotting down notes, waiting for a nod. "He was a good friend of yours, wasn't he?"

"Yeah, best friend." Merlin's voice was shaky. He looked away from Tory as his eyes welled up with tears.

Tory didn't know quite what to say and, as she collected her thoughts, impressed Merlin that she was being considerate. "I'm sorry. I know this is horrible." Merlin nodded. "I'm sorry to have to ask you so many questions, but can you fill me in a little more on what happened when Kevin disappeared?"

"There *aren't* any more details, that's the problem. He disappeared. Period."

"No reason?" Tory asked.

Merlin shook his head. "No. Nothing. After he was gone a couple of days the police came around, asked a lot of questions. Felt we were wasting their time. They lost interest when they couldn't find anything."

"Tell me what you remember about the day he disappeared. Did he work that day?"

"Yeah. He did. I was on the trauma service—twelve on, twelve off. Shift change was at nine. Anyway, Kevin was on the general surgery service and called me in the ER and asked if I'd stay an hour late to cover him while he spent some . . . uh . . . quality time with Jan . . ."

"Who's Jan?"

"His girlfriend. Jan Wolkin. She was an OR nurse. They would've ended up getting married."

"You spell her last name W-O-L-K-I-N?" she asked as she block printed the letters.

"Right. Your time off is really precious; you sort of guard it. Anyway, the last time I saw him he handed me his beeper. He had a silly grin. That was about nine P.M. He was supposed to page me at ten-thirty—Jan was on eleven to seven—and he and I'd go home together. At eleven o'clock I went up to fourteen, where the on-call rooms are, heard they were still busy, and left his beeper outside his door. I left without him. Jan said she left the on-call room around 11:45 and, we assume, Kevin left shortly after."

"You said Jan is an OR nurse?" Tory asked.

"Used to be. Not anymore. She's back in Bridgeport."

"Do you know how I can reach her?" Merlin shook his head. "How old was Kevin?"

"Twenty-eight. Almost twenty nine."

"Was Kevin in trouble? Drugs . . . ?"

"Maybe he smoked a little grass on weekends to relax. No different from anyone else. I mean, he didn't deal, if that's what you mean."

"There was never any reason to believe he was dead?"

"After Kevin had been missing for a couple days his dad came in—I remember his mom dying when we were in med school. Mr. Hoover's from upstate New York. Anyway, he camped out in my apartment waiting. Every day I'd come home from the hospital and Mr. Hoover'd be sitting there reading or staring at the TV, always gave me a smile. You know the type. Optimistic to a fault. Then one night I came home and he was packing Kevin's things, and he just looked at me and we both knew. That's when we assumed he was dead.

"He wasn't the type to run away, leave someone he loved, and go off to Tahiti. Jan hung in for a couple of months, but then she went back home."

Jake walked in. "Excuse me, Miss Welch. I'm Jake Barnhouse; I'm in charge of the labs. Dr. Olsen asked me

to drop off this fax from City General. He said you wanted
a copy.'' He handed her a photocopy of the fax. ''When
the bodies come in I just embalm 'em. I don't even look
at them. I—I had no idea.''

Tory took the copy of the medical record and started to
read it.

Jake turned to Merlin. ''Merlin, I'm sorry, really.''

Tory looked up from the photocopy, toward Jake.
''When do you embalm the bodies? Right away?''

''They're either embalmed at the referring institution or
we do it here, usually within twenty-four hours. Mostly,
they're done here. The law.''

''Who actually does the embalming?''

Jake hesitated for the briefest moment. ''I do. That's
my job.'' He sounded like a child accused unjustly of
stealing some candy.

''Thanks, Jake. Listen, I'll need to sit down with
you . . . maybe sometime tomorrow.''

''Yeah, yeah, anytime. You know, I didn't even know
him. I haven't been here that long.'' Jake turned and left
as abruptly as he had entered.

Tory looked back at the photocopy of the death record
Jake had handed her. It was obvious to her untrained eye
the cadaver she had seen wasn't a sixty-seven-year-old.
Merlin broke the silence, ''He sounds suspicious.''

''Who?''

''Jake.''

''He sounds upset, like everyone else around here
does.''

''Miss Welch, why are you here? I mean, where are
the police?''

''It's departmental. Like I told Dr. Olsen, sometimes
the police will ask us to examine a case. Don't worry—
I'll requisition all the files from their initial investigation.
I'll have them by morning.''

Merlin did not look reassured. ''Answer one question
for me. What're the odds of solving a year-old murder?''

Tory thought a long time before answering. No one had used the word "murder" until now, but it was becoming obvious that, indeed, she was investigating a homicide. "I don't know."

Six

After talking with Merlin, Tory arranged with the police to have the Kevin Hoover file faxed to her office, then went home to bed. She slept poorly, forcing herself to wake from an uncomfortable dream.

She was dancing, feeling elegant and beautiful, wearing a long sequined gown in an ornate ballroom. Every time the music stopped, her partner, whose face she could not see, bowed deeply. When he stood up, it was Kevin Hoover. Naked from the waist up. And suddenly, Dr. Olsen appeared and asked if he could have the next dance. But when the music started again it was Dr. Olsen and Kevin who moved gracefully across the dance floor.

No hidden message, no ominous warning, just a frightening rehash of her unsettling evening. The dream repeated itself like a record skipping back on itself. Over and over. Louder and louder. Finally, when it was still dark, and she could no longer face the nightmares, Tory showered and dressed, then drove to her office.

The police file, seventeen pages in all, sat on her desk—thin, shiny fax copies so curled up Tory had to spend several minutes photocopying them. Reports were filed from two uniformed officers and one detective. Physicians, nurses, and family members, none of whom lived in Pittsburgh, were interviewed and briefly documented. Tory read the entire file twice and quickly developed a short list of people she would interview. The only name Tory placed on her list that did not also appear in the police file was that of Jake Barnhouse.

Then an image of Julian Plesser popped into her mind. How many nights had she stared up at the ceiling, thinking about her first trip to the medical examiner, never capturing the essence of her visit? Too many, she thought. The woozy vertigo in the hallway before she went in. The acrid smell that stung her eyes and never seemed to leave her clothing. Dr. Plesser's finger sliding in and out of the esophagus. Those were the middle-of-the-night worries she couldn't shake.

But she also remembered being swept up in the fascinating details of the case, losing that sick feeling in her stomach as her mind clicked away in synch with Dr. Plesser's, trying to piece the facts together into something that made sense. And she left the medical examiner's office that first and only time particularly intrigued with Julian Plesser. He was someone no doubt worth getting to know better.

By the time Tory made it over to the medical examiner's office, it was almost nine o'clock. It was a crisp, cool morning. Tory bought a *Post-Gazette* from a corner vendor. There was no mention of Kevin Hoover, but she realized it was just a matter of time before the press would swoop down on the Medical Center. It was also just a matter of time before Mark Peters would realize that this case, which could become increasingly sensational, could have catapulted him into the national news media and take him anywhere he wanted to go.

When Tory finally pushed through the frosted-glass doors to the medical examiner's autopsy room she was struck by how little the room had changed in the past year: three tables, running water tinkling in the background, even the Forrest Gump poster.

Julian Plesser, alone, was standing in front of the middle autopsy table, greasy gloved hands comfortably tucked into his armpits. A body was lying, face up, behind him. His chest was opened in the manner she'd seen before, but she could not see his face. It was a small effort to look away.

"Dr. Plesser. I don't know if you remember me, I'm—"

Julian smiled. "Tory Welch. I remember you. Your buddy Olsen called me about you last night. Twice."

"He scared me."

"You handled it fine."

"You probably think I'm getting in over my head, right?"

"You would've been if you'd let him do the post. Let me ask you a question."

"Sure." Tory took a second look at the body and saw it. "Oh, my God. What—" It looked to her as if his head had been chopped off. How could she have missed it when she first walked in? "Is that Kevin Hoover?" she asked, clutching her little brown notebook tightly.

"It's the body you saw last night."

After a few seconds the initial shock abated and allowed her to process things a bit. The head wasn't *gone*. It had been opened. The top of the skull was removed, sitting on the table by the right shoulder like a shallow bowl, and Tory was able to look down into the base of the empty skull. Empty. Lined with light blue mother of pearl. It reminded Tory of a horrible life-sized Pez dispenser with the top snapped off. No brain. Tory's eyes flitted about the room. *The brain. Where's the brain?* The desk. No. The bookshelves. No.

"Tory what are you looking for?"

"What happened to his brain?"

"You okay?"

"I'm fine. This is a helluva lot easier than the last time I was here," Tory said with a forced laugh. Then she spotted it, a large gray cauliflower with blue veins running its surface, sitting alone on the third autopsy table.

"How'd you ever get those good 'ol boys to give you a high-profile murder case?" Julian asked pleasantly.

"I didn't. At least I don't think I did. What I got was

a case of mistaken identity Mark Peters didn't want at six P.M.'' They laughed.

"If this was just a case of mistaken identity, why'd you call for my drivers to meet you at the Medical Center?''

" 'Cause I'm green, and maybe I subconsciously didn't want to go alone . . . I don't know. I guess it's better to be lucky than good.''

"Trust me—you won't go through this unscathed. You'll make mistakes, but you won't make 'em twice. You trust yourself?'' Plesser asked.

Tory thought about her confrontation with Dr. Olsen. "I think so,'' she said with a trace of pride.

"Good. Enough lecture. You ready to get started?'' Plesser asked. Tory nodded. "First of all, the paperwork. What I got from the Medical Center is basically toe tag number 4-1-7, which corresponds to the documentation sent with him. The name on the Medical Center records, Robert Gardner, age sixty-seven, nickname 'Red.' '' Plesser paused, looked at Tory. "This kid here probably was in his twenties, maybe his thirties. Unless that's a typo, there's been a switch of paperwork. Or the bodies. Anyway''—Julian flipped the page on his clipboard—"I got this faxed to me from City General, this Red Gardner was homeless, an alcoholic. He died of a GI bleed in the ER at City General. Not much information, but that's not Red Gardner. It doesn't say where he was embalmed—probably the Medical Center. And the birthmark—my drivers called me—actually a café au lait spot, is unique. I took photos.''

As she got involved with the details of the case, she relaxed the death grip on her leather notebook, and it was left with a dark, wet imprint of her hand. "So, do you think he's Kevin Hoover?''

"With the positive ID from that resident and that birthmark, yes, I'm going to call him Kevin Hoover. We'll get dental records later today, but that's just to confirm something I think we already know. And by the way, he was definitely murdered, a single blow to the back of his head. Someone strong."

"Back of the head," Tory said, absently. She bit her lower lip and thought about Olsen. "Tell me more about the injury."

"I haven't done cross-sections on the brain, but the base of the skull is crushed. An epidural hematoma and herniation."

Tory looked confused, "What's that?"

"He was hit so hard the impact crushed part of the skull and ruptured an artery under the bone. It continued to pump blood, but unlike a water balloon, the skull has no room for expansion—solid bone—and the pressure built up. That's the epidural hematoma. In Kevin's case the pressure came on quickly, within minutes, and pushed his brain until it herniated out of the skull and down toward the spine."

"Oh, my God." Tory's knees felt wobbly.

Julian watched the color drain from Tory's face. "Fortunately, he died quickly. He'd be on a ventilator in some chronic-care facility if he'd survived."

"Could you tell about the injury just from looking at him? I mean from the outside?"

"Oh, yeah. The back of his head was indented, the skin discolored from the bleeding. Hard to miss. Why?"

"I'm not sure."

"A curious thing I noticed, Tory. Most embalmings involve a single site. The neck, for example, where the infusion catheter is placed. It usually takes a few hours. Kevin has three injection sites: neck, groin, and left arm."

"Meaning what?"

"Well, multiple injection sites usually mean the embalmer had trouble pushing the embalming fluid through the body and had to switch locations. A young healthy kid like this should've been easy to do. Maybe someone was in a rush and wanted to do him quickly."

"You know the last time I was here there was a body

fished out of the river, and it was embalmed. You called it Margery . . . something like a girl's name . . ."

"I wondered if you'd make the connection. You've got a good memory. I called it a Mallory–Weiss tear. Fancy name for a GI bleed." Plesser picked up a file from his desk and talked as he read from the typewritten pages. "Uh . . . red hair . . . sixty to seventy years old . . . GI bleed . . . sound familiar?"

"Certainly does."

"Here's the scenario: Kevin Hoover disappeared a year ago and was murdered—probably in the hospital—embalmed, and tucked away in the gross anatomy lab. A simple switch of bodies. The first-year students dissect the face. Once they hack him up a bit you'd have—"

"A perfect murder," Tory whispered.

"That's right. A perfect murder. The anatomy lab has the correct number of bodies. The extra body is dumped in the river and, even if it's ever found," Julian smiled, "died of natural causes."

"You're fantastic. You figured the whole thing out."

"It all fits, doesn't it," Dr. Plesser said, sliding his hands together, smoothly interlocking his fingers.

"Buy why? Now take me one step further. Why was Kevin Hoover killed in the first place?"

"I don't know, but let's think it through a bit. A random killing? No way. Why bother with this elaborate plan to hide the body if you had no connection to it."

"What about a psycho? A serial killer?" Tory asked.

"If there'd been any missing hospital personnel since then, maybe. But with only one, I don't think so."

"Okay, then what?"

"Let's agree that he was killed within the hospital. It stands to reason one wouldn't bring a murdered doctor back to his *own* hospital, right?"

Tory nodded.

Julian continued, "Okay, then it's either business or pleasure. They all are."

"Business or pleasure?"

Julian nodded. "Business. Kevin owed money, didn't make good on a deal, saw something he shouldn't have seen. You know, that sort of thing." He paused. "Pleasure. He got caught having a good time with someone's wife. Something like that."

"Tell me a little about Olsen."

"He's actually an impressive guy. Jonathan wrote the definitive anatomy manual that practically every medical school uses. He's also a mean-spirited bastard, and the next time you run into him he'll give you a hard time, guaranteed. Oh yeah, in 1950 . . . maybe '51 . . . he was captain of some collegiate debating team. Won some trophies. Loves to talk about it."

"Nice to get a look at his playbook."

"How's that?"

"Oh, you know what they say. The best defense is a good offense." Tory thought for a minute. "Can I run something by you?"

"Absolutely. You're going to need a sounding board on this one. Feel free, unless you'd rather huddle with your buddy Peters." Julian laughed.

Tory rolled her eyes. "Anyway, last night I noticed Dr. Olsen staring—I mean bent over, staring intently—at the back of the head. It's obvious now what he was looking at. But when I asked him what he was examining he wouldn't tell me. Flat-out refused. I also asked him if he'd examined the body before I got there, and he denied that. But the way he flew off the handle when I insisted on sending the body to you . . . well, what do you think?"

Julian nodded. "I'll give you two possibilities. One, just what you're thinking. How awfully convenient it would be to do the autopsy on a body you killed. You could generate whatever cause of death you want, destroy evidence, substitute evidence.

"However, let's consider a second possibility. Olsen, a pompous sonovabitch who loves to take charge, spots the indented skull and assumes, correctly, the method of murder. But he can't bear the thought of relinquishing a juicy case. So he plays dumb when you asked him about the back of the head, and explodes when some young *girl* stands up to him.

"Besides, Tory, going back to the first scenario, if he murdered Kevin Hoover, why call attention to himself by examining the skull?"

Tory thought for a moment. She'd seen Dr. Olsen display a terrifying outburst of emotion that certainly demanded closer inspection. " 'Cause he's a debater, and debaters play the odds, taking calculated risks at times. At that point he knew there was an excellent likelihood you were going to examine the body. Right? And a good debater knows something about psychology, and sometimes pointing out the obvious can be an effective means to an end.''

Seven

Demasi's Produce was the largest produce warehouse in Pittsburgh's Strip District, a riverside stretch of buildings where fresh produce, meats, cheeses, and breads were distributed throughout the entire city. Taking up one entire block, Demasi's had been around for seventeen years and had become successful for one reason: Mike Demasi. A combination of personality and integrity fostered enormous growth as Demasi's routinely undercut its competitors.

Mike Demasi worked from 4:30 A.M. to late afternoon, Monday through Friday, and oversaw every aspect of his business. Although the warehouse was busy throughout the early-morning hours, no office personnel arrived until nine o'clock giving Mike a couple of hours to catch up on paperwork. This was the only quiet part of his day, and he thoroughly enjoyed sitting in his dark little office eating fresh cinnamon rolls baked right down the street. An occasional employee might stop upstairs to ask for an advance on his next paycheck or confide some family news to Mike, but otherwise Mike spent the time alone.

So it was no surprise when Mike heard someone walking up the wooden stairs to his office. Mike looked up from his correspondence and was startled, however, to see a man standing in his doorway whom he had never seen before. The cane-backed wooden swivel chair that had been Mike's father's creaked loudly as he sat forward. "Can I help you?"

"You Mike Demasi?" the man said. His voice was

low and confident. He took a bite of a perfect apple and crunched loudly.

"Yes. What can I do for you?" Mike asked, then cleared his throat. Although just standing in the doorway chewing an apple, this man was physically frightening. Like a body builder in off-the-rack dress clothes, his dark suit emphasized huge thighs and powerful biceps. The jacket, sort of matching the pants, couldn't be buttoned without giving him the look of a dressed-up hippopotamus, and his shoulders nearly spanned the entire doorway, leaving only a tiny slip of space for Mike to spot a second man lurking in the shadows.

There was a microphone on the desk, an old-fashioned one that sat on a little round base. It was used to page his men when a personal telephone call came in and it was only about eighteen inches from his right hand. Mike looked at it momentarily.

"Good apple," the man said as he worked his tongue behind his upper lip to loosen a piece of fruit caught between his teeth. Then he took another bite.

Mike stood up. There was something about conducting business face to face, not looking up at the guy, and Mike sure as hell didn't want to invite him to sit down. As he pushed up from his chair, the man eating the apple took a single step forward toward the desk. Only a couple of dozen words had been said in their brief conversation, but much more than that had be communicated, and the big man smiled as he saw Mike sit back down.

"Who are you; what do you want?" Mike asked quietly.

The man walked over to a wall filled with framed photographs of his family. "This your wife?"

"Uh-huh. It is."

"Tennis player. Nice looking. Your daughter, huh? Pretty, like her mom."

Now he was really frightened. "What's this all about?" Mike asked, his voice trembling.

The man noted the change in Mike's voice and the way Mike was sitting in the chair, slouching as though he was being compressed by something. That was the man's cue to continue. *I gotcha now, Mike. You work for me.* "I work for Mr. Bevel. He wanted me to talk with you."

Demasi rubbed his forehead. "Oh." The name Bevel was widely known to everyone in the Strip District. Feared more than hated, Frank Bevel controlled several important pieces of real estate. Mike knew immediately why Mr. Bevel had sent some muscle to his office. *Grab it. Grab the goddamned microphone.* But his hands gripped the sides of his chair, and he was unable to move. He wanted to scream for help, but it was too late and he was too frightened. The room got very quiet. There were sounds of the trucks rumbling on the cobblestones outside, but they seemed in another world, and the warm aroma of cinnamon was replaced by the sweet odor of cologne. "I know who Mr. Bevel is. What do you want?"

"I don't want nothing. You know," the man smiled. "Mr. Bevel wants something." Another bite of the apple.

"Okay. What does Mr. Bevel want?"

"Mr. Bevel wants to make an offer on Demasi's Produce."

"I guessed so," he said weakly. It really wasn't a surprise. Demasi's was profitable, and Mike had feared this moment for the last several years. It had happened to two other businesses. Both had sold.

"This is a good apple. You grow 'em in Pennsylvania? What do you call this kind? I might want to get some." The big man took a step toward Mike. The second man stayed in the doorway, said nothing.

"They're—uh—they're called McIntosh," he said quietly.

"You don't mind if I take a few on the way out do you?"

The microphone could be grabbed in an instant, his voice screaming for help even before his thumb found the black button to broadcast his cries. But he knew what would happen. The apple would be thrown aside as the man thundered toward him. *Stay calm. Pretend it's a business proposal.* "Sir," Mike's voice high like a truant collared by the principal, "I don't know what you've heard on the street, but we're not for sale. We've never been for sale. Are you certain—"

The man ignored what Mike was saying and continued with his business plan. "Mr. Bevel would like to get more involved in the fresh-produce business. He would propose a very reasonable price. You tell him what would make you happy, and Mr. Bevel would even relocate you to a desirable location someplace else."

Although wearing an open-neck shirt, Mike tugged at the collar. The big man with the apple liked what he saw. He never released Mike's eyes from the grip of his stare.

"Could I think about it?"

The big man grinned. The deal was all but consummated. "Absolutely. Mr. Bevel specifically said, 'Don't rush Mike Demasi.' You and me'll have another meeting, let's say . . . what's today? Tuesday, huh?" He turned to the guy in the doorway, a skinny guy wearing a leather jacket, his face lost in the shadows, and got a nod. "Okay, let's say you'n me on Thursday, about eight."

"Okay. I guess that—"

"P.M.

"Eight at night? There's nobody here at—"

"Hey look, I don't want to interrupt you when you're making big fruit deals, or bopping your secretary, or what. Yeah, eight at night. You'n me."

Mike Demasi didn't say a word. The big man ate his apple. Two more bites and it was gone. He flipped the core with a gentle arc and hit Mike in the chest. As it bounced off and started to fall Mike caught it.

"Nice catch. You play some ball in your time? Oh, one more thing, Mike. Let's meet alone. A couple of businessmen like us don't need no distractions, you capice?"

Mike's mouth was so dry he couldn't talk. The man turned toward the door and his partner turned to start down the stairs. "Hey, I almost forgot. I'm sure you know a lot about Mr. Bevel. Things get said. Street shit." The man took a step toward Mike and lowered his voice until it took on a menacing quality. "I want you to know something. What you hear around the Strip is true," the man said and pointed a fat finger at Mike and emphasized each word with a flick of his stubby baton. "Don't fuck with Mr. Bevel. You think things over, Mike. Then we talk. Alone. You got a nice family, Mike. A nice produce stand in Cranberry or the South Hills wouldn't be so bad. Think about it. My name's Erno, by the way. That's Satch." Erno and Mike looked over to the doorway. Satch was nodding his head. "He don't smile much. Hey, thanks for the apple."

Long after Erno Pantuzzi creaked down the old stairs his cologne lingered behind, and Mike Demasi sat there holding the apple core.

Eight

The Allegheny County Courthouse is a massive castlelike building, full of archways and turrets, built entirely of cut stone. Seemingly dropped into a crowd of taller office buildings, it actually predated most of them. There was a time when the district attorney's offices, on the third and fourth floors, commanded excellent views of the Mon River and the hills beyond it, but Mother Nature had long ago been replaced with steel and concrete edifices.

The brief walk back from the medical examiner—not the circuitous one she had taken with Mark Peters the first time she met Julian Plesser—hardly gave Tory a chance to review the case. She entered the imposing Romanesque structure at street level, which originally had been the basement, and only became the entryway when construction lowered Grant Street about a dozen feet.

Quite by surprise, she rode the elevator with Mark Peters, who stepped in just as the doors were closing. Peters looked sharp in a tailored brown suit, light blue shirt, and a blue and red tie. The *Wall Street Journal* was in one hand, a leather briefcase in the other. "Morning, Tory. No loose ends on your mistaken identify?" he said, suppressing a grin. They stood side by side, looking above the shiny brass doors at the lighted numbers. Despite the presence of several other people, mostly clerical staff, Peters wanted to talk business.

Tory spotted the smirk in his reflection. "You don't

know, do you, Mark?'' Tory queried in a tone of voice
designed to attract attention.
    "Know what?'' he asked casually, expecting to be re-
galed with minutiae from her trip to the anatomy labs.
    "That was no mistaken identify. Didn't you check your
voice mail?''
    Peters turned slightly and faced Tory. "Tory, cut to the
chase.'' His tone seemed urgent.
    She'd gotten to him.
    Tory leaned closer to Peters and stage whispered, "The
body.'' Tory turned around, in an exaggerated motion,
ostensibly to make certain their conversation was truly
private. "We think it might be *Jimmy Hoffa*. Not sure yet.
Wait 'til we get off.'' Tory looked at the brightly polished
door and caught Peters's eye in his reflection as he turned
away from her. She winked coyly. Someone behind them
giggled. He could wait until the fourth floor.
    Tory stepped off the elevator first and waited just out-
side the heavy glass doors adorned with simple black lettering: "District Attorney.'' Peters was intrigued but
wouldn't dream of tipping his hand. "Okay, Tory, whatcha
got?'' he asked with a hint of annoyance in his voice.
    "Mark, this wasn't a mistaken identity.''
    "Then what is it?'' He sounded irritated.
    "Maybe you remember about a year ago, a doctor dis-
appeared from the Medical Center.''
    Peters nodded his head in obvious recognition. "Go
on.'' He had no idea what Tory was talking about.
    "Well, his name was Kevin Hoover. He was a resident
in surgery, and they never found him. Nothing. It was in
all the papers.
    "Last night his buddy spots him in the gross anatomy
lab being dissected by the medical students. I just left Dr.
Plesser. Kevin Hoover was murdered. Evidently he was
hidden in the lab for the med students to destroy.''
    "Wait a second.'' Mark Peters was at a complete loss
for words. "Have you told anyone about this?''

"No."

"Why am I finding out about this at—" Peters looked at his watch—"eight-thirty? Never mind. My office. Five minutes." Peters grabbed the door handle. "Tory, talk to no one."

"There's more."

"Not here," he said crossly.

Peters pulled open the heavy glass door and walked through quickly. He needed to be alone, to think, to regroup. His secretary, a fifty-year-old woman who always wore her hair in a bun and favored sweaters draped around her shoulders and closed at the neck by a small silver chain, stood as he streamed past. She had a neat little stack of messages, but Peters held out his right hand like a traffic cop to warn her not to bother him as he disappeared into his office and closed the door. Before his secretary could sit down, he opened the door partway, stuck his head out and said, "Sue, no calls. *No calls.* I don't want to talk to anyone. Not my broker, not my mother. No one. And when Tory arrives, buzz me." He closed the door, loudly, for emphasis.

Office size, location, and window view are the most reliable ways to determine pecking order within many organizations, and Peters's was third-best in the department. His two-window view was better than most, but the last time he bothered to enjoy it was six months ago. It was after a string of successful trials—and coincident with the sudden retirement of a colleague—that he was rewarded with a promotion at the weekly Friday wrap-up meeting. When the meeting broke up, Peters, wanting nothing more than to run into his new office and jump up and down like a kid, held his throbbing ego in check and forced himself to saunter into his new home with humble pride. Although carefully staged by Peters, as if but one more rung on the very tall ladder of success, it was the only time he ever walked over to his window and, knowing others watched him from the doorway with burning jealousy, savored his view. It was one of those wonderful snippets of time he would reflect on with great pride.

The office was very bright, modern in furnishings, the centerpiece of which was a large blond wooden desk sitting directly in front of the window overlooking the river. A computer terminal and phone sat on the otherwise uncluttered desk and an annoying cluster of wires spilled off the back of the desk and down into a hole in the light brown carpet. Simple conduits for electrical impulses hadn't progressed in the exponential fashion technology had. A chocolate brown leather chair behind the desk was complemented by two smaller ones facing the desk. One wall was taken up with a large wooden credenza rendered by the same craftsman as the desk, complete with a tastefully stocked bar and private fax. Two framed photos of Peters shaking hands with the mayor and one of him with Mario Lemieux at a charity function adorned the opposite wall, arranged around his Princeton diploma.

Finally alone, he threw his briefcase onto one of the smaller leather chairs so that it came to rest standing on one end, leaning awkwardly against the armrest. Then he dropped his frame into the desk chair, spun it around, and focused his gaze above the buildings to the trees atop Mt. Washington. He couldn't get comfortable. His right hand beat a nervous rhythm on the armrest and he put his right, then his left foot on the window sill. He shifted in his chair, tried rubbing his temples, and finally closed his eyes. *I gave away a . . . goddamned . . . fucking . . . murder case. But you can make order out of chaos; you've done it before. C'mon. Try. Look for the silver lining; it's gotta be out there. Dig in hard. Do it. There's an opportunity. SEE IT. DAMNIT.* A successful burst of inspiration was required, and Peters talked to himself and reviewed the sketchy elements of what he knew.

A murdered doctor turning up in the anatomy lab. What a field day the press would have. But this case was attractive for one simple reason: It would never be solved. Peters smiled to himself. Although time erodes memory, dramatic events, like a witnessed shooting or rape, were etched into one's mind forever. But, unless someone came forward with key testimony, this case was likely to remain a mystery. And if there were witnesses to the victim's disappearance, something had kept them from contacting the authorities. Police records needed to be scanned, friends and relatives needed to be interviewed, and hours needed to be wasted.

Yet the array of press conferences, possibly on a national level, would showcase someone from his department. A clear voice of reason and authority would be noticed. Pithy sound bites for the evening news could also become eye-catchers in weekly magazines, printed in large type within the text of the article.

"Mr. Peters, Tory is here," Sue said by way of the intercom.

"Thanks, Sue; send her in," Peters said, with a tone of confidence. His hand had stopped its rhythmic beating on the armrest, and he nestled himself comfortably into the supple leather of his chair. Twirling his chair around so he would face his visitor, he picked up his phone and began to speak, "Yeah, I think Hilton Head would be great. Let's call Chip and make this a reunion . . ."

His door opened and Tory stood in the doorway holding a brown accordion file. Their rapid-fire exchange outside the elevator left her uncertain what Peters would say to her, and she tapped her knuckles timidly on the jamb until he waved her in as he continued to prattle on. Tory had always been put off by people who insisted on sharing their end of a personal phone conversation with strangers. For the next minute she endured a discussion of restaurants, bars, and golf courses before Peters ran out of monologue and ended the soliloquy.

". . . Thursday morning we can get eighteen in before you buy the first round. Hey, I've got someone to see me, lemme call you back. Right. Bye.'' Peters hung up with satisfaction. ''Tory, sit down.'' He sounded cordial.

As Tory sat in the only empty chair in the room she looked, momentarily, at the briefcase, obviously thrown into the chair next to her. It looked out of place.

''I brought the police file. I didn't know if you would want to see it,'' Tory said.

Peters reached across his desk, took the file, and perfunctorily began to read it as he spoke. ''So this kid—what was his name again, Hoover?—disappeared a year ago.''

''About thirteen months.''

''The police find anything?'' Peters asked.

''Nothing.''

''No one hate him?''

''No.''

''No previous record?''

''No. Mark, I know it doesn't make sense, but he vanished into the night.''

''What do you mean 'into the night?' ''

Tory thought briefly, not certain how much of her conversation with Merlin she was ready to reveal. ''The last person to see him was his girlfriend before he left the hospital around midnight.''

''The girlfriend check out all right?''

''The police seemed to think so. She's not living in Pittsburgh anymore.''

''Check her out. Is this an active case? I mean, can the police take it?'' Peters wanted to know.

''Look at the last page.'' Tory waited while Peters flipped the stapled pages and quickly read a statement on the last page. ''They signed off about six months ago. It's ours.''

''You said there's more.''

''My first day here you and I went to the morgue and saw the body of a red-haired man pulled out of the river.''

''Yeah.'' His memory of that day was still painful.

''His name was Red Gardner, and his body had been

donated to the medical school for gross anatomy dissection. You remember, he was embalmed when they pulled him out of the river. Anyway, his body was found the day *after* Kevin Hoover disappeared. Probably a switch of bodies.''

Peters was taken aback. With each layer of detail it became increasingly obvious how tantalizing the case was. ''This is big. I mean a career-maker. You know this type of homicide is tough.''

''Mark, give me a chance. I've got a couple of—I don't know if they're really leads, but—things to check out.''

''That's great that you're on top of things, but I'm a bit concerned. If this were domestic violence, a robbery, or even drug related I wouldn't feel this way. But a doctor, turning up in the anatomy lab, switched for God-knows-who. That's dicey.''

''You gave me the case. And I've handled things correctly so far. I think it's mine.''

''But it's my ass, too. As you said, *I* assigned you the case.''

''Why did you?'' Tory asked, then looked away from Peters almost embarrassed to hear his response.

''You've asked a couple of times for something more challenging. When the call came in I thought of you. It's quite a bit more''—Peters searched for a word—''high profile than I originally thought.'' Then, almost as an afterthought, Peters added, ''You haven't talked with anyone, have you?''

''I told you already, of course not.''

''The police?''

''No.''

''The press?'' Peters asked with the precise cadence and tone of voice he'd been using.

''No, Mark. I've talked with no one.'' Tory sounded irritated.

''Tory, we HAVE to make a statement to the press for a couple of reasons. One, to show we're in control and two, to establish that we—not the police—intend to handle it. Have you ever done a press conference?''

''Don't patronize me. You know I haven't.'' Tory sensed what was coming next. ''You're going to take this case away from me, aren't you?''

''Absolutely not. But you tell me, are you ready to handle a press conference? Are you ready to go under the magnifying glass?''

''I've gotta start sometime.''

Peters closed his eyes and rubbed them with his thumb and forefinger. ''Tory, what would you say is the biggest case you've handled since joining us?''

Tory stared at him, tight-lipped, for several seconds before answering. ''Probably the Burger King robbery.''

''Right, the Burger King robbery.'' Peters raised his eyebrows and pursed his lips as if he were stunned. ''That the one where those punks got a couple of hundred bucks, ran outta gas in the parking lot?''

''Right.'''

''We win it?''

''No.'' Tory got the message.

He, playing the role of mentor, slowed the pace and thought things through from a variety of angles. ''All right, Tory, it's yours. I want you to run this case. Take it as far as you can.

''You've got my support. But I don't know if the boss will buy it. I just don't know.'' He ran his hand through his hair, putting on a show. ''Maybe you'n I can work something out, though. As long as you're hunting down leads you can go at your own pace with no one looking over your shoulder.

''Let me be frank. You're not ready for the media arena. I think you and I both know it. A press conference throws you right to the wolves.

''How does this sound? I'll handle the press for you, but that's it. You run the show. I'll talk with the boss, make things right with him. You get the credit.''

Tory hesitated and took a deep breath. She was clearly disappointed. "It's your call, Mark."

"Oh no, it's up to you. As I said, it's your case. If you want to go it alone, just say so. But if *your* press conference, which will happen today whether or not we want it to, doesn't go well, I pull you off it entirely."

"You made your point, Mark." Her voice betrayed her irritation.

"Good. We'll need to talk daily. You call the shots but I've got to know what's going on."

Acting more like a scribe than the senior attorney, Peters sat quietly and took notes as Tory described the events in the anatomy lab and the preliminary findings of the autopsy. When she stopped talking he clarified several points, sat back in his chair with his fingers clasped behind his neck, and asked, "Okay, so where do you begin?"

"With Dr. Olsen. With the way he exploded at me, I want to see how he reacts when I tell him about the head injury."

"Let me give you my expanding-circle theory. When you don't have a solid lead, start as close to the victim as you possibly can, then broaden your investigation with a wider and wider circle of supporting players. Olsen is clearly second tier. Start with"—he looked down at his notes—"this Barnhouse fellow. I'd learn as much about him as you can, then follow any leads he generates or, if he doesn't pan out, broaden and talk with Olsen. Here, let me see your notebook." Peters shifted forward in his chair while Tory slid her brown leather notebook across the desk toward him.

He opened it and at the bottom of the first page drew what appeared to be a target. In the center he wrote "Hoover," around it he drew a circle and, turning the book several times to keep his print on the curved line, wrote "Barnhouse," around that a larger circle with three words: "Olsen," "Merlin" and "Jan." He also wrote "6-6-2-6" before he slid the book back to Tory.

Tory studied Peters's expanding circle theory. "Thanks."
She stood and started to leave.

"That's my private extension. Call me before six. And
Tory, will you ask Sue to step in here?"

The press conference was a done deal.

Nine

It was just after noon when Tory parked her Saab in the multilevel parking garage two blocks from the Medical Center. All steel and concrete and opened widely on each of its four sides, the garage had a pleasant breeze blowing through it. Nevertheless, the central stairwell was poorly lit, and although parked on the second level, Tory chose to wait for the elevator. She looked trim in a dark green suit, white silk blouse, flats, and her gold bangle.

When she joined the District Attorney's office her father, a retired cop from Philadelphia, had sent her a small canister of Mace, which was stowed deep inside her Coach bag. Never in a million years would she admit it, but her ritual in parking garages, which always felt particularly claustrophobic to her, had become to palpate the bottom of her bag until she identified the cylindrical bulge of the Mace.

The walk to the Medical Center and up to gross anatomy took nine minutes, but the doors were locked. A handwritten sign on yellow-lined paper, turned sideways and taped to one of the swinging doors read: FIRST-YEAR STUDENTS: GROSS ANATOMY LAB CANCELED UNTIL NEXT WEEK. JAKE BARNHOUSE. Tory read the words twice. *And now for the second tier of the Mark Peters expanding-circle theory.*

The hallway was quite empty. Dark walls, gray linoleum floors, and infrequent globed lights gave it an abandoned feeling. Directly across from the anatomy lab was the express elevator to the loading dock. To the right was a short hallway and a metal fire door leading back to the Medical Center; to the left a longer hallway leading to the medical school elevators Tory had just taken, as well as an open doorway apparently leading to an office. Light spilled out into the hallway, and Tory drifted toward it.

The door to the office, a tall one going almost floor to ceiling with a single, rectangular semiopaque pane of glass that at one time must have been considered attractive, was fully opened. A small plastic sign on the wall, just to the right, said, "Jonathan Olsen, MD, PhD, Chairman, Department of Anatomy." Tory stood for a minute and listened to what she assumed was Dr. Olsen's secretary talking on the phone.

". . . Yes, I'll give him the message, but he told me not two hours ago he would not grant any interviews. Absolutely not." There was a short pause. "I'm sure it is important. Why don't you try administration?" Another pause. "No, I don't have the extension. Good-bye." Tory heard the phone being cradled as the words "Good-bye" were being uttered. Dr. Olsen's secretary sounded about as warm as her boss. Tory tucked her hair behind her ear, a nervous habit from high school, and walked into what was a tight, windowless anteroom. The door to Dr. Olsen's office, eight feet straight across the room, was closed. The walls were blank except for an art poster that said I LOVE YOU VERY MUCH. To the left, a narrow coat closet door was opened halfway and several crisply laundered white coats, each encased in plastic and on a separate hanger, hung precariously from the top of the door. A low black metal file cabinet, piled high with charts, was pushed up against the wall. To the right, behind the gunmetal gray desk, sat Dr. Olsen's secretary typing at her computer. She was about fifty, attractive, and had a no-nonsense look. As soon as Tory walked in, she pulled off her half glasses and let them hang from a chain around her neck, giving her the aura of a stern elementary schoolteacher.

"May I help you?"

"I'm Tory Welch. I'm with the district attorney's office."

"I *know* who you are, Miss Welch. You're lucky he's not here. I've never seen him in such a mood."

"Actually, I was looking for Jake Barnhouse. The anatomy lab is locked."

"Oh, I just assumed . . . Well, I'm afraid you've made a trip for nothing, Miss Welch. Jake won't be in today. Look, Jake was pretty upset last night. Dr. Olsen really laid into him pretty good, then he wanted him to take the day off. Otherwise, it's business as usual here."

"So Mr. Barnhouse will be in tomorrow?"

"As far as I know. Can I have him call you?"

"That's okay." Tory exhaled loudly. "What about Dr. Olsen? Is he around?"

"Miss Welch, take some friendly advice. Let him cool off. Let me give you a call next week, set something up."

Tory looked at the brass nameplate sitting on the desk. Rita Barnhouse. "Barnhouse. Are you related to Jake?"

"His wife."

"Were you here last night?"

"No, I'd just left. But when Jake got home he was pretty upset. We talked for a good long time. I'll tell him you want to speak with him."

"Did you know Kevin Hoover?"

"Never met him."

"Not when he took gross anatomy?"

"Jake told me Dr. Hoover took gross before I came to the department."

"I know how Dr. Olsen feels about me, but I've got no choice. Where can I find him?"

There was a long pause. Rita put on her glasses, then scrutinized Tory very carefully, sizing her up. "Okay, you do what you want. But don't say I didn't warn you," she said, picking up the phone as if she had a call to make.

"He's doing Man-in-the-Pan in the small amphitheater on seven."

"Man-in-the-Pan?"

Rita flipped through a Rolodex, talking to Tory but making no eye contact. "Dr. Olsen is known for many things, but he's probably most proud of Man-in-the-Pan. Once a week, mostly for third- and fourth-year students, he examines all the organs from a recent autopsy. He goes in cold. It's a case he's never seen, and he *dazzles* the students with what he figures out about the patient." Rita looked up. "Why don't you catch him after he's done? But remember, I warned you."

Tory stood outside the door to the little amphitheater trying to hear what Dr. Olsen was saying. His words were garbled through the heavy doors, and Tory eventually felt conspicuous eavesdropping. Gently pulling the door open she was surprised to see how steeply banked the room was. She was looking down from the back of a medium-sized room, but unlike a gently sloping movie theater, these seats seemed to be carved into a hillside, two stairs between rows, one student's feet at the head of the student one row down. The room was silent except for the monotonous sound of Dr. Olsen talking about coronary artery disease. The seats were in darkness, and it appeared that only about half of them were taken, the students choosing to sit in small groups in every row except the bottom two. Dr. Olsen, professorial in his white coat, stood before a metal table, brightly lit from above with a dozen organs laid out before him in a large metal tray. From a distance they looked like lumps of colored clay, different sizes and shapes. He held something in the palm of his right hand that could have been a big chunk of fat.

Tory slipped inside, careful not to fall down the stairs or cause a commotion, and chose to sit anonymously in the semidarkness of the top row. With slow, deliberate movements Tory eased the seat down just in case it was going to embarrass her with a squeak. Finally, her hand holding the seat firmly in place, she sat down, placed her bag and leather notebook on her lap and noticed how quiet the room had become. For one horrible second she thought she'd been caught sneaking in and shot a glance toward Dr. Olsen only to see him place the chunk of fat down on the table and look over the various organs, touching some lightly, like a child choosing a chocolate from a Whitman's Sampler. Eventually, he decided on a large, dark brown organ, and picked it up carefully with two hands as if it might break if handled roughly.

"Now, the liver," he said, and paused dramatically. "This liver is grossly enlarged, but notice, if you will, that it is homogeneously big. The edge is not sharp, but smoothly rounded, and is, of course, consistent with the diagnosis of congestive heart failure. The differential diagnosis of an enlarged liver includes . . . what?" Dr. Olsen looked about the room for a volunteer. The audience seemed to shrink in their seats and play the junior high school game of hiding behind a classmate. Well before it happened, Tory sensed the danger of his roving eye. The pH of her stomach dropped a point, her heart picked up speed, and, during her final, fleeting moments of freedom, she wished she had never ventured into his domain.

Wearing dark clothes in a poorly lit portion of the room she seemed relatively well camouflaged, but he detected her like a cheetah spotting its prey. Once he focused on her it became obvious to the rest of the herd they were, at least temporarily, safe, and they sat a bit straighter, some even turning around to watch. Tory felt their eyes on her, anticipating a moment of high drama, and her cheeks flushed hot. Olsen waited—made her wait, actually—until all eyes were on her, then he placed the liver back in its place on the metal tray. He then placed both hands on the table and leaned forward slightly. "Ahhhhh, *Mzzz.* Welch. I didn't see you slink in. Welcome to Man-in-the-Pan.'' His voice was powerful. "Please join us down front.''

"I'm sorry, I didn't mean to interrupt your lecture. I was just waiting for you—"

Dr. Olsen held out a hand as if showing a guest to a comfortable chair in his living room. "Come. That's a terrible seat. You won't see anything. I don't want to be accused of putting on a less spectacular show than Julian Plesser.''

There was no graceful out. Tory stood, clumsily clutched her bag and notebook to her chest, and walked down three rows before slipping quickly into the aisle seat next to a young man with a ponytail. As quickly as possible she got settled and gave Dr. Olsen a subtle nod, hoping to convey that she was sorry for interrupting him.

"*Mzzz.* Welch, you're our guest of honor. All the way down front. Please.''

Something exciting was about to happen and the students were salivating. The sibilant sounds of excited whispers broke out in several areas of the room as her mind vainly coaxed her legs to make a run for it. Instead she drew more attention to herself, reluctantly walking down to the first row, ensconcing herself right in front of Dr. Olsen. It felt like she was floating in the classic dream, walking into class to take an exam she hadn't prepared for.

Olsen, fine-tuning the moment, milking every drop of drama from it, waited until Tory adjusted her notebook and bag comfortably. He then picked up—and for the first time Tory realized he was wearing fleshtone latex gloves— a small organ that looked like a giant kidney bean and considered it briefly before replacing it. Apparently not satisfied with the assortment in front of him, Dr. Olsen reached under the table and produced a second large tray covered with a white cloth. After placing the tray on the metal table next to his multicolored organs, he removed the drape and revealed the large intestines. Picking up the long, ungainly organ and holding it with both hands several feet in front of Tory like some huge dripping fish, he tweaked a small fingerlike projection, snapping it back and forth several times until a clear drop of fluid flew off in the direction of Tory.

"This is the large intestines—the bowels, *Mzzz.* Welch—of a man who died from complications of heart disease. Would you identify this projection from the proximal end of the large intestines for us?"

Tory was stunned, certain she had heard him incorrectly. This wasn't a dream, it was a nightmare. Dr. Olsen was giving her an oral exam she had definitely not prepared for. Her own bowels rumbled beneath her jacket. She felt trapped and was madly reviewing what little anatomy she could remember from freshman biology. "Uhhh, Dr. Olsen," she said in a hoarse whisper, "I really didn't mean to disrupt your discussion, and I'll just wait—"

"Don't be silly," Olsen said loudly. "Visitors are always welcome . . . but are expected to participate." He gently massaged the projection between his thumb and index finger rhythmically, up and down, up and down, until another tiny drop of clear fluid—visible only to Tory and Dr. Olsen—formed at the very tip, catching a twinkle of light for just a second. "What does this look like to you?" he said with a clinical tone of voice that belied the phallic nature of the discussion.

Tory felt woozy and thought she might vomit. Her breathing was so fast her chest heaved noticeably. *And the next time you run into him he'll give you a hard time, guaranteed.*

The twenty-nine medical students were experiencing a variety of emotions—mostly disgust—and two women were able to muster the strength to leave. But some of the men were enraptured with the control Olsen had.

Slowly, Tory stood to leave. "I don't know. You win, Dr. Olsen. Now we're even. I concede. I'll leave now."

When she turned to walk back up the stairs the students saw a face full of anger and determination. Before her foot hit the first step Dr. Olsen shouted, "Sit down, *Mzzz.* Welch. This is quid pro quo, but we're not finished."

Tory turned back toward him but remained standing. "All right, Dr. Olsen, you've had your fun. Just like a fraternity hazing. Get someone out of their element and humiliate them." Her voice was strong and clear.

Dr. Olsen pulled his head back in shock as if he had been smacked in the face. "Come, come, now, *Mzzz.* Welch. You weren't at a loss for words last night. You had an answer for everything. Let's have an answer before you run and hide."

Tory stood absolutely still and waited until it was dead silent in the room. Timing was everything. She spoke directly toward Olsen, but in a voice that could be heard throughout the room. "The question is, if I recall, what is that little thing dangling from the intestines, that flaccid, limp projection you massage until juice comes out. Is that right, Dr. Olsen? Okay. I'm not a physician," she said, pointing to herself, "so asking me a technical medical question is patently unfair, but I'll give it a go. I don't have one of those things, but if you drop your trousers I'll tell you right now if you've got one."

Someone whistled in the back, and the rustling sound of twenty-seven students leaning forward forced Olsen to wait a few seconds before answering. She'd stepped in it and was going to pay. "*Mzzz.* Welch, what a pity. A valiant effort, I might add, to turn things around, and I'm certain those left in the room with double-X chromosomes applaud your courage. But you are one misinformed girl if you think this is phallic." Olsen gave out a little laugh. "Actually, I feel for your boyfriend—"

"No, Dr. Olsen, you're the one thinking about genitals. I never said anything about phallic. That's an appendix. Mine was removed when I was seven, and if you lower your pants, even my untrained eye can spot an appendectomy scar."

Dr. Olsen and Tory stood facing each other until the

students, quick to gather their books, filed out at the top
of the amphitheater. At the sound of the door closing, Dr.
Olsen, still holding the large intestines, gently placed them
on the tray and recovered them. He seemed to have aged
twenty years in the blink of an eye, and his movements
were slower, more deliberate, lest he do something foolish.

Understanding what it meant to lose in front of subordi-
nates, Tory sat down in the first row and waited for Dr.
Olse to remove his gloves. She knew he wouldn't sit and
fully expected him to continue standing in front of her.
"Dr. Olsen, I've got a suggestion. Let's start over. We've
got to talk, and I won't take up much of your time."

"What kind of a stunt was that you just pulled?" he
asked. His voice was calm.

Tory stared him down. "Why did you try to embarrass me?"

"Ahhh, a question with a question. You held your
ground last night. You don't back down, do you? And
today, letting me go on like that, you knew it was an
appendix all along. I should have seen it coming. You
really sucker-punched me, you know that? And you think
too damn fast on your feet for a first-year ADA. Do you
know what the word 'polemic' means, Ms. Welch?" Dr.
Olsen asked.

Tory smiled. He didn't call her "*Mzzz.*" "That's a hard
word to work into a conversation. Yes, I know what it
means, and no, I didn't debate in school. I know a little
bit about your debating career, though—"

"Julian, what a gossip," Olsen said, shaking his head
knowingly.

"Actually, I'm one of six kids. My father was a cop
just to the right of Rush Limbaugh, my mother a social
worker who leaned way to the left, and our dinner table
conversation was always lively. My father loved to let us
go off on a tangent, really get some momentum going,
and then spring a trap on us."

"Then your father would have been proud this morning," he said, his anger muted, replaced with sarcasm.

Tory hoped there was some common ground where they could meet. After she opened her leather notebook and readied her pen, she said, "I spent some time with Julian Plesser this morning. He completed his examination."

"Blunt trauma to the head."

"You called Jules?"

"Nope."

"You knew last night, didn't you?" Tory said gently.

Dr. Olsen took a deep breath and wiped the side of his hand across his forehead. "Of course I knew."

"Then why did—"

"Why'd I get so upset last night? You're not that naive. Put yourself in my shoes. I've got a former resident in *my* anatomy lab. Damnit, *I* want to investigate what the hell is going on. And don't tell me you're surprised."

Tory bit on the end of her pen. She noticed, for the first time, the faint odor of formaldehyde. "Tell me about embalming."

"You met Jake Barnhouse last night. He's the diener. That's his area. Why don't you ask him?"

"His wife told me you gave him some time off."

"I had to. The guy was a wreck. Look, embalming's easy. I mean, all you do is dump a body in a vat and twenty-four hours later—presto, the body is embalmed. It wouldn't take a genius to have embalmed Kevin Hoover."

"Vats. You mean the medical school doesn't use arterial infusion pumps?"

Dr. Olsen scratched behind his right ear. "Ahhhh, the old courtroom adage: Never ask a question you don't already know the answer to. So why don't you tell me about embalming. What's going on?" He sounded irritated.

"I'm not trying to jerk you around. Kevin Hoover had three puncture sites from infusion catheters."

"So?"

The common ground seemed to be shrinking fast.

"If I understand the basic process—which I'd like to see as soon as possible—multiple sights are necessary when circulation is poor. Maybe multiple sights were used to speed up the process. How many pumps do you have?"

"Two. One's a backup. Anything else?"

"How long has Jake Barnhouse worked for you?"

"I don't know. Six, seven years. Used to be over at Mercy in the pathology department."

"Any problems with him?"

"None. Pretty much keeps to himself. He knows his job and does it without much interference from me."

"Did he have any sort of a professional or personal relationship with Kevin Hoover that you know of?"

"No. Look, Ms. Welch, you'll have to talk with him. He'll be back tomorrow. You know his wife is my secretary."

"What about her?"

"Been with me five years. Jake's the reason I hired Rita. She's efficient, types well, but can't spell worth a damn. She and I have lunch once a year on Secretary's Day, but I don't really know her. Talk to her if you want."

"How many people know how to embalm, work the arterial infusion pumps?"

"Jake does all the embalming. But it doesn't really require any more skill than catheterization. I guess any physician who has seen it done could probably do it. Is that it, Miss Welch?"

"Almost. Let's talk about Kevin Hoover for a second. How well did you know Kevin Hoover?"

"Am I under suspicion?"

"I'm just gathering information."

"He was a lab assistant in my research lab the summer before he started med school, and of course he took gross anatomy as a first-year. That's about it. Now, if you'll excuse me, Miss Welch, I've got my own problems. Half the first-year class is terrified to take gross anatomy, afraid someone's grandmother is going to turn up."

"One more thing, Dr. Olsen. Tell me about the grant."

Dr. Olsen's lips tightened, and he looked almost straight up at the ceiling for a second. She'd obviously struck a nerve. "The grant. Oh, the grant. Indeed, you've done your homework, read the police reports late last night, I bet. Look, that detective crawled around here . . . Let me give it to you in a nutshell. I don't know how much you know about grant writing, anyway," Dr. Olsen said, sounding a bit confused about which facts he would include. "Kevin was leaving the lab one afternoon, and I gave him the grant request to mail. That's all he had to do—just drop it in the mail."

"And Kevin forgot to mail it."

"Right, he shoved it in his backpack and forgot to mail it. Without that grant money we had to let three technicians go. And, I'm sure you know, Kevin got a C in anatomy."

"Your course."

"Right." He looked at Tory sadly.

"And Kevin protested the grade and the dean raised it to a B. Were you biased against him?"

"Honestly, I don't know. I've asked myself that question a thousand times. Kevin was clever. He outmaneuvered me. He used his blunder with the grant to convince the dean of students I downgraded him. I hated him after that—why don't you jot that down—hated. But rational, SANE human beings do have the ability to hate without killing, don't we, Miss Welch? By the way, I was in Philadelphia lecturing—not merely attending—at the academy meetings at Penn the week Kevin disappeared. That didn't make the police report, did it?" Tory shook her head. "Check it out."

"I will. Thanks for your time, Dr. Olsen." Tory closed her notebook and stood to leave. As she mounted the stairs Dr. Olsen leaned forward on the metal table, his right hand, ungloved, absently grasping one of the kidneys. His grip tightened as he watched Tory climb the steep stairs, and as she pushed through the door, without so much as a hesitation, he squeezed hard and macerated the organ until it squirted through his fingers like soft, red modeling clay.

Ten

Pittsburgh had always been a city of neighborhoods. Three miles up from the Strip District, tightly sandwiched between different ethnic communities, was the Italian section of Bloomfield. Generations of families lived along crowded city blocks, staking claims to parking spaces with old kitchen chairs strategically left in the street, and every corner had a good restaurant. Several streets behind the Pleasure Bar, wedged between two clapboard homes, was a two-chair barber shop, the kind with *Spiderman* comics for the kids and—if you knew where to look behind the cash register—*Playboy*s for the men. Two brothers owned the shop, always operating in slow motion. No one remembered who was Gaeton and who was Carl. A cardboard American flag, a glossy portrait of Bill Clinton from the Sunday supplement, and a photograph of the Apollo moon landing were proudly displayed between the two huge mirrors facing the chairs. Above the old-fashioned cash register was a one-dollar bill and a five-dollar bill in a cheap black frame. The white-smocked barbers—not stylists— had been cutting hair for more than a quarter-century and would be happy to tell anyone who would listen that hair salons were for faggots. They would never have one of those peculiar sinks you lie back in, with the U-shaped cutout for your neck.

Anthony—"Antony" to anyone who knew him way back—stopped in each morning for a hot towel wrap and a shave. He was the kid from the neighborhood who had made good, the first family member to earn an MBA. His ascension within the Bevel organization was rapid. Graduate school had taught him to examine business situations creatively, and as he successfully applied his sophisticated techniques to a somewhat stodgy family business, his biggest reward was the opportunity to work independently much of the time.

Business was conducted in a variety of locations. Financial affairs were attended to in the warehouse in the Strip District, but street business happened on the street. At 4:15 P.M., just as the floor of the barber shop was being swept clean for the night, Antony walked in. He wore a silver-gray suit, double vented, and a custom white shirt with a silk tie knotted perfectly. When women would describe Antony the morning after a glorious night they'd say it was like being with a movie star. Olive skin. White teeth. And thick black hair combed straight back.

Gaeton looked up from his broom. "You want a trim, Antony?" Carl, counting the take from the cash register, nodded. They would clearly be happy to accommodate Antony.

"No, I'm okay," Antony said as he looked at himself in the mirror, fine-tuned his hair with a sweep of his hands just above his ears, and walked to the back of the long, narrow shop. The routine had happened before and the brothers knew what to do. As Antony settled in the back with last month's *Playboy,* and the sun's last rays were filigreed on the linoleum floor by the oak tree across the street, Gaeton and Carl finished their end-of-the-day routine and went home. No good-byes. No reminder to lock up. They never even bothered to close the door when Antony was there, and knew, when they reopened in the morning, it would be business as usual. It was simple. If they couldn't trust Antony, then who could they trust?

Antony enjoyed the quiet for several minutes. He conducted street business as far from the Strip as possible and never included Frank Bevel's name in any discussion. Bevel met with Antony; Antony handled the rest.

"Yo, An-to-ny." Erno's voice was low and smooth. He walked the length of the shop with a smile, his heavy gait rattling the glass bottles of tonic on the shelf. Satch followed, and without handshakes or cocktail party palaver, the three were seated on red chairs in the back corner. The leatherette seats were cracking and wisps of white stuffing stuck out; Antony sat against the rear wall, Erno and Satch against the side.

Antony looked comfortable leaning back, his legs crossed like an Armani ad. Always graceful, he flipped the *Playboy* onto the matching chair to his left, then ran his fingers down the leg of his pants, appreciating the fine material.

Meanwhile Erno shifted his large frame a couple of times to get his shiny sportcoat out from under his massive rump. His pants rode up and exposed a swath of white skin above his socks. The big brute seemed a bit oafish in Antony's polished presence, and he quickly slipped into an obsequious role.

Satch, always uncomfortable with his body, hunched forward, dropped his head to avoid participating in the conversation, and sagged his shoulders until he looked like someone who should be nicknamed Vulture.

"How'd the meeting go with Mike Demasi?" Antony asked.

"He . . . gave it his fullest attention," Erno replied. Satch nodded, still looking at the floor.

"What'd he say, Erno?"

"He wanted to, you know, think about it. Like you told me, I said it was okay for him to think it over, that Mr. Bevel said—"

Antony held out his hand to stop Erno from rambling. "Erno," he began with a smooth voice, "we don't want to talk specifics . . . names. You know what I mean. How you handle Demasi, well, that's up to you. I don't care what you say, but we don't mention *his* name between us." He pointed a manicured finger at Erno, not menacingly, but the big man took note nevertheless.

"Sorry, Antony," Erno said. His upper lip showed a few beads of sweat, and he wiped it with a folded white handkerchief he pulled out of his jacket. This was followed by a hard swallow. "Anyway, me'n Satch are having another meeting with Demasi this week." Satch nodded.

Antony leaned toward Erno and collected his thoughts. "I want a clear understanding. This deal with Demasi is to be completed in two meetings. Not three or four. Two. If he wants to sell, then you set it up for Demasi to come see me. You got that? *He* comes in, *he* sees me, *he* tells me *he* wants out." Antony waited for Erno to nod.

Then there was a silence that went on until Satch looked up and realized Antony was looking at him. Satch gave a single nod and went back to counting the linoleum tiles. Antony continued, "If he dances around, gives you the sad eyes, wants to meet with the man, end it. Quick and clean, right there. Demasi is Demasi's. He's got no one to step in. Saves us money."

Antony stood, buttoned his jacket, looked at himself in the mirror, and smoothed his hair. The other men could not help but admire his cool. "Looking good, Antony," Erno said.

"Check out Miss August before you lock up." Antony walked out of the shop, stepped onto the narrow sidewalk, and looked both ways before walking smoothly down the street.

Erno picked up the *Playboy,* flipped the pages to find the staple, and a white business envelope—no writing, sealed with tape—slipped out onto the floor. Antony once told Erno the feds could trace DNA in the spit you use to lick an envelope.

Erno counted the money before they left the shop.

Eleven

Mark Peters had set himself up to have a perfect day.

After he trumped Tory, getting control of the press conference, Sue was sent to the *Post-Gazette* archives to dig up whatever it had on Kevin Hoover. The next hour was spent daydreaming, feet up on the windowsill, lazily watching the sun reflect off the roof of the Civic Arena.

The first order of business was to start a mental checklist. *Redistribute my caseload around the office.*

He was in shirtsleeves, a white oxfordcloth Brooks Brothers shirt, cut full so it puffed out slightly in the back, giving him that Bobby Kennedy jacket-slung-over-the-shoulder look.

Maybe dash home after lunch and set the VCR.

His first impulse—usually the wrong one—after Tory left his office, had been to alert the media immediately, get on the midday news. But then he forced himself to slow down, really think things through. By six o'clock, when the evening news aired—the *real* news—the media would already be a well-organized machine. There would be video interviews from a dozen different people, including the medical examiner. He didn't want to compete with Julian Plesser.

If I go home to set the VCR, what about putting on suspenders? Yeah, the red ones.

It was important, therefore, to control the news, establish himself as *the* source on Kevin Hoover. When new information was available in the next several days and the media needed a sound bite, he wanted to be the one called first. *The Today Show. Hard Copy. The Evening News with Dan Rather.*

Maybe skip lunch, look thinner.

Therefore, he decided, his first Kevin Hoover press conference had to be late enough in the day to prevent metastatic live broadcasts from sprouting up around the city. But it was equally important not to be too late and risk missing the news altogether. Then he'd be relegated to the *Post-Gazette* in the morning. The TV crews needed ample time to edit the videotape so his would be the lead story. Four-thirty seemed perfect.

When he got bored daydreaming, Peters made the obligatory trip to inform the boss that he had ordered an investigation into the Kevin Hoover murder and that Tory Welch was running leads for him.

A folder, thick with photocopies from the *Post-Gazette,* was waiting for him when he got back to his desk. Peters picked up his phone and beeped Sue on the intercom. "Uh, Sue, will you call a press conference this afternoon, say four-thirty? You can let them know it involves a murder. Don't mention anything about the Medical Center. Thanks."

Reading glasses on when I walk in, off just before I start to speak.

Maybe get a haircut at lunch.

Then he pretty much stayed in his office reading news clips on Kevin Hoover until he was off on his busy lunch agenda.

A thousand different ways to tell the same story, and Peters struggled to find the right combination of accuracy, detail, and command of the situation to make them come back for more. His tie, a thin colorful silk, allowed several different knots, and he settled on a half-Windsor, pulled down at the neck slightly, exposing an unbuttoned top button. His shirtsleeves were rolled up and down half a dozen times before he settled on all the way down, buttoned.

And a shave, definitely a shave.

Vest on or off? Off.

Don't drink after two o'clock, and pee at four-fifteen.

At four-thirty precisely, Sue knocked on his door, and let herself in. "We're ready in the media room. Nice suspenders."

Peters tried not to, but he looked down at the red suspenders and blushed. Having checked his watch several times in the last half-hour, he was expecting Sue. The police report and the newspaper photocopies had been strategically placed in several piles on his usually neat desk. A quick look at his watch confirmed what he already knew. "Oh, I lost track. Sue, tell them I'll be there in five—no, better make it ten minutes," he said and picked up his pen, looked down at his work, and underlined what must have been an important passage.

Sue rolled her eyes and quietly retreated to the media room where she dutifully explained that Mr. Peters was on his way.

At 4:42—he had debated the time element throughout the afternoon and decided 4:40 might look contrived—Mark Peters strode into the media room. If nothing more, he certainly looked the role of district attorney. He carried a thin leather folder up against the side of his chest like a college professor and took his place at the podium. In a practiced gesture he hooked his thumb on one of the suspenders and slid it up and down.

The small media room, really a windowless conference room with a pull-down screen emblazoned with the seal of Allegheny County, had a dozen seats arranged around a rectangular oak table, half of which were now filled with reporters. The anchorpersons were back at the studios keeping their clothes from getting wrinkled, while the name-brand reporters waited at remote locations around the city to report on breaking stories. At 4:42 in the afternoon only wanna-be reporters were available for a press conference in the media room. Empty Styrofoam coffee cups and a couple of sandwich wrappers were scattered on the table, little spiral notebooks sat open, and polyester jackets were slung over chairs. Standing at the opposite end of the room were three men, each with video and sound equipment. Peters noticed them and worked hard to suppress a smile.

"Good afternoon. I have a short statement to read, and then I'll be happy to answer any questions you have." With his leather folder opened, glasses on, and rehearsed facial expression in place, Mark Peters read: "I'm certain you remember two stories you covered about a year ago. I have a copy of *The Post-Gazette,* dated August 24, 1995." He pulled a stack of photocopies from his leather folder, handed the stack to a reporter he did not know, and waited for them to be spread through the room.

He looked about, saw the faces for the first time, and realized he didn't recognize anyone in the room. *Oh, crap. These are second-stringers.* "By the way, for those who don't know me, I'm Assistant District Attorney Mark Peters. As you can see, around midnight on the night of August 21, 1995 a resident, Kevin Hoover, disappeared from the Pittsburgh University Medical Center. Although an exhaustive search was mounted by the City of Pittsburgh Police Department, no trace of him was ever found. A second story, buried in the second section, also ran the same day and described a John Doe pulled out of the Allegheny River. What was noteworthy about this John Doe was that he came out of the river embalmed.

"Let me tie them together. Late last evening, September 16, 1996, a resident surgeon, and former roommate of Kevin Hoover, a Dr. Jack Merlin, discovered the body of Kevin Hoover. Dr. Merlin was working in the gross anatomy laboratory—the first-year medical students dissect the cadavers there—and discovered the body partially dissected. We've been in contact with the medical examiner today, and the cause of death—blunt head trauma—has been ruled a homicide.

"The John Doe, it turns out, was a man named Red Gardner. Mr. Gardner's body had been donated to the Pittsburgh University School of Medicine for purposes of medical education. It had been stored in the gross anatomy labs and Dr. Hoover's body was apparently switched with his."

The room became a flurry of activity. Notes were furiously scribbled, the photocopy of the *Post-Gazette* report was scanned for details, and hands shot up. One reporter was on a cellular flip phone, talking quickly in hushed tones. The cameramen trained their cameras on Peters.

"Uhhh, okay, why don't you go ahead," Peters said to an intense female reporter with too much makeup who wrote in her notebook while she raised her left hand.

"Mr. Peters, are you saying the body of Kevin Hoover was in the hospital since his disappearance?"

"We believe so."

"So is the focus of this case on the Medical Center?" she continued.

"We are working on several leads."

"Are these leads *within* the Medical Center?" she asked.

"Yes, they are, but we are by no means limiting our investigation—"

"Then may we assume you have not ruled out the possibility that someone within the Medical Center committed the homicide?"

"Uh, no. Nothing has been ruled out." Peters looked at a second reporter, this time a male in a sportcoat and tie.

"Mr. Peters, how would you characterize the relationship between"—he read from his notes briefly—"Jack Merlin and Kevin Hoover?"

"They were roommates. Beyond that I have no further information."

"Let me get this straight. Was Kevin Hoover killed *in* the Medical Center?"

I don't know. "No comment," Peters said, hoping to sound as if he had sensitive information, something he was working on that he couldn't share.

"What's the hospital say about all this?"

I don't know. "We have someone there right now. Tory Welch, a member of this department, will be the lead investigator at the Medical Center."

Another reporter, also a male, spoke up. "Who is responsible for the bodies at the medical school?"

"Uh," Peters paused. *I'm blocking on his name.* "Until we've completed our initial interviews I'm not prepared to release names."

"What about Kevin's family? What was his relationship with them?"

Damnit. Should've had Tory call them immediately. "You have the newspaper articles in front of you. That's all that I'm prepared to say at this time."

The barrage of questions continued for another ten minutes, but it was clear after the third or fourth question that Mark Peters shot his wad in his opening statement. His carefully worded speech contained everything he knew about the case. Once he handed out the newspaper articles the reporters quickly became acquainted with the historical perspective, and new details were scarce.

They knew as much as he did before he took the first question. *So why the hell am I holding a press conference?* Peters noticed that hot, flushed feeling he remembered only too well from law school, when a professor, favoring the Socratic method, grilled him with an endless stream of questions.

Even the most tenacious members of the press lose interest when the answer to every question is "No comment." The meeting seemed to end abruptly right after a fat reporter asked, "Mr. Peters, if the body was discovered last night, why the late press conference? I mean, all we got here is a teaser. There's no time to put a story together.''

Peters looked serious. "I've spent the day coordinating the efforts of this office. That's my first priority. But I realize you have your own agenda. I'd be happy to schedule all future press conferences earlier in the day.''

For what seemed an hour, Peters found himself standing at the podium watching the reporters gather notebooks and jackets and he felt distant, as if watching the scene on a television monitor. The group didn't gravitate toward him to discuss the case on a more conversational level. It would be a race for these reporters to get back to the newsroom and secure a slot on the news or front-page space in the morning paper.

The woman who'd asked the first series of questions fussed with her briefcase and waited for everyone else to leave. It became obvious she was wasting time, and Peters, sensing she wanted him alone, and no slouch at squandering time himself, managed to fiddle with his papers, and step toward the door precisely as she did.

The female reporter made her move. "Mr. Peters?" Her thick black hair was cut short. And her nose had been professionally reshaped so that it looked as if her ears were having a tug of war and her beak got in the way. Obviously she was of the belief that the shorter the hair the heavier the jewelry, and her earlobes strained under the weight of thick gold earrings.

Peters stopped, feigning surprise at being asked yet another question. "Do you have another question?''

"Sandy Keller, KDKA.'' She handed him her card, which confirmed her affiliation. "Let me ask you something. Is this bigger than it seems?'' She spoke quickly, like a drill sergeant.

"Why'd you ask?''

"I don't know. You seemed kind of . . . nervous, maybe holding something back. I'm going for the emotions be-

hind the story—you know, human interest. Just wondered why.''
   "No, I've been tied up with this since I walked in today.
I've been swamped.''
   "So tell me. A year-old murder? C'mon, if you're holding a press conference, you've got something. If you
didn't, this would start out as a press release. So like the
fat man said, all we got is a teaser, right?''
   "You got what I had to give you, Miss Keller.''
   "I mean, you being with the department nine years,
senior guy. This press conference with a lot of 'no comments.' '' She lowered her voice for the last part.
   Seven years. "You've got a point?'' *Don't talk. Don't
talk. Don't talk.*
   Sandy walked over to the door and closed it. "You call
a press conference, late afternoon, too late for us to interview anyone before six o'clock, give out old clippings,
and don't answer any questions. Level with me. You're
watching somebody, seeing how he reacts to the reports?
I can feel it. What do you got?''
   Peters thought a minute. This woman was aggressive,
even a bit intimidating, and certainly had the potential to
be obnoxious, but at the same time she was the only one
who showed a spark of interest in him. "Let me level with
you. This press conference was designed to disseminate
information. We have more than I can say. Obviously. But
we don't have a killer. Obviously. And—I know, I know—
a year-old murder without any leads''—Peters tilted his
head, raised his eyebrows, and put both his hands out in
an effort to demonstrate there really were leads—''may
seem a bit of a long shot. But let things play out a bit.
There is a method to the madness.''
   "Then you didn't deny you're watching someone.''
   "I didn't confirm it either.''
   "I want an exclusive.''
   "I don't have an exclusive to give you.''

Keller thought for a second. "How 'bout a late bite? Say Morton's, about 11:15."

"Everyone's gonna want an exclusive. I know what's in it for you—"

"Here's what's in it for you, Mark—may I call you Mark? Look, the story here is the murder of a doctor named Kevin Hoover, not the people investigating it. This is a spectacular murder. It'll make O. J. look like frozen concentrate. The press will cover every detail, interview anyone with a shred of information, and put Pittsburgh on the national map. And when you catch the guy—and I know you will—then every headline in the country will blare the murderer's name. He's the guy on *People* magazine. He's got the book deal, the made-for-TV-movie deal. Not you.

"Don't you know, the perp gets the glory. We remember Jeffrey Dahmer. But, who prosecuted hm? Other than Marcia Clark and Mark Peters, can your mother name any other assistant district attorney in the country? And when this is over, regardless how it turns out, I write an up-close-and-personal about you."

"And all you want me to do is keep you one step ahead of the pack."

"That's right. Maybe I run an idea or two by you and you either deny it or . . . you don't."

"So I've just made a pact with the devil."

Sandy Keller laughed. Maybe a bit too loud.

Twelve

September 18, 1996

Erno and Satch sat in a booth in the back of a diner. They met for an early breakfast before they spent the day at the track, anxious to get there well before post-time because Erno knew a trainer who had a couple of sure things for a friend. The greasy odor of bacon lingered in the air and a talk radio station played quietly from a radio behind the counter. Most of the breakfast crowd was blue collar, and Erno enjoyed a smoke while reading a racing form and the sports pages. His wallet still bulged with hundred-dollar bills from Antony, and he used a stubby pencil, which he stored behind his ear, to circle the names of horses that looked good. Every couple of minutes his right hand drifted over his plate, and his thumb flicked whatever ashes had accumulated, sprinkling dots of black onto the bright yellow remains of several egg yolks. It was a scene from an anti-smoking commercial that no dedicated smoker could ever understand.

Satch, wearing a porkpie hat and black leather jacket, chose the front section of the *Post-Gazette* over the comics. He was going for worldliness, but Erno didn't notice. While he drank from a large ceramic mug of coffee he read the headlines, skipping anything with a word like "Bosnia" or "Clinton."

"Holy shit," Satch whispered. "Hey, Ern, listen to this." Erno continued to mark his racing form. Satch folded the newspaper down to quarter size. "The body of a former Pittsburgh University Medical Center resident was discovered late Tuesday evening following an intensive year-long search by Pittsburgh police.

"The body of Kevin Hoover was found in the ninth-floor anatomy laboratory of the medical school. The discovery was made—"

"Kevin Hoover. Shit. Gimme that." Erno grabbed the paper and spread it out on the table, covering his racing paraphernalia, and hunched over it. He wiped the back of his hand across his nose and read to himself until he came to the point where he'd interrupted Satch. "The discovery was made by Dr. Jack Merlin, 26, a senior resident and former roommate of the deceased.

"According to District Attorney Mark Peters, Dr. Hoover was first reported missing August 22, 1995. He was last seen by his girlfriend, Jan Wolkin, a nurse in the hospital.

"Allegheny County Coroner Julian Plesser has ruled the death a homicide. Cause of death was blunt head trauma." Erno looked up at Satch and made a tight fist with his right hand. His skin tightened and his eyes became slits. The veins on both sides of his neck bulged out like steel pipes. "Jesus fuckin' Christ. That's the kid. The doc on the elevator."

"You sure that's the kid?"

"I can't tell you the last three pieces of ass I had, but I can tell you everything about Kevin Hoover, M.D., General Surgery." *Pop. Pop. Pop.*

"That night's a blur to me. What are you gonna do?" Satch asked. He was frightened.

"What am *I* gonna do? How much money you got in your wallet right now? Five, six hundred bucks? Not *me*, Vulture. We. What are *we* gonna do, Satch? Here's the answer, we ain't gonna do nothing. That's what we're gonna do."

"What about that Demasi guy? Maybe we should wait," Satch said slowly, thinking things through. "We don't do Demasi, we gotta tell Antony. Then Antony's gonna ask a lot of questions. About why he didn't find out last summer. Forget it. There's no connection to us. We're clean. If Demasi don't sell, we do him, just like Antony said."

Erno stared past Satch and watched an overweight waitress in a greasy uniform clear dishes from the booth across the aisle. As she stacked plates and saucers high atop one another and walked toward the kitchen, Erno opened and closed his massive fists like a weight lifter getting ready to grab the barbells. "Okay, Satch, you, me, and our friend up the Med Center are the only ones who know about the kid. Let's find out what's going on."

Erno picked up his cellular phone and punched a series of numbers so forcefully he kept hitting the wrong pads and had to redial three times. "Yeah, operator. I want you to voice page Dr. Antony. Right, Dr. Antony." He scratched his cheek. "Yeah, yeah, yeah, I know you got no listing for him. Just voice-page him, will ya?" After a minute of silence, Erno jerked his head up and spoke quietly. "Hey, asshole, what the fuck did you do?" Pause. "Yeah, well, disposal's your job. What do they got?" Pause. "Look, you act cool, real cool, nothing ties you to this. You blow your cool, we cut you loose." Pause. "What about this Peters guy from the DA?" Long pause. "Oh yeah, what's her name?" Erno scribbled something in the margin of the newspaper. "Okay. Business as usual. We may even have something for you, end of the week." Pause. "Hey, shut the fuck up. You do what we tell you to do. You jus' be ready." Pause. Erno cut off Dr. Antony with a push of a button. "Fuckin' asshole."

Confusion. Thoughts ran through his mind like loud voices in his ear. Words screaming. *Dr. Antony. Satch. Antony. Now. Now. Now.* Then he heard a new one: *Tory Welch.* He wanted to reach out and grab a voice, grab it around the neck, and choke it into silence. It was foreplay to Erno. His heart beat against his chest wall so he could feel every thump, and his skin burned and tingled with the sensation of a thousand needles. *That stupid fuckin' Dr. Antony.* Erno wanted to kill him. *No way. No fuckin' way.* And Satch. *What am I gonna do? Why is it always what I'm gonna do?* Satch was such a nothing. He could control Satch, make him do what he wanted. Why couldn't Satch get his hands dirty? And the deal with Antony was sweet. A couple of thou every time he met with him. *Keep Antony out of it.*

Faster and faster the impulses raced around his brain. Louder and louder the voices. Tory Welch. *Keep her away. Take her out before she has something.* That was the right decision. *Yes. Yes. Yes. Ohhhhhh.* The business decision. *Now. Do it now.* The voices quieted.

A warm glow crept up from his loins and he exhaled loudly. He lit a cigarette and blew a stream of smoke right toward Satch. It was so obvious, so clear that it felt very comfortable.

This was Erno at his most dangerous. He was on automatic pilot.

Erno slid the phone across the table to Satch, thought for a second, and grabbed it back. "You know your buddy over at DMV. Give him a call on the pay phone. Tory Welch. W-E-L-C-H. See what she drives, get a plate number."

"Sure thing, Erno." Satch got up, hitched his pants to his waist and fished in his pocket for change. He went over to a wall-mounted phone in the front of the restaurant.

Erno began to beat a rhythm on the table with his hands. The indecision had grown into a plan. He was feeling good. And he'd get Satch laid in the process.

Thirteen

All Sandy Keller had to do was mention she had secured an inside source and that there was a suspect under investigation, and she was a celebrity. And to top things off she had purred and cooed at everything Mark Peters said at Morton's and he was hers.

The next morning, while the other networks repackaged Sandy Keller's story, KDKA dispatched a white minivan with a directional antenna and a full news team to the Medical Center. Sandy, a cameraman, and a young producer in his early thirties were in place while it was still dark. Although most mobile news teams didn't include a producer, one was sent at Sandy's insistence. She was hot right now, had been for almost twelve hours, wanted prima donna treatment, and as long as she delivered would be granted the perks of celebrity. The Kevin Hoover story had immense tabloid-type appeal, and the legitimate news media hungered to tap into this sensational story.

After the marvelous coup she pulled the night before when she scooped everyone with the news of an actual suspect under investigation, Keller basked in the glow that came when a correspondent transcended the basic reportorial duties and became the news story. That high praise came in the form of interview requests from rival colleagues, and she'd obliged every one of them with a brief chat on the phone.

It was a two-pronged attack. Peters belonged to her and could be counted on for any leads. What would keep the year-old murder alive was a continuous procession of witnesses and friends who knew the victim. Sandy wanted first crack at Jack Merlin. Once he'd been grilled three or four times his answers would become pat, sound rehearsed. Keller wanted him raw. She'd planned her ambush carefully and even secured the services of a nurse at the Medical Center who knew Merlin's schedule and would identify him when he arrived.

The thrill of the hunt was almost too great for Sandy Keller. Hyperactive as she was, she fussed with her hair, checked her heavily applied makeup, added a bit more here and there, adjusted a heavy gold earring, and gave her cameraman too many suggestions in a futile attempt to channel her nervous energy. Occasionally she would stop moving, whispering quietly to herself, *"It* might help Kevin. It *might* help Kevin. It might help *Kevin."* She'd already decided on the grabber; now she was fine-tunning it.

The lookout nurse, standing off to one side, checked her watch every couple of minutes, hoping Merlin would not be late. She was getting antsy.

At ten minutes of seven Jack Merlin bounded, not from the direction of the multilevel parking garage as had been expected, but from a local bagel shop. It was a cool morning, but he was without a jacket and stood out from the rest of the more appropriately dressed early-morning foot traffic in Oakland. Every couple of steps he stopped to take a bite of his bagel or a sip of coffee from a Styrofoam cup.

The nurse spotted him immediately as he rounded the corner—"Miss Keller, there he is"—and at once Sandy Keller focused him in her sights and grabbed a microphone. She brushed past the nurse like the high school prom queen passing the pimply-faced girls in the bathroom. Her cameraman trotted behind her. Traffic was still light and wouldn't be a distraction. Two women joggers came up out of nowhere, and Sandy bumped into one of them, nearly knocking her over.

Merlin crossed the street toward the Medical Center,

never stopping for oncoming traffic, but dodging cars and locking eyes with the various drivers in his New York City bravado. As Merlin stepped up onto the curb Sandy walked right up to him, microphone subtly held down at her side. Her cameraman lingered somewhat behind her and shouldered his heavy equipment, looking toward the cluster of medical buildings, pretending to adjust one of the dials on his camera. Although it was getting steadily brighter from the morning sun as it skipped across the tops of the buildings, the camera had enough automatic controls to adjust to the changing conditions and did not require any manual fine-tuning. The producer hung around by the minivan, not knowing what to do with himself, talking on a cellular phone to the studio. "Dr. Merlin, I'm Sandy Keller, KDKA. Let me first offer my sincere condolences. I'd really like to talk with you about what you found the other night."

Merlin shook his head. "I don't think so. I'm late for rounds anyway." He started up the steps, taking them two at a time.

"It *might* help Kevin," she said delivering the line expertly. Merlin stopped abruptly. She'd hooked him, and winked at her producer who mimed a fisherman reeling in a fish.

Merlin walked back down the steps and faced Sandy. "Is there really a suspect under investigation?"

"My sources say so. The DA said we might be able to jog someone's memory. Maybe you could encourage somebody to come forward."

Merlin took a bite of bagel. "My emotions are a bit frayed. I'm afraid I'd babble incoherently." He put the coffee cup to his lips but didn't take a drink.

"C'mon. Let's give it a try. We can stop any time you like," Keller said in that soothing voice a therapist uses when breaking the ice with a new patient. A good street reporter must be a good actress, and Keller could slip in and out of character effortlessly.

Merlin liked the way she sounded, and her smile seemed

reassuring. "Okay. I'll give it a shot." He balanced his bagel on his coffee cup as he quickly ran his fingers through his hair.

The young producer nodded his head as he finished his conversation. "Great timing, Sandy. We can go live whenever you're ready."

The cameraman readied his camera and on some subtle cue nodded to Keller who stood facing him directly. Merlin saw the little red light, just below the lens, glow brightly, and he felt trapped.

"Paul, I'm standing in front of the Pittsburgh University Medical Center, where an investigation into a bizarre murder is taking place. I'm with Dr. Jack Merlin, the surgical resident who made a gruesome discovery two days ago." Then, turning to Merlin, asked, "Dr. Merlin, can you make some sense out of this? What exactly happened?" With balletic precision Keller turned to her left and looked at her interviewee while her cameraman took several slow, graceful steps to his left and moved into a position to shoot Merlin over Keller's right shoulder.

The transition was done seamlessly, and Merlin barely noticed the camera as he started talking. "A couple of nights ago I found the body of Kevin Hoover, a former resident in surgery—"

"Where exactly did you find the body?"

"Well, I was working in the gross anatomy labs in the medical school and I found him . . . there." His eyes were getting wetter and caught the headlights from an oncoming bus for a moment.

"Where was he?"

Merlin fidgeted. This question made him uncomfortable. It was an invasion of Kevin's privacy. He looked across the street and watched the bus disgorge a group of hospital workers who smiled and laughed as they got off the bus.

The surgical ICU was a twelve-bed unit, a large rectangular room with every bed occupied and arranged around a central nursing station like the spokes on a wheel. The sickest post-op patients spent varying amounts of time there, and as a new admission was wheeled into the unit, the least-sick patient was bumped to the regular floor. Each bed sat in its own port, and privacy was a curtain that closed in such a way as to provide passersby both complete anonymity and a generous view of a patient on a bed pan. Shelving above the head of each bed contained a variety of monitoring equipment. Each patient had his or her own TV suspended from the ceiling, and the only thing shared was the nursing staff, each nurse being responsible for two adjoining patients.

Morning bedside rounds were almost finished. The surgical team consisted of medical students, interns, and residents at various levels of training. It was the chief resident's responsibility to run these rounds, and the senior residents reluctantly trailed behind showing a spark of interest only when their own patients were discussed. The philosophy in medical training was "See one, do one, teach one," and it was never more evident than on the surgical floors, where even the most inexperienced medical student was permitted to insert needles and catheters into every imaginable part of the body. The students enthusiastically took their places in the front of the group, hoping for a spot on the scut list of invasive things to do.

Medicine dripped with tradition. One of the most sacred was the custom of directing any questions to the lowest-ranking person in the group, usually the third-year students, because they were least likely to know the answer and would create an opportunity for the highest-ranking member to dazzle everyone else with medical minutia gleaned from the latest *Annals of Surgery*. Martin Wheeler had wisely dispensed with that age-old practice in the ICU because the patients were more complicated, and dazzling the senior residents was almost impossible. So each morning, as rounds began, he would mention that he needed to move things along because of some important commit-

ment, and when he questioned the senior residents, rarely
offered anything more than a nod of approval.

The large group congregated around the foot of Mrs.
Weinstock's bed, and Wheeler accepted the metal chair
handed him by the ICU nurse who accompanied them on
rounds. Mrs. Weinstock was now two days post kidney
transplantation, and each morning the team spent several
minutes discussing her complicated fluid and electrolyte
balance. As Wheeler engrossed himself in a series of laboratory data attached to the front of the chart, he said,
"Okay, Merlin, you're on." That was Wheeler's signal
for Merlin to begin a concise description of everything
that happened to Mrs. Weinstock in the previous twenty-
four hours, as well as the treatment plan for the next day.

". . . I was working in the gross anatomy labs in the
medical school . . ."

It sounded like the right voice, maybe a bit tinny and
distant, but Wheeler thought he was overhearing a private
conversation Merlin was having during chief resident
rounds.

"Merlin!" Wheeler scanned the surgical team quickly.
"Where the hell is Merlin?" The sting from Merlin's stunt
in the OR still smarted, and Wheeler looked around a
second time hoping to find his resident snapping some
nurse's bra. It wasn't so much that Merlin had poisoned
him, but that the bastard had bragged about it and wrote
a memo to the OR nursing staff asking them to "remind
Dr. Wheeler to go potty before surgery."

One of the medical students, eager to answer an easy
question for the chief resident, brightly replied, "He's
not here."

"I can see he's not here."

Mrs. Weinstock pointed a bony finger in the direction
of her TV. "There's my doctor. See, he's a celebrity. Did
such a good job . . ."

As soon as the surgical team recognized their missing
compatriot being interviewed on the morning news, they

squeezed tightly against each other at the head of Mrs. Weinstock's bed, craning their necks and leaning against each other at odd angles, silently watching together. Wheeler looked more concerned with the cramped viewing conditions than anything else and held Mrs. Weinstock's metal chart like some hapless upper-crust businessman unexpectedly forced to ride a crowded subway, clutching his expensive briefcase dearly to his chest lest some heathen grab it.

Merlin's head, eerily floating in the Zeniths above each bed like a disembodied spirit, was not the same relaxed, confident practical joker they knew. He was tight lipped and uneasy. The questions came from a female voice off-camera. "Where was he?"

A nerve had been struck, and wounds not yet allowed to heal were casually displayed. "He—uh—he was on a dissection table."

"He was being used as a cadaver, is that right?"

Merlin nodded. His mouth was dry.

"Doctor, what are the cadavers used for?"

Merlin swallowed twice to get his mouth working again. The camera eased in for a close-up and clearly showed his thyroid cartilage bobbing up and down. Keller watched for it, the Adam's apple, which she'd come to rely on as a telltale sign vintage emotion had been uncorked. Tears couldn't be far behind. Gritty passion. New information would be icing on the cake, but raw, unrehearsed emotion would suffice until her unnamed source called her.

"Part of the first year in medical school," Merlin said, his voice raspy, "involves learning human anatomy. The medical students dissect cadavers—human cadavers—in the anatomy lab for hands-on experience."

"And the coroner has confirmed Kevin Hoover was murdered."

"Right." Merlin nodded twice.

*   *   *

Dr. Olsen, his crisp white coat wrapped tightly around his pear-shaped body, was snugly wedged in a narrow armchair like an egg in a carton. He was joined by a trio of serious-looking men in dark suits. The four of them were also fascinated with KDKA's live broadcast, watching in the comfort of a small, cocoonlike conference room next to the administration offices. They sat motionless, coming alive only to lift their glasses of ice water to moisten their dry lips, afraid to shift in their chairs and chance missing a word. Olsen rapidly puffed on his pipe until he'd created a wispy haze of smoke through which they watched the TV. The rest of the quartet—the CEO, the Medical Center's lawyer, and the chairman of the board of trustees—looked like cookie-cutter businessmen. Perfect WASP-straight hair, great posture, country-club tans, and first names that the working class thinks of as last names: Banks, Knox, and Carter. The three sounded more like a stuffy law firm or an old-money jewelry store.

It was no secret that KDKA's stunning revelation would prompt a media stampede, and the early-morning meeting had been hastily called by Banks, the hospital's CEO, to "charter a course through the quagmire." They had met at 6:30 A.M. in the CEO's office and, at Olsen's insistence, the pompous trustee, Carter, who fortunately also sat on the board of KDKA, telephoned the station manager. After a series of pointed questions relating to Sandy Keller's reliability, he stood up, took charge, and adjourned the meeting to the nearest available television.

Following some initial fumbling with the remote control, Merlin's face filled the screen while they hastily found seats around the teak conference table.

Keller shot rapid-fire questions, ready with a new one as soon as Merlin finished his answer. "Doctor, why? Your best friend, Kevin Hoover. Why would something like this happen to your friend?"

Merlin ran his hand through his hair. "God. I don't know." As if prompted, he wiped a tear from his eye. "I have no idea." Then Merlin clenched his jaw and said, "But you know something, we're gonna find out. This is just the beginning."

Sandy's voice didn't hide her surprise. "You said, 'we,' doctor. Are you involved in the investigation?"

Merlin looked down, pensive. "Can we stop now?" he asked. He sounded defeated, tired. She'd sucked every telegenic emotion right out of him.

Olsen was the first in the room to speak, "Oh, shit. This is getting out of hand. We're gonna need to plug him up."

"It can't come from us," Carter stated.

"Who's his chief resident?" Banks asked.

"Martin Wheeler." Olsen said.

"Ahhh, Martin. Sewickley Country Club. Low handicap. I'll give him a call, see what he can do." Banks smiled.

The surgical ICU looked the way most older Americans remember those frantic hours after Kennedy was assassinated. Every patient, doctor, nurse, and orderly had found a spot, comfortable or otherwise, to watch a TV. The largest crowd remained around Mrs. Weinstock's bed. Every set was tuned to KDKA and Merlin's voice came from every direction in the quiet room.

"Just one more question, Doctor. As a physician who must deal with death on a daily basis, how does it feel to Jack Merlin to discover your best friend being dissected by a group of medical students?" Sandy's voice became soft. Now she was Barbara Walters conducting one of her trademark intimate interviews. As long as the question was asked very slowly, and with a sensitive tone of voice, the most personal privacies could be invaded.

The quiet that followed seemed appropriate for such a sensitive inquiry.

But time was a precious commodity on the morning news, and the moment of reflective quiet quickly became a pregnant pause and soon was an uncomfortable ear-piercing silence. Even the poor quality of the TVs in the ICU showed the crimson in his face. He looked as if he was trying not to explode.

Merlin took one step toward the camera, and for a split second was out of focus. "How does it feel? *How does it feel?* That's why you wanted to interview me. The facts are just foreplay. I'm your emotional climax." Then his voice become phony deep, and he mimicked an interviewer. "Ma'am, sorry, you've just lost your family and home in a tornado, but *how does it feel?*" Then Merlin returned to his own voice, an angry one. "You just want me to cry on camera. Is that what this is about?"

The cameraman wisely pulled back and moved slowly to the right, bringing Sandy Keller's face on camera. "Thank you, Dr. Merlin, this is Sandy Keller reporting live from—"

Merlin was clearly not through. "Goddamnit, don't cut me off. Here comes the emotion you wanted. You are full of—"

The TV picture immediately switched back to a startled anchorman in the studio. He wore a blazer, conservative tie, light blue shirt, laminated smile, and the same phony deep voice Merlin had just imitated. "Uh, thank you Sandy Keller, and obviously, emotions are running high at the Medical Center, and we will, of course, follow this developing story throughout the day . . ."

Peters sat at his desk, feet propped up, watching the news.

He'd arrived early, before any of the nosy secretaries, carrying his small bedroom Sony TV.

The night had been mostly sleepless. He'd recorded the eleven o'clock KDKA news while he dined on Caesar salad and prime rib at Morton's. When he got home he watched, and rewatched, the Sandy Keller segment, which was, of course, the lead story. The video of his news conference had been edited nicely, but coupled with Kel-

ler's remarks about her "anonymous source" and a suspect under investigation, Peters felt frightened that maybe
things had gone too far. But then the phone rang, and it
was Sandy calling to say goodnight, and how great he
looked on TV with the red suspenders. And when he hung
up the phone he felt a lot better.

The next morning he'd awakened early, before his
alarm, and used the extra time to arrange his clothing for
the next week, a shirt–tie combination selected and laid
out in sequence on his dresser, to avoid the possibility of
being caught on camera in the same outfit. The decision
to bring the Sony was never debated, only the mechanics
of getting the device into his office and securing it inside
his credenza without being caught.

Now the television reception was terrible, what with the
forest of steel and concrete buildings surrounding the court
house, but he could hardly have Sue look into cable for
him. Despite the moving vertical lines and white snow,
Peters could see the pain on Merlin's face, and Sandy
Keller was responsible for that. She went for the groin,
asking the questions the viewers wanted her to ask. He
watched the television, even as the news went to commercial, and thought about his evening with Sandy Keller.

With his eyes closed he could see her clearly. When
she wasn't pumping him up he could view their relationship with a measure of objectivity. Suddenly it felt like
he was being tangled up in the sheets with a big-mouth
nymphomaniac who wasn't going to be satisfied with a
quickie. She'd want more and if he didn't produce she'd
turn her cameras, and big mouth, directly toward him.

A McDonald's commercial, with an annoying jingle
played over scenes of happy families racing into a restaurant, distracted him and emphasized just how complicated
his life had become in a very short amount of time. The
TV went dark and he flipped the remote onto his desk.

But he also loved seeing himself on TV, and the promise of an in-depth interview. It was also nice the way

Sandy Keller hung onto every word he said. Maybe the show stopper was when he really got a good look at her in the dim lights of Morton's, with her blouse unbuttoned enough to catch a couple good peeks of her lacy bra. She was much better looking than he originally thought.

He was halfway up the mountain. A quick fall down would hurt more than a climb the rest of the way up.

At that moment he reminded himself that it would be quite an easy thing to sever any relations with Sandy Keller, *if he wanted to, which he didn't.* Ignore her calls, offer no special treatment at press conferences, and if cornered by her, boldly accuse her of reading between the lines when they were, in reality, tightly single spaced. *Look Miss Keller, I don't know what you're referring to; I don't even want to hear what you thought you heard. But, if you're gong to embellish the news without regard for the truth, I will personally contact the network executives.*

However, Sandy Keller was as important to him as he was to her. She had been correct that the Kevin Hoover murder was the story people would remember, and knowing that a murderer might not be found without a genuine piece of luck, Keller was the one who would wring the last drop of emotion from each of the supporting players and keep The Kevin Hoover Show in the news.

Peters's answer was simple, not for its correctness, but for its ability to solve the problem at hand, never mind what effect it might have tomorrow or the next day. For the time being he'd pound his pitons higher up the mountain and enjoy whatever pleasures the media could bestow. The district attorney's office clearly needed to turn things up a notch. No way was he going to be a sideshow, trotted out when things were soft. Forget about scratching the surface; he wanted things cracked open.

Peters picked up his phone and hit the intercom button. "Sue, you out there?" No answer.

Cradling the phone with his shoulder, he looked up Tory's voice-mail extension. As he punched in the number he rehearsed the tone of voice he would use. Tory's smooth voice came on the line and informed him she wasn't at her desk and told him to leave a message at the beep. "Beep."

"Tory, this is Peters. I want to see you in my office immediately."

He ran a variety of scenarios in his head. *Tory, are you the anonymous source KDKA is talking about? Tory, I'm sure you've seen the news, and this bullshit. . . . Tory, I know what's going on with KDKA and I don't like it. We've got to heat things up before this is thrown back in our faces, and I need to stay more involved in the day-to-day issues. Tory, what's this about an anonymous source at KDKA?*

Once the plan was in place Peters let his mind drift. He thought of a variety of things, but whatever consequences his strategy might have were not among them.

Someone said, "All right, Merlin, let her have it!" One of the residents, pushed up tight against the wall next to Mrs. Weinstock's bed, gave a thumbs-up sign in the direction of the TV, and the group slowly migrated back to the foot of the bed. The ICU had a powerful intensity, death visited weekly, and any diversion, fleeting that it might be, was always welcomed. The news of Kevin Hoover upset and frightened even those who hadn't known him. The Medical Center didn't feel safe any more, although it was somewhat reassuring to see Jack Merlin refuse to be reduced to an emotional wimp.

"Doctor?" Mrs. Weinstock's frail voice, raspy from the endotracheal tube, tried to get Wheeler's attention.

"Enough!" Wheeler was furious. His rounds were a shambles and no one knew Mrs. Weinstock well enough to present her case. The surgical team quieted. "What is it, Mrs. Weinstein?"

"Is Dr. Merlin coming to see me today?"

Wheeler thrust the metal chart into the hands of a startled medical student. "You're in charge," he said with sarcasm. "Don't worry—you couldn't possibly do worse than Merlin."

After he furiously strode out of the ICU, Mrs. Weinstock said, "I don't think I like that doctor."

"You just want a prostitute, don't you? Suck my emotions and walk away. Why don't you crumple up some money and throw it on the ground." Merlin started after Sandy Keller, who was beating a hasty retreat toward the mobile news van. He had dropped his coffee in the emotional melee and his pants were stained with ugly blotches of moist java.

"Hey, cool down, everything's cool, man," the producer with the sportcoat said as he stepped directly in front of Merlin in a failed effort to appear calm and reclaim control of the situation. He walked backward, step for step with Merlin.

"Fuck you," Merlin hissed, as he pushed the producer out of the way. The door to the news van slammed shut and Keller disappeared. Merlin's hands were clenched tightly as he walked to the front of the van and peered through the front window. The morning sun caught the windshield and the only thing Merlin could see were the streak marks from the squeegee someone had used to clean off the city muck. He cupped his hands on the glass and, as if looking through imaginary binoculars, tried to see into the far reaches of the news van. He never spotted Sandy Keller, who kneeled uncomfortably behind a back seat, combing her hair.

The cameraman pivoted and continued to beam footage to the KDKA news room. This wasn't news but it was great drama. A lone producer sat in the semidarkness of the control booth, transfixed to the monitor. He stroked his cheek absently, ignoring the thin line of smoke drifting past his face from a smoldering cigarette in the ashtray. It wasn't often that news footage shocked or surprised anyone in the industry. Pictures of death and starvation were almost hackneyed, and it was a struggle to repackage the news each night giving calamity a fresh approach. But live footage with out-of-control anger was mesmerizing, and the producer made a mental note to remember Dr. Merlin. It seemed clear that he had not been heard from for the last time.

Fourteen

Erno and Satch arrived in the Strip District early. Hours early. They'd driven by the church in the old neighborhood before heading down Penn Avenue to the Strip. Only one time they stopped and went in, not dressed very nice, and ran into the priest. Now they never stopped or anything, just drove by before a job, just in case.

Erno wanted to get a sandwich at Primanti's, the Pittsburgh landmark in the Strip District where the steak on Italian bread is served with the fries and coleslaw *on* the sandwich. They talked about broads. Had a couple of beers. And they smoked.

When it was getting toward quitting time for the hourlies on Penn Avenue, Erno and Satch walked up Smallman Street, past St. Stanislaus Church and City Banana to Twenty-first Street, and down a block toward the river. Railroad Street.

They climbed into the unmarked panel truck, the same one that could be decorated with the magnetic Pittsburgh University Medical Center logo. Parked only a block away from the Demasi Produce building, Erno could look out the front windshield and have an unobstructed view of the front entrance and seven loading docks on the side. The small parking lot was empty. If he looked in the rearview mirror, he could catch a glimpse of the Bevel Building, a two-story brick begging for a sandblasting. He watched as a silver-haired gentleman stopped to chat with some young women in aprons. They all seemed smiley and happy.

Then the silver-haired man got into a big Chrysler and drove off.

"Hey, Ern, why we always gotta be so early? Jesus, my legs are stiff," Satch said, massaging his long bony legs folded off to one side.

"It's like I tell you every time, we don't want to walk into something. Maybe this Demasi has some muscle with him. Maybe even the cops. You're making what—seven, eight bills?—for this job. What're you complaining? I never got you arrested."

"Yeah, well, I still don't like sitting in a car that's not moving. Starts to smell after a while."

Erno rolled down the window. "You getting carsick?" he laughed.

"No, I jus' don't like doing it."

Erno reached in the back and pulled out a bunched up newspaper and pushed the mess on Satch's lap. "Shut up and read this."

Satch started to read. Erno drank from a half-gallon cardboard container of iced tea and watched the trucks rumble by, listening to oldies on the radio. At 7:45 P.M. he spotted him. "Satch, there he is, getting outta that red station wagon." Actually a red Volvo wagon with a bike rack. Mike Demasi, khaki pants and a golf shirt, looked around before he unlocked the front door and disappeared inside.

"All right, Satch, my man, it goes like Antony said. If he ain't interested, we do him."

"You don't think I was at the meeting at the barbershop?" Satch said with a hint of anger.

"You're never at the meeting, even when you're at the meeting. Look, if you don't have nothing to say, which is all the time, shut the fuck up. I don't want to go in there like a couple of assholes and not know what we're doing."

They sat another twenty-five minutes. Erno scanned the neighborhood. He checked every window on the second floor of the Demasi Produce building. The feeling was starting. He was getting in the mood.

Then he caught the signal: Mike Demasi looked out one of the windows. Not a quick, confident look to confirm his reinforcements were in place, but a long up-and-down-the-street gander. Like a skinny kid would do, told by the bully to meet him after school.

"He's alone."

"You sure?"

"He's looking for us. He's scared. I think he's gonna say yes so he don't pee his pants."

Erno opened his jacket and took out the syringe. Not your ordinary tetanus-shot syringe. These were special. Spring-loaded, automatic-injecting with the needle hidden up inside the black plastic tip. It looked like a cross between a fat ball-point pen and a cigar tube. Not at all intimidating. But a little pressure on the business end engaged the spring action with an audible click, ramming the needle half an inch through a tiny hole in the black plastic tip, into the skin and emptying the syringe. They were mostly used by the military so soldiers in battle could self-inject atropine, an antidote for nerve gas. They were also loaded with adrenaline for life-threatening bee-sting allergies. And, with some modification, they were just what Erno needed.

He shook it and saw the clear liquid, some kind of nerve medicine that paralyzed the nerves and muscles so the diaphragm didn't work, and the victim suffocated. Antony had explained, more than once, that you couldn't drop off a bunch of stiffs to the Medical Center with bulletholes and bashed-in skulls. Everything had to look right. So Antony had a bunch of the auto-inject syringes made up special by some guy who substituted the atropine with pancuronium bromide.

But Erno didn't trust the stuff at first, said it looked like water. So he and Satch went out in the alley behind Satch's building and jammed the syringe hard in the rump of some dog. The mechanism clicked loudly and the syringe emptied in less than a second. The dog limped away, then stumbled to the ground like a discarded rag doll, whimpered for a second, and was gone.

The only mistake Erno and Satch ever made with the stuff was the first time they used it for real. The same dose that dropped the mutt in eight seconds took a bit longer to work in a fat guy who owned a nightclub. Erno injected him in the thigh while Satch held him from behind. The guy was struggling, his fat belly jiggling up and down, scared to death, and after the syringe shot its load Erno and Satch stepped back to watch him go down. But the fat guy got up and started running. And screaming. Down two flights of stairs with Erno and Satch chasing him, all three of them scared to death. The fat guy almost made it out the front door of the nightclub before he fell, working hard to breathe for a few seconds before he went out.

Now they were a little more careful.

"I gotta take a leak before we go in," Erno said taking the last swig out of the iced tea.

"You getting the willies?"

"No, I drank a couple quarts of tea."

"What else is new?" Satch said sarcastically.

" 'Harry, you looking at me?' " Erno asked.

"I see you Ern, but I thought you were calling me Vulture. Where'd you get Harry from?"

"I want you to keep looking right here, 'kay?"

"What's the hell's wrong with you?" Satch said, sounding irritated. "Are we going in or what?"

"Vulture, you know who Chili Palmer is?"

"I heard of him. Where's he live, Bloomfield?"

"Shit. You didn't rent it, did you?"

"Rent what?"

"The movie I told you about."

"Oh yeah, a Quarter-Pounder with Cheese is a Royale with Cheese. I saw it."

"Wrong movie. How're the Buccos doing? Who's been taking the snaps for the Steelers? Man, like I told you, I can't talk wit' you. You couldn't hold up your end of a conversation with Helen Keller. C'mon, let's go," Erno said, showing his disgust.

Erno and Satch crossed the street, letting Demasi watch them if he wanted. Satch waited by the front door of the Demasi Produce building while Erno went around back. There were always some weeds and brush behind warehouses, and Erno liked having a restroom wherever he conducted business. Afterward, still hiking up his pants and adjusting his personal equipment, he walked all the way around the building. "All clear."

The front door was open, and their footsteps echoed loudly off the concrete. The warehouse smelled good, like a glass of cider. One huge room, stacked high with wooden and cardboard cases of fruits and vegetables, had a walk-in cooler in back. Erno eyed an open case of McIntosh apples. It would be nice to load up a few cases when they loaded up Mike Demasi. In Erno's mind it was becoming a forgone conclusion. *Pop. Pop. Pop.*

The stairs to the second floor were old wooden ones, slightly bowed. It came up often enough in this line of work that if you wanted to go up quietly you knew to walk on the outside aspects of each step where the wood was reinforced. Much quieter. Erno, followed by Satch, placed his feet squarely in the middle of each step. Squeaks and noises at this point were part of the negotiations.

Mike Demasi was sitting behind his desk, trying to position his hands in a natural way. The remaining light of the day illuminated the room poorly.

Erno didn't knock. "I like a guy who arrives on time. Why you driving your wife's car?"

"She had . . . ," Demasi hesitated. This man knew too much. "She had garden club and wanted to take mine."

"The BMW, right?"

Demasi didn't answer. He was used to discussing his car at backyard barbecues. But this didn't feel like cocktail-party talk. He averted his eyes from Erno's for a second and looked down at his pencil drawer.

Erno followed his eyes down to the edge of the desk. The pencil drawer was open enough—maybe three or four inches—that Erno could see the edges of it protruding out toward Demasi. Erno knew damn well what was inside.

The two intruders drifted to opposite sides of the room. While Demasi waited, Erno took a few moments to look at some framed photos on the wall. "Hey, Mike, what was the name of them apples?"

Demasi let out a little sigh. "McIntosh. They're called McIntosh apples." He didn't want to deal with bullshit.

"You mind if I take a few more on the way out?"

"Help yourself," Demasi said, his voice weak. "Your friend can have some, too."

"Satch don't eat fruit. That's why he's always constipated. Right, Satch?"

Satch put a finger in his right ear and shook his ear canal violently. "You got it."

"Hey Mike, I betcha a guy like you working with all this fruit is real regular." His voice hit a certain rhythm. *As long as it takes.*

"Look, sir—"

Erno acted surprised. "Sir? C'mon, *Erno.* That's Satch over there."

"Look, Erno, what's this all about? You didn't come here to talk about fruit."

"Maybe you let me buy one of them boxes of apples? Save me a trip to the Giant Eagle."

"Go ahead, take whatever you want. Look why don't we talk about whatever—" Demasi's voice was getting an edge to it.

"Maybe you can write down the name of those apples so I remember."

Demasi didn't answer and he didn't reach for paper. He

was irritated. His eyes got intense and his jaw muscles tightened.

Erno heard the chair creak as Demasi sat straighter. This was good. Erno had played with him long enough, gotten him pissed off so he wouldn't try a song and dance.

Now Erno was ready to conduct some business. "Okay, Mike, Mr. Bevel wants you to consider an early retirement from the Strip District. You thought about it, right?"

"Yeah, I thought about it." All of a sudden Demasi sounded like he was trying to run the meeting. "I thought about having you thugs come in here and tell me what you're gonna do. I thought about how you scared the crap outta me. And if Mr. Bevel wants to do business with me, why doesn't he call me?" His hands were still on the desk, fingers spread slightly like he was waiting for a manicure.

Every conceivable permutation had run through his mind. He didn't even know for certain Frank Bevel was behind this. For all he knew, Erno was some independent using the Bevel name to muscle in on him. But Mike Demasi had hoped—maybe a better word was prayed—that this was a friendly offer. *Hey, I thought about it but I think I'll pass. Timing's wrong.* And the monsters would leave. *Yeah, right.* What he really should have done was planned better how to handle these bastards. The gun in his drawer, a pearl-handle pistol with only two bullets. *I shoulda called the cops.*

In the movies, he would do it blind. The move. Pulling the drawer open wide with the left hand, grabbing the gun with the right and pointing it at the big sonovabitch in the leather coat. Deceptively simple was the only way he could describe it. Over and over he'd worked on it. Hundreds of times. Sometimes the drawer jammed and didn't open enough to get his hand inside, but if he pulled too hard the gun would fly out onto his lap, or sometimes would twist around and he'd end up pointing it at himself. *Pull it out straight, medium force. Don't rush.*

Now! Demasi looked down, slid his chair back, pulled

the drawer hard with his left hand, fumbled for a second, grabbed the gun and stood. The creaky old chair scooted out from behind him and banged into the wall. His thigh caught the pencil drawer as he stood and ripped his pants. A trickle of blood ran down his leg.

Satch jumped back as the gun moved herky-jerky back and forth. Erno took a step forward. Confusion. *Get control and end it. Just like Antony said.*

"Get back, you bastard! Get the hell away from me!" Mike said loudly, almost yelling.

"Nice-looking gun." *Keep talking.* "What's it, a .38? Hey, you don't want to do the deal you say so. Put the gun away."

"No. Get the hell outta here. I'm gonna call the cops."

"Mike, listen to me. We own the cops. They *know* we're here. Call 'em if you want. C'mon, sit down. Let's talk this thing out. We'll make you good."

"I'm not afraid to use this." Demasi looked back and forth between Erno and Satch, his head like a metronome.

"You want to use it, go ahead. But I gotta tell you, I got one of them Kevlar vests on. Bulletproof. You gotta do a head shot, Mike, so raise up the gun a little. A little more. Yeah, that's better. You got it in you to do it?" It was working. The gun was trained on Erno. *You and me, pal.*

Demasi wiped some spittle from his mouth with the back of his left hand. He was listening to Erno, hearing the patter more than the words and sweating heavily. "I'm protecting what is mine. No one's gonna take what's mine."

"No one's taking anything. Mr. Bevel wants to make you a wealthy man. You don't see no gun in my hand. We coulda come busting in here, bang, bang." He was talking smooth. Sleight of tongue. Almost hypnotic.

"Get out. Now."

"Then pull the trigger. You see that picture behind me, the one of your daughter in the tennis outfit? Nice-looking

girl. What is she seventeen, eighteen years old?'' He
waited for effect. Demasi looked at the photo. ''She's
gonna have the back on my head splattered all over her
white tennis dress. She'll look like she's having her
fuckin' period. Thirty-eight bullet makes a big hole out
the back.'' Erno made a circle with his thumb and forefinger for emphasis. ''What're you gonna tell your
daughter?''

Crack. The awful crunching noise of the collar bone
snapping. Satch hit him, both hands together, fingers inter-
laced, with a downward blow to his right shoulder. The
gun vanished somewhere under the desk and Demasi stumbled down into his chair. He slumped to the right and used
his left hand to support his right arm. For a few seconds
he almost blacked out from the pain. Satch wheeled him
around to the front of the desk and into the middle of the
room and took his position behind the desk chair. One
hand on Demasi's throbbing right shoulder was more than
enough to secure him.

''You shoulda said yes,'' Erno said without emotion.
Pop. Pop. Pop.

Demasi started to cry. ''My family. Please let me go.''

Erno opened his jacket and pulled out the automatic
syringe.

''We can't. Not now.''

''*Yes. Yes,* goddamnit,'' Demasi screamed. ''YES, take
it. I'll sign it over to you. Just let me go!''

''You're a nice guy, Mike. I bet you're a good dad,
probably don't fool around on your wife. This is business.'' Erno coolly pressed the syringe against Demasi's
thigh, the one with the rip in the pants. A clicking noise,
a pricking sensation, and the syringe emptied.

''What is that? What did you do to me?'' Demasi
said hoarsely.

Erno stood in front of Mike, placed a hand on each of
the armrests and leaned in close. His voice softened. ''Listen to me, Mike. You want me to tell your wife some-

thing? I'll do it. I'll find her if you want me to. I won't
give her a hard time or nothing. I promise you. You want
me to tell her you love her?''

"Please, I want to talk to my kids. Lemme go home,
make a call.'' Demasi felt out of breath, like he'd sprinted
a mile and was sucking air.

"There's no time for a phone call, Mike. I'll call her
later, tell her you love her.''

Demasi tried to squirm. It was starting to grab him, like
sliding into a hot bath, making him relax. His muscles
softened; it became hard to close his mouth and he
drooled. His head was a weight he couldn't control. Long,
slow breaths, each taking more effort. He thought he was
having a stroke. "Helllllll.'' He couldn't close his lips to
make the "P" sound. "Helllllllll . . .''

"Satch, that's okay, let him go. Mike, you don't got a
lot of time, you want me to say something to your kids?
Blink your eyes if you want me to. Mike. Mike.''

Demasi slumped forward and Erno caught him before
he fell. His last three breaths were filled with the sweet
perfume of Erno Pantuzzi.

Fifteen

September 20, 1996

Tory never left a conversation with Mark Peters feeling anything other than frustrated or angry. Today she added a new emotion to her file: used.

Her morning was spent on the phone, first talking with the medical school at the University of Pennsylvania and then with the central office of the American Academy of Pathology, finding out that, indeed, Jonathan Olsen was registered to attend the meetings in Philadelphia, but no one knew whether or not he had been a featured speaker or merely part of the anonymous audience.

The conversation with Jan Wolkin in Bridgeport was much more difficult. Locating Kevin Hoover's former girl-friend involved a single call to directory assistance and telephoning the only J. Wolkin listed. It wasn't a surprise when she answered the phone, knowing Jan was a nurse and probably worked shifts.

"Hello." A quiet voice. Timid.

"Hello. Is this Jan Wolkin?"

"Yes, it is. Who is this?" Jan's voice sounded distant, almost hesitant.

"My name is Tory Welch, and I'm with the district attorney's office in Pittsburgh, and a Dr. Jack Merlin gave me—"

"Oh, God. Oh, no." Jan cried out and started to cry.

Tory heard the phone drop to a hard surface and listened for almost a minute to Jan sobbing.

"Hello." Jan was back on the line, sniffling loudly.

"Jan, are you okay?"

"It's just that . . . you're calling about Kevin, aren't you?"

"Yes. Kevin was found a couple of days ago. I'm so sorry to have to tell you over the phone like this. Jan, Kevin was murdered."

"Oh, God." Jan started to sob again, this time only for a few seconds. "You know, every time I answer the phone, I expect it to be the police. I wanted to be ready for the call. It was just a matter of time. I didn't expect a woman, I guess. Where did they find him?"

"He was hidden in the anatomy labs."

"The anatomy labs? Was he there all along?"

"We think so."

"It happened that night, didn't it? The night he disappeared."

"We think that's what happened."

"Who did it?"

"Oh, Jan, we don't know. I wish I had answers for you. I guess that's why I'm calling. I was hoping you could help us. Would you mind telling me what happened that night when you saw him last?"

"What's your name again?"

"Tory Welch. If you'd like, I can call you back."

"No. No. I've known he was dead. I've known for a long time. You know what I mean. That last night I went to his on-call room . . . you know . . . for about an hour, maybe a little longer. And we were . . . together, and he went home. I thought he went home, and I finished my shift in the OR. That was the only time I'd seen him the whole day. I didn't know there was a problem until the next day, when someone called looking for him."

"Nothing else happened when you were together? No phone calls?"

"No, not that I remember."

"Did he seem distracted?"

"No. But I was on a three-week stretch of nights and Kevin was . . . um . . . you know. So I came in early so we could be together. He was definitely not distracted."

"When he left the room did he—"

"Wait a second. Merlin. That's right, Merlin interrupted us. I mean, it was nothing, but Jack Merlin was holding Kevin's beeper for him and—I guess we took longer than Merlin thought. He came up to the fourteenth floor and banged on the door, and finally he opened the door—the on-call rooms don't have locks for some reason. I screamed and he threw the beeper on the bed where Kevin and I were . . . you know . . . He was furious with Kevin—the way one friend gets mad at another—and said something really nasty and slammed the door. At that point, I guess all three of us were angry."

"Jan, can you tell me what he said?"

"You know, Miss Welch, they were really good friends, but they said things to each other. Like a couple of brothers. You know, it didn't mean anything."

"I understand. I'm not accusing anyone of anything— in fact, just so you know, it was Dr. Merlin who found Kevin. He was pretty shaken up. But I still would like to know any detail you can recall."

There was a pause as Tory waited for Jan to find the courage. "I never told the police. When they came to talk with me, you know, Kevin wasn't . . . dead. I probably didn't think about it."

"Never told the police what?"

"There was a doctor, Martin Wheeler, a real worm. Anyway, he gave me a hard time . . ."

Tory was confused. "Jan, what kind of a hard time? What did he do to you?"

"He touched me. Squeezed me on my breast."

"When did this happen?"

"I'm not really sure. Maybe three or four months before Kevin disappeared."

Tory sat forward, her posture rigid. "Did you ever report it?"

"No."

"Did you ever tell anyone?"

"Kevin."

"What did Kevin do?"

Jan chuckled briefly. "He handcuffed Martin to his on-call bed when he was sleeping. Then he unplugged the phone and left him there. When the cleaning lady found him the next day he'd wet himself. Martin was furious, threatened Kevin. Said he'd get him back. But as soon as Kevin told Martin this was to get him back, Martin told Kevin he didn't know what he was talking about. He denied the whole thing. He's a worm."

"Did Dr. Wheeler ever do anything to get Kevin back?"

"No way. Martin's a wimp, and Kevin never let anyone have the last word in an argument. Whatever Martin did, Kevin would have topped. As horrible as it was when Martin grabbed me, I'm certain it was worse for Martin when housekeeping found him in a wet bed."

"And you never told this to anyone?"

"No. And to be truthful with you, I don't know why I'm telling you. I mean, I don't think Wheeler would kill anyone."

"Has Dr. Wheeler made any effort to contact you since Kevin disappeared?"

"No."

"Jan, it took courage to tell me. Let me sort through things. Would it be okay if I called you back sometime?"

"You be careful how you use this. I don't want some reporter to call me."

"And if you think of anything, anything at all, you'll call me."

"Miss Welch, what Merlin said."

"Only if you're comfortable."

"He was mad—you know I've never told anyone this—and he threw the beeper right on the bed, and Kevin looked over at him and Merlin said something like, 'I'd say "Fuck you" but I can see it would be redundant,' " Jan said, and quickly hung up the phone.

Tory was off to the Medical Center, but not before running into Mark Peters again in the hallway.

"Hey, Tory, listen. About our little conversation before."

"We're not gonna go through that again, are we?" Tory frowned.

"I wasn't accusing you of talking to KDKA or anything." Peters slipped his hands into his back pockets, trying to look casual.

"Mark, when you asked me if there was any possibility that I was KDKA's source, you were asking if I had leaked false information. Why wouldn't that be an accusation?"

"I thought we might have a leak, I just had to ask, it didn't mean anything, you know I trust you, you're not pissed, right?" Peters rambled, blurting out his run-on sentence quickly.

"Mark, it's not that important. Relax. One reporter mouthing off. I don't think it's that big a deal. I would have preferred sitting down, like colleagues, to discuss it, rather than be summoned to your office and then asked point-blank, 'Have you been talking to KDKA?' Forget it. It doesn't impact our investigation."

Peter was relieved. "Yeah, maybe you're right. Probably someone at the Medical Center, anyway."

"Hey, I'm late. I'll try and catch up with you later," Tory said and started to walk toward the elevators.

"What's up? You reach Hoover's girlfriend?"

"Just now," Tory said trying to be brief.

"Well, what gives?" Peters asked, wanting a nugget of information.

"Look, she didn't want to tell me anything, but some-

one—I don't know who—was coming on to her with unwanted sexual advances. That's all I know, Mark. I gotta
go.''

Tory turned and walked away from Mark Peters.

Sixteen

Martin Wheeler was in the doctor's lounge when his beeper went off. Sitting in an overstuffed green leather wingback chair, legs crossed just so, a copy of *Barron's* draped over his thighs like a giant napkin, he was listening to Jonathan Olsen's version of the Man-in-the-Pan incident. Wheeler had already been treated to several hilarious renditions of the details and now endured a carefully rehearsed rehash that Olsen hoped would spread with equal dispatch.

"I was having a little fun with her, that's all, after what happened in anatomy—absconding with the body like that when I was on the phone. I took it upon myself to show her there were no hard feelings. So I asked her to identify the appendix," Olsen said, shaking his head. "She turned it into a big deal. Tried to embarrass me."

Wheeler, a master at agreeing with the right people, shook his head in sympathy.

"Take some friendly advice, Martin. She attacks with a vengeance. Probably weaned on *Murder, She Wrote.* Every time she interviews someone she's certain he did it. Real pain in the sphincter." Olsen laughed uncomfortably.

Beep Beep Beep. Beep Beep Beep. Beep Beep Beep. Wheeler's yellow beeper chirped away and would continue to chirp until a small black button was depressed. Then a short message played back from the paging system. "Dr. Wheeler, please call your office. Dr. Wheeler, call your office."

"Jonathan, let me take this. I'll see you at eleven-thirty," Wheeler said.

Olsen looked confused.

Wheeler continued. "The meeting with Banks, and the lawyer, and Carter from the board."

Banks, Knox, and Carter. The stuffy trio who controlled the politics of the entire Medical Center. Olsen tried not to show his concern. *Think. What the hell do they want Martin Wheeler for? It had to be about shutting up Merlin. Who the hell do they think suggested Martin Wheeler, anyway?* Olsen would later recall countless times the off-handed way Wheeler said, "See you at eleven-thirty," like Olsen was one of the power elite and of course would be at a pivotal meeting.

Why was it the most important things you learned about yourself came on the heels of an offhand comment?

"Oh, right, I forgot," Olsen lied. One thing was certain: He was no longer in the loop.

As Wheeler punched in the extension to his office, Olsen made his exit, mumbling something about a conference call he was late for.

The goddamn Man-in-the-Pan incident.

"Edna, what's up?" Wheeler said in the clipped tones of authority he worked hard to perfect.

"Dr. Wheeler, a Tory Welch from the district attorney's—" Edna, Martin Wheeler's secretary, was interrupted in mid-sentence, which in no way surprised her because Wheeler always cut her off.

"What does she want, Edna?" Wheeler asked, urging her to cut to the chase. On those occasions when Edna immediately cut to the chase, Wheeler would say. "Whoa, Edna, slow down, time out, start from the beginning," like she was some scatterbrained schoolgirl overreacting to the situation.

"Here, let me put her on," Edna said before Wheeler

could protest. Only several months into Martin Wheeler's chief residency and Edna was already catching on.

"Hello, Dr. Wheeler?"

"Yes." *Short, professional, IN-CONTROL answers.*

"I need a few minutes of your time, either here in the hospital or at my office, if you prefer, to discuss the Kevin Hoo—"

"I'm busy now. I just finished a case and I'm in recovery with a patient."

"When would be a convenient time?"

"It's never a convenient time. Look I'm very busy today. I can give you a few minutes." Wheeler paused, picked up his copy of *Barron's*, rustled the papers, and checked a quote. "Oh, how 'bout ten of two? The solarium on eight." Martin Wheeler hung up the phone, picked up the TV remote control, and turned on CNN.

The meeting with Banks—it turned out Carter and Knox weren't there—was nothing more than a short conversation. Wheeler was ushered into Banks's office, an impressive room with a trophy cabinet loaded with golf trophies.

"Martin, thanks for coming," Banks said, coming around his desk to shake Wheeler's hand. They settled into comfortable chairs covered in a flowery chintz fabric. "I saw your father at the club over the weekend," Banks said, picking an invisible piece of lint from his trousers.

"He's still working on his backswing, swiveling his hips," Wheeler said with a smile.

"Your game's pretty sharp. What're you, a seven?" Banks said, having checked with the pro in the last half hour.

"Just a ten," Wheeler replied with a humble smile. He liked the single-digit reputation of a seven.

"Martin, I need your help."

For a second Wheeler thought about a witty response. Like saying, "Irons or woods." But instead he remained true to form. "Name it."

"I want you to keep Jack Merlin busy. This whole thing with Kevin Hoover is a tragedy, and I don't want to do anything to impede the district attorney from bringing this to a close. I don't know if you saw him on KDKA the other day, but the last thing we need is someone saying inappropriate things to the news media."

"I agree with you completely. What about farming him out to do one of his community hospital rotations?"

Banks spoke slowly, choosing his words carefully. "We have to be careful not to give Jack Merlin the impression we're putting a muzzle on him. I've talked with Carter Wallace—your father knows Carter quite well—and we're pretty much in agreement that you should keep Jack busy. Less free time. More consultations or whatever. I know you'll use discretion."

More golf talk, a promise of a round sometime soon, and Banks ended the meeting precisely seven and one half minutes after it began and joined Carter Wallace in the conference room for a private lunch. The soup wasn't even cold.

After her brief phone conversation with Wheeler, the only satisfaction Tory got out of a quick trip to the anatomy labs was fifteen seconds rattling the locked doors. Now she sat alone in the hospital cafeteria, one of those complicated eating centers with a variety of food stations scattered about and no hint of the traditional food line that offered all elements of a meal. And there was a wide variety of table sizes to break up the monotony of military-style seating. It was 1:15 P.M. and most of the visitors had completed lunch and gone on to whatever afternoon activities the Medical Center offered. The remaining tables were filled with an assortment of medical personnel sitting within their species—medical students, nurses, and doctors clustered with their own kind. Convivial conversations were welcomed between tables, but segregation was usually the rule.

Good gossip spread quickly, and several of the tables were abuzz with whispers of the marvelous put-down Tory affected on Dr. Olsen. Tory, too, was stuck on that topic, but for different reasons. It was, at times, impossible for her to put her verbal acumen on hold, much like a black belt in karate getting pushed around in a bar by a drunk. There was no way to stop the reflexes from taking over. She was in danger of becoming mired in the details of her Dr. Olsen imbroglio, rendering herself impotent as an investigator.

A reasonably appetizing chef salad sat untouched while Tory sipped her Diet Coke. Two oatmeal raisin cookies would wait forever. Unaware she was the topic of more than one conversation in the room, she stared at her little leather notebook. Absently she played with her gold bangle bracelet on her right wrist.

Mark Peters's expanding-circle theory boldly stared up at her. Her first dart hit Olsen squarely, touched a nerve, but probably was a dud. She was frustrated, not knowing what to do, and not having anyone in her department to guide her.

Tory never felt more alone. Not since she first went off to Yale had pangs of homesickness rocked her stomach this way. Failure terrified her more than it did others who failed regularly. What would happen if she interviewed each of the people on the expanding-circle theory and had nothing to show for it? Would Mark Peters take the case over and reopen the investigation? Would she become a joke with the let's-grab-a-beer-after-work crowd? "Hey, 'member Tory Welch? What a loser."

While Tory worried herself out of an appetite, each card-carrying member of the expanding-circle club made an appearance in the cafeteria.

Merlin had something going with one of the checkout girls. He whizzed through the grill line, a loaded tray in one hand, two cartons of milk in the other, and after paying about half of what his meal cost, he headed for a large table in the middle of the room, where a small group of surgical residents was finishing lunch. Before he put his tray down he noticed Tory over by a huge picture window, her back toward him, sitting alone. After begging off his colleagues' attempts to have him sit down, Merlin smoothly made his way over to join the assistant district attorney.

The view through the picture window was almost stunning. A small courtyard with large ceramic flower boxes proudly displayed sturdy mums, and a trio of Japanese maples offered shade. Meandering through patches of lush green myrtle was a brick path that led to the centerpiece of the garden: a formation of rocks with a small waterfall. Several nurses' aides with teased-up, moussed-up hair ate their lunches in the arbor of the maples. One of them stubbed out her smoke and flicked the butt in the general direction of the trash bin. They seemed out of place, like plastic tulips planted among the myrtle. *What's wrong with this picture?* Tory wondered, taking a respite from her notebook.

Merlin circled the table and was pulling out his chair before Tory noticed him. "Hey, you're the talk of the Medical Center."

Tory was taken aback. "What?" she asked.

"Great appendix story. You're quick."

"That's what I was afraid of. On replay it seems foolish to get pulled into an argument with Dr. Olsen," Tory said with a trace of regret.

"There aren't many who can tangle with him. Anyway, I wanted to talk with you about the other night. Up in anatomy I—uh—I gave you a sanitized version of what happened that night Kevin was killed," Merlin said with a tone that sounded more appropriate for a confessional than a hospital cafeteria.

Oh my God, he's going to confess. Tory's heart skipped a beat. The croquet game with the cherry tomato in her salad stopped, and she picked up her pen. "Are you comfortable talking here?"

"Look, it doesn't matter where we talk. I need to set the record straight."

Hospital cafeterias are noisy places, but suddenly Tory noticed the background sounds of other conversations had become as distant as the ocean in a conch shell. Tory brushed the hair from her face and tucked it behind her right ear. *Don't say a word; let him talk.*

"Remember I told you I was carrying his beeper so Kevin and Jan could go up to his on-call room before Jan's shift in the OR?"

Tory nodded.

"Well, when Kevin was late I waited and waited and got pretty pissed off. When I went up to fourteen to return Kevin's beeper I knew darn well what he and Jan were up to. Like a jerk I opened the door anyway—for some ridiculous reason there're no locks—and deliberately caught them in the act and screamed some embarrassing obscenity at them.

"I've been racked with guilt ever since Kevin disappeared, like I might have had something to do with his state of mind when he left. Maybe I caused him to go off and do something he wouldn't ordinarily have done, and maybe that got him killed. Shit. I never told anybody about it, never even talked about it with Jan. I mean, it makes me feel terrible."

That's it, that's the whole confession? Disappointed, Tory waited, hoping for more.

"Outside page Tory Welch, one-seven-one-two. An outside page for Tory Welch, please dial one-seven-one-two," a paging operator's voice intoned over the intercom system.

Tory heard her name and looked around the cafeteria.

Merlin pointed to a wall mounted phone ten yards from where they were sitting. "Over there, just dial one-seven-one-two."

Tory walked over to the phone—*Who knows I'm*

here?—figuring Mark Peters would be at the other end of the line to pump her about the sexual harassment angle, and reluctantly punched in the four numbers.

"Hello, this is Tory Welch," she said in the same professional tone of voice she would have used at her desk.

"Tory Welch?"

The voice was low and muffled, a horrible connection. Tory could hardly hear it over the din of the cafeteria. She put her finger in her left ear and held the receiver tightly against her right. Tory closed her eyes to concentrate.

"Yes, this is Tory Welch. Who is this? You'll have to speak up," she said, turning up her own vocal cord volume, assuming the caller was having the same difficulty.

"A friend. And I've got a friendly message for you." Suddenly the voice was louder and more distinct. The connection was fine. The caller was disguising his voice, a crude caricature of a voice, like a child trying to make a phony phone call. "Don't let his cutsie-pie shit fool you. He'll do you next."

Every muscle in her body tensed. "What? Who is this?"

"Merlin did it," the voice said.

Reflexively, Tory shot a glance at Merlin. He looked up momentarily as he squeezed little packets of ketchup onto a burger.

Whoever she was talking to had been in the cafeteria in the last five minutes; he knew she was sitting with Merlin. Maybe the caller was still in the room. Tory scanned the cafeteria, looking for someone on a cellular telephone.

Then she spotted her only possibility. On the other side of the room a doctor, three-quarter-length white coat, was talking on a wall-mounted hospital phone. He was hunched over the phone, his back toward Tory, talking privately.

Tory studied him as she spoke, "Uh, how do you know all this about Merlin?"

"I saw him that night."

"I'm sorry, could you talk louder—it must be a bad connection."

"I said, I saw him the night it happened." The voice now spoke in a deliberate, loud tone. The one used to give directions to foreigners who do not speak English.

Across the cafeteria the doctor remained comfortably hunched over the phone, his white coat stretched tightly across his broad back.

"Tell me what happened that night," Tory said, reducing her voice to a whisper. Playing. Teasing. Hoping to frustrate him, make him turn around to see what's going on.

Produced, Written and Directed by Tory Welch. The gambit worked! HE TURNED AROUND, just like it said in the script. Tory could see his face—Dr. Jonathan Olsen. He didn't smile or acknowledge Tory. He looked about the room briefly, making it look like he was searching for a colleague. Then he turned back to the phone.

"No games, Miss Welch. We're not at some slumber party, having fun with a telephone."

Dr. Olsen hung up the phone and walked out of the cafeteria, hands thrust deep within the patch pockets on his white coat. Not even a glance in Tory's direction. As if he never saw her in the first place.

Her heart raced in her throat. *I've got him.* Tory was about to hang up the phone. "Hello, hello," she said, confirming the line was dead.

"I'm still here," the voice said, maintaining the same cartoonish tone. Tory's posture slumped; she looked like a deflating balloon. "I work the graveyard shift, came in a little late that night, and saw Merlin pushing that other doctor. Then he hit him."

"Please tell me who you are," Tory said, her voice

as lonely as a little girl talking to her out-of-town dad before bed.

"That's it, you're on your own. Good luck."

Click.

The voice was gone, but one thing was clear. The Kevin Hoover murder investigation was anything but a dead end.

Tory slowly replaced the receiver. Thoughts raced through her head and she needed to be alone to sort them out. Someone had been in the cafeteria to see them together. But what good was an anonymous indictment? And why did an eyewitness to a murder wait so long? But the thought that screamed in her ear until it gave her a headache was that maybe, just maybe, Merlin was unloading half his emotional baggage and leaving out a second conversation with Kevin Hoover that ended in a violent act.

"You okay?" Merlin asked.

Tory found herself at the table, seated across from Merlin. *How did I get here?* "Yeah, I'm fine. Why?"

"The color's gone from your face and your voice sounds . . . sort of shaky. You just get some bad news or something?"

Determined to end the conversation Tory sat up straight and spoke confidently, "No, I'm fine. I just spotted my good friend Dr. Olsen and thought he might walk over. That's all. Anyway, I appreciate you straightening out those details from the other night." Tory looked at her watch. "Look, I've gotta go."

Merlin ignored the hint. "Miss Welch, the reason I told you what happened is so you'll understand exactly what I'm up against. If in any way I'm responsible for starting some horrible sequence of events that ended in Kevin's death, then I've got to help unravel what happened. I know my way around the Medical Center, and of course I'm familiar with medical terminology . . ."

Tory listened as Merlin detailed his credentials.

"Merlin, tell me about Jan. What was their relationship like?" Tory asked, attempting to redirect the conversation.

"They had a great relationship. Hey, if you think Jan could be involved, you're way off."

"How can you be so certain?"

"I may be a surgeon, but my advisers in med school said I'd make a great shrink. I size people up pretty well. Jan adored Kevin, and vice versa. No way was Jan involved. Period," Merlin said with the confident swagger of a surgeon.

Beep Beep Beep. Merlin's yellow beeper. "Dr. Merlin, please come up to Eight South. Merlin, we need you ASAP," a female voice said.

"I gotta go. Anyway, what about me getting involved? I need to help. I need to be a part of things."

"I appreciate your offer, but I don't think that's a very good idea," Tory said apologetically.

"Why not? You need someone on the inside."

Tory swallowed hard. "Dr. Merlin, I don't know you. I really don't think we could team up."

"What do you need to know? I spilled my guts out to you."

"The other night you left out a significant part of the story. So does that mean I get the truth only when it benefits you?" Tory asked.

Merlin hesitated for a second, pulled his head back. "Of course not. There are some nights I can't sleep. Telling you what I did was very difficult."

"I understand. This isn't about you, Dr. Merlin. This is about your friend. I appreciate how much it hurts to have lost him."

"You appreciate it? Like hell you do. Not unless you've had a friend murdered. Not unless the last thing you can remember you did for your friend was barge in on him, cursing like a maniac at him, inflicting a case of coitus interruptus. Tell me you've had that experience, then tell me you appreciate how much it hurts," Merlin said, raising his voice slightly for effect.

"Look, Dr. Merlin, the last thing I want to do is upset you—"

"You've already done that. What's the first thing you want to do?" *Beep Beep Beep.* The chirping continued ad nauseum. Merlin pressed the black button.

"Merlin, please come up to Eight South; we need you for Scott Gordon."

"I'm outta here. You can say it's none of my business, but that phone call you got had something to do with me, didn't it? I don't know what you were hearing, but you gave me a look when you sat down that could paralyze. What the hell's going on?"

Merlin stood, his face red with anger, and gathered his milk cartons on his tray. He held the tray in one hand, then looked down at Tory.

Sitting at the table with her chef salad, Tory felt vulnerable. She wanted to stand and face him directly, but the timing was wrong. The argument might escalate to raised voices. She remained seated. "You're right. The phone call *is* none of your business, and it didn't involve you."

"Wrong. You're not being truthful. Am I a suspect in your investigation?"

Tory stared at Merlin. There was no safe answer. She opted for the safety of silence.

Merlin flipped his tray back on the table with a loud clatter, an open carton of milk slid across the tray and spilled its contents onto the table. "That's what I thought, goddamn you," Merlin said and walked away from the table. The back of his hand wiped his right eye.

All eyes were on Merlin as he crossed by the residents' table on his way out of the cafeteria. Once he walked through the doors and disappeared, the attention shifted to Tory, sitting alone at the table, concentrating on lachrymal duct control. The wandering puddle of milk had worked its way across the table and was dripping in Tory's lap. Her brown skirt lapped up the milk like a hungry kitten.

Seventeen

It probably would have been smart for Merlin to spend half an hour sitting in a stall in the bathroom, walled off from the rest of the world, just like Tory did, staring at the floor while she absently pressed paper towels against the huge wet spot in her skirt. There were no tears but her lower lip throbbed from where she bit it to keep from crying.

When Merlin hit Eight South he was in what psychiatrists call a "highly agitated state." He was pissed off as hell and stomped up to the nursing station and demanded to know what the emergency was.

No one was anxious to talk with him. Finally Joyce, the head nurse on the pediatric unit for as long as anyone could remember, said, "We have a situation."

"What are you, the Pentagon?" Merlin asked sarcastically.

"No, Scott Gordon—"

"Wait a second, I'm not Scotty's physician. Unless this involves putting his central line back in, you'd better call his oncologist."

"Merlin, no one cares about him like you do. He's a lymphocytic leukemia to his oncologist. He's Scotty to you. And we've got a problem."

Merlin rubbed his eyes. "Joyce, I've got to get out of here, I'm coming down with something."

"Merlin, he's in a lot of pain."

"What about some Demerol?"

"Had it two hours ago."

"Increase the dose."

"Damnit, Merlin," Joyce said, not afraid to raise her voice to a doctor, "he doesn't need Demerol. His mother's giving up on him. Don't you dare turn your back."

A slap in the face couldn't have been more effective. Merlin looked around the nursing station and realized all activity had stopped. Silently they listened, not understanding the pain Merlin was in.

"Okay, okay, so I'm a jerk. Let me go see him."

Merlin started to walk down the hall in the direction of Scott's room. "Hey, Merlin." It was Joyce. "You're not a jerk. I know you've had a lot heaped up on you recently, but sometimes you're our last hope."

Scott was on his bed watching TV with the sound turned off. Nine years old and not a hair on his head, he lay on his side in a fetal position and didn't look at Merlin when he walked in. "Scotty baby," Merlin said in a tone that made him sound like a sportscaster using a nickname for a popular athlete. "Where's your Pirates cap?"

"Over there."

Merlin could see Scott was crying, staring off at the TV, working hard not to look at Merlin.

Martin Wheeler, walking down the corridor toward the solarium, briefcase in one hand, stopped for the briefest moment and chuckled to himself at the sight of Merlin walking into an hour of social service duty. As he continued past the room he licked the tip of his index finger and made an imaginary line in the air. Wheeler: 1, Merlin: 0.

"Your mom taking care of your sister?" Merlin said softly.

"That's what she says."

"How 'bout if I call her and see what time she's coming?"

"Don't bother. No more needles. That's all I care about."

"Pretty bad, huh?"

"I'd rather be dead than have my IV put in again."

Merlin sat down on the bed, looked at Scott's skinny arms, polka-dotted with purple bruises from failed IVs, and his throat tightened.

"I know. They really hurt. You ever put one in?"

Scott turned his head and looked at Merlin for the first time. "What?"

"You heard me, Scotty."

"I'm a kid."

"I'm a kid, I'm a kid, I'm a kid," Merlin said in a high-pitched voice that made Scott smile. "You want to try'n put one in me, or lie around watching Barney?" Scott sat up. "Holy moly, for a second I thought you were gonna smile. Don't scare me like that."

"Do you really mean it?"

"Sure. How much do you hurt?"

"A lot."

"Lie down."

Scott obeyed and Merlin stretched out on the crinkly hospital bed next to his young patient, rolled Scott on his side, and started to rub his back.

"Hey, Merlin, will you teach me the ball trick?"

Eighteen

For a second Tory wondered if all the nurses on Eight North were related. The same hairstyle, tight white pants revealing the outline of underwear, and nightclub-thick makeup. Fat, skinny, ugly, attractive, it didn't matter. It was the uniform of the Medical Center nursing department.

"Excuse me, I'm looking for Dr. Wheeler. He's supposed to be in the solarium," Tory said. Actually, she had to ask the question three times, three *different* permutations of the same query, before someone acknowledged hearing her.

"At the end of the hall, past peds," an overweight nurse said, eyeing Tory, then quickly walked away, her overextended panty line bunching up sections of her derriere like the tectonic plates of the earth.

Tory walked down a long corridor, past orderlies and candy-stripers, all walking with purpose. Reddish-brown walls were painted the color of used bandages. Room after room of narrow-faced, toothless old people in wheelchairs or traction, and beds that looked like cribs. TVs talking to no one. Bedpans scattered about like some cruel joke on the senses. Scatological air fresheners.

Suddenly the ambience changed. It was like flying out of a dark cloud into the bright sunshine. The walls went to bright blue and on the floor a meandering path of yellow bricks was inlaid in the linoleum. *Gee, Toto, I don't think this is geriatrics anymore.* Tory passed the Eight South nursing station and followed the corridor toward the solarium. Then she heard Merlin's voice, the same voice that had just made her cry. But it sounded gentle and relaxed. For a moment Tory thought Merlin must have followed her to apologize and accommodated his gesture by slowing her pace while digging through her handbag, giving him ample opportunity to catch up. The voice continued, and Tory quickly realized it was coming from one of the patient's rooms. That's when she spotted him, lying on a bed with a small boy who had no hair. Merlin in white pants and blue scrub shirt, the boy in an oversized Penguins T-shirt with his toothpick legs sticking out. Merlin was rubbing the boy's back and talking to him.

Tory eased her way to the door, standing off to one side, the occupants of the hospital bed unaware of her eavesdropping.

"Hey, Merlin will you teach me the ball trick?" the boy requested.

"I thought you were gonna put an IV in me," Merlin said.

"How about both?"

"I don't know. Can I trust you, Scott?"

"Yes. Please," the boy pleaded.

Merlin sat up on the bed, dug a couple of red sponge balls out of his pocket, and proceeded to make them disappear and reappear. Coming out of Scott's ear. From under his pillow. And even from Merlin's nose in a hugely phony sneeze. Then Merlin gently taught the small boy how to do a fake hand-off with the sponge ball.

Watching the scene changed everything. It was amazing to see the good Dr. Merlin after her horrible luncheon with Mr. Hyde. Then Merlin looked up toward the doorway—years later he would insist he smelled her perfume, but Tory always laughed and said he was full of it—and saw her standing there. He made a funny face and smiled.

"Uh, the solarium?" Tory said, fumbling for the words.

"Follow the yellow brick road. Just before you get to Oz."

As she walked away Tory could hear Merlin singing "Follow the Yellow Brick Road" in a weird Munchkin voice to the giggling delight of Scott.

Maybe he was a horse of a different color.

The solarium was painted green and was used mostly by parents of the children on the pediatric unit, who camped out on uncomfortable loveseats for nights on end until their spines took on the peculiar contours of the sofas. A couple of women sat on plastic chairs watching an afternoon soap on a wall-mounted TV. On the other side of the room, sitting alone on a plaid sofa, was a doctor, full length white coat, button-down shirt, yellow and red silk rep tie. Perfect hair. Cordovan wing-tips. And he was reading the *Wall Street Journal.*

My God, it's Mark Peters with a stethoscope.

"Are you Dr. Wheeler?" Tory asked, approaching him tentatively.

"None other," Martin said, not immediately looking up at Tory but checking one last quote before folding the paper, not the least bit self-conscious with his fiduciary passion.

"I'm Tory Welch—we spoke on the phone." Tory sat down and pulled out her brown leather notebook, placing it on her lap over the wet milk stain. Wheeler had positioned himself on the seat at such an angle that his MARTIN WHEELER, MD, CHIEF RESIDENT, DEPARTMENT OF SURGERY nametag was prominently displayed on the lapel where his coat billowed out around his chest. Tory noticed Martin wore his pants high and guessed it was an attempt to hide his gut. She figured he was probably the kind of guy who undressed pants first, even alone, in a vainglorious attempt to keep his abdominal shelf of flab from hanging over his belt.

"Miss Welch, before you go into your *forensic hyper-space mode* let me tell you I understand your agenda. But you must understand mine. I have thirty residents to supervise, and in several minutes a dozen medical students will come through that door to learn everything there is to know about the acute abdomen, so . . ."—He pushed two buttons on his watch—"you've got four minutes. Go."

He even had that obnoxious imperious tone, the one Tory always said had to be perfected over years of being a prick.

Tory organized her thoughts quickly and chose to begin gently. The conversation with Jan Wolkin, her ace in the hole, would be saved. "I wanted to talk to you about Kevin Hoover."

Wheeler said nothing.

"What was your relationship with Kevin Hoover?"

"I was his senior resident. His boss. Actually, he was on my service, trauma, when he disappeared. And no, if you're wondering, Kevin Hoover wasn't a friend. Quite frankly, Miss Welch, Dr. Hoover was a bit immature for me."

"Was he a good surgeon?"

"He was okay. Merlin and Kevin, they were quite a team. Practical jokes, feeling up the nurses, making things tougher for those of us who take medicine seriously." Martin leaned closer to Tory and spoke in a conspiratorial tone, "When Dr. Hoover first disappeared quite a few of us thought he skipped town, he was that much of a flake. I was relieved . . . I mean, he was out of my hair." Martin thought twice, realized he sounded happy his colleague had been murdered and quickly tried to repair the damage. "Don't get me wrong, this whole thing is a tragedy, a black eye for the University. Christ, we didn't fill his spot in the residency so we've all had to work a bit harder. Heck, if the funeral wasn't in New Jersey I'd be there."

"I thought Kevin was from New York."

"New Jersey, New York. I don't know. The funeral's far enough away that I won't be there. Make sense?"

Tory sat silently for a few seconds and hoped that

Wheeler was feeling like a jerk. "Anyone dislike him enough to want to hurt him?"

"Have you talked to Merlin yet?" Wheeler asked tightly.

"Couple of times."

Wheeler gave a tight-lipped smile, the kind you use when the hired help are being difficult and you don't want to lose your temper in front of them. "He can be a pain in the *gluteus maximus,* if you know what I mean," Wheeler said, chuckling at his own joke, "but no one was out to get Dr. Hoover."

"Do you know anything that might shed some light on what happened on August 21, 1995?"

Some birds flew by the large windows of the solarium. Wheeler watched them, thinking back, waiting to launch into his rendition of what happened that night. "Maybe I do have something. You ready?" he asked, waiting for Tory to ready her pen and notebook. "I was on the resident's on-call floor, up on fourteen, late that night. I was coming out of the bathroom when Merlin stormed off the elevator. He walked right past me. Ordinarily I'd have thought he was being rude—he can be that way—but I could see he was mad as hell. He walked down to Kevin's on-call room, listened at the door for fifteen seconds. Then he opened the door, watched Kevin and his girlfriend— oh, what *was* her name? Jane or Jamie or something— you probably should talk to her but I don't know how you'd ever track her down. Janet, I think, maybe it was Janet—anyway, they're having sex, and then Merlin yelled an obscenity, threw something into the room, and bolted."

Martin sat back and straightened his white coat. He was pleased with his oratory and even more pleased to watch Tory scribble away as he spoke.

"You know, Dr. Wheeler, I've reviewed the police reports, which included listings of all the medical personnel in the hospital that night, and I don't remember reading that you were on call." Tory jotted some meaningless gibberish in her notebook and underlined it twice for emphasis.

Martin tried desperately to read her upside down scratchings.

"As a matter of fact, no, I wasn't. I had a few consults to do and it was late, so I had a bite to eat in the cafeteria and decided to spend the night. As a senior resident I was expected to be here later than anyone at night and earlier the next morning."

"Did Merlin ever *tell* you Kevin and his girlfriend were having sex?"

Martin scratched the back of his head, careful not to disturb his perfect hair. "Merlin and I don't talk, Miss Welch. And besides, what else would she be doing in his on-call room?"

"How did you know Kevin's girlfriend was in his on-call room?" Tory asked, her voice carefully modulated. No hint of the importance of the question. *Dr. Wheeler, were you stalking Jan Wolkin?*

"Come to think of it, we might have taken the elevator up to fourteen together—yes, I believe we rode up together. Miss Welch, I don't know what you're driving at, but if you're planning any of that crap you pulled with Olsen, forget it. I don't have time for your verbal one-upmanship. Let's get on with this."

"And do you think Merlin had it out for Kevin?"

Wheeler put one finger under his chin and tried to look aloof. "In Heinlein's *Stranger in a Strange Land* there was such a thing as fair witnesses, observers of events who did not interpret what they saw, only reported facts. It is your job to assign meaning to my observations." His smile showed Tory he was pleased with himself.

Just answer my questions. "Do you think any more came of that confrontation?"

"I don't know. My specialty is surgery," Martin said in a haughty tone.

"Actually I've heard that narrative before. Twice, as a

matter of fact. Merlin told me the whole story, felt pretty bad about it being the last time he spoke to his friend.''

"Oh," Wheeler said, disappointed. *Twice?* "As I said, Miss Welch, it is up to you to interpret the facts."

Martin checked his watch. In the brief silence that followed he caught a buzzword on the TV: "Medical Center." Reflexively, he looked up at the wall-mounted TV. The increasingly ubiquitous Sandy Keller was standing in front of the main entrance to the Medical Center, enthusiastically giving the teaser for the five o'clock news. "At the Pittsburgh University Medical Center the investigation continues into the murder of surgical resident Kevin Hoover. I'll be live at five with a report on Jan Wolkin, Kevin Hoover's girlfriend, who has revealed information to the district attorney on sexual harassment in the operating room. KDKA has the exclusive story. Stay tuned to Channel Two, live at the Medical Center." Of course "live" meant that Sandy Keller would be standing near where the event took place, never mind the alleged harassment was a year old, no charges were filed, and no interviews were to be televised. Jan Wolkin's wisp of news had turned into the top story of the day. All Sandy had to do was mention a new headline and rehash the Kevin Hoover saga, and she could milk a couple more exclusives in the next forty-eight hours.

Martin stared at the TV for a few more seconds after Sandy Keller's face was replaced with the instant drama of *The Guiding Light.*

Tory studied Wheeler's body language. He crossed and uncrossed his legs twice and looked like he'd just received the news of a death in the family. The fortuitous timing of Sandy Keller's report had an amazing effect on Martin Wheeler, and Tory almost forgot how mad she should be at Mark Peters.

"Dr. Wheeler, I spoke to Jan this morning," she said gently.

Beep Beep. Beep Beep. Beep Beep. Martin deftly pushed

a single button on his watch and silenced the beeps. A few medical students strolled into the solarium and relaxed on the remaining chairs, some within earshot of Martin and Tory.

"*Jan,* that's right. Nice girl. Good nurse. *Excellent* scrub nurse."

"Dr. Wheeler, I need to ask you a couple more questions," Tory said, speaking in a conversational tone that could be easily overheard. She could feel the momentum build.

He felt trapped and swallowed hard. There was no graceful way to end or postpone the interview. It was like being strapped in tightly on the way to the top of the steepest roller coaster.

Martin leaned closer to Tory and spoke in a hushed tone, as if he might be explaining some confidential medical news to a young mother whose child was on the pediatric unit.

"Okay, Miss Welch, no more questions. Let me tell you what you want to know. First of all, if you think I had anything to do with this tragedy, you are wrong. I wasn't crazy about Kevin Hoover, but that's it. In truth, *he* hated me; I didn't hate him. But I fell in love with Jan. It wasn't supposed to happen, but it did. I wanted her so badly it hurt. And I did something really stupid, writing those love letters like a schoolboy. I was a jerk.

"And for the record, Kevin got me back with an endless barrage of humiliating practical jokes. And I've worked hard to put these memories out of my mind. It was quite painful. I sure as hell didn't mean to hurt anyone. Things got out of hand . . . I never touched her or anything."

Wheeler was breathing hard. He whispered, "Didn't they ever teach you about Willie Sutton? Go where the money is, Miss Welch. Ransack the gross anatomy labs."

He was spent. The lie was obvious. Like her dad always said, if you wait long enough they always step in it.

"Miss Welch, look, about that news story, is uh . . . my name . . ."

"No. It's not . . . yet."

Martin looked at her with gratitude and let out a sigh. "If this silliness comes out, my reputation as a surgeon, a member of the community, my friends . . ." He covered his mouth.

He looked pathetic, and Tory had to remind herself that he had grabbed Jan, that he was no better than those disgusting congressmen in Washington.

"Miss Welch, you do believe me. Look, I've cooperated with you, and I swear I've told you the truth. Just keep my name out of this."

"Deal. But if you've lied to me in any way, I'll splatter your name all over the *Post-Gazette*."

Martin nodded.

"One last question, Dr. Wheeler. Take a minute before you answer. Have you lied to me about anything today?"

The room was filled with students. Wheeler couldn't help but look around. Everyone was watching him. Surely they didn't hear anything.

One look at Tory's face told him everything. She knew. She knew everything about Jan. There was no sidestepping it now.

"Once, I touched her. Once! Don't you dare embarrass me by asking for an anatomical blow-by-blow because you won't get one. You win; you know everything. Now stay the hell away from me."

Tory scribbled a few more notes, snapped her notebook shut, and walked out of the solarium. She realized how much easier it was as a kid when all you had to say was, "Colonel Mustard in the library with the candlestick." So what if you were wrong?

At least for the moment it appeared that Jan Wolkin unwittingly vindicated Martin Wheeler. If his obsession with Jan had led to murder, why would he turn off his efforts after successfully eliminating Kevin Hoover? That didn't make sense. Or were Wheeler's emotions set *against* Kevin Hoover for the cruel practical jokes? And if so, why concoct such an elaborate scheme? Tory was more mixed up than ever.

In any event there was a well thought-out plan to hide the body—certainly premeditated, not spur-of-the-moment. Did Martin Wheeler have it in him? Tory didn't think so.

In the end she decided Martin Wheeler was probably right. Go with Sutton's rule. But how?

Nineteen

Only a resident could enjoy being that tired.

At 6:30 P.M. Merlin moved like a running back through the ER. He was on his way home and scurried around stretchers, cute nurses, and medical interns looking for curbside consults. At its worst, the ER wasn't quite as bad as an average workday on a TV medical drama, but the buzz of activity usually waxed and waned well past midnight.

After a terrible night on call, Merlin loved being alone in his own bed when he could feel the cool sheets on his naked skin, sink into his own pillow, and savor, maybe for half a minute, that wonderful feeling just before he fell asleep. There was just so much hospital air Merlin could take before he started to go a little crazy. Thirty-six hours of Betadine disinfectant and enough purulent drainage to choke a man was his limit.

The cafeteria thing really bugged him, haunted him all day, and not because he'd blown his cool, but because of the way Tory Welch had looked at him. That look. Suddenly turning toward him and staring right through him. Practically accusing him right at the table of killing his best friend. Making him feel as though he had to defend himself. Tory Welch scared him a little. *What the hell was she hearing? Who was she talking to?* Was he really a suspect?

And his hand was still throbbing.

The double doors opened automatically, and the cool

evening air tasted delicious. Merlin stopped and stretched and tried to clear his head. He pulled his shoulders back until the muscles in his chest burned. His stomach growled and reminded him he'd thrown his lunch away. For a moment he even thought about stopping for a bite before heading home to an empty refrigerator, but his first priority was getting as far from the Medical Center as possible.

The residents' parking facility was a trek, all the way on the other side of Pitt's Cathedral of Learning. Merlin walked quickly and joined a small group of hospital-types crossing Fifth Avenue. He decided to make a quick detour to The Original, grab a couple of dogs and a beer, and eat them while he walked to his car.

A face in the crowd eyed Merlin. Ichabod Crane sucking on a cigarette. Pitted skin, long hair. A gust of wind pulled the smoke from his lips and into Merlin's face. Their eyes met for the briefest of moments, and Merlin wondered if they'd ever met before. A black leather jacket, the belt dangling sloppily from two loops, hung from his anemic frame. Merlin knew the type. Probably wore the jacket year round, turned the collar up in the winter, never complained about the cold. Maybe kept his hands warm cupping his cigarette. He was certainly ugly enough to remember, but not worth the effort to try.

What caught Merlin's attention, however, was a bouncy head of hair, shiny in the streetlights, walking right in front of the ugly man. Tory Welch.

And as luck would have it the wind wafted a mouthful of smoke over Tory's shoulder. Just as she turned to give the smoker a look, she noticed Merlin. She thought about a quick nod, or maybe a curt "hello" before marching away, but then she remembered that little boy with the skinny legs and the bald head and slowed her pace as she stepped onto the curb.

There was no avoiding a conversation now. "Dr. Merlin, three times in one day."

The ugly man, now walking almost in step with Tory,

narrowly avoided a collision. Again he looked at Merlin, took a long drag on his smoke and dropped it, still smoldering, between Merlin's feet. Before he turned and walked away he did a curious thing. Tory didn't notice, it was a guy thing meant for Merlin. Something that would scare the crap out of Merlin, but not for twenty-four hours. He gave Tory a once-over with his hollow eyes and ran his tongue around his lips to wet them. The kind of bullshit an ugly punk did behind a bouncy head of hair.

Merlin saw the back of his greasy hair and was grateful he wasn't a dermatologist or a plastic surgeon. *Paging Dr. Sisyphus.*

"You found the solarium okay?"

"Yeah, thanks. Listen, I wanted to apologize about earlier. Maybe I misjudged you."

"Word around the Medical Center is this is your first murder investigation, and by some fluke—"

"What's your point, Dr. Merlin?"

"My point is this: You've got to use a little common sense. I found the body, remember? In two days his face would have been dissected beyond recognition. I didn't have to identify him. I coulda waited. You must watch too many made-for-TV movies. It's always the friend who's overly helpful to the police who did it.

"But this is not a movie. It's real and it is happening to me." Merlin's anger was picking up momentum. "I don't give a flying fuck what you say about it being about Kevin. As far as I'm concerned it's about us. I lost my best friend *and* I've spent a year racked with grief and guilt. If you can't see that, then go back to the DA's office, or wherever you came from, and prosecute little old ladies who jay-walk."

A group of Pitt undergrads talked and joked as they walked by.

For the second time since breakfast Tory concentrated on controlling her tears. This time she was unsuccessful. A single, glistening tear slid down her right cheek. She turned and walked up Fifth Avenue toward the parking garage. By the time she'd gotten half a block from Merlin, her nose was running and both eyes were flooding.

Merlin watched Tory hurry away. "Shiiiiit!" he said in exasperation. He shook his head a couple of times, upset with himself for going too far.

Catching up with Tory was the easy part. Merlin accomplished that before she reached the corner. "Hey, betcha we're both hungry."

They were walking quickly past pizza shops and book stores. The emotional teeter-totter was difficult to stop. It would be easier if they could be mad simultaneously rather than this yin-yang approach to fighting.

"Haven't you been cruel enough to me for one day? I don't need your cutsie-pie shit," Tory retorted.

Cutsie-pie? "Okay, so now you're mad at me. You sling an insult my way and we'll be even."

"Which part of my wardrobe are you gonna ruin this time?" Tory questioned, balancing on the brink of forgiveness.

"What are you talking about?"

They stopped walking in front of Sweet Loretta's.

Tory looked down at her skirt. The stain had faded, and with the darkness of evening setting in, was all but gone. "You dumped your stupid milk all over my skirt." She sniffed away some tears.

"I'll pay the cleaning," Merlin offered. "You don't think it's ruined, do you?"

"It's not ruined."

"Good. It's a nice color—what's it called, 'harvest wheat' or something?"

"It's called brown."

"Where'd you get it?" Any segue involving women's fashion was of course dangerous, what with running the risk of alienating any heterosexual females within earshot. Merlin nervously waited for her answer.

Just as she was about to roll her eyes and walk away Tory hesitated. "Joseph Banks."

Whew. "Store or catalogue?" Merlin asked.

Tory felt like she was knee deep in cutsie-pit shit. "Like I have any time to shop."

"The most precious commodity, isn't it?"

"I could use a few more hours in the day."

"All my shirts are Banks. It's great to shop from my on-call room. I haven't been in a store, 'cept for my unmentionables, in a couple of years."

Tory did one of those cry-laughs, the kind kids do when they're trying to stay mad, but someone says something to distract them. "I didn't see that one in the catalogue."

Merlin looked down at his own shirt, a blue V-neck scrub tucked into his white pants. "Not this one. But all my Banks shirts have these little rectangular labels in the collar, and the corners stick up just a little and tickle my neck. Drives me nuts. I have to tear them all out."

"Don't you ever rip the shirt?"

"Couple times. Hey, you ever eat at Sweet Loretta's?" Merlin asked, already walking to the door.

"You'll keep your dinner out of my lap?"

Sweet Loretta's was an Oakland landmark on Bouquet Street and was filled with a generous cross-section of the hospital and university. A sprinkling of tweed-coated professors who could remember when elbow patches weren't decorative sat elbow to elbow with first-year medical students showing off their first short white jackets. Everyone loved Sweet Loretta's: dark and crowded, a dozen beers on tap, and great food. It was long and narrow like a giant railroad car. The entire right-hand wall was a smoky mirror with shelves of bottles in every color and shape. A wooden bar, complete with a polished copper top and several dozen bar stools, was always in great demand. Straight down the center were two columns of maroon vinyl booths separated from one another by a wooden lattice laced with fake ivy that afforded a modest degree of privacy.

Tory and Merlin slid across from one another in the only available booth, a four seater near the far end of the bar. A TV perched in the corner above everyone's head droned on with the evening news. Suddenly, Sandy Keller's face appeared for yet another live broadcast from the Medical Center. All she had to report was the nugget Tory tossed to Mark Peters after speaking with Jan. Just a single sentence—"Someone—I don't know who—was coming on to her with unwanted sexual advances"—and Sandy expanded it into a hard-hitting bit of fluff. No one at the bar noticed. Sandy Keller was losing her cachet, and her stories were relentlessly moving later and later into the broadcast. If they kept pushing them back, in another week or two she'd be on Andy Griffith reruns, or whatever followed the evening news.

A waitress appeared. "Hi, Merlin. Haven't seen you for a while," she bubbled in a perky voice usually reserved for cheerleaders addressing quarterbacks.

"How 'bout a couple of beers, Melanie? You got Sam Adams?"

"Merlin, I always have Sam Adams for you."

Tory noticed Melanie's nipples poking through her pullover like a pair of light switches and felt a twinge of jealousy.

Merlin turned toward Tory, raised his eyebrows, and got an immediate nod of approval from Tory. Melanie ignored the tight-lipped smile from Tory and instead giggled, "Okey-dokey, a couple of beers, coming right up."

When Melanie disappeared Tory retrieved a small packet of Kleenex from her pocketbook and blew her nose.

"Hey what's up?" Merlin asked.

"My father used to say, 'Sometimes the faucet drips long after the pipes burst.' I'm fine."

"No, you're not. What's going on?"

"You're right about everything. This is my first case. And I'm not sure I know what the hell I'm doing half the time." And with that admission Tory started to cry again.

The syrupy music for the Pennsylvania Lottery blared from the TV. "Hey watch this," Merlin said as he picked up the Kleenex pack from the table. "Move over."

Tory obeyed and Merlin slid out of his side of the booth and joined Tory so easily, so relaxed that not for a moment did it seem awkward. They looked like a couple.

Merlin plucked one of the tissues from the pack and rolled it into a tight little ball. He shifted to face Tory. "Now watch."

"What happened to your hand?" Tory asked, spotting the purple bruise on the back of his right hand from one of three failed attempts at venous access.

"Slipped on a bar of soap. Now pay attention." Holding the pink ball between his right thumb and forefinger, he placed it in the palm of his left hand and closed his fingers around it. Then Merlin held up his left hand, clenched tightly. In that magical second, when Tory's eyes left his right hand for his left, Merlin flipped the tissue-ball— which he had deftly retained in his right hand—over Tory's shoulder *and* out of sight over the fake ivy divider. A classic rendition of Tony Slydini's paper-balls-over-the-head routine. Then with a flourish, Merlin opened his left fist, pinkie first, then ring finger, then middle finger and so on until the hand was opened and quite empty.

Tory, having seen sponge balls worked by amateurs in bars time and again, looked at Merlin's right hand, which he now held a bit more tightly to "hide" the tissue ball. Again, with the pinkie-first flourish, Merlin showed his hand to be empty. It was close-up magic at its purest. No fancy props. He didn't have to go to his pocket to drop anything off. Poof and it was gone.

"This time pay closer attention," Merlin said as he plucked a second Kleenex and repeated the trick, again flipping the tissue over the divider at exactly the right moment.

Tory smiled. Merlin noticed how white her teeth were.

"Merlin," Tory said, leaving out the "Doctor" for the

first time, "once more." And as Merlin repeated the magic for the third time Tory leaned in a bit closer, which as any magician knows makes it easier to effect the sleight of tissue disposal over the shoulder.

It was Tory who noticed the man first. Not a waiter or a bartender. This was a giant of a man. Huge, maybe 275 pounds, with a shaved black head and one earring. Big John, still in uniform, his gut straining against his wide black belt. And he was standing there holding a heavy ceramic bowl with two pink balls of Kleenex sitting on top of his chili.

Always the entertainer, Merlin quipped, "Ahhh, here's my lovely assistant," then stage whispered to Big John, "Aren't you supposed to be in your sequined outfit for the chili trick?"

"Merlin, is this one of your damned magic tricks?" Big John demanded, dropping the ruined bowl of chili on the table. It wobbled and spun for a few seconds, like a coin to determine heads or tails, and, mercifully, none of the steamy contents spilled. The bowl came to rest in front of Merlin, who, along with Tory, was devoting all his attention to Big John.

Tory pressed herself back into the soft seat, sinking in as deep as she could, wishing she could vanish as easily as the Kleenex balls did. Merlin smiled at the very upset Big John.

"Merlin, who the hell did this?"

"She did. I told her not to," Merlin said, quite seriously pointing to Tory with his thumb, then burst out laughing.

Tory said nothing. She tried a smile, but it failed.

"Hey, aren't you the DA lady from the anatomy lab?" Big John's tone softened.

Tory nodded.

"I watched you handle Dr. Olsen the other night. Right on. You're one tough lady. I hope you catch the sonava-bitch who did Kevin." Then, turning to Merlin, he added,

"And you keep your goddamn magic tricks outta my dinner."

The waitress arrived with the beers just as Big John scowled at Merlin and walked away. The Beatles were on the jukebox and laughter erupted from the bar. Merlin ordered Buffalo wings.

"One more thing, Merlin." It was Big John, back again, this time sans scowl. "It must've been tough finding Kevin like that. I'm sorry for you, man."

Then he was gone. But his comments sent Merlin back to the anatomy lab. That feeling of recognition. The pain. His eyes filled with tears.

"Tory, if you don't let me help I'll toss that entire pack of Kleenex in his beer."

Tory sipped her beer and placed it on the cocktail napkin. "At lunch today, when I got that call. You were right. It was about you. Someone knew we were eating together, must have seen us sitting together. He said he saw you kill Kevin."

"That explains the look you gave me. The person identify himself?"

"Of course not. I think it was a man. He disguised his voice. It wasn't Olsen. I spotted him in the room at the time."

"What about Wheeler or Jake Barnhouse?"

"I don't think Wheeler was in the cafeteria when I was on the phone, and I'm not sure I'd recognize Jake Barnhouse; only met him for a second the other night."

"So I'm in the loop, not a suspect anymore."

"Yes." Tory said tersely to keep from smiling.

"So we're, what, partners?"

"No. You're my contact in the hospital."

"Let me get this straight. I've gone from suspect at lunch to *trusted* contact person at dinner. Why?"

"That little boy. The one you taught the magic trick to."

"The same one I just fooled you with. You caught me

in a moment of weakness. Back rubs work better than chemo.''

A steamy oval dish of Buffalo wings arrived, decorated with celery and a small tub of blue cheese dressing.

"It was like a Norman Rockwell painting. Merlin, if you killed Kevin you're way too clever for me.''

"So you think the guy you were talking to did it and called trying to throw you off his trail.''

"Makes sense. But this is between us. I don't want this all over the news.''

Merlin thought for a second. "This *is* news. That Sandy Keller would probably sleep with someone for a scoop this big.'' Merlin laughed.

"Now you know how my boss thinks,'' Tory said with a smile.

Merlin said, "The murderer is in the hospital. Not an outsider. And he's scared shitless or he wouldn't have done something as stupid as calling you. But why the hell would someone go to that much trouble? I mean, why not hit Kevin in the head and leave him? What about Jake? Why haven't you talked with him?''

"Who, the phantom? I keep stopping by to talk with him, and the doors to the anatomy labs are always locked. Where does he go?''

"Can you meet me in the ER around eleven tomorrow?'' Merlin asked, suddenly feeling infused with energy.

The Buffalo wings smelled delicious, dripping in a wicked red sauce. Merlin started on one and savored the burn on his lips. Tory chose a piece of celery, dipping it in the blue cheese dressing.

"You can get me in?'' she said between crunches.

"Aren't you gonna have a wing?''

"Wait a second. Can you track down Jake Barnhouse tomorrow?''

"You eat a couple of wings, then we talk shop.''

Tory picked up a wing and tapped off the excess sauce. Taking a modest nibble of the crunchy skin, she asked,

"How hard would it be to run the arterial infusion pump?"

"Any physician could insert the catheters, just like putting in an IV. A nurse could do it, for that matter. Setting up the pump, that's a different story. I've seen it done a couple of times, and it looks pretty easy. I guess anyone who has seen it done could stumble through it."

"Did Jake Barnhouse have any relationship with Kevin?"

"Not that I know of. The guy's behind the scenes. Maybe you see him around once in a while. He's creepy. I mean, who wants to work with dead bodies, anyway?"

They drank their beers, ordered a couple more, and eventually had bacon cheeseburgers. Tory said something about how much she loved a good bacon cheeseburger, and they talked about their careers and their childhoods, and got very comfortable with each other. After the second beer, Merlin even told Tory about the second-worst day of his life, when a dog charged up the third-base line, attacking him as he hit the bag in a Little League game, and took out a chunk of his rear end as he turned and tried to run into left field. By the time the story was over, Tory had somehow put her hand on top of his, touched the purple bruise gently and coaxed Merlin into an explanation.

Merlin never made it back to his side of the table.

Twenty

After he concluded it would have been presumptuous to escort her all the way to her car—it wasn't a date or anything—Merlin waved to Tory as she walked into the University Parking Center. Merlin lingered on the sidewalk and checked his watch—10:51 P.M.

Twin elevators were located centrally, the first floor was well lighted with an intense white light from rectangular lamps that buzzed softly, and Tory felt quite comfortable walking up the ramp toward the elevators. At this hour the first floor was relatively full of cars, with the 11 to 7 nursing shift just arriving and filling up all the desirable first floor spots. Tory passed several nurses scurrying down the ramp and off to the hospital.

Tory took two steps backward after pressing the "up" button and reflexively patted her bag hanging from her right shoulder until she felt her canister of Mace. *Thanks, Dad.* The evening had been unexpectedly appealing, and her thoughts drifted as she waited. Merlin had first humiliated her, and her face tightened as she recalled his harsh words. But as quickly as he'd attacked her, he'd rescued her with his unique brand of humor and magic, and she'd even forgotten herself toward the end of the evening and felt as if she could say something really stupid, like, "Where have you been all my life?"

The elevator doors lurched open. It was empty and Tory stepped inside. She was alone now. A cigarette butt on the floor, squashed with a circular toe motion, continued to emit a thin blue line of smoke. She pressed the button for the fifth floor and turned to read the work of a graffiti artist. SUCK ME was scrawled in huge black letters on the back wall of the elevator, but the artist—probably working furiously between floors—gauged his spacing wrong so that the "e" had to be miniaturized into such a tiny sliver of space it looked like a blob of black. Tory wondered why anyone would write "Suck M." and whispered aloud "Suck M. Suck M." several times. Before the doors finally jerked closed Tory thought she spotted Merlin turning and walking down the street.

The overhead numbers lighted in sequence to indicate what floor the elevator was passing, but the numeral 5 lighted six or seven seconds before the elevator actually stopped moving. Tory had already taken several steps toward the front of the elevator and had to slow her momentum.

The fifth floor wasn't as hospitable as the first. Yellow light spilled out of the small elevator and onto the dark cement floor. Were the elevator doors in a hurry to close behind her? Tory wondered. And where were those miniature carbon-arc lamps that buzzed so brightly on street level? A series of three-foot fluorescent bulbs every twenty feet or so gave her skin an eerie mottled glow. Street noises filtered in from the perimeter of the garage which was open at every level to the outside, but the occasional car horn or friendly shout she could hear seemed distant and no more reassuring than if they were broadcast on hidden speakers. If she had been with a friend she might have joked, "Toto, I don't think we're in Kansas anymore." It would have been nice to hear a friend laugh.

It was late enough that at this level the garage was less than a third full. The remaining cars belonged to nurses who arrived late afternoon and would not leave the hospital for another twenty minutes, and doctors who manned the ER and ICU. It struck her how lonely she felt. Her breathing quickened and she tucked her hair behind her ears to maximize her peripheral vision, but instead of double-timing it, she crossed to her car very slowly, the way a frightened child might walk when trying not to excite a frisky dog. Her car was as far from the elevators as it could be and, at the rate she was going, it would take her almost half a minute to get there. She peeked between the cars and shifted her bag in front of her so her right arm could press it against her chest. A clump of hair popped off her ear and flopped in her face. Without glancing down into her bag her right hand slipped deep inside to find her keys. *Why the hell didn't you get them before?* Her fingers found her pen, then her Mace, then a pack of Kleenex, then back to the Mace. *Damnit, where are they?* An old pack of Wrigley's Spearmint. The pen again. Walking a bit faster now, Tory shook her bag to hear the rattle of her keys. "Where are they," she said aloud, softly, with an edge of panic in her voice.

Then she thought she heard something. A wolf whistle. Not a cool, smooth practiced one like the construction workers used when she'd pass by on a cool spring day, but a dry-lipped version of the same. She usually hated that obnoxious mating call and charged down the street in defiance. But late at night, alone on the fifth floor of a parking garage, it had a totally different ring. It wasn't a misguided compliment. It was menacing.

Tory stopped walking and spun around. No one. Shadows were everywhere. She carefully scanned each one but none seemed to be moving. After she'd convinced herself she was alone and the whistle probably drifted up from the street, Tory stood there, and opened her bag to look inside. Her hands were shaking and her fingertips were numb. The lighting was terrible and every time she leaned in for a look her head created a total eclipse and the contents of her bag were in a dark well.

"You lose something, baby?"

A man's voice. Tory froze. Every woman's nightmare. The stuff made-for-TV movies are full of. Her eyes darted about but she dared not move her head. She held her breath and listened for footsteps. If she heard any she would've run. Drop her bag—maybe he'd go for that—and run. Nothing. It was quiet. She slowly turned around. Nothing. *Nothing. Nothing.*

This wasn't coming up from street level. Whoever it was had called her "baby." A coarse whisper she'd recall for the rest of her life as she'd pull the covers up to her neck and drift off to sleep. Her fingers ransacked her bag looking for the Mace.

Immediately she found her keys.

For a second she fingered her keys and found the one to her Saab. The one with the rubbery grip that distinguished it in the dark from her house key and the key to her file cabinet at work. She gripped it firmly between her thumb and forefinger and considered making a dash for it. She could see the rump of her dark green Saab sticking out forty yards away. Getting to her car wouldn't be a problem if someone was chasing her. She was in shape, and fast, and probably could outrun a man if she had three or four steps head start. Unlocking the door, pulling the keys out, opening the door, jumping inside, closing the door and locking it. *That* would take an eternity.

One more look around. No one. Empty. A horn sounded off in the distance. Tory started to walk again, quietly sliding her keys out of her bag. The Kleenex package was stuck to one of her keys. As they pulled free of the bag, then dangled in the air, the plastic package of tissues dropped to the cement floor. Tory didn't notice.

"You dropped something."

Tory continued to walk, acting as if she hadn't heard the voice.

A man's voice, soft and hoarse, one that needed to be cleared. "Pussy pie."

Oh, my God. Tory sucked in her breath. She turned around and he was there. A skinny, ugly man standing in the shadows, coughing up a bit of phlegm, like a man racked with consumption. A cigarette was cupped in his hand as if he'd always lived hiding his habit from authority figures. Greasy hair, deeply pockmarked skin, and a halfhearted attempt at a mustache. Tory had seen the look before, a hundred times even. At the bus station. Maybe the gas station. There were probably two or three in her high school class. They never had names, just a look, but they were always there. He took a drag from his cigarette and expertly flicked it between two parked cars.

"Shake it, baby," he said with his multicolored smile.

"What do you want?" Tory tried to sound angry, but her voice trembled.

"I said shake it." He smiled again, and pursed his lips into an air-kiss.

"Get the hell outta here 'fore I call the cops."

"On the fifth floor? Go ahead. Hey, I just want to get to know you. Nice shiny hair. I like that. I bet you smell real fine." He walked over to a sedan and grabbed the antenna. Gently at first, he started to bend it back and forth until it snapped off in his right hand. Using it like a riding crop he smacked it hard against his right lower leg and took his first slow step toward Tory.

Maybe she should have run immediately, but she stood there, shifted her keys to her left hand, and jammed her free hand back into her bag and madly grabbed for her Mace. Before he had taken his second step her fingers found the familiar canister deep within the bag and yanked it out. Her pen and a wrapped Kotex also flew out of the bag and scattered to the floor. Then she dropped her right shoulder, letting her bag slip off and fall to the floor with a thud, and Tory forced herself to square up with the man. *Hide your fear. Look at the bastard in the eye. Let him know YOU mean business.* Her hands were shaking and Tory had to use her left hand to grasp her right wrist and steady it. The keys, still in her left hand, cut into her wrist. Thankfully the trigger of the Mace was thoughtfully designed so you could only engage it with the nozzle pointing away from you, preventing accidental discharge in your own face.

"You get the fuck out of here. This is Mace and—"

"Tough talk, but I *know* what you want. I know you like it wild, baby." He whipped his calf hard and made a loud slapping noise. "And what? Whatcha gonna do, pussy pie? You gonna shoot me?" He reached into his pocket and Tory thought he was going to pull out a gun. She edged back until she was butt-flush with a Chrysler minivan and was almost relieved when he pulled out a surgical mask. This mask provided physician *and* patient protection. It was equipped with a clear plastic eye shield surgeons favored to protect themselves from blood splattering. The four ties dangled down and he temporarily stowed the antenna between his legs, like a pencil-thin erection, while he tied the mask onto his head.

He smiled and delivered a line he'd memorized from a porno movie, "Safe sex."

He took another step toward Tory. Her right arm was extended and visibly wavering. "Help, *fire*! There's a *fire*!" Tory yelled. At the insistence of her father she'd attended a woman's safety course and knew what all women were taught: People were afraid to respond to someone's call for help if it involved an assailant.

He'd stopped walking when she started to scream and looked around. They were alone, and he was in control. "You can yell all you want, no one's gonna hear you. You know what they say, why not lie back and enjoy it? After, we'll share a cig. You'll like it." His voice was raised now and had an edge of anger. There was no rush. And when he looked at Tory he licked his lips, moving his tongue in and out of his mouth in little flicking movements that made him look like a snake.

"*Fire!* Help, there's a *fire!*" Tory looked about desperately and he could sense she was about to run.

"Hey, I'm Satch. What should I call you?" Satch said.

He turned slightly, away from Tory, as he rubbed himself. His bulge was obvious in profile.

Tory was on the balls of her feet, leaning forward slightly, in the starting blocks about to run the race of her life.

Satch slapped the antenna against his leg while he waited. "C'mon. What, I introduced myself. Waddya want me to call you?" He paused and held Tory's gaze.

Tory said nothing. Each breath she took was an effort.

He continued to talk, babbling on in increasingly cruder language about her body, but nothing he could say could stun Tory more deeply than what he said next. "Miss Welch or Tory?"

Tory let out a loud gasp. He said her name. He— Satch—was waiting for her. Stalking her. Thinking about her.

Her hair was in her face. It was wet with perspiration and behaved when she tucked it behind her left ear. This was a planned ambush, and if she stood there it was going to happen. *Run. Goddamnit, run.*

Satch took another step toward her and Tory sprinted. She turned, a quick pirouette to the left, bent forward and left Satch in midstep. Keys in the left, Mace in the right. Tory had taken three long strides before Satch yelled "Fuck" and took off after her.

Satch was wheezing through the surgical mask and fogging up his windshield as he ran as fast as his cowboy boots would allow. Their striking difference in physical shape notwithstanding, Tory was wearing low-heeled shoes and was outdistancing him. Then she made a mistake.

The sign for the exit ramp was in front of her, but the adrenaline was pumping and she couldn't think straight. Instead of running hard and racing down the ramp Tory rounded a corner, and in that brief moment before Satch made the turn, ducked between two cars and hid in the shadows.

A split-second later Satch ran past her, his heels clicking madly on the concrete. She had disappeared, and he wasn't stupid enough to keep running. Relieved to stop, Satch rested, just out of Tory's view, gasping air through his mask, making it move in and out with each sucking breath.

"All right, pussy pie, *where the fuck are you?*" he yelled. His breathing wasn't slowing, and he erupted in a violent smoker's cough as he bent down on one knee to look under the cars. Shadows. Black shadows. *Where the fuck was Erno?* Satch stood and slowly walked into the row of cars, spitting distance from Tory. "All right, you come out now, real nice-like, and I won't hurt you." His voice was suddenly soft, but he couldn't hide his cruel intent. A tone to mock every child who ever played hide-and-go-seek. He'd all but forgotten he was going to screw her. He wanted to kill her and watch her die.

Tory crouched in the safety of a black shadow and knew it was a matter of time. Waiting it out wasn't an option. In fact, it never occurred to her to hope for the elevator to open and unload someone to scare this monster away.

She looked out between the cars, across the aisle toward three cars parked flush against the perimeter of the garage. A glimpse of the night sky loomed invitingly above the cars, but what Tory noticed was a sign that stated "Physician Parking Only." The cars were late-model, clean and polished. Two BMWs and a Lexus. *Doctor's cars on the fifth floor. At night. One of them would be equipped.*

It seemed that Satch was moving away from her; his wheezes were harder to hear. Tory put her head to the oily cement and caught a glimpse of the back of his boots walking along the wall, moving slowly and methodically, like he was trying to sneak up on her.

This was an opportunity, maybe her only one. Tory duck-walked in an uncomfortable crouched position as she edged her way toward the "Physician Parking Only" sign.

Crack. Her right shoulder was stung by a powerful swipe of the car antenna. Satch was behind her, standing tall, infused with a new vigor at having found her. "Get up. Now, goddamnit."

Tory was ready with the Mace. Slowly she got to her feet, but her hands were shaking uncontrollably.

Satch shifted his angle and swung hard, hitting Tory's right gluteus maximus and sending Tory into a short sprint like a quarter horse smacked on the rump.

In a second she was across the aisle, twenty feet away, next to the Lexus. She turned and saw Satch slowly walk toward her. "Get the fuck away from me!" she screamed.

Satch kept coming. "Satch wants a little snatch. Satch wants a little snatch." His eyes were hidden by the fog in the mask and he looked like a robot.

Tory hopped on the hood of the Lexus and jumped up and down. Nothing.

Satch was at the bumper. Tory looked like a kid jumping on a bed, and he paused to watch her. After two jumps she leaped to one of the BMWs, and as she landed a loud piercing siren cut the night air, and the headlights flashed on and off.

"You fuckin' bitch," Satch said as he took several steps toward Tory. His body hit full force on the hood of the car and Tory stumbled backward, falling against the second BMW, setting off a grating cacophony of twin sirens at slightly different ear-splitting pitches.

Before Tory could recover, Satch was between the two BMWs, pinning her to the hood of the car. Leaning in close, his face inches from her nose, Satch forced her legs apart and pressed his groin hard against Tory's and spoke in her face with a low, guttural sound that was the voice of death. "We don't have long. I'm gonna fuck you, then cut you up in little pieces." The sirens continued.

His rancid breath oozed. Every word he spat at her ballooned out the loose surgical mask and Tory thought she would vomit.

Holding both her hands within his left one, pressing them hard between her breasts, he barely let Tory breathe.

With the wailing sirens, this was surely a time-erosive opportunity, but Satch's hormones were running the show. *Fuck her. Do her.* Testosterone tunnel vision. He eased his body back and reached up under Tory's skirt and made quick business of hooking his fingers around the elastic waistband of her panties. His fingers lingered for just a second before grabbing the silky material firmly and ripping them off her body in one motion. He released the devil's grip on her chest and held Tory down with his groin and moved rhythmically against her while he lifted up his mask and brought the panties to his nose. Taking in the essence of her female charms in one long whiff, Satch got dizzy with excitement.

A tactical blunder. This violent foreplay didn't come close to making Tory a passive participant. Before Satch could possibly realize she wasn't his victim, that there was no way she'd given up, he was turning himself on, sniffing her panties, turning them over, pushing his nose into them.

Tory seized the opportunity and grabbed his fogged-up windshield and pulled it away from his face and blasted the Mace in his eyes from close range.

Satch reeled up and clutched his eyes, the mask getting in the way, the panties falling silently to the cement. He was blinded. "Oh, shit. You goddamned bitch," he hissed.

He took a single step away. The siren deafened her ears and Tory could barely hear him cursing her. In those seconds that he fumbled with the searing pain in his eyes and reached into his right pocket for his switchblade, Tory braced herself. Stretching her arms widely apart and digging her fingers hard into small crevasses in the BMW's front hood where it rolled down toward the grille and where it stopped at the windshield, she drew both legs up, knee to chest. If Satch hadn't been stung with the Mace he would have enjoyed the bare-bottomed view.

Satch pulled out the knife and the blade swung out of the handle silently, but Tory's feet were already moving toward him in a powerful thrust that caught him squarely in the chest. His arms flew out for balance, he stumbled backward, dropping the knife in the process, and hit the wall waist high and toppled out of the garage. But before he disappeared completely, his body somehow turned slightly and he was able to grab onto the edge of the wall with one hand. With a single swinging motion his second hand was thrust up onto the ledge, and Satch was hanging seventy feet above street level. It would be impossible to determine after the fact, but he messed his pants as soon as he looked down.

Tory got off the car, her ears ringing wildly, and saw the ten fingers clutching desperately at the slippery enameled wall. The bastard was still screaming obscenities at her. The antenna and the knife had been dropped between the cars. Tory looked at both and picked up the three-foot antenna and walked toward the fingers.

One swing, moderately firmly, like a nun might do to a misbehaver's knuckles with a yardstick, was all it took. She caught eight of the ten fingers, which might have swollen up like so many Vienna sausages if he had lived, but Satch released his grip, and his final scream blended in nicely with the blast from the BMWs.

Sobbing uncontrollably, Tory retrieved her underwear, her shoulder bag, the pen and the wrapped Kotex, then threw everything, including the car antenna, into the back seat of her Saab.

The sirens were still wailing as she drove out of Oakland.

Twenty-one

September 21, 1996

Fortunately, Tory missed the breaking story near the end of the late news. Teetering on the edge of a nervous breakdown, the graphic reports of Satch dangling and dripping from the tree would have pushed her over. She was lucky to be alive.

The next morning she opted for the ridiculously expensive valet parking the Medical Center offered, and now sat in the ER waiting room next to a fat woman who smelled horrible. Her two overweight, hyperactive children buzzed about like annoying gnats but Tory hardly noticed them. Maybe someday the graphic details would blur together in her subconscious like a distant nightmare, but just thinking about the attack filled her eyes with tears. The horrific events that took place twelve hours earlier were replayed over and over in no particular order.

Somehow she'd made it through the night, showing up at her next-door landlady's back porch looking a mess. The gruff old woman, Mrs. Kincaid, took her inside and said, "You want to tell me, you'll tell me," and handed Tory a cup of coffee with several shots of Kentucky bourbon. Mrs. Kincaid, from the old school of medicine, soaked a Kleenex in iodine, and cleaned off a nasty scratch on Tory's cheek. Then Tory soaked in a scalding hot bath until the water turned so cold she shivered and plunked herself, soaking wet, into one of Mrs. Kincaid's beds for a few hours of horrible nightmares. When it was light, Tory went home and took a shower. Mrs. Kincaid walked with her, just keeping her company, and sat in Tory's living room watching the television. Her horribly ugly mutt, Pepper, curled up at her feet and went to sleep.

The question of going to the police wasn't considered until Tory was more than a mile from the garage. The Saab had swerved a couple of times, narrowly missing oncoming traffic, and she finally had to pull over. While sitting on Fifth Avenue sobbing, cars zipping past her, honking at her, their headlights distorted by her tears, the reality hit her: She was too frightened to go to the police. It was too easy to dismiss her heroics as luck, and Tory felt just as vulnerable and emotionally naked as those pathetic young girls she'd seen when she volunteered at a shelter for battered women.

The way you dressed, you were asking for it, baby, a man's voice whispered in her mind and laughed. *You wanted it bad.*

Now Tory knew why so many women never reported rape. How could she ever describe the things he said, how he put his hand up under her skirt, the way he made her feel like filth. And then Tory remembered a night several years earlier, when she was a first-year law student. The time she accompanied a Pitt coed to the ER after she'd been date raped. The girl clutched Tory's hand, begged her not to leave, and Tory stayed and got to see how they collected samples of semen from her vagina and rectum. And how the girl covered her face and cried so pitifully that Tory burst into tears just watching. *There's no way I'm going through that.*

Now, in the relative safety of the ER, as Tory stared off in the distance, past the fat woman and her two kids, she thought about killing him with her hands. Squeezing his neck hard, stretching it like putty, holding her grip so tight her hands would go into spasm. She'd keep it up until he went limp, tighter and tighter, his head wobbling back and forth like a broken doll, waiting for his tongue to ooze out of his mouth. Then she'd release him, let him slip to the ground, watching for him to start breathing again, the spark of life not completely smothered from his disgusting body. And she could start all over again.

There was some solace in this revenge, and Tory found herself smiling until her body reminded her just how much pain she was still in. She ached everywhere. Her groin, where he'd forced her legs apart and gave her a nasty rope burn ripping her underwear off. And her chest, the pectoral muscles especially, and both forearms from the death grip she'd maintained on the hood of the car when she kicked Satch in the chest. Worst of all was the sick feeling she had in her gut every time she remembered: He knew her name.

No one would have blamed her if she'd gone to the police and quit her job. Mark Peters would have loved it: A juicy press conference, the Kevin Hoover investigation would fall in his lap, *and* he'd be able to make some sexual jokes at Tory's expense. And Tory's father, the retired cop, if he'd ever found out about it, would have driven all the way to Pittsburgh to take his little girl home.

But Tory wasn't a quitter, and she wasn't going to say a word about it. Never. Maybe Tory knew it all along. Maybe that's why the first thing she did after collecting her torn underwear from the oily concrete was use them to wipe off the hood of the BMW.

At 11:20 she looked at her watch: Maybe Merlin had forgotten her. It was hard to focus her thoughts on Jake Barnhouse, the center of her expanding-circle theory. It had occurred to Tory more than once that each interview had been a nice exercise in polemics but hadn't opened up any leads. If something didn't come of her interview with Jake Barnhouse she'd have to go back to Mark Peters and risk having her case taken away from her. By 11:45, the fat woman and her brats were gone, and she decided to inquire at the desk.

The line for the registration desk looked long and amorphous. A clot of people, none looking too terribly ill, milled around and wondered if maybe they should come back to the ER later when it wasn't so crowded. Tory looked like she was in the wrong line. A couple of people wearing grimy coats, too heavy for the weather, turned around and eyed her crisp dark suit, checking out the red scratch on her right cheek. One woman even mumbled something to her husband about the prima donna and her teensy-weensy scratch. She looked like a yuppie princess and these people resented her in their ER.

Someone pulled her hair from behind. Tory startled, more than she should have, and turned around to see Merlin, white pants and clean blue scrub shirt.

"Let's go; sorry I'm late." Immediately he started to walk out of the ER registration area and into a crowded hallway with Tory double-stepping to keep up. "Strangest thing. I got a STAT call to the ER to sew up a couple of lacerations any intern coulda done. They're working me to death. Maybe I'll have to walk around catheterized like one of the astronauts. Hey, did you hear about that guy fell off the parking garage last night?"

"Yeah, I did. Must've happened just after I left. I didn't hear any sirens."

"Tried to call you."

"You did?" Tory said, feeling a burst of excitement like a schoolgirl.

"After I heard about that guy I wanted to make sure you got home okay. You're T. Welch, Ninth Street, right?"

"Actually, I went to a friend's house."

"Boyfriend?"

"Friend," she said firmly and suppressed a smile. It was nice having the upper hand.

They wound their way past the gift shop and vending machines, through a throng of candy-stripers, to the first floor of the medical school, and finally stopped in front of a pair of elevators, alone, in a dark foyer.

"You know, when I heard about that guy in the garage I felt like I shoulda walked you to your car. It was late when we left Loretta's."

Before Tory could respond the elevator doors opened and they stepped on. Tory felt like a jerk for not saying anything. But she didn't want to gush. The light caught Tory's face and Merlin looked at the scratch on her cheek, the one the woman in the ER thought was teensy-weensy, and said, "Ooooh, what happened?"

"My cat."

"What, a cheetah?"

"A tabby named Holly."

"If you didn't go home last night how'd your cat scratch you?"

He's quick. "This morning. I had to go feed her."

"If something's none of my business, tell me. I'm a surgeon and that scratch is more than a couple hours old."

"Okay, you're right," Tory said with a let-me-have-my-privacy smile. "It's none of your business."

The rest of the ride to the ninth floor was quiet, Tory certain Merlin knew exactly what had happened. That she'd almost been raped, and she'd killed the guy in the garage.

Merlin, on the other hand, his hormones getting the better of him, indeed did think the worst. That Tory had a boyfriend and in the process of wild sex got her face scratched.

The doors to the anatomy labs were wide open, the banks of fluorescent lights dark, and only the ambient light of a cloudy Pittsburgh day illuminated the dissecting tables. Tory looked over the rows of cadavers covered with yellow tarps. None of the tables was empty. Tory only cared about one: third table, second row, where it all started. But the table wasn't vacant. A yellow tarp, bulged here and there, covered what Tory assumed was a replacement for Kevin Hoover. Otherwise the room was empty.

Merlin called out to Jake a couple of times. There was

no response. The second of three doors on the opposite wall was opened partway. A sliver of bright light cut across the dark linoleum floor and up onto one of the tarps. Tory followed Merlin across the room. A small black sign with white lettering, EMBALMING ROOM, and the distinct aroma of formaldehyde put Tory's stomach on notice.

Beep-beep-beep. "Dr. Merlin, please call OR at extension 5-4-4-1." Merlin's beeper had become a nagging lover, about to summon him to some nonurgent crisis.

He ignored the chirping and stopped walking. "Tory, you gonna be okay going in there?"

"I'm getting used to it. I'll be fine."

"Hey, before I forget, did you a favor. You know Kevin and Wheeler were working together when he disappeared?"

"So?" Tory cocked her head just so to catch the best view of the embalming room. It was easy to see a white-coated man through the six inches of space between the door and jamb. He was bent over something and seemed to be working with some clear plastic tubing that reminded Tory of chemistry class.

"Are you gonna be able to stay?" Tory asked.

"I have to call and find out. Anyway, I had Medical Records pull all the files that Kevin wrote an order or note in for two weeks before it happened. Must be fifteen or twenty of them. Probably'll give you a feel for what his workday was like."

"You did?" Tory was surprised by Merlin's thoughtfulness.

"You know where Medical Records is? Basement, old part of the hospital. Be available around three or four. Don't be too late; I don't know how late they stay open on weekends. Ready?"

Merlin pushed the embalming room door open and walked right in. Tory waited in the lab, carefully testing the waters, watching through the doorway. Jake stood to his full height when he saw Merlin. He was wearing the same type of white coat Olsen wore but with no fancy nametag. Light blue shirt, no tie. A drone. He seemed taller than Tory remembered, very lean and wiry. He had powerful, big hands and strong shoulders. It looked to Tory as if Jake could have stuck a pencil in his hair, anywhere on his head, and leave it there all day if he wanted.

Behind Jake was a stainless-steel dissecting table bearing a man, supine, his head uncomfortably turned to the side, looking away from Tory. A device, just bigger than a mixmaster, sat on a small stand next to the dissection table. Quarter-inch plastic tubing, coiled around the machine, spiraled its way over the naked chest to the neck.

Tory quickly scanned the windowless room and saw gray metal shelves lining three of the walls, straining with the weight of large metal canisters and thick glass bottles. A huge poster was tacked up on the only visible patch of cinder-block wall: a human skeleton standing at a table, contemplating a human skull, its bony hand holding the skull on its side. Around the skeleton's feet were rocks and sprigs of wildlife, which always seemed odd to Tory. She remembered seeing the work before, knew it was Andreas Vesalius, and even recalled sitting in Sterling Library at Yale, an art history book in her lap, getting all philosophical over it. But standing guard over a dissecting table with a real dead body lying there infused the poster with new meaning. Death imitating art. The head of the corpse and the bony skull in the drawing were turned away from Tory in exactly the same way.

"Merlin. Been expecting you."

"You remember Tory Welch."

Jake nodded, humbly or nervously—Tory couldn't tell—and said, "Miss Welch, sorry you had trouble tracking me down. Rita told me."

After difficult interviews with Olsen, Wheeler, and even Merlin, Tory did not know what to expect and would not be surprised if Jake treated her as an intrusion.

"Mr. Barnhouse, I need to ask you a few more questions. I'm trying to piece things together and I want to be familiar with the embalming process.''

"Look, I want to help, but when Dr. Olsen found out you were coming up here he kinda went ballistic.'' Jake looked around.

Tory decided he was definitely nervous. "Would you be more comfortable coming down to my office? No one needs to know.''

"We're down a cadaver. This one just came in and he wants it embalmed, prosected, and ready for the students tomorrow. With all that's happened I'm afraid the ax is gonna fall on me,'' Jake said, making a slicing motion with his index finger across his neck.

Tory looked from the drawing to the corpse and wondered if Jake's decapitation worries were a deliberate reference to the poster.

"This is my area,'' Jake continued. "I'm responsible and when something like this happens, someone's gonna get canned. Me,'' he said, swallowing hard. "I can't be going back out on the street, looking for work. I got benefits, been here awhile,'' Jake said starting into a singsong babble.

Merlin interrupted. "Jake, calm down. All Miss Welch wants to do is talk to you and see how you embalm. No biggie. Ten minutes. Is Olsen even around?''

Jake scratched his cheek like he was thinking about his options. His demeanor was different from any of the doctors Tory had talked with, and she assumed his status had a lot to do with it.

Beep-beep-beep. "Merlin, call the OR. Now.'' Even through the miniature speaker in the beeper, a tone of exasperation could be heard. Merlin went directly to a phone.

Jake began to explain the embalming process to Tory, pointing first to the shelves with the metal and glass containers, and saying that a mixture of chemicals, mostly formaldehyde and glycerin, was what he mixed up each

time for embalming fluid. Then he started to explain about
the device on the side stand, which turned out to be the
elusive arterial infusion pump.

Merlin finished his phone conversation and slammed
down the receiver. "Gotta go," Merlin said, and Tory
wanted to say, *No wait, please stay with me until I finish
here.* "Gonna hold hooks for Wheeler while he does a
gallbladder. What the hell do we have medical students
for? See ya, Jake." Then, turning to Tory, he added,
"Don't forget, between three and four. The old building."
And before the sound of his footsteps disappeared down
the hall, Tory heard his beeper go off again and Merlin
said, "Shit."

Jake poured a clear liquid, the embalming fluid, into a
glass reservoir and flipped the switch on the arterial infusion pump. It shuddered and hummed and began to draw
the embalming fluid from the reservoir through a short
segment of tubing and into the pump itself. The fluid then
inched its way through the curled-up plastic tubing and
toward the cadaver's neck.

Running without resistance until it hit the neck, the fluid
caused the coils to unwind, and Tory swore she saw the
cadaver shudder and shake.

"That's it. The embalming fluid is pushed through all
the tissues; takes about two hours. Preserves everything.
Don't even drain the venous blood, that way the veins
plump up nice, like a whatchamacallit—a rigatoni. Makes
it easier for the students to see 'em."

Tory jotted in her notebook as Jake spoke. "Where did
this body come from?" she asked.

"Most come from City General. Poor people mostly,
bums who can't afford a decent burial. Some from people
who want to donate their body for science—not many.
Getting chopped up by medical students isn't what I'd call
science. Anyhow, this one's from City General."

"Can I see the documents you receive when the body
arrives?"

"Yep." Jake looked around. "Oh, shit. Olsen's got all the paperwork in his office. Lemme grab it."

Tory was alone in the embalming room for almost a minute, the quiet hum of the infusion pump pushing the embalming fluid into the neck of some guy who couldn't afford to be buried. The acclimation period shortened each time. Looking at the body didn't make her dizzy. It had the same waxy gray skin and purplish lips she'd seen before. In fact, there were no surprises until she noticed he was clean shaven. And his hair, uncombed and wild, was trimmed shorter and shorter as it tapered down toward his sideburns. No scars. No tattoos. Trimmed nails. A white band of skin that never saw daylight on his left ring finger. Tory thought back to her first encounter with a corpse. The red-haired man looked more like a mangy dog. This one didn't have that forgotten look to it.

Jake returned with a clipboard and read from it. "Uh, Eugene Fletcher . . . donated by his sister in Florida . . . chronic liver failure . . . came in yesterday."

"Who has access to the cadavers? Keys?"

"Everybody from Dr. Olsen to maintenance and housekeeping. Thought about that myself. It's an inside job, isn't it?"

"It looks that way. Who else does the embalming?"

"No one."

"When the cadavers arrive at the Medical Center, are they ever embalmed?"

"Not unless they come from a funeral home, which is rare. Look, Miss Welch, you want my read on this? Maybe Kevin Hoover was into something he shouldn't be. Drugs, I don't know. Someone whacks him and makes a switch. It could've been anyone."

"Was Kevin Hoover into something he shouldn't have been?" Tory asked pointedly.

"How do I know? Like I said the other night, didn't know him, that's why I didn't recognize him. Been here only six years. He woulda done gross about seven, eight years ago. When he was a first-year. I only get to know the first-year students and the resident instructors like Merlin.''

"So you never met him," Tory said and realized she'd goofed. *Piss him off, why don't you?* Asking once whether Jake knew Kevin was okay, informational, reasonable. Repackaging the question, especially if Tory didn't know otherwise, was the red flag of desperation. If she'd pulled a similar stunt with Olsen he would have smelled the vulnerability and pounced on her.

"That's what I said. You don't believe me, ask your buddy Merlin. I don't hang out with the docs. I'm an enlisted man, if you know what I mean. Maybe I passed him in the hall sometime, wouldn't even know. If you're coming in here looking for information, fine. Ask what you want. But be logical. Hell, if I were gonna kill one of the hospital docs I'd do it as far away from the hospital as possible.''

"Who could have embalmed him?"

"Two dozen people, including me, if that's the body was delivered to the embalming room from City General. You know what I mean? Maybe Kevin Hoover was delivered here, with phony paperwork, and *I* embalmed him. The paperwork doesn't come with a photo ID. Olsen taught me the Jonathan Olsen technique. He's real picky. All the teaching residents have spent time in here. It's not that difficult.''

"Kevin Hoover had multiple catheter sites on his body.''

Jake hesitated, then smiled. "Then it wasn't me. I'm a pro. Whoever embalmed him didn't know what the hell he was doing. Mine have one puncture, two if I don't get good flow from the artery. Never three.''

Tory jotted something in her notebook. "How many pumps do you have?''

"And you know what, I've got twenty-eight witnesses out there," Jake said and motioned with his head to the anatomy lab. "You wanna examine the stiffs? Maybe count the puncture marks, because in three days the hackers are gonna do head and neck and grind those babies up. Hey, I know," Jake said sarcastically, "Why don't you stroll into Olsen's office all la-di-da-like, and demand he cancel anatomy lab and ship *all* them bodies to the coroner's office? You do that, people'll believe you got an appendix and more," Jake chuckled.

Tory wasn't new to bullshit schoolyard dares. It was one of those "Have you stopped beating your wife—yes or no?" challenges. Only a fool would jump at the bait, and backing down was just what Jake wanted. But maybe there was a diamond in the rough concealed somewhere in the rhetoric. No one had considered examining the remaining bodies in the lab to see if they matched their paperwork. This would require more thought than Jake would allow. *Don't let him think he's getting to you.* The slightest hesitancy would be lethal. *Ignore him.*

"What I'm curious about is how many pumps you have, Jake?"

"This and a backup. The backup's broke."

Tory put her notebook on a small cluttered desk and stepped closer to Eugene Fletcher.

Tory looked at the body again. "Mr. Barnhouse, do you know if this Mr. Fletcher was one of those indigent patients?"

" 'Spose so. He came from City General. If I was hit by a car and was bleeding to death in the street, in my last dying breath I'd say, 'Not City General.' Who'd go there if they didn't have to?"

Tory nodded. "I haven't seen too many dead bodies, but something doesn't look right." Jake turned and looked at the body. Tory pointed toward the head. "His hair looks cut, his nails. Looks like he wore a wedding band. He doesn't look like a bum," Tory said.

"We got a barber at the Med Center, cuts the patients' hair. They probably do, too. I don't know, maybe you should check out City General, maybe even the transport service. Like I told you the other night, I don't look at the bodies; I just embalm 'em.'' Jake spoke matter-of-factly, not raising his voice, as he added some more embalming fluid to the reservoir. "I gotta get back to work."

Tory felt dismissed, mumbled her thank-yous, and walked out. She'd probably gotten all she could from Jake Barnhouse, the disappointing center of the expanding-circle theory. Jake might be physically closest to Kevin Hoover but if a motive existed, it certainly was well hidden. And Jake seemed so confident that the multiple puncture sites were a sign of sloppy work.

Tory was at the elevators before she realized her precious notebook was on the desk in the embalming room.

As she crossed through the darkened anatomy lab she could see Jake standing next to the pump, wearing glasses now and reading her leather notebook. Jake turned a page, read for a few seconds, and flipped to the next.

He kept reading even after she walked into the embalming room, and it was obvious that she was there. A little throat clearing from Tory; Jake kept on reading.

"Excuse me, I'm always forgetting that thing,'' Tory said, encouraging Jake to give her a look and shake his head like she was some ditzy broad. The thought crossed her mind to leave, forget the book, and get the hell out of there.

"My name's in here. On this page twice, and in the center of all these circles. Let me ask you a question. Why are you focusing on me? City General is a real shithole. Why don't you give them the hairy eye?

"And I'll tell you another thing. Wanna know why the hell you couldn't find me, ask Olsen. Night you took the body he laid into me pretty good in front of everybody. Made me look like a simp. Like it was my fault you took the body. Like I shoulda somehow stopped you. When he's done I'm shaking—you saw me that night. So I go into my office and I'm sitting there, trying to calm down, stopping my hands from shaking, waiting for everyone to leave so I can go home. Five minutes later *he's* standing in the doorway, says he's sorry he was so hard on me. Says to me, 'Take some time off.' He talks to my wife the next day—you met her—says I need some R&R.

"So I come back yesterday, all *my* paperwork's gone. He's been through my desk, got my paperwork on *his* desk for safekeeping, he says. Took me an hour to straighten up. Half my dissecting tools are missing. Where the hell are they?" Jake turned abruptly to the side table holding the arterial infusion pump and yanked out a shallow drawer, spilling a scalpel onto the floor. The blade was shiny clean, probably never used, and bounced on the floor a couple of times before coming to rest near Tory.

Tory jumped back and clutched her hands to her chest.

"Goddamnit," Jake said, almost hissing his words. He bent over and picked up the scalpel.

"I'm okay, it didn't touch me," Tory said, her voice an octave higher.

"I know goddamn well it didn't touch you."

Tory watched Jake handle the scalpel, holding it comfortably in his right hand, his index finger resting on the top of the blade for leverage. He was standing close to Tory, less than an arm's length away. The way he was staring at her, looking like he was making up his mind about something, made Tory want to take a step back. But she wondered—if she did would she be just falling into his little game? Was this just a game? Was Jake looking for an excuse to explode, wanting to lash out at Olsen but settling for second-best? His emotions were boiling and he used his hands for emphasis as he spoke. Tory held her ground, and could smell the coffee on Jake's breath.

"Two scalpels are missing and a pair of scissors. Olsen's been through my stuff. What's next? Maybe I'm getting set up. One of them blades is gonna turn up someplace with my prints. Then everyone here will breathe a little easier when they cuff me, huh?" Jake could see the terror in Tory's eyes, the way she recoiled each time he waved the scalpel in the air. "I'm feeling desperate, but what I want to know is, do I scare you, Miss Welch?"

"A little."

"Good, now you know how I feel. Scared shitless," Jake said and threw the scalpel back in the drawer. He took a rest for a few seconds.

"This is the only chart I can get my hands on," Jake said, holding up the paperwork on Eugene Fletcher. "Why? And when I come back this body's waiting for me. Olsen accepted it. So if you don't like the way he looks—he's too pretty or his dick's too long—Olsen's your man. He wanted me outta here. I don't know what the hell's going on." Jake was breathing hard. "I'm not taking the fall for nobody, most of all him," Jake yelled and turned away from Tory and fiddled with his arterial infusion pump.

Tory watched him for a few seconds, not knowing what to say, and finally grabbed her brown notebook and left.

Twenty-two

The medical records department was badly in need of more space. It reminded Tory of the stacks in the Pitt law library. Thick metal racks stuffed solid with brown medical charts overfilled the room, giving it a claustrophobic feeling. A corridor, barely wide enough for two wheeled carts to pass by each other, separated the two massive squadrons of racks organized in tight formation. The aisles between chart racks were narrower yet, leaving only enough room between them for an average-size person to squeeze through.

The crowded room was full of activity. Phones rang constantly and a variety of Medical Records employees— men in shirtsleeves and bland polyester ties, women in yellowed blouses—walked slowly like people do who work behind the scenes and rarely see the light of day.

Tory was surprised at how heavy the wooden door was, and, as she stood inside the threshold waiting for someone to notice her, wondered if some of the relics who worked in the department struggled each day just to get inside. As the door slowly thudded to a close behind her, Martin Wheeler appeared at the far end of the room dumping off a huge stack of charts to a frail woman who struggled under their weight. As the chief resident continued to give instructions to her, she accompanied him toward the door, several steps behind him, walking hunched over like she might drop her load any minute.

An encounter was inevitable and Tory braced herself.

"Ah, Miss Welch, slumming it?" Wheeler said with a practiced touch of condescension.

"Just reviewing some records, Dr. Wheeler. Have you seen Merlin?" Tory said blandly.

"Elusive sonovabitch, isn't he? I'm not Jack Merlin's social secretary. Enjoy," Wheeler said as he pushed open the door and strode out, making no effort to introduce the woman to Tory.

"Oh, Miss Welch, I'm Paula Blatt. Dr. Merlin told me to watch out for you," she said and plopped her load of charts on a nearby table before offering a bony hand to shake.

"Call me Tory."

"You're better off in the Jack Merlin camp than our esteemed chief resident's. Sometimes I'd like to take a belt to that boy. Anyway . . ." Paula said, letting her voice trail off, and Tory took an immediate liking to her.

Paula led Tory down the wide corridor that separated the two flanks of chart racks. In the back of the large room there were two clusters of wooden cubicles, one group behind each regiment of chart racks, intended for doctors to dictate and sign off their charts. Most were stacked high with charts and each had a telephone for dictating. Paula stopped at the second cubicle they came to, an aisle seat, flanking the corridor and considerably brighter than the ones off to the side.

"Of course you know, Miss Welch, access to medical records is restricted—I don't know if Merlin told you— but when he called I just couldn't say no after what he did for my niece. He operated on her, you know—thought it was her appendix the way she was all hunched over and everything, but it was really her ovary. It got all twisted up like a rubber band and Merlin unraveled it. It's fine, but did you know you only need one ovary? I wonder if a woman has her period every other month if she's only got one? Hmmm. I'll ask Merlin. Anyway," Paula said recounting a story she obviously loved to tell and probably told each time a new intern ventured down to Medical

Records, "here are the charts, twenty-three of them that Dr. Hoover wrote orders or notes in between August 7 and August 21, 1995. I'm not quite certain what you hope to find, but I pray there's a clue buried somewhere."

Tory was surprised to see three stacks of charts, each a foot tall, tucked in the recesses of the cubicle. While Tory extracted her brown notebook from her bag, which she'd hung on the back of her chair, Paula got her a glass of ice water, then wheeled a small metal cart next to the cubicle.

"When you're done with a chart just load it here, so they'll be out of your way. Oh, yes, dial nine if you need to make a call," Paula said and smiled. "If you need anything I'll be around."

Paula discreetly left and Tory sat in the cubicle, her notebook opened in front of her, and stared at the stacks of charts. The uncertainty of what she was actually looking for, and her unfamiliarity with medical terminology, made the task daunting.

This is what her dad called detective grunt work, hunting down a thousand ideas just to score with one. But she also remembered hearing her dad say that most cases weren't solved by clever detective work but by fortuitous circumstances that started the dominoes falling. *Started the dominoes falling.* That was one of her dad's favorite expressions and Tory said a silent prayer for them to start tumbling soon.

The first chart, an inch-and-a-halfer, clunked heavily to the desktop as Tory slid it off the top of one of the piles. Casually, almost timidly, she flipped through it and saw almost a hundred pages of handwritten notes, as well as an endless supply of computer printouts of lab information. Suddenly, Tory had the urge to run an idea by Julian and decided to take a quick break and give him a call.

"Hello, is Dr. Plesser available? This is Tory Welch."

"Dr. Plesser is in court. Be out the rest of the day. Can I have him call you?"

"He can reach me at the courthouse or leave a message in my voice mail."

That felt about as satisfying—and wasted only as much time—as sharpening her pencils before doing her homework in grade school. Tory went through the first chart slowly, first familiarizing herself with its organization into four main sections (in decreasing order of legibility): Lab Data, Nursing Notes, Physician Orders, Physician Notes. After twenty minutes of deciphering abbreviations and arcane terminology, Tory discovered the discharge summary, a two-page *typed* narrative of the entire hospitalization. She quickly discovered that if she read the discharge summary it was easier to follow the handwritten documentation in the body of the chart.

The charts were incredibly boring. Each page had notes from several different doctors saying the same thing:

8/8/95 6:15 A.M. POD 2. Wound OK. U/O 350. BP 135/ 87. No temp. Lungs clear. Abd benign. Start PO.

Tory spotted Kevin Hoover's signature and followed his notes more carefully.

No controversy. No unexpected deaths. Just an endless chronicle of a day in the life of a surgical resident. Some of Kevin's notes were written as early as 5:30 A.M., while others were as late as 11:30 P.M. There were even a couple from Merlin that Tory found herself reading most carefully of all.

Tory was through the first stack of charts, nine in all, when Paula Blatt appeared at the cubicle wearing a light jacket, her pocketbook over her shoulder. "It's five-thirty. I'm leaving now. Is there anything you need?"

Tory looked at her watch, surprised she had been sitting there almost an hour and a half. "You're locking up?"

"Heavens, no. We're open twenty-four hours for emergencies. Lila, the night girl, will be around if you need her. I think she's at dinner now.''

"I'll be fine, thank you."

Tory listened to Paula's footsteps grow softer and disappear completely as the wooden door softly closed. The phones had stopped ringing. For a few minutes Tory enjoyed the quiet and listened to the occasional interruption of the hospital paging system. Standing to stretch her legs Tory walked in a lazy circle around the cluster of cubicles and realized she was alone.

It was boring. None of the charts had any revelations and Tory was beginning to wonder if she was wasting her time. It was either this or wander back to the courthouse and face a grilling from Mark Peters. With that perspective in mind, her chart review didn't seem quite so horrible. But her back was getting stiff, and she tried various sitting positions to get comfortable. The reward for finishing a chart was a reshifting of her posture and that worked for a while, getting Tory through the next dozen charts.

As it got later the paging system broke the quiet at increasingly longer intervals. Tory had three charts to go when she heard the sound of the door closing, that unmistakable thudding noise, wood tapping on wood. Then there was nothing. No sounds of footsteps or voices. Nothing.

Tory grasped the side wall of the cubicle and peered down the corridor and had an excellent view of the front door. It was closed, the room still empty of people. Tory breathed very quietly and listened as carefully as she could, even turning her head, looking down at the floor, pointing her right ear directly toward the door. The fluorescent lights gleamed brightly in the marble floor, and a large dustbunny sat motionless next to the end of one chart rack. She concentrated for a while, silently admonishing herself for hearing things. Nevertheless her left hand delved into her bag and removed her small canister of Mace and placed it next to the empty glass of ice water. Then she picked up a chart, a thick one. The name typed on the yellow label was Margaret Emont, which surprised her and made her smile. Tory started to read the chart with a renewed enthusiasm, wondering if she might learn anything about herself.

The discharge summary quickly dispelled any notions of that. It was dictated by Kevin Hoover, but signed off posthumously by Martin Wheeler. The first sentence of the typed summary clearly read, "This is the first Pittsburgh University Medical Center admission for Margaret Emont, a 33-year-old black female admitted for biopsy of a lump in her left breast . . ."

Tory laughed out loud. Emont was an unusual name but—

There was a loud slapping noise, the sound a coffee-table book would make if dropped squarely on the ground. Tory drew in her breath and held it. "Merlin? Is that you?" Tory said quietly, hopefully.

There was no response. More importantly, there was no way Tory could convince herself she was hearing things. If she just sat there she would scare herself to death. She had to take a look. No sideways Kilroy this time, Tory silently slid her chair backward and slipped down to the cold floor on hands and knees. The angle was wrong for the front-door view, blocked by a chart rack, but Tory could see most of the corridor.

The first thing she saw was the dustbunny spinning wildly, caught in a windy vortex. Her eyes followed it across the marble floor as it settled down and disappeared in a shadow. But in the middle of the corridor, where several minutes before there had been nothing, was a thick brown chart. *How the hell did that get there?* It was too far from the shelves to have fallen from one of them.

Her stomach started to churn out acid. That sick feeling came back to her, the one from the parking garage when she heard the wolf whistle.

Even if this was an embarrassing false alarm, Tory decided to leave Medical Records in a big hurry. She was off the floor, out of the starting blocks, and walking quickly toward the door, her shoes making tiny squeaking noises. Halfway there she shot a glance down one of the aisles between chart racks. In the shadows she spotted a shrouded figure, lingering in the darkness. The head was swathed in something giving it a peculiar shape. It made no effort to come at her, standing there like a statue, as if its presence alone would serve a purpose.

That's when Tory sprinted for the door, to hell with anyone who might see her and think she was nuts. A half-dozen graceful strides and she was there. Breathlessly, more from fear than exertion, she hit the door and expected to run right through it, straight arming the heavy wood like a running back powering through a linebacker. The door didn't budge and Tory clumsily crumpled into it and bounced off. She struggled to regain her balance when she heard the voice.

"It's locked," the voice said with a familiarity that Tory recognized but didn't have the luxury to identify.

Tory turned around and saw the shrouded figure. A surgeon—dark blue sterile gown over scrub pants, cap, mask, and light blue surgical gloves—walked out of the shadowy aisle and stood even with the end of the chart rack, just at the edge of the bright lights. The cap was a disposable one, pulled down below the eyebrows so that two eyeballs, dark as night, were all that Tory could see. The figure was medium height, narrow in the shoulders. The small rectangular label on the end of the chart rack, telling which letters of the alphabet were housed in that row, was just about even with the top of its head.

Tory frantically looked around, up and down the corridor, terrified she'd see other figures slink out of the dark.

"Don't worry, Miss Welch, it's just you'n me," the surgeon said.

The voice. Tory had heard it before. Maybe the identity would pop into her head. "What do you want?"

"It's what do *you* want?"

"If you know I'm down here, you know what I'm reviewing," Tory said evenly. *That's good. Confident but not snotty.*

The surgeon's right arm came up into the light and a glint of reflected light flashed from something in his hand. A shiny piece of metal, a small knife of some kind. *Oh, my God. It's a scalpel.*

Her mind raced. She could practically hear Jake Barnhouse screaming about his missing scalpels. Was this one of them?

The surgeon's hand came up again, provocatively waving the razor-sharp blade. The scalpel was held crudely, the way a street fighter would a stiletto in a rumble, fingers wrapped tightly around the handle, the thumb overlapping for strength.

The grip was distinctly different from Jake's. That was obvious. Jake had seemed so relaxed and comfortable with the scalpel in his hand, the way he grasped it, pressing his index finger on the top of the blade for pressure.

The build was wrong, too. She was certain the surgeon was not Jake.

Tory's bag was still hanging on the back of her chair, the Mace sitting next to the empty water glass. She didn't even have her ballpoint pen to use as a weapon. In a second she'd reviewed her options. The door behind her was locked solid, and any thought of attempting to run past the armed surgeon to get her Mace seemed ridiculous. Tory decided to engage him in conversation. Maybe he was just trying to scare the hell out of her. And if he approached—only if he approached—would she try to kick the knife free and make a break for her cubicle.

"The person who works here will be back from dinner shortly."

"You haven't met Lila. She's a three-desserter, with a half-pack of cigarettes. We've got lots of time. Why are you reviewing charts?"

"I'm not really sure," Tory said innocently.

"Save the cutsie-pie crap. You don't spend two hours in this dungeon for nothing."

Cutsie-pie. Less muffled, but this was the voice from the cafeteria. *Keep him talking.* "No, really. I'm just trying to see what Kevin Hoover's life was like before he was killed." It seemed ridiculous having this conversation with the person who probably killed Kevin.

"See anything that interested you?"

"No. I don't understand half of what I read."

"Take any notes?"

"*No.* My notebook's back there. Take a look."

"I told you on the phone. Merlin isn't what you think. He's not your friend. He'll do you."

"And you're my friend?"

The surgeon took two steps toward Tory. "Right. Now I'm your best friend in the whole world. You're alive, aren't you? I'm doing my best to keep my good friend alive, but I can't promise that forever. Look at that table over there." He gestured with the blade to the table Paula Blatt had unloaded Wheeler's charts.

Tory saw a key sitting on the corner of the rectangular table.

"Let yourself out and stay out. You come back here with the cops I'll know, and then you won't be my friend anymore."

Tory unlocked the door, had to jiggle it a little to work the cylinder, pushed it hard so it opened quickly, and immediately started to run down the narrow hallway. Walls on both sides, no stairwell or even a doorway to slip inside. Tory knew the elevators were around a sharp bend thirty yards away and she took the turn at full speed.

"*Ahhhhhhhhhhhhh,*" Tory screamed. Before she realized what happened, she'd run into an enormous man with a dark blue shirt on. The same dark blue color the surgeon had been wearing. Tory kicked him hard in the shin and clawed wildly at his chest, ripping something off his shirt and hearing it clang off the floor. Every part of her en-

gaged in the fight, like a cornered animal lashing out at
a predator.

"Hey, hey, calm down!" the man's voice said, and two
enormous black hands clamped down on Tory's forearms
and backed her away from him.

"Get the fuck off me, you bastard. I'm gonna kill you."

"Hey, you ripped my shirt. *Cut it out!*" he said, tight-
ening his grip until he was hurting Tory. "You're the DA
lady. What're you running from?" he asked, his voice
softening. He released his grip and Tory stepped back and
criss-crossed her hands to massage the throbbing muscles
in her arms.

Tory saw his face for the first time. Big John. "Oh my
God, help me!" And she fell into his arms, trembling, her
blouse sticking to her skin with perspiration. Suddenly, in
a hurried gesture, she wriggled around to make certain she
wasn't followed. She looked up again to see Big John and
was so relieved gave him a hug. She smelled his after-
shave. "Oh, thank you. He was gonna kill me." Then
Tory stepped back and wiped her eyes and smoothed her
hair.

Big John reached down and retrieved his gold shield
and pinned it on his shirt, covering the small patch of
ripped fabric. "Who was gonna kill you?" he said calmly.

Even after a couple of cleansing breaths it was difficult
for Tory to speak coherently. As Big John heard the story
he popped the safety strap on his holster and removed his
service revolver. Tory rambled a bit but her attention to
detail convinced Big John the scalpel had been real.

"Okay, you take the elevator out of here; I'll check
things out," Big John said as he punched the elevator
button.

"No, I left my bag in there and my notebook. It's . . .
it's important to me. I've got to get them."

"I'll bring them up to the information desk."

"Please let me get them."

"Look, I wouldn't tell you how to do your job—"

"John, I wouldn't tell you what to do. I'm asking you. Please let me go with you."

"All right, but if there's any trouble you're gonna scram," Big John said, sounding irritated.

As they walked the hallway toward Medical Records, Big John removed a small halogen flashlight from his belt. He pulled open the doors effortlessly and they stepped inside. Tory spotted the chart in the middle of the marble floor but the surgeon was gone. She noticed that Big John had his service revolver chest high in a shooting position.

"Anybody in here?" Big John yelled. When he got no response he clicked the flashlight on and shined it down each darkened aisle between the chart racks. Tory huddled next to Big John, like Dorothy and the Cowardly Lion approaching the Wizard, as they slowly made their way toward the back of the large room.

"Is there another way out of here?" Tory asked.

"Yeah, a fire exit in the back."

When they reached the cubicle where Tory had been working, Big John continued further back as Tory picked up her bag, dropped her Mace inside, and rummaged through it. Finally she pulled out a six-inch clear plastic ruler. In less than a minute Big John rejoined her.

"Whoever it was is gone, most likely out the back," he said.

"Oh, my God. My notebook's gone." Tory looked around frantically, scattering several of the charts from the side table. Big John shined the flashlight around as Tory pulled the chair out of the way and kneeled on the floor. "He took it. I don't know why, but he took it."

"Look around; see if anything else is missing."

"I checked my bag, everything seems to be . . . wait a minute. There was a chart here. Yeah, I was looking at a chart. A woman. Emont. E-M-O-N-T. I remember because my mother's maiden name was Emont. I can't remember her first name. What was it?" Tory began rummaging through the charts, checking each one twice and finally giving up. "The chart's gone. What the hell was in that chart?"

"C'mon, Miss Welch. There's nothing left down here for you to do. Why don't I see you to your car?"

"You don't know where Merlin is, do you?"

"Up on fourteen, the resident's on-call floor, about a half hour ago. Probably still there. I'll ride partway up with you."

"I have to measure something first."

Tory walked back to the chart rack where the surgeon had been standing. With Big John watching her, Tory knelt down on the floor, and in six inch segments measured the distance up to the rectangular tag that had marked the top of the surgeon's head.

Afterward, they walked through the dark hallways of the basement, past storage rooms, the laundry and the boiler room, into the new part of the hospital. Big John explained that he chose the elevator in the new part of the hospital because Tory could get an express to the fourteenth floor.

The doors opened and Big John pressed 14, no other buttons, which seemed odd because he said he would ride only partway with Tory. Tory looked at him as if to remind him he'd made a mistake.

"I'd feel better if I let you off on fourteen. You don't mind, do you?"

"I ripped your shirt."

"Don't worry about it."

"You're really very nice. I don't know what I would have done without you tonight. I know I'm babbling, but you're very kind. You make me feel safe, after the way you scared me the other night in the restaurant."

"Over at Loretta's, c'mon." Big John burst out laughing and by the time the doors opened Tory was smiling broadly.

"I owe you a shirt."

The fourteenth floor was a long hallway with a series

of dormitory-style rooms, a communal bathroom at one end of the hallway, and a small resident's lounge at the other. Big John pointed Tory in the direction of the lounge, which wasn't really necessary because she could hear Merlin's voice engaged in a chatty monologue.

As the doors to the elevator started to close Big John said, "I'll take a Hawaiian shirt with lots of color."

As Tory approached she realized Merlin was on the phone. It was easy to hear what he was saying and Tory lingered in the hallway. With its spartan walls she felt like she was in her freshman dorm. Even the way it smelled, a hint of cigarette smoke and garlic from a pizza.

". . . what's going on. I mean, I'm called to do every scut job around here. Like a 'tern. I'm even drawing blood in the ICU . . . no, that can't be it. Wheeler doesn't know about the Lasix . . . oh she's something, I can't stop thinking about her. I almost feel I'm cheating on Kevin. I'm down in the ER couple of hours ago, and I'm sewing up this kid in that motorcycle accident, and all of a sudden I can smell her." Pause. "Yeah, smell her. I look around like an idiot, but she wasn't there. She smells so great . . . Kevin's playing matchmaker . . ."

That's when Tory walked into the lounge and saw Merlin slouching on a sofa, one leg dangling over the armrest, a phone cradled by his shoulder. As soon as he saw Tory he sat bolt upright and said, "Oh that's my beeper," and hung up the phone.

There was an uneasy silence as Tory took a seat next to him.

"You hear any of that?" Merlin asked nervously.

"Any of what?"

"Hey, don't ask. I've got secrets, too."

Tory smiled, letting Merlin know maybe he didn't have any secrets.

"Anything good in Medical Records?"

Tory's eyes welled with tears. "Oh, God, everything's falling apart. I don't want any more secrets from you Mer-

lin. I've got to trust somebody. I'm in over my head,"
Tory said and started crying.

"What happened?" Merlin asked as he slid closer to
Tory and put his arm around her.

"Someone almost killed me."

"What!" Merlin tightened his grip on Tory's shoulder
and pulled her a little closer. "Are you okay?"

"I'm fine, but it's the second time in twenty-four hours
someone's come after me."

Merlin turned to faced Tory, placing his hands on her
shoulders, forcing her to look him in the eye. "That's
enough. Are you gonna tell me the truth about what the
hell happened to you last night?"

"You already know. That creep they found in the tree.
He was waiting for me in the garage just after you left
last night. Tried to rape me. I got lucky and kicked him
and he lost his balance and fell over the railing."

"Holy shit! He hurt you?"

"No."

"You go to the police?"

"No, but I've got good reasons," Tory said firmly.

Merlin thought for a second and smacked his hand hard
on his thigh. "Shit!" Tory startled, and Merlin jumped to
his feet. "Oh God," he said and covered his eyes with
his hands. "When we were crossing Fifth Avenue last
night, before we saw each other, there was a guy, a creep,
walking right behind you. He was looking you over, then
he looked at me and licked his chops like the wolf in Red
Riding Hood. He was telling me what he was gonna do,
and I was too stupid to listen. Must have been the guy."

"You couldn't have known," Tory said softly. "I really
could use you sitting next to me."

Merlin sat down. "But why didn't you go to the cops?"

"I've seen the interrogation a girl gets. And besides, he
knew my name."

"Stalkers *know* their victim's names. That's not a
surprise."

"Suppose it was meant to look like a rape but it was really a set-up to kill me, get me out of the way. I feel like I'm really close to something."

"So you're gonna dangle yourself and get yourself killed. For what? Why not go to the cops?"

"My boss is the one on the news. He salivates just thinking about this case. If things heat up I'm history. Too dangerous or some such nonsense. This is my chance to prove myself."

"If this creep had more in mind than rape, whoever sent him is gonna send someone else."

"*Now* I realize that. That's the breakdown in my logic. What I did was stupid."

"When's the second time you were almost killed?" Merlin said, slipping his arm around her shoulders.

"I'll get to that. A lot's happened since you got beeped out this morning. I left my notebook in the embalming room and Jake read it and saw his name. *Then* he kinda freaked out and blurted out all sorts of stuff about Olsen, how he gave him some time off and confiscated all the paperwork. Some of his scalpels were stolen. He frightened me.

"Then I went to Medical Records. It got late and everyone left. The charts were so tedious. I thought I was all alone and I heard a noise and there was someone who was all dressed up in a surgeon's get-up. Gloves, mask, everything. And he had a scalpel. It was the same person who called me in the cafeteria. I recognized his voice. He was five-eight, five-nine maybe. And he held the scalpel like this." Tory stuck out the index finger of her left hand and grabbed it with her right in the same crude manner the surgeon had done. "That's not the way I saw Jake hold one earlier today. I thought this guy was going to kill me. He said some bullshit about being my friend, and he was keeping me alive, and how you were the one who killed Kevin. Then he let me go, and I literally ran into Big John. When I went back with Big John to get my stuff, he hadn't touched my bag, but he took my notebook and the chart I was starting to read. Someone named Emont. There must have been something in that chart.''

"Emont. Doesn't ring a bell.''

"Margaret! That's her first name. Margaret. Kevin dictated the summary and Martin Wheeler signed off on it. I didn't get a chance to read it. Anyway, I've got to find out what was in that chart.''

"Let me see what I can dig up for you.''

"Merlin, let me run something else by you. Remember that cadaver Jake was embalming?''

"A little.''

"The guy died of chronic liver disease, but he wasn't yellow. I don't know anything about medicine, but I know one thing. Liver disease. My mother was an alcoholic. She died of liver failure and she looked like a pumpkin before she died. He was supposed to be some derelict from City General, but his haircut had a styled look to it. He also had a white ring on his finger where a wedding band had been. Something wasn't right. Anyway, when I pushed Jake he got all huffy and told me to have Olsen ship all the cadavers down to the coroner's office. I know it sounds crazy, but think about it. Do all the bodies match their paperwork?''

"Now you're getting out of my league. I'm not a pathologist,'' Merlin said.

"I know. I know. And I know I can't ask Olsen. I was thinking about Julian Plesser. Maybe he'd come down here, let's say in the evening, and give the anatomy lab a once-over. That's it. You know everything. No secrets,'' Tory said.

"I want one promise from you. Tomorrow you talk with your boss, come clean about getting attacked, and get some kind of police escort. If you don't talk to him, then I will.''

"Oh great, now you're threatening me.''

"You got it. You have someone you can stay with to-night? Someplace safe?" Merlin asked.

"I think so," Tory said wistfully.

"I *could* page Big John. He could get you to your car."

"Worried about me?"

"Why the hell do you think I've been sitting here, my arm falling asleep," Merlin said, but made no effort to untangle himself from Tory.

"I betcha I don't smell so great right now."

"Oh, you did hear. How much?"

"Enough to embarrass you for years," Tory laughed.

Merlin gently touched the red scratch on Tory's cheek and for a moment she closed her eyes. "It must've been horrible last night. I'm glad you're safe."

"By the way, Merlin, you were so damn nosy this morning, I was afraid to go home last night. I stayed at my landlady's house."

"If you walk out of here right now it'll ruin my night." Then Merlin leaned close to Tory and breathed her in. They kissed, tenderly at first, then with a hungry passion. He retreated slightly, his tongue tracing the circle of her lips. "Want to see my etchings?"

"After you see my appendix scar."

Merlin took Tory's hand and led her to his on-call room. As they kissed they slowly undressed, dropping a small pile of clothes next to his narrow bed. Kissing his way down to her appendix scar, Merlin knelt in front of her and slid her silky panties down, stopping his pursuit only long enough to caress the rope burns from her violent undressing by Satch. But Tory whispered, "I'm okay. Just don't stop."

And there seemed to be no hurry. Although there was always something special about the first time with a new lover, this was different. Once they were undressed they held each other, Tory's breasts snuggled tightly against his chest, feeling safe for the first time in days, Merlin's fin-gers gently stroking her, moving lightly from the nape of her neck to the small of her back. When Tory murmured "Oh, my God," Merlin's lips found hers and they kissed deeply. Then Merlin gently turned her around and cupped her breasts from behind, nuzzling her hair out of the way, kissing her neck. Finally Tory took his hand and they slipped between the sheets.

Except for an occasional moan their mouths were otherwise preoccupied. Even though they'd each had lovers before, Tory and Merlin felt part of one another, their souls melding as he entered her.

After they made love, Tory made Merlin roll over and touched his jagged scar from the dog bite. They giggled like kids when she said in a cute little-girlish voice, "Let me kiss the boo-boo, make it all better."

Then Merlin felt her lips and tongue caress him and he said something about wishing he never turned around just before the dog attacked, because the scar would've been on—

But Tory interrupted him and said maybe we can just pretend . . .

Twenty-three

September 23, 1996

Coincidentally, he hoped, Erno was summoned to meet with Mr. Bevel as he walked out of his apartment on the way to Satch's funeral.

"Mr. Bevel? Wants to see me?" Suddenly his voice was weak. Bloomfield had many dead-end streets and this one was lined with clapboard houses with well-trimmed lawns and hedges. No teenage bullshit on any street where Mr. Bevel's man lived. The elderly neighbors loved Erno.

"Yeah, Erno, the big man wants you." Einstein was pointing a pudgy finger at Erno—Uncle-Sam style—and smiling. He was one of those guys—always a little slow—from the neighborhood who, despite being bald and in his mid-thirties, would always be known as a kid from the neighborhood. He was standing a safe distance from Erno, as was his habit. Before he became Mr. Bevel's delivery boy he was used to being the butt of jokes and random beatings and knew to keep a buffer zone around himself. Now he was just called Einstein. Everyone knew his real name, but if you asked Erno he would tell you he couldn't remember. Einstein wasn't worth the effort. Until today.

"Why's he want to see me, Carmine?"

It was late morning. A covey of pigeons was eating some scattered bread several feet away from the two men. Erno didn't notice. Neither did Einstein; he was talking with the authority of Frank Bevel.

"He's pissed. Really, really pissed. Wants ta talk wit-cha, Erno, big man to big man." The stubby finger, again. He couldn't hide his glee at being called "Carmine."

"What's he pissed about?" Erno was stunned by the message. He shifted his shoulders. His suit was binding him. The enormous pseudo-Windsor knot at his neck dug into his Adam's apple. He pulled at the knot.

He was being called on the carpet. Why did Mr. Bevel want to see him? For what? *What the hell is Mr. Bevel pissed about?* Erno racked his brain. *Probably the thing with Satch. Yeah, that's it. Probably wants to offer his condolences.*

"You'll know in about an hour, Erno. He's waitin' for you. Wants ta see you at eleven."

"What about Satch's funeral?"

"Business before pleasure, Erno," Einstein laughed. Satch had always been cruel to Einstein. This was no day of mourning for him. "He wants to see you, Erno."

"Jesus Christ," Erno said, and thought better of his comment. Einstein was a direct pipeline to Mr. Bevel's ears. "And Carmine, you don't have to go back to Mr. Bevel and tell him that."

"You better go, Erno. It's almost eleven."

"His office, huh?" Erno had never met directly with Mr. Bevel. He'd always had a boss who gave him Mr. Bevel's orders, usually in some diner. Or barbershop. Antony was his third boss.

"No, Heinz Hall, stupid." Einstein cackled.

Respect was one thing when the messenger was delivering shocking news, but Erno wasn't about to let the neighborhood dimwit tease him. Erno took a step toward Einstein. One step. Right foot forward, weight shift. That was it. Einstein stepped back off the curb and stumbled backward between two parked cars, landing on his rear.

Erno started down the street mumbling, "Fuckin' Einstein."

Einstein sat in the gutter brushing himself off. He called

out to Erno, "Hey, Erno, you look like the Incredible Hulk in that suit. Whereja get it? Hey, don't worry, he won't do you in his office. He loves his office."

Everyone knew Frank Bevel loved his office. Always a private man, this had been *his* sanctuary, and since his wife died Mr. Bevel spent his only happy moments in his second-floor office. No, he would never kill anyone *while* he was sitting in his office.

Erno was having trouble thinking straight. The sting of missing his cousin's funeral wouldn't hit him for hours.

At eleven o'clock Erno walked into the Bevel Building after lingering on Penn Avenue for about twenty minutes.

He'd been in the Bevel Building once before, not getting past the first-floor secretary, to pick up an envelope from Antony and deliver it to some judge. The first floor of the small building was a single large room, poorly furnished, some chairs and sofas scattered about. Meetings were evidently held in this room, but Erno had never been invited to any. The secretary, quietly working alone in the back corner, told him, "Go right up, Mr. . . . Erno."

After quietly climbing the thickly carpeted stairs to the second floor, he found the richly appointed office vacant, lights on, and the door wide open. Several minutes of standing in the doorway, shifting his weight from foot to foot, was about all Erno could take. He gently knocked on the jamb with one knuckle and even said, "Uhhh, Mr. Bevel, uhhh, you there?" in a thick voice. Slowly, and with great reverence—or maybe brutal fear—Erno shuffled his way over an oriental rug and seated himself in a worn leather wingback chair directly in front of the massive desk. The room was filled with the rich aroma from a Cuban cigar smoldering in the heavy ceramic ashtray.

The private office was on the second floor of an anonymous warehouse in the Strip District where Mr. Bevel controlled the family's operation in relative comfort. An expensive teak veneer covered the walls and ceiling, hiding the old pine boards, and the hardwood floor was

stained to bring out the brilliant grain of the wood. Photos
in tasteful black frames lined one entire wall, and as so
often is the case with the criminal element at the top of
the food chain, included shots of Mr. Bevel with a former
president, two former mayors, and in a foursome with
three Penguin hockey players. Erno's and Satch's like-
nesses did not grace the wall. A huge bookcase blocked
what was once the only window and contained leath-
erbound copies of American classics, which a sharp eye
would note were indeed creased along the bindings. One
entire shelf was devoted to first editions of Mr. Bevel's
favorite works and had been on loan to the Carnegie Museum for the past year. Frank Bevel had embraced litera-
ture about the same time he truncated his name so that it
ended in a consonant rather than a vowel. Then he moved
to a large brick Victorian home in a North Hills suburb
and joined a country club. He'd eased his family into
everyday life effortlessly, but ran his business with a vision that set its sight on one goal at a time, hammering
away until his competition folded.

Satch had been dead almost three days now. He never
hit the ground. Instead he crashed through the upper
branches of a maple sapling so that his upper chest was
impaled on the narrow trunk, severely bending the tree,
and dangling Satch's feet eighteen inches above the
ground. He looked like a bloody marionette. It took almost
an hour for the police to order the tree cut off at the base
so that the body could be extricated.

Fortunately, his criminal record, coupled with the evidence of a fifth-floor scuffle, provided a neat denouement:
a drug deal gone sour. He was the lead story on all three
networks, each one offering footage of the bloody tree
stump. One story, one night, no follow-ups. And no connection. Erno hoped that Mr. Bevel was upset that one of
his men was dead. *Yeah. That's it. Or maybe the rape.*

The rape. Why the hell did Satch have to fuck her? How the hell did Mr. Bevel find out?

In truth, Frank Bevel couldn't care less that one of his men was down. Business casualty. That's all. Only a family member could tell for sure, but Frank Bevel was upset. He'd gotten sketchy details of the Medical Center deliveries and didn't like what he'd heard. Control was important in any organization, and his seemed to be slipping.

Quietly Mr. Bevel entered his office from a small bathroom off to one side, methodically wiping his hands on a white linen towel. Silently Erno watched him fold the towel and place it neatly on the desk.

Erno's shiny suit had always been snug. Ninety-nine bucks off the rack, no vents, no vest, forty-two long. But he was eating too much pasta and probably should have taken the forty-four. Cheap suits didn't come with directions any more than thousand-dollar ones did, but owners of a well made three-piece knew how to two-finger unbutton the jacket *before* they sat down. This somehow eluded Erno.

Now his was cinched tight across the flanks, creased from the button to the small of his back. Of course he ended up sitting on the tail of the jacket, and the fabric snagged on the deep cracks in the worn leather of the chair. As Mr. Bevel placed his hands on the desk, delicately like a piano player about to perform, Erno slid back in his chair, the jacket holding tight to the leather as the slippery pant material pushed back against it. Tighter and tighter the jacket became on his shoulders, pulling at him, until Erno felt like he was wearing a straitjacket.

Mr. Bevel said nothing. His hands seemed to interest him for the moment and he stared at his fingers. This was the most uncomfortable silence Erno had ever known. Mass was tedious but at least he could think about sex and make the time pass. Funerals were the same way.

The silence was choking him. Had he gone to hell before he'd even been ordered killed?

"Erno, I've spent so much time reading about growth these past few years," the old man began, his head tremoring slightly as he talked. There was no trace of an accent. He had a full head of silver hair and wore his expensive suit well. Frank Bevel could have been a senior VP in a Fortune 500 company. Or *of counsel* in a large law firm. But he chose to run the most powerful family in the city. "More is not always better. But we've grown over the years. Bigger means delegation of power and that means trust. I've tried to do right." His was the voice of an old pundit, quiet, but with sentiments and wisdom that signaled a clarity and precision of thought. These were not the musings of a senile old man, but they missed their mark if Erno was supposed to understand them. *What the hell are you talking about?* Erno was confused. The straitjacket tightened and his jugular veins bulged from the tourniquet effect as Erno leaned forward in his chair and concentrated.

"But things have . . . for lack of a better word, slipped. My fault. I guess I really don't know what's been going on in my own organization lately. People I've trusted with my life and my reputation haven't lived up to my expectations." He picked up the cigar and gently tapped off an inch of silver ash before placing it to his lips and taking a measured drag of the fine smoke.

"You ever have a Cuban?"

Erno shook his head.

"Smooth, really smooth," Bevel said, holding the cigar out, regarding the shape. "How about the Jersey shore? You ever get out there?" he asked and looked at Erno directly for the first time.

Erno blinked and stammered. No words, just sounds. Finally he managed a "Yeah" and swallowed hard.

"Waves," Mr. Bevel went on, speaking slowly, waxing cerebral, lingering between phrases like he was sipping a good port. "You watch the waves, don't you? Sit out on the beach, maybe in Margate. I like Margate. You look out far enough over the water and you don't see any waves, just the ripples of the ocean. But then a wave starts, out past the seagulls, small at first, but picking up strength. Sometimes the wave grows steadily as it makes its way to shore; others grow suddenly when two smaller ones merge together. No matter how big—I'm talking about those towering monsters they get in Hawaii—they eventually reach the shore and die. We together?''

"Yes, Mr. Bevel," Erno said. He tried to pay attention but instead noticed how wet his collar had become.

"Only thing is, I didn't think we would hit some kind of barrier reef and come crashing down." Mr. Bevel nodded his headed slowly, rolling the cigar along the edge of the ash tray. "Now, I need you to fill me in on the details of the barrier reef at the Medical Center."

There was a hesitancy to Erno's breathing. "Well, ya see, me'n Satch figured we'd take care of this broad from the DA's office and—"

Erno's grammar was hard for Mr. Bevel to take and he winced. "Erno, that's the *end* of the story. We'll get to what happened in the parking garage later. What I'm interested in are those deliveries to the Medical Center. When did you make your first one?"

Erno looked up at the ceiling and thought. "Oh, I guess about a couple a years ago. When Antony come back from school, yeah, that was it. He knew some guy up the Medical Center—"

"Okay, good, that's what we need to focus on. This man Anthony knew at the Medical Center. What's this man's name?" Bevel asked, careful to pronounce his nephew's name correctly.

"I don't know."

"You don't know," Mr. Bevel said.

"No. I really don't."

"But you made all the deliveries, right?" Mr. Bevel was confused.

"Yeah."

"Then, Erno, who contacted him when it was time to make a delivery? Did Anthony arrange the delivery?"

"No. Antony had me do everything. He wanted to stay out of it. I called on the cellular phone Antony game me."

Mr. Bevel forced an exaggerated calm in his voice. "Then how did you contact him? What did you call him?"

"I never met the guy. Hell, I never even *saw* the guy. I'd page him. I'd call the hospital operator, and say 'Can you voice page Dr. Antony?' Ya see, Antony set this up, and he said that would be a good code name, easy to remember. And this guy would answer. I don't know, I guess he was a doc up in them labs or something. Look, Mr. Bevel, Antony had something on this guy, he owned him. Maybe you should talk with him."

"I'd like to talk with Anthony. We haven't been able to reach him over the weekend. That's why you and I are having this little talk."

"Oh." Erno suddenly felt naked. He looked over his shoulder toward the door. They were still alone.

"Finish your story, Erno."

"I . . . I . . . I . . ." Erno stammered.

Mr. Bevel was growing impatient. "Oy, yoy, yoy. You sound like an old Jew."

Erno took a deep breath. "I know how you always wanted things done. And I never questioned anything, Mr. Bevel. Antony said it would look bad if the dump was ever discovered. He wanted us to play it safe. So Antony fixed it up that we'd take the guys we whacked—you know, people someone might recognize—and deliver them to this guy at the Med Center. Then he'd put the bodies out for the medical students to hack up—they carve up everything, even the face, I think. And then we'd get one of the Med Center bodies and bury it in the dump. A bunch of unknowns. Nothing to tie us to anything."

"Did you ever meet this 'Dr. Antony'?"

"No. Like I said, we'd bright our stiff in a body bag. Fifteen hundred bucks in his mouth. And then me'n

Satch'd take this special elevator up to the ninth floor and switch the bodies. There was a stretcher waiting right at the elevator. It was always dark, no one around.''

"And what happened with the doctor? He walk in on things?"

Erno thought for a couple of seconds. "That night, I took the body up. Satch stayed with the truck. The doc must've been hanging around the elevator. I don't know for sure what happened.

"I guess Satch thought he would've seen me bring the stiff *out* of the damn place at midnight and . . . and . . . I don't know. Satch got spooked. The doc asked him what he was doing there so late and he took him out. Satch told me he had to do him. I told Antony about it.''

"So Anthony knew. Hmmm. Why'd you send the doctor's body up for the med students?"

"That's just it. I didn't. No way, Mr. Bevel. You gotta believe me. I'm more careful than that. I been wit you ten years and I never fucked up." Erno spotted Mr. Bevel cringe at the coarse language. "Sorry. Anyway, this Dr. Antony must've done it. *He* must've taken him up to the lab and switched him for the body they found in the river. I don't know why. That wasn't the plan.''

"Why didn't *you* take him with you and dump him?"

"Taking a stiff out of the Medical Center in a body bag on a stretcher is one thing. Carrying one over my shoulder . . . I don't think that was too smart. I lifted his wallet and his watch, left him on that loading dock. It was supposed to look like a robbery. I mean, if Satch hadn't panicked, and Dr. Antony left him alone . . .''

"Is that it?"

"I guess so."

"So, Anthony had you *deliver* bodies—*identifiable* people whose pictures were no doubt in the *Post-Gazette*—to the Medical Center. Then the medical students would dissect the faces—and hope nobody would happen to recognize any of them. Shrewd, very shrewd.''

Mr. Bevel had summarized their clever plan in such a way as to make it seem childishly stupid, and Erno was embarrassed.

Bevel continued. "I assume that was your last delivery."

"Which was?" Erno was easily confused.

"The one the night you disposed of that doctor—I think his name was Hoover—that was your last delivery, right?" Mr. Bevel's voice was raised.

Erno wanted desperately to lie. *Yessir, we've been using the family dump ever since.* Mr. Bevel might be a soft-spoken gentleman now, but he'd ordered every murder that Erno had carried out and wasn't shy about fixing problems.

And Erno figured Mr. Bevel probably already knew they'd made more deliveries.

"We—uh—delivered a couple more times since then," Erno said, his mouth dry and sticky.

"When was the most recent?" Mr. Bevel snapped.

"The night Satch was killed, I had a body in the truck, been sitting there over twenty-four hours. That's why we were in Oakland. I'd already called Dr. Antony *before* Satch. I waited around until the ambulance and the police left. I sat in a coffee shop across the street—I musta had ten cups—and made the delivery. I didn't have any choice."

The room seemed very quiet. "You didn't have *any* choice. *You* didn't have *any* choice," Mr. Bevel said. "Shrewd. Who was it?"

There was a long pause. "Mike Demasi."

"Help me, God." Mr. Bevel took off his glasses, heavy dark frames, no tint to the lenses, and placed them on the desk. His thumb and forefinger squeezed the skinny bit of nose cartilage between his eyes. "The press is full of the most sensational murder this city has ever seen, the cops are probably living in the goddamn anatomy labs, and you decide to deliver Mike Demasi, whose face is now also all over the paper. *You,* Erno, are my barrier reef." He stared at Erno, waiting for an explanation that could make some sense out of this ridiculous story. "What about Satch?"

"I was reading the *Post-Gazette*. It seems this broad from the DA is the only one hanging around the Medical Center. No cops or nothing."

"And you figured if you dispose of the investigator the whole investigation would go away. Jesus Christ. I deserve to go to jail for employing such *stupid* people."

Again, Mr. Bevel had reduced a clever plan to its base value.

"I know this don't sound too good, but I was trying to help. Look, you know I'll do whatever you tell me. I been loyal to you, Mr. Bevel." Erno had become Willy Loman begging not for his job but for his life. If he had the requisite salesman's dress hat he would have looked down at it and gently rotated it in his hand for effect. Instead, he spotted a picture on the wall, just above Mr. Bevel's right shoulder, of the Pope. It seemed a safe place to rest his eyes.

Mr. Bevel's eyes followed Erno's gaze and they both admired the pontiff. "I'm sure he knows how lucky you are to have been loyal." More ashes were tapped from the cigar and Mr. Bevel stood and came around the desk and stood in front of Erno. He leaned back on the desk. "Erno, time was all I had to do was ask what happened, and I got told. I never had to ask twice, wonder if I was getting the truth. I don't know. Anthony disappears. Satch screws up, but he's dead . . . it doesn't matter. We're not gonna pursue it. I'll go to my grave wondering what really happened at the Medical Center."

"Mr. Bevel, it's like I told you."

With a single wave of his hand Mr. Bevel silenced him, then took a long drag on the cigar. "I want you to do something for me."

Thank you, Jesus. Erno breathed a sigh of relief. His death sentence had been commuted. Frank Bevel was a straight shooter. No games. No phony assignment and then a bullet in the back of the head when he was walking out. There wasn't going to be a hit. At least not yet. Mr. Bevel wanted him to do something. *Thank you, Lord.*

"First of all, don't touch the woman from the DA's office. Miss Welch, I believe. Leave her *the fuck* alone. If she disappears they'll send ten more." He rubbed his cheek.

"I'll leave her alone. No problem." Erno thought better than to mention the note that was being delivered to Tory Welch even as they spoke.

"I'm not going down. Not like this. No one's at our door, and we can contain this. There's always a solution. It's a game we can win. Okay, now our real problem is this Dr. Antony. He's the liability. He can sink us. I'm gonna assume our Anthony had something good on him to get him to put his neck out for something like this. So I'll bet he's the only one in on this. He's the loose end we've got to tidy up." He paused and waited for a nod from Erno. "Here's what I want you to do. I want you to page Dr. Antony and tell him you want to make a delivery."

"Mr. Bevel, that may not work. He gave me a hard time about the Demasi delivery."

"Good, he's scared. But you tell him Anthony wants this to be the last delivery. Other arrangements have been made for the future. Whatever. Tell him a final payment of, say, fifteen grand. Something like that." A hint of an Italian accent crept into his speech.

"Got it."

"Then arrange a time for the delivery. Late night, like usual. But you get there first, up where the switch takes place. Find someplace to hide, where you can watch the elevator. Have someone else—maybe Carmine—make the delivery. Take a body bag—stuff it with old rags or something—make it look good. When this Dr. Antony shows up to take the body, take care of him. Use a Saturday Nighter. Get him in the fuckin' head, maybe the shoulder, too, and put one or two in the wall. I want it to look sloppy.''

"Sloppy?" Erno was confused.

"Yeah, sloppy. Like some, I dunno, some orderly or janitor wants to ice him. And he don't know shit about guns, so he uses Grandma's pistol that's been in the back of her panty drawer. Sloppy.''

Erno nodded.

Mr. Bevel continued, "You never been printed, right?"

"How'd you know?"

"Drop the gun, don't wipe it."

"What? But they'll have my prints. I get picked up for something.''

"Don't worry about the prints. You're through in Pittsburgh. I hope you've saved something over the years. You're heading outta town. Once you leave, don't come back. Go to Hawaii, maybe, and watch some of those monster waves.''

Bevel handed him an envelope. There was a half-inch of money inside.

Erno stood to leave. "Thanks, Mr. Bevel." His voice was barely audible.

"And Erno, don't worry about your mother. I'll personally stop by now and then and check on, her.''

The message was clear.

Twenty-four

August 22, 1995

It wasn't planned for a moonless night, but the clouds rolled in before midnight, and, except for the single light all the way at the end, the alley was pitch black. The panel truck backed up slowly to avoid scraping the walls on either side. PITTSBURGH UNIVERSITY MEDICAL CENTER DELIVERY was printed in small letters on both panels. Silently, the truck stopped at a loading dock lighted by the single overhead floodlight and its headlights darkened. An elevator connected the loading dock to the gross anatomy labs on the ninth floor of the medical school and made no stops in between. Although the Medical Center had almost a dozen loading docks scattered about the seven-building campus, this one was used the least. The delivery of cadavers to the gross anatomy labs happened infrequently, only several times a month, but the planning committee for the medical school was concerned with the public viewing this particular type of delivery. So a small loading dock was constructed in a deep alcove. When a delivery vehicle was backed in, no one crossing between hospitals could catch a glimpse.

Once Erno was out of the cab his hand automatically pulled his jacket down in the back and he hoisted himself up onto the loading dock with a grunt. As soon as he stood up again he had to pull his jacket down in back. Then he scanned the night and smoothed his hair before pressing the combination to signal the elevator. All the outside elevators at the Medical Center had numerical touch pads for security, all set to the same "5-7-3-4" combination, and were designed to keep pranksters and kids out. Erno then banged on the truck's back door twice to signal Satch. With a squeak, the back door of the truck swung open and Satch started to roll the stretcher off. A black body bag, bulged wide at the shoulders and cinched tight at the feet, was strapped to the stretcher. The loading dock was awkwardly small, and Satch could not step off the truck until he could push the stretcher onto the elevator. The two men waited. Erno leaned against the brick wall looking down the alley while Satch hunched over the stretcher uncomfortably, his nose close enough to the body bag to smell the guy's after-shave through the nylon.

They listened as the metallic rumbling of the descending elevator slowly grew louder. Street noises, a block away on Fifth Avenue, were drowned out as the rumble picked up. Erno gave a quick last look around as the elevator shuddered to a stop and hesitated for a split second. So familiar was Erno with the timing of the creaky old elevator door, he would start his step onto it just as the doors began to open.

A flash of white, an unfamiliar face, and Erno reared back an instant as he came face to face with a kid in his twenties. Instinctively, Erno's right hand slipped inside his jacket pocket and he took a step forward, forcing the kid to take two steps back. The kid, wearing white pants, white jacket, blue scrub shirt, and an L.L. Bean backpack slung over one shoulder, was instantly intimidated by this large man, and sucked in his breath loudly. Erno had seen enough TV shows to recognize an intern. Never before had the two men seen anyone while making a delivery, and it took great self-control for Erno not to say, "What the fuck are you doing here?" Erno stepped aside and looked at his watch. In a second he had regained his composure and let the kid pass by.

" 'Scuse me," Erno grunted. He noted an ID badge: Kevin Hoover, MD, General Surgery.

"Kinda late for a delivery," Kevin said, squeezing past the stretcher.

Erno locked into Kevin's eyes. "Kinda late to be leaving the hospital," Erno paused, "Dr. Hoover." Erno's voice was low and very quiet, and he said the words "Dr. Hoover," out of the corner of his mouth, but Kevin heard every syllable as if it were screamed into his ear.

Kevin stopped walking and let the stretcher slide fully into the elevator. Satch walked by him, head down, no eye contact. The two delivery men stood on opposite sides of the stretcher. Erno never took his eyes off Kevin's, hypnotizing him with fear. The kid backed up against the brick wall as his backpack slipped off his shoulder and fell to his elbow. Erno liked what he saw. *I've gotcha kid. You're mine. Now, get the fuck outta here.*

Kevin's thoughts were scrambled. Finally, he blurted out, "Late shift in the ER," as the doors closed.

Kevin exhaled loudly. "Holy shit," he said aloud. He had lied and was certain it had been transparent. His thoughts went to Jan. Now, as he shouldered his backpack, Kevin wondered if it was obvious he had just gotten laid. Before he hopped off the loading dock he patted his right rear pocket, and realized he left his now-condomless wallet in his on-call room. "You stupid, horny bastard," he groaned as he punched "5-7-3-4" several times on the keypad, then paced back and forth.

Almost immediately he could hear the elevator approaching. For an instant, Kevin could hear the delivery man's voice say "Dr. Hoover." Over and over, low and guttural, "Dr. Hoover . . . Dr. Hoover . . . Dr. Hoover." When in doubt what to do, physicians gather information. Reflexively, Kevin placed his right index finger under his jaw and took his pulse. One hundred forty.

He debated walking to another entrance to avoid the possibility of running into the delivery man again. It was almost 12:15 A.M. and Kevin didn't want to waste the time. He was required back on rounds in six hours. As the doors creaked open for the second time he bolted onto the elevator, and this time Kevin ran right into a wall of muscle. Erno's chest, the pectorals in particular, had been pumped to perfection on a bench press and Kevin bounced off and stumbled. He took several steps backward to steady himself, and the look on Erno's face sucked all the air noisily from his lungs. Erno's jaw muscles visibly tightened as he glared at Kevin.

Trying not to look at this horrible man was impossible. Kevin had no idea Satch was even there watching his cousin in action; Erno seemed to fill the entire elevator, squeezing out any oxygen to breathe. No delivery had ever taken so long. Satch began to feel the tension and decided to keep things moving by pushing the stretcher off the elevator.

Look away. Don't look at him. DON'T LOOK AT HIM. The stretcher sliding past seemed the obvious place to focus his attention, but as Kevin did so he was confused by what he saw.

Satch wheeled the stretcher onto the truck without realizing the prologue was over and the real drama was about to unfold.

Erno must have noticed something. Maybe Kevin's eyes got wider, and he took in a couple of breaths more quickly. Or maybe it was the way Kevin followed the stretcher all the way onto the truck. But, now, Erno was confused.

It usually started this way. Confusion. *What to do? What to do?* And then Erno's breathing quickened and he could hear the pulse in his neck. *What the fuck is going on?* There was only one conclusion he could make *This motherfucker knows.* There was no self-doubt. No short list of options. No thought of a verbal coverup. No finesse. *The kid saw the stretcher. Jesus fucking Christ. He knows.* In a split second Erno decided Kevin knew. Now it was easy.

No decisions to make. Only one way to thread the needle. Erno was on automatic pilot. *Pop. Pop. Pop.* He stopped thinking, his pulse slowed, and he relaxed.

Satch pulled the back doors to the truck closed, leaving Erno alone with Kevin. Not a word had been said. Erno waited and listened to Kevin breathe. Kevin made no effort to push the "up" button, but moved back into a corner, as far away from this beast of a man as he could go, and tried to gaze innocently away from Erno. Before the elevator doors might close spontaneously, Erno reached behind his back with his right hand and pulled out a length of pipe ten inches long, then held it at his side. It was wrapped in unstained, light tan, braided leather. Someone had told him prints couldn't be lifted off leather. His thumb absently shifted the light braiding back and forth and it creaked like a saddle being mounted. Erno took a step forward to move within Kevin's peripheral vision. *Get him out of the corner.*

Kevin could feel Erno moving closer.

"You don't smell like no 'late shift in the ER,' Dr. Hoover."

It was at that moment when Kevin knew, beyond any shadow of a doubt, this man was going to give him a hard time. It was inescapable, and he decided he wasn't going to let the doors close. He wasn't going to ride up with this man. He wasn't going to ride in a metal box with an animal. Counting to three, nodding his head in rhythm, Kevin jammed his elbows as hard as he could into the back wall, and shot himself to the front of the elevator. Erno knew he would, as if he'd been through it before. The opportunity was now. *Pop. Pop. Pop.* Erno raised his right arm like a maestro about to conduct and ferociously brought the length of pipe down on Kevin's head. There was no need for a sweet spot, the mass of the pipe easily smashed the skull, the leather stretching the skin just enough to avoid a deep laceration of the vascular scalp. Sometimes he wasn't so lucky and it was a bloody mess. When the skull was hit squarely and it imploded, a noise like a glass Christmas ornament dropping on the floor could be heard. The first time Erno heard a skull pop he had no idea what it was, no idea he had made it. In fact he'd looked around thinking it might be the popping of a small handgun, and it wasn't until he'd heard it two or three times that he recognized the sound of death.

Kevin slumped to the floor in a limp heap. In the pitch black of oblivion Kevin could smell the sweet cologne of Erno Pantuzzi for his last three breaths. He was dead before Erno finished inspecting the leather braiding to see if it had been stained.

After a quick check for a pulse in Kevin's neck, Erno punched the "up" button, hopping off the loading dock just as the elevator doors closed. He looked at the body folded up on the floor one last time.

Erno slipped back in the driver's seat, flipping the murder weapon up on the dashboard. Satch sat quietly listening to the radio. Erno glanced to his right and saw Satch's hand shaking ever so slightly as he lit a cigarette. Erno knew his cousin had watched, probably in the rearview mirror. Before they were out of the alley, driving slowly in the dark without benefit of headlights, Erno was speed-dialing a number on a hand held cellular phone. "Operator, yeah, voice page Dr. Antony. Yeah, yeah, I know you don't have a beeper number for him, just voice page him, will ya? Yeah, I'll wait."

Satch turned off the radio and sat quietly. Always seen, never heard. This was the key to his survival in the business: He knew when not to talk.

Erno made the turn onto Fifth Avenue as he was connected. "It's Double Jeopardy and the category is . . . Hey asshole, we just sent you another package. Check the elevator." Erno paused as he listened. He nodded his head several times to speed up the conversation. Erno was getting annoyed. "Yeah, well, I don't give a

264 JAMES TUCKER

fuck about inventory numbers. You dispose of the body any way you want." He clicked off the phone and only after Erno started to laugh did Satch allow himself a chuckle.

Twenty-five

The fourth floor of the Allegheny County Courthouse was arranged in podlike groups of offices that roughly corresponded to the pecking order within the DA's office. Tory was as far from Mark Peters's flashy corner space as she could get without leaning out a window, which she didn't have anyway. Peters referred to a trudge down the hall as "slumming it." It was after six when Tory breezed into her office, really a fancy cubicle, one of three clustered around a secretary's L-shaped desk. The secretary was already home cooking dinner when Tory switched on the lights in her office. The other two offices were alive with activity, serious work being done at the expense of a personal life. Trying to move up a pod or two.

Tory hadn't seen her office in days and the mail was piling up. Her desktop looked like the skyline of a medium-sized city. Tory's diplomas adorned one wall and a small color photograph of Tory crossing the finish line of the Boston Marathon was hung for inspiration across from her desk. An empty ceramic planter sat unused on the black file cabinet in the corner, indisputable evidence of a series of botanical fatalities. Had she planted wheat, corn, and oats instead of the rubber tree and Christmas cactus, Tory liked to joke, she could have been a cereal killer. *Ba-dum-bum.*

Sunday the twenty-second had begun in Merlin's on-call room. From the moment Tory woke up she experienced an

invigoration she had never known before. Merlin found a
pair of small scrubs that Tory had worn down the hall to
the bathroom. They shared Merlin's toothbrush, then
shared a shower. Once again, this time with the benefit of
light, they explored each other as they took turns soaping
and kissing every body part in *Gray's Anatomy,* including
a couple old Mr. Gray never dreamed could be eroge-
nous zones.

After breakfast in the cafeteria—Merlin suggested they
sit at *their* table—he took Tory to the department of surgery offices, where copies of operative summaries and discharge summaries were kept for departmental use.
Margaret Emont's file was a thin one, the hospitalization
in August of 1995 being her first Medical Center surgery.
Merlin spent several minutes reading the file and told Tory
that Mrs. Emont had two lumps that were biopsied and
found to be benign. The only reason she had been admitted
in the first place was that she had a history of a bleeding
disorder and admission was advised as a precaution. There
were no complications, no reason why someone wouldn't
want Tory to know what was inside the chart. Merlin even
looked up Mrs. Emont's phone number and called her,
identifying himself as one of her doctors from her hospital
stay, and politely inquired about her health. They chatted
for several minutes. Finally Merlin hung up the phone. He
got up and started to pace around the small office. "We're
getting sidetracked. This chart is nothing but misdirection.
A red herring."

Tory watched him and frowned. "Can we afford to
be wrong?"

"We're not wrong. Whoever was in Medical Records
grabbed your little notebook and scooped up whatever else
was on the table. The Emont chart was probably dumped
in a trash can two minutes after it was taken. If the chart
meant *anything* it would have disappeared long ago."

"Maybe you're right."

"Maybe? Think of it like an elaborate magic trick. How

'bout the one where they saw the girl in half. The magician comes out with a couple of pretty assistants in skimpy dresses. Pretty soon they're flashing around those huge guillotine-like blades they push into the box to cut it in half. And your eyes are looking here and there and you don't quite know where to focus your attention. You wonder if the blades are really made of metal, and the sequined dresses are catching the light." Merlin danced his fingers around in front of his face like shimmering sequins, "There's probably some bouncy music in your ear, and by golly, you don't notice the girl in the box scrunching up inside so she fits in one half. All the extra stuff is just that. Extra stuff. That's what the Emont chart is. A goddamn sequined dress." Merlin did one of those little triumphant moves—one step forward, right hand extended palm-up toward Tory, like you see after a snappy dance number.

Tory smiled. "That's what I like about you. Everything can be reduced to a magical metaphor."

Tory went home—after making plans to meet later—for a couple of hours, changed her clothes, and had grilled cheese and tomato sandwiches with Mrs. Kincaid. They sat in the Kincaid kitchen, the huge mutt named Pepper curled up under the table waiting for scraps. Tory delicately explained that she'd been accosted twice, careful not to divulge too many details of the case. True to form, Mrs. Kincaid didn't ask a series of questions, but listened attentively and promised to keep a watch out for trouble. Tory knew what that meant. Mrs. Kincaid would give up Regis and Kathy Lee and *The Price is Right* to sit at her back door, watching. Tory pitied the United Parcel man if her latest shipment from Joseph Banks arrived in the next day or so.

She picked up Merlin at the Medical Center and they went to his apartment to spend the night.

Before going back to the office on Monday, Tory took a chance and dropped by to visit with Julian Plesser. She felt so comfortable around Jules that she ended up staying most of the day, going through every phase of the investigation. Jules didn't know Jake Barnhouse and wasn't able to comment on Olsen's motive for taking the paperwork. But he was impressed that Tory recognized the cadaver as a phony and told her so.

Then Tory presented her plan to Jules. Somehow—the details hadn't been worked out yet—she'd get her hands on the paperwork for all the cadavers in the anatomy lab. And, if someone knowledgeable in pathology agreed, she'd meet that someone in the anatomy labs late at night, avoiding Olsen, and do a cursory check to see if the bodies matched the paperwork. Julian, of course, agreed, admonished her to be more careful, and said he couldn't think of anything more appealing than helping Tory and scooping Olsen simultaneously.

Things were starting to fall in place.

By the time she walked over to the courthouse it was getting dark.

Traffic would be horrible for the next half-hour, so Tory sat down at her desk and flipped through her correspondence. One white business envelope immediately caught her attention. It was handwritten. PERSONAL was blocklettered across the bottom. It had not yet been opened.

Inside was a prescription, wrinkled and missing a corner, from the Emergency Department at the Medical Center. "Pancurmonium bromid" was scrawled across the paper and was signed "Dr. Antony." The signature was carefully written and easy to decipher. Tory wrinkled her brow. She read and reread the script, over and over, like it was some kind of brainteaser, hoping for a burst of inspiration so the answer would pop into her head. The ink was black, and each time the pen had come into contact with the paper to start a new letter a small blob of ink was left behind. Flipping it over, looking for a clue, Tory spotted an innocuous smudge of brown on the back. She verified it was her name on the envelope and the

prescription. Twice. *Dr. Antony. Pancurmonium bromid.*
She smelled it. Sweet as a note from a feminine lover.
But the handwriting was unmistakably masculine, big letters, firmly pressed into the paper. After flipping the prescription over a second time, Tory gently ran her fingertips
over the raised letters like she was reading a palm. She
was scared. Absently, she rubbed her neck. Gooseflesh.
Who the hell is Dr. Antony?

"You busy?"

Tory looked up. Mark Peters casually walked in, tie
loose, shirtsleeves rolled partway.

Oh, shit, Tory thought, remembering her promise to
Merlin. "No, c'mon in. I'm falling behind on paperwork,
just trying to catch up."

Peters had to move a bulging accordion folder from the
visitor's chair before he could sit down.

"Know The Pennsylvania Polka, Mark?"

"What?"

"The folder, looks like an . . . Never mind," Tory said.

Peters looked down at the accordion folder. "Oh, I get
it. Funny. Anything to report with the investigation?"

"Not really."

"Hey, you hear about that guy, Pantuzzo or something,
fell out of the parking garage in Oakland last week?"

Tory carefully took a deep breath. "Yeah, I read something about it. Druggie or something."

"Do you have any firsthand knowledge of what happened to Mr. Pantuzzo?"

This was a perfect opportunity to tell Peters everything
she'd told Merlin the night before, but for some reason,
probably the fact that Tory truly detested her boss, she
decided to play games with him. "Firsthand knowledge?"
she asked innocently.

"You know what I mean."

"Are you deposing me?"

"No. I'm asking you a simple question. Were you involved? That *is* the parking garage for the Medical Center, right? I mean, correct me if I'm wrong.''

Information whirled in her head. Peters knew something, and Tory wanted to milk him to see exactly what he knew. Things needed to be handled delicately or her presence on the case would be a distant memory. She knew to rely on her debating instincts and forced herself to think things through. There was always an opportunity that would lead her to a win. She needed more information, needed a peak at Peters's hand.

"Of course not. Mark, they're saying he was killed over drugs. How would I be . . . what, because I might have parked in that lot? Are you investigating *everybody* who parks there?''

"No. No, it has nothing to do with where you park. In fact, I didn't know you park there. Initially we thought it was a drug deal gone bust.''

Tory stood and played her measly four flush with gusto. She looked hurt and had the temerity to say, "Mark, I have no idea what you're driving at, so why don't you tell me. I don't do drugs—you can run a tox screen if you want.''

"I'm not doing a tox screen. Maybe you don't remember. You were fingerprinted when you joined the DA's office.''

Tory sat down. "So?'' Her voice didn't sound so confident. *Damn, he knows or he's a better bluffer than I am. Did I leave prints on the car? How many? Where were they? How could I have missed them, I wiped down everything. Not more than one or two.*

Now it was Peters's turn. "Actually, it was your buddy Jules who noticed Pantuzzo had been sprayed with pepper spray or Mace. Something to do with his eyes. Not typical of a drug deal. So the police went back and looked around. They went level by level. Then it got easy. Some doc who owns a nice, new shiny car reported to the police that his baby had scratches all over the hood. A dark green

Beemer. License plate SJT2. Had your prints on it. From what the doc tells us, it was parked where we believe Mr. Pantuzzo—"

"Look, Mark, the creep tried to rape me. And he tried to kill me. So I defended myself. I Maced him and he fell off the ledge. End of story."

"No Tory, that's the *beginning* of the story. Why didn't you go to the police or come to me?"

"You would've pulled me off the case."

"No, I wouldn't."

"Baloney. The case is too dangerous, you're too new, you're a girl. Forget it," Tory said in a sing-song voice. "And I bet you could come up with a few of your own . . . right? That's what's gonna happen now, isn't it?"

"You didn't think it might be germane that you were attacked *at* the garage connected to the Medical Center *while* you were investigating a murder at the same Medical Center?"

"Oh, my God, it never occurred to me," Tory said. "Honestly, I defended myself and it resulted in the death of a creep. Big fucking deal. Oh, yeah, I can say the word just like you can. I screwed up. Rookie mistake. But humor me and think this through. If I go to the police and tell them the story and that I was afraid you'd pull me from the case, the focus of this whole thing shifts from Kevin Hoover to me. This case will spin hopelessly off track. Now, would justice be served?"

Peters didn't like the scenario. He realized he'd look bad. "I agree with you. The focus must stay on the investigation. That's why we're here," Peters said with a phony tone of altruism.

Tory noticed the way Peters had said "we're here"—still including her on the team—and felt a twinge of optimism.

"But that doesn't excuse what you did," Peter continued. "You're working under me. Chain of command and all that." Peters pointed to himself. "I'm in charge. I need

to know what the hell's going on. You know we discussed
all this. I *should* pull you off the case and teach you
a lesson.''

"You're right, Mark, you should. I'm sorry. But who
benefits? You told me I'm not ready to be thrown into the
media arena, and I don't want to be out there.''

"Right,'' Peters said, pleased that Tory remembered his
little speech.

"The whole thing scares the hell out of me, Mark. So
we find a compromise. Justice is served.''

Peters bit his lower lip. "Not so fast. This isn't a neat
and simple case anymore. I need to think about it. Give
me until tomorrow.''

Tomorrow. No way. Tory didn't want to chance giving
Peters a night to mull things over. "Tell me what's really
bothering you.''

"I don't know if this Pantuzzo thing has anything to
do with Kevin Hoover, but maybe you've stumbled onto
something. Maybe you know too much and someone's
trying to shut you up.''

"I doubt it—I don't know anything. That's the problem.
I feel like I'm spinning my wheels. Hey, I got an idea.
Let me go step by step, review everything I've done on
this case, every detail. Give you a full accounting.''

"What about the Pantuzzo incident?'' Peters asked, sitting back in his chair. "Start there. Flesh out the details
for me.'' He could see the broad strokes but had trouble
actually getting from point A to point B.

Tory could smell victory and dared to change the direction of the conversation. "I'm curious. How many prints
were on the car?''

"One set. Everything else was smeared.''

Then Tory proceeded to fit things together logically.
"Pantuzzo was a low-life wiseguy, and I bet the police
really don't think I was involved. They were just checking
with you, right? It got dropped on your desk. And if it

gets out the DA's office was practicing renegade justice it looks bad." Now it was Tory's turn to bite her lip.

"How would *you* suggest we handle this?"

"That I was parked next to the BMW and must have accidentally touched the hood. Can you live with that, Mark?"

"Maybe. And if I do you're gonna agree to a uniform accompanying you until this case is over."

"Agreed."

"And that *I'm* in charge and need to be kept informed."

"Agreed."

They were both thankful for a moment of quiet. Finally Peters said, "You weren't hurt, were you?"

"Just this scratch on my cheek," Tory said, touching her cheek lightly. Tory still had the prescription in her hand. She handed it to Mark Peters. "You know what pancurmonium bromid is?"

Peters shook his head. "No. Where'd you get this?"

"The mail."

"This script has no directions, just 'pancurmonium bromid.' Phony."

"Obviously it's phony."

"You know any Dr. Antony?"

"No."

"Call your friend Merlin. See if he knows him." Peters slid the script back across the desk.

"How do you know about Merlin?"

Peters didn't answer.

Tory dialed the phone, making a mental note that Peters had ignored her question. The sound of laughter emanated from the hallway as the various offices slowly emptied for the night. "Hello, would you please page Dr. Merlin?"

While she waited she looked at the prescription. The recorded Disneyland voice assured her she was indeed very important and someone would be with her shortly.

*   *   *

"Merlin, hello, it's me."

"Hi, Tory, you okay?"

"Yeah, why?"

"Your voice sounds funny. Someone in the room?" Merlin asked.

Tory smiled.

"I can hear you smiling," he said.

Tory giggled.

"Now I hear you giggling."

"All right, enough." She loved having a private joke in front of Peters.

"Ooday ouyay antway emay ootay alktay inay Igpay Atinlay?" Merlin asked, as if he were bilingual.

"Listen, I need some help. Pan-cur-mo-nium bro-mid? You ever hear of that?"

"Yeah, it's a drug used in anesthesia. But it's pronounced pancu-*ron*-ium bro-*mide*. What's going on?"

"I got a prescription in the mail, Medical Center logo, and it's for pancuronium bromide. Spelled wrong."

"What the hell is going on? You don't write a prescription for pancuronium. It's only used in the OR. I don't like this, Tory."

"What's it for?"

"It paralyzes all the goddamn muscles." Merlin's voice was raised. "If someone sent you a script for pancuronium bromide someone's trying to scare you. Who sent it?"

"Someone named Dr. Antony. Ever heard of him?"

"Tory, he spelled it wrong. Whoever wrote it isn't a doctor. And I don't recognize the name, anyway. Definitely not in the department of anesthesia. Sounds off the wall to me."

"Just to be sure, how can I check the name?"

"I'll check in the morning . . . no, I know, call the paging operator. They've got it all on computer."

"Okay, thanks—"

"Wait a second. You tell your boss you want some police protection."

"I already arranged it. Call you later. 'Bye."

Tory pressed the button to clear the line. "First of all, it's called pancuronium bromide. That's a misspelling. Second, it's a drug used in anesthesia to paralyze the body. It's deadly."

Peters smiled and gave the thumbs up sign. "You definitely stumbled onto something. Yes. Yes. Yes. Now we've just gotta figure out what it is."

"I'm glad that having my life threatened excites you so much. Will you be able to contain yourself if I get killed?"

"Tory, you know what I mean—I'm excited we've got a break on the case. That's all. What about Dr. Antony—he ever hear of him?" Peters said, smoothly changing the subject.

With Peters's sudden gush of enthusiasm, Tory knew she was back on the case. "Nope. I'm calling the paging operator right now, but Merlin says the name's a phony." Tory dialed again and waited a few seconds.

"Hello, paging operator, I wonder if you could tell me if you have a certain doctor on staff at the Medical Center?"

"Who is this?"

"My name is Tory Welch; I'm with the District Attorney's office. This is official business. Would you like to call me back at the county courthouse to verify?"

"No, that won't be necessary. Who do you want to know about?"

"Dr. Antony."

The answer came instantly. No rustling of phone book pages. No plastic taps of fingers on a keyboard. "He's not on staff at the Medical Center."

"Are you sure? I mean, don't you have to look it up?"

"Okay, I'll double check, but he wasn't on staff at four o'clock."

"What do you mean? Someone else checked on him earlier?" Tory's voice squeaked with excitement.

"Who? Who? Who?" Peters couldn't contain himself. He put his hand out as if it were his turn to talk.

Tory ignored him.

The operator said, "No, I mean someone paged him earlier today, or at least he tried to. I told him there's no Dr. Antony on staff and he told me—he wasn't very nice—to voice page him. And I did. But this time no one picked up the page."

"This time. What do you mean 'this time?' "

"He calls every once in a while. Insists we voice-page Dr. Antony. But since he's not on staff we couldn't beep him anyway—"

"What's your name?"

"Rayma."

"Rayma, how late you working?"

"Eleven. Is this about that murder investigation?"

"I'll see you in an hour."

"I'm going down there," Tory said, speaking fast. "There's no Dr. Antony on staff, yet he gets calls. *Now* we've stumbled onto something."

Twenty-six

"How do I reach you if I think of anything else that might be important?" Rayma said as Tory and Peters walked into the windowless room that was the communications center for the Medical Center. The phone operators were tucked away near the service elevators in the basement of the hospital.

Tory was still angry from her conversation with Peters. Not the one where he cross-examined her about her knowledge of the Pantuzzi incident. That had gone very well, and Peters still did not know that Mr. Pantuzzi knew her name.

It was the other conversation—the one when he announced he was coming along to interview the phone operator. When he informed her it was too late in the evening to arrange a police escort, so he'd tag along. Just in case. Wouldn't be in the way or anything.

The drab room with its drab denizens wasn't used to visitors. Tory and Peters, at the *end* of their workday, looked dazzling, bigger than life, almost as if by some digital magic they could be seen in color but their surroundings were stuck in black and white. Three telephone consoles, a series of computer monitors, and an assortment of business phones were arranged along a long table spanning the middle of the room. Rayma obviously sat at the first station and stood nervously beside her chair. Actually, she'd been standing so long, anxiously awaiting her visitors, a bicuspid smile frozen on her face, that her canines were bone dry, her upper lip stuck at the gumline. As soon as Rayma saw Tory and Peters walk in she worked her upper lip down like a shade being drawn to hide her crooked teeth. A second chair had been arranged next to hers for her company. The middle seat was unoccupied and another woman, introduced later as Dotty, sat at the other end of the table, working her console and looking at Rayma longingly.

"Hi, I called about an hour ago. I'm Tory Welch. Are you Rayma?" Tory asked.

"Yes, I'm Rayma. Rayma Elizabeth Ryan. Do you need my address?" she asked with a spirit of anticipation as she awkwardly stepped forward to shake Tory's hand. Rayma wasn't used to this business ritual. She looked down at Tory's hand rather than her eyes and immediately stepped backward toward her desk after a few seconds of vigorous pumping. Rayma was what people called an old fifty. Years of sitting had widened her posterior, giving her torso a pear-shaped appearance. Although Peters didn't take notice, her gray dress was adorned with a small gold pin commemorating fifteen years of service to the Medical Center. It was the first thing she did when she hung up the phone after talking with Tory. Put on the gold pin, the one she kept in her wallet in the zip-up compartment. The one she only wore to the holiday party.

"Oh no, that won't be necessary. Rayma, this is Mark Peters. As I told you on the phone, we're with the district attorney's office. We just would like to ask you a few questions."

"Nice to meet you, Mr. Peters." Rayma repeated her version of shaking hands.

Tory smiled. Peters nodded.

"Mrs. Ryan," Peters started, "We're doing some background investigation—"

"About that body they found in one of them labs?" Rayma wanted to know. "What a shame."

"I'm not at liberty to say," Peters said, using any stilted

movie expression he could think of, "but we would appreciate anything you can tell us about one Dr. Antony." Tory rolled her eyes.

Rayma admired the way Peters talked and got her lip stuck on her teeth again. She thought he had the dashing look of a TV anchorman: the dark blue suit with the thin white lines, his clean white shirt and the bright red tie, still knotted tightly at the neck. "Okay, I can tell you everything you want to know. Uh, I guess we need another chair."

Peters—quite deliberately—made no effort to help provide adequate seating. Tory quickly rolled the vacant seat from the middle communications station to Rayma's and the three sat down. Peters sat next to Rayma. Each desk area was personalized with odds and ends. Rayma had several small ceramic figures and a sandwich tucked away on a small shelf, wrapped in a piece of waxed paper, heavily creased from previous outings. A glass of water, the rim stained with lipstick, waited for Rayma.

"Do either of you want a glass of water or anything?"

"No, that's very kind. Here," Tory said, fishing a business card out of her leather bag, "this is my card. I hope you do call me if you think of anything." Tory reached back in her bag for her small notebook and came out empty.

Rayma accepted the card and gently ran her thumb over the lettering, several times, appreciating the raised letters. "Thanks."

"Mrs. Ryan, on the phone you told Ms. Welch about some calls that came in for Dr. Antony," Peters said.

"Yes, I did. Why don't I start at the beginning?" Rayma said, at least temporarily feeling a little like Cinderella at the ball, determined to dance until midnight. "This is the AT&T System 85," Rayma began, gently patting a sleek, black console with multiple rows of labeled buttons. "All phone calls to the Medical Center come into the System 85. When I took the call from that man today—I told Miss Welch he wasn't very nice, didn't I?—he said to page Dr. Antony. Now I didn't think we had a Dr. Antony on staff at the Medical Center—I have a pretty good mind for names—and besides, I've talked to that man before, and Dr. Antony wasn't on staff the last time I talked to him.''

"Rayma, how do you check to see if a particular doctor is on staff?'' Tory asked.

"That's a good question.'' Rayma slid her keyboard in front of her and began to type. "See, I type the name 'Antony' into the computer, hit enter, and . . . there.''

The blue screen had a boxed message: "There is no beeper number issued to ANTONY. Please check the spelling and reenter.''

"I've checked other spellings *and* I asked the man to spell the name but he just got mad.'' Rayma sat up straight and put on a "mad'' facial expression. "Just voice page him, for Christ sake. Forget the beeper,'' she said in a mock angry man's voice. "Now we're always supposed to use the beepers,'' she continued back in her earnest phone operator voice, "so as not to use the paging system 'cept for real emergencies, but I paged Dr. Antony on the overhead just the same.''

"And did Dr. Antony answer his page?''

Afraid this might be a single-elimination conversation and her company might find a better party at the other end of the table, she answered, "I suppose so. See, when a call comes in one of these lights goes on to tell which number the call will be answered on.'' She pointed to the console and a light next to 1711. "There's a call waiting for someone on outside line 1-7-1-1. When that light goes off, the call has been completed. If I voice page Dr. Antony and the light stays on for a couple of minutes, then I can pretty much bet they're talking.''

"Rayma, this is important. Do you specifically know whether Dr. Antony picked up his page earlier today?'' Peters wanted to know.

Rayma hesitated. "No," she said quietly, lowering her eyes, certain her fifteen minutes of celebrity were about to end.

Tory thought Rayma was about to cry. "Rayma, that's okay. Don't worry about it. When a call comes in, and a doctor answers the call, is there any way to—I don't know—listen in?"

"Yes. Yes, there is," she blurted out, feeling almost giddy. The more excited she became the faster she talked. "Sometimes at night when the doctors are doing emergency surgery or something and they need to get informed consent, they call down to us to set up the call and be the witness for the informed consent.

"First we call the family at home and place the call on hold on the extension phone." A regular business-type phone sat on Rayma's desk under the shelf holding the sandwich. Rayma slid the phone to center stage, picked up the receiver, and hit the hold button.

Dotty was salivating, turned sideways in her chair, trying to answer incoming calls, her AT&T System 85 lit up with blinking lights. As a new call came in it was abruptly added to almost a dozen incoming callers already waiting, hearing the Disneyland voice soothe them every thirty seconds, telling them how important their call was and that someone would be with them shortly.

"Then we page the doctor to the same phone, different line—extension 5-3-2-6—and create a three-way conference call. That way we can hear the doctor explaining the surgery to the patient."

Tory was intrigued. "So if a call from Dr. Antony came in and you transferred it to the extension phone, you could listen in. Would the two parties know you were listening?"

Rayma answered by hitting a button on the extension phone that said "MUTE." "Now I can listen all I want." Confidently, she crossed her arms and leaned back in her chair. She was in her element. An expert witness who knew what she was talking about.

Tory wondered how often the hospital operators passed the time listening to the soap opera of the Medical Center. "The next time Dr. Antony gets a call, could you record it?"

"Yes, but you hear those little beeps every few seconds."

Peters turned to Tory. "Simple, we get a court order to have these lines tapped, record the call and try to identify—"

Peters was interrupted by the sound of rapidly snapping fingers at the other end of the table. "*Rayma! Rayma!* He's calling for Dr. Antony. He's on the line now!" Dotty screamed, stealing the show. Rayma frowned. Dotty was wearing her phone operator's headset and gesticulating wildly with her hands for Rayma and her guests to join her. "I've got him on hold on the extension. He wants Dr. Antony," she said, her voice calming a bit as she got everyone's attention. "Hi, I'm Dotty, I work with Rayma," she said a bit coquettishly. Dotty gave a little wave. A wallflower no more.

Dotty beamed as she was suddenly surrounded by Rayma, Tory, and Peters. Rayma was not about to relinquish the spotlight. Dotty could join the party but Rayma was still the hostess. "Dotty, leave him on hold on the extension. Okay, good, now page Dr. Antony on the overhead," Rayma ordered.

Peters patted Rayma's right shoulder at the same time he said, "Great work, girls."

Dotty punched in a series of numbers on the console's keypad, took two very dramatic breaths, and spoke into the tiny mouthpiece conveniently positioned in front of her mouth, "Dr. Antony, outside page, extension five-three-two-six. Dr. Antony, outside page, please call five-three-two-six." She hit two more numbers, apparently to disconnect. "How was that?"

"That's great, Dotty," Rayma said and looked at both Tory and Peters for nods of approval. Tory smiled appreciatively; Peters took a subtle step forward, standing a bit closer to Rayma and Dotty and gave them each a wink. "Okay, now hit the mute button."

Dotty obeyed and a small red light, the beacon of their anonymity, lit up next to the mute button. "Now, what do we do?" Dotty wanted to know, looking up to Peters who posed himself, standing tall with each hand holding one of his lapels like some modern day Napoleon leading the conquest of the Medical Center.

"We wait," he said powerfully. Rayma and Dotty admired Mark Peters. His looks. His confidence. His Y chromosome.

The four waited less than a minute before the extension phone in front of Dotty rang with a muted sound while a white light blinked in unison. Dotty swallowed hard. She and Rayma would discuss the nuances of these moments and the unexpected tragedy that would soon follow for the rest of their lives. Even the excitement of being questioned, and exonerated, by the police. And at the service, which of course they both attended, they rehashed everything that happened that night. But one question would always linger. Was it just a miscommunication?

"Patch Dr. Antony in, and we'll be on three-way conference," Rayma said, an able cocaptain who looked again to Peters for approval.

"Hello, Operator," Dotty said, her breathing quick. She nodded and smiled, indicating that indeed Dr. Antony was now on the line. "Yes, Dr. Antony, I have an outside call. Please hold and I'll connect you." Dotty pressed two buttons, swiveled in her chair, looked at Mark Peters, and said, "We've got 'em."

Tory needed to wrest control of the situation. She felt like Peters's secretary, like she should be standing there taking notes while he patted people on the back and made eyes at Rayma and Dotty. "Dotty, could I listen to the conversation?"

"Sure." Dotty took off her headset and handed it up to Tory.

Peters took a second step forward and intercepted the pass. "Give it here, Dotty." Mark Peters took the headset and held the ear piece up to his right ear and listened. To hold Tory at bay he held up his left hand, fingers splayed. Mark Peters—the Mark Peters who could spot an opportunity and pounce on it like no one else in the district attorney's office—was now in charge.

All three women were silent. Rayma stood, hands clasped to her bosom. Dotty sat in her swivel chair, white-knuckling the armrests in tense anticipation. Tory fumed.

In seconds it was over. Peters handed the receiver to Dotty. "Thank you ladies. You'll both receive citations of service from the Justice Department for your help. And I know I don't need to tell either of you that absolute secrecy about Dr. Antony is a must." Peters was in a great mood. He pulled out his wallet and extracted two of his business cards and handed one of the heavy-stock cards to each of the two operators. Now it was Dotty's turn to feel the raised letters.

After they all said their good-byes and Rayma and Dotty went back to their AT&T System 85s, Tory hit the EMERGENCY STOP button halfway between the basement and the ground floor and the elevator bounced twice before coming to a stop. Fortunately they were alone because Tory was about to explode. "What the hell is going on, Mark? I thought you were tagging along for my protection."

"Look Tory, I'm sorry. It's just that I detected—I don't know—a connection with those women and I thought I could expedite things. You know, keep the ball rolling."

"By grabbing control? By making me feel like your

secretary? Why didn't you send me out for coffee for you and your two friends?''

"You may not want to hear it, and I think it's wrong, but these kind of women respond better to a man.''

"How can you rationalize such moronic behavior?''

"We—you and I together—just broke this case wide open. You'd better decide what you're gonna wear on national TV. We're a good team. Let's not bicker.''

"The end justifies the means. You can't see what you are. Oh, you can see yourself on TV, giving interviews, and probably riding down Fifth Avenue in a ticker-tape parade. But you can't see how pathetic you really are. And if I didn't stop this elevator, when exactly were you going to tell me what you heard on that line?''

Peters said nothing. His right hand stroked his evening stubble in a contemplative fashion. He had a lot to think about. *Pathetic. Pathetic. Pathetic.* There was no way, no reasonable way, to salvage their relationship. He could see the hatred in Tory's eyes. She saw him for what he really was and now he knew it. His face flushed red. *With enough effort and creativity order can be made of chaos, the proverbial silver lining can be visualized, and an opportunity can be realized from a hopeless situation.* It was becoming his mantra. Solo suited him just fine.

After an appropriate amount of introspection Peters faced Tory. He puffed up his cheeks, Dizzy Gillespie-style, and—with Tory watching—blew out a long stream of air. His demons were exorcised.

"Okay, Tory, here goes,'' he said, his tone conciliatory, even humble. "You may not like it—and I know where you're coming from—but the reality is we have to work together on this. This is a big case, and it means a lot for the department, and for me, *and* for you. For better or for worse we've got to see this through together, then we'll go our separate ways, and I hope we can find some way to be friends. It's all going down Friday night.''

"What's happening on Friday night?'' Tory demanded.

"A delivery," Peters said confidently.

"A delivery of what?"

"A body. The caller—guy with a rough voice, on a car phone I think—told our friend to expect a delivery, 10:00 P.M. Dr. Antony was reluctant, but the caller said the delivery was the final one, with a final payment of fifteen grand. Said it'd be stuffed in the mouth; it's gotta be a body. Dr. Antony acquiesced. It's all set. Friday at ten. We've hit the jackpot. Ba-bing, ba-bing!"

"It all makes sense. The body I saw Jake working on. Are we turning this over to the police?"

"What are you, nuts? This is your case, Tory."

"Then I should arrange police backup for Friday."

The final piece of the puzzle fit well. "Or maybe *I* should. I gotta call that lieutenant from homicide back on the parking garage thing, smooth him over. Maybe I can kill two birds with one stone.

"This sting'll be handled entirely by our department. No input from the Medical Center. I don't want some dumb-ass security guy who couldn't get real police work to screw this up. You wouldn't believe how bad the Medical Center's board wants this mess brought to a close. They'll be happy to cooperate. I'll get a master key for the medical school and arrange for hospital security to stay the hell away from whatever floor anatomy is on. We'll handle this ourselves. Tory, you just sit tight, spend some time with your boyfriend, and wait 'til Friday."

"How do you know about Merlin?"

"Don't worry about it."

But Tory thought about Big John, how she'd hugged him that night in the basement. Maybe it was better for Peters to handle the arrangements. She couldn't tell Big John to stay away.

Twenty-seven

September 24, 1996

A man's heart always beats faster when he gets a gun. It doesn't matter if it's bought, stolen, or gifted. A man's heart can't distinguish one gun from another. A $45,000 Purdey side-by-side shotgun only fired at the club. A Crossman CO_2 pellet pistol used to plug pigeons. Or even the lowly BB gun. A gun is a gun. And that gets a man's juices flowing.

Erno never had a new gun, except for his BB gun, which was also the first weapon he ever owned. Eighteen years ago his dad had given him one for Christmas. A Daisy Model 25 pump action, with the long thin magazine that took forever to load and was threaded into the end of the muzzle. Erno had ignored his other gifts when his dad reached behind the couch and pulled it out. As if he were a new father timidly holding his new baby, Erno cradled the rifle and bent over to take a whiff of it. How could any kid ever forget the smell of his first BB gun?

It seemed to take his sisters forever to open their presents, boring things like sweaters, but finally his mother went into the kitchen to start breakfast. That's when his dad said to him in a low voice, the one he used to tell dirty jokes after Mass, "You want to give this pop gun a try?" Mr. Pantuzzi opened the front door and sat down next to his son. From the couch Erno had a clear view of the metal trash cans sitting next to the front walk. Erno's mouth went dry when Mr. Pantuzzi said, "Go ahead, pop 'em."

BBs were scattered all over the worn carpet as Erno placed the wooden butt of the gun hard in his gut, puffed out his cheeks, and tried to pull the pump back, trombone style, and force enough air into the chamber to power the rifle. He couldn't. The harder he'd pull the more the barrel would wiggle from side to side. His abdominal muscles ached but he kept trying.

"Gimme that," his dad said, grabbing the gun. Mr. Pantuzzi was big, having worked for Conrail his whole life when he wasn't tormenting his wife. He secured the gun in his left hand and effortlessly pumped it once, snapping the mechanism back against the barrel with an impressive metallic crack. Now the gun was ready to shoot. Still sitting on the couch next to Erno, the old man confidently brought the junior-sized rifle to his shoulder, like a harmless toy, and aimed it around the living room as if preparing to shoot the lamp or the TV.

Erno couldn't wait. This would be the gift *and* the Christmas he would remember forever. Arms outstretched, trembling, he waited to be handed the gun. His gun. The moment he'd waited for his whole life. "Dad, c'mon. Lemme try it."

Mr. Pantuzzi ignored the boy.

Mrs. Pantuzzi was walking back and forth in the kitchen now, wearing her new bathrobe and singing Christmas carols. Her generous rump could be seen crossing back and forth between the stove and the refrigerator, the terry cloth stretched to its limit. Erno's sisters played quietly with all their Barbies, new and old, on the floor in front of the Christmas tree. The front door, still wide open in anticipation of the young marksman's first shot, let in a blast of bitter December air. The branches on the Pantuzzi Christmas tree, shaking ever to slightly, bounced the ornaments and the tinsel blew back and got tangled on neighboring branches.

Suddenly, aware her feet were turning blue, Mrs. Pantuzzi appeared at the kitchen doorway. Her arms were crossed under her bosom in the traditional maternal sign of feeling cold, and she asked, "Who opened the door? It's freezing. Erno, dear, close it now." She turned and went back to the bacon and eggs sizzling in the cast iron frying pan.

Little Erno continued to sit next to his dad, arms outstretched, quietly repeating the question, "Dad, can I have a turn? Please, Dad, can I try it now?"

By now Mr. Pantuzzi had turned his attention to Mrs. Pantuzzi's rump. No one told the men in the Pantuzzi household what to do. And this would be a good excuse to pop her. As he sighted her right gluteus maximus—the size of a small watermelon—he chuckled once and said to Erno, "Hey, watch this."

Erno knew what was about to happen. He would remember his father whispering "Pop. Pop. Pop," just before he pulled the trigger.

POP. The metallic popping noise filled Erno's ears. He looked toward the kitchen. *Holy shit.* Immediately there was a scream and a loud clang as the heavy frying pan banged to the kitchen floor. Mrs. Pantuzzi grabbed her buttock as she tried to jump out of the way of the splattering grease.

Mr. Pantuzzi laughed. He tipped the Daisy Model 25 toward the ceiling and blew gently across the muzzle, western style. What was great about being a male in the Pantuzzi household, never mind that it was the Seventies, was that the females did all the domestic chores. Wyatt Earp made no effort to get up and clean up the scalding mess. He sat on the couch and laughed. That's when Mrs. Pantuzzi hopped out of the kitchen and realized she'd been shot. She was crying. "What the hell is wrong with you? Erno, shut the goddamn door like I asked you."

She came across the room with a fire in her eyes. A

hundred eighty pounds of Italian fury wanted to kill her husband with her bare hands.

Mr. Pantuzzi dropped the gun and stood up just as his wife, both arms extended, reached him. Like the neighborhood bully he'd always been, he grabbed both of her forearms and held them in his massive hands. The harder he laughed the more she sobbed.

"Let go of me, you dumb bastard!" his mother screamed at his father. His sisters hid behind the tree. Erno picked up his Daisy Model 25, still wearing his pajamas and leatherette slippers, and closed the front door behind him as he stepped out onto the small stoop and started to cry.

For some reason that's what Erno was thinking about when he walked into the apartment building that morning. Already a warm day, Erno wore a light leather jacket and was sweating. The heat and sweat must have activated his sweet after shave and he positively reeked.

It was a nondescript building near where Erno grew up, three stories, the ground floor windows boarded up. A sign on the elevator said "Broke" and Erno took the stairs, two at a time for a single flight, and quickly slowed down to single steps for the remaining one. The walls were a dark brown, camouflaging years of grime, and a series of sixty-watt bulbs enhanced the gloom of the building. Suddenly he heard the faint cry of a baby. And the drone of a TV. He was breathing hard; his wheezy breath sounded like the bray of a donkey, echoing back, reminding him how out of shape he'd let himself become.

Apartment 3G. The white gluey remains of long-ago removed stickers decorated the brown door, probably not the original one. It was poorly held in the jamb and had half an inch of play to it. Erno grabbed the knob and shook the door noisily back and forth. Music, muffled to obscurity, filtered through the door, and it was more than a minute before he heard footsteps.

"Yeah." A voice on the other side of the door.

"Open up, Poldy. It's me." *Poldy.* Leopold, actually. Poldy was one of those dread nicknames that wasn't shed at puberty. Poldy Escobar.

Two deadbolts were unlocked loudly, and the door opened several inches, still protected by a chain. The pungent smell of marijuana leaked out. Two sleepy eyes blinked in the darkness. "Hey, Erno." He was stoned and didn't remember he had an appointment.

"C'mon, Poldy, open up." Erno looked down the short hallway. A cat, skinny and hungry, picked at a white garbage bag left on the floor; otherwise the third floor was vacant.

The door opened and Erno stepped inside. After he took in three or four quick sniffs he wished he hadn't. Stale weed. Not until the door banged closed and the deadbolts were secured did Poldy turn to greet Erno. He wore an undershirt and blue jeans, no shoes or socks, a poorly trimmed goatee and the stench of body odor. One of those homemade tattoos, a lopsided cross, adorned his right bicep. "Erno, what brings you here, my man?" he said, with a Spanish accent that always became more exaggerated as he got high. He put out his balled up fist and Erno returned the greeting by taking his own fist and clicking knuckles like a couple of beer mugs.

"Why the fuck are you stoned, Poldy?"

"Why the fuck are you always straight, Ernu?" He laughed at his mispronunciation.

"Don't you 'member I called? I need a piece, man," Erno said.

Poldy kept his fist out and popped out his first two fingers in a peace sign. He laughed at his own visual comedy. "You want a beer?"

"No. No beer. No weed. No jokes. Just a piece."

"You seem pretty uptight, man. Maybe what you really need is a nice piece of ass. Sit down, sit down," Poldy said, his hands always in motion. "Take a load off, Erno, let me get the box of stuff.'' Poldy walked off to the bedroom.

"Hey, Poldy, you been printed, right?"

"More'n I been laid," he yelled from the bedroom.

"They lift a print from something in one city, they have a way to check it in another?"

"What the fuck do you think they have computers for?"

"Yeah, that's what I thought. Fuckin' computers."

The living room was filthy. And hot. Erno took out a wad of Kleenex and mopped his brow and neck, leaving tiny pieces of white tissue stuck to his wet face. A pizza crust peeked out from under a stained sofa which sat in the middle of the room. Greasy waxed paper, the kind that lines a pizza box, was stuck to an armrest like a doily in an elegant sitting parlor. Other than a wobbly coffee table, there was no other furniture.

Erno wisely decided not to sit down. Instead, he looked at the TV and listened as Regis told Kathy Lee about his vacation. *Why the hell is he watching this crap?* No fan or air conditioning. Just a couple of double-hungs, opened wide, with shades pulled halfway down, slapping noisily against the windows as an occasional breeze lifted them for a refreshing moment before disappearing and dropping them loudly.

"All right Erno, feast your eyes," Poldy said as he carried a large cardboard box into the room and placed it on the coffee table in front of the TV. "Man, it's hot for September. Why'nt you take off the leather, Erno?"

With the precise movements of a junkie trying hard not to look stoned, Poldy spread out a light green bath towel, carefully and slowly, almost like a jeweler laying out a fine piece of black velvet to highlight his sparkling diamonds. Poldy sat down on the edge of the sofa, his butt using no more than six inches of cushion, and began taking an impressive assortment of handguns out of the box. Many were wrapped in oily rags. Each was placed on the towel. When he was done, Poldy straightened several of the pieces and completed his demonstration by stacking half a dozen boxes of ammunition off to one side.

Erno had something specific in mind. Twelve guns were displayed. All were semi-automatic weapons, some new, none more than twenty years old. Poldy removed the cardboard box from the table and placed it on the floor.

Thump. The sound of one final weapon banging against the side of the box caught Erno's attention. A Harrington and Richardson, .38 caliber.

A Saturday-Night Special.

"What's this?" Erno said, as he bent over and picked up the small weapon. Not even a pound of metal, it looked like a child's toy in his hand.

"That's a piece of crap. Are you crazy, man? That's a fuckin' Suicide Special. No power. I should throw the fucker away."

Right arm fully extended, Erno was sighting Regis Philbin, and as he squeezed off an imaginary round, he jerked his hand upward in an exaggerated recoil. Then he held it in both hands and studied it. It was old and rusty. But wasn't that supposed to be its appeal? Sloppy.

A Saturday-Night Special was the perfect weapon. Although tens of thousands of cheap pistols were manufactured in the early 1900s and sold for a gentleman's protection on his Saturday night excursions, Erno thought they were so named because you could purchase one quickly to kill someone on a Saturday night. Now you could pick one up at a garage sale.

If your next-door neighbor needed elimination, why buy a registered gun? Why endure the state-mandated waiting period? Just rummage around the attic. The choice of the nonprofessional.

Erno squeezed the trigger. It had a cogwheel feel. Jerky. "It needs some three-in-one, Poldy."

"Why do you want that gun? I mean, a man in your line of work . . . well . . . you need something with some muscle. Who you gonna do?"

Erno gave Poldy a hard stare, like a character out of an Elmore Leonard novel. "Don't ask what you don't want to know."

"Yeah, well, as your personal gun expert I don't want to see you buy the wrong piece, Erno."

Erno looked out the window. He was tired. Mr. Bevel's voice replayed in his mind. Some noisy kids ran by on the crowded street below. Resigned to the fact that this was his last job and he would never see Poldy again, Erno turned around and said, "Look, I'm doing a job, and I don't want it to look like a hit. Get it? So I want something . . . sloppy."

"Look, Erno. If that's what you want, gimme ten bucks. But I wouldn't use it. If that barrel's rusty it'll go up in your hand." Poldy picked up a Browning Hi-Power. Solid black. Forty ounces. "Take a feel of this, Erno. This is a fuckin' gun. Brand new. Thirteen-round clip. A lot more bang."

Erno accepted the gun. It fit comfortably in his right hand. He liked the heft. This was a serious weapon. The side-by-side comparison was striking. Harrington and Richardson. Browning. Harrington and Richardson. Browning. If the hit on Dr. Antony was to be his last in Pittsburgh, it was going to be done correctly. Putting a bullet or two off mark was acceptable. Using an unreliable weapon was not.

Poldy was lighting a joint. Once he saw how comfortable Erno was with the Browning he had a reason to celebrate. Between draws on the reefer Poldy started his sales pitch. "Those are five and a quarter new. Picked that one up last week—it's never been shot, smell it. It's clean. Gimme," Eddie pause for effect, "Gimme two bills."

"What are you figuring? Two bills. I'm not some junkie running crack you can take advantage of." Erno smelled the weapon. It smelled like the Christmas he'd never forget. "I'll give you a hunnerd bucks."

"That's a new gun, Erno. Absolutely clean—"

"Buck and a half. Otherwise I walk."

Poldy traced his goatee with his thumb and forefinger, starting below his nose, encircling his mouth and down to his chin, where he pulled on his scraggly whiskers. Before he finally agreed to the transaction he repeated this half a dozen times.

"Hey, Poldy, why you trying to grow something on your chin grows wild on your ass?" Erno laughed.

"Okay. Buck and a half. You got the money wit' you, right?"

Erno placed the Browning on the table and produced a thick wad of new bills tightly wrapped in a rubber band. In one slick move he snapped the rubber band off the money and onto his own wrist like a cheap bracelet. A quick lick of his thumb and he was ready to start counting.

"Oh yeah, one more thing," he said, almost as an after-thought. "I want you to silence it."

"Oooooo. Big time. That's gonna cost you, man. Five bills."

"What?" Erno said, his voice surprised. "The gun's one-fifty, a little silencer is five hunnerd?"

"Man, I get caught with a box of guns, the PD gets me walking the same day. A silencer—no way, no fuckin' way. I do hard time for a silencer. I got responsibilities. You gotta make it worth my while."

"I'll give you three bills, Poldy."

"Four. Look, Erno, me'n you go back a long way. But I can't do no hard time. You don't want to pay me, fine—"

The last thing Erno wanted to hear was a speech. "Okay. Okay. How long?"

"Couple a weeks."

"Couple a weeks? Man, I need it this week. Couple a weeks, shit."

Poldy had a box of 9mm ammo in his hand. He removed the clip from the Browning and fumbled loading the bullets. "Then you get it without a silencer. Guy I know with a machine shop. Has to put the threads on the barrel. He's busy. You want to drop some serious dough, then maybe he can rearrange—''

Erno was irritated at the explanation, but watched closely as Poldy slid each bullet into the clip. It was reassuring the way Poldy's fingers weren't working smoothly, and the stoned businessman dropped a couple of bullets in his lap and had to fish them out with his bony fingers. ''Forget it. Just gimme the gun. What are they, 9mm?''

Poldy held one up, rolled the shiny brass shell between his thumb and first finger. ''Beauties, huh? I betcha this is that one that does the guy, huh, Erno?''

Three crisp fifties were peeled from the wad, squeezed and excessively wrinkled lest an extra bill be included as a generous tip, and thrown on the table. Erno picked up the Browning Hi-Power and grabbed the loaded clip from Poldy. Never mind he was angry that the gun wasn't going to have a silencer. He'd bought a gun. A new gun. He was in tachycardia heaven and it felt great.

There was someone else in the room. All of a sudden *there was someone else in the room.* Erno spotted her as she walked in from the short hallway that led to the bedroom. Early twenties, he estimated, and pregnant. He figured she could have been pretty if she didn't have so many pimples. And if she wasn't knocked up.

''Who the fuck is that?'' Erno was shouting.

''Gina. We're gonna have a baby.''

''What the hell's she doing here? We're doing business, man. I'm talking a deal wit' you.''

Gina wore a soiled maternity T-shirt that said BABY UNDER CONSTRUCTION with an arrow pointing down to her belly. She walked slowly, one hand on her belly, and sat next to Poldy.

''She shouldn't be here, Poldy. And you sure-as-shit shouldn't of asked me what I was gonna do wit' the gun.'' Erno towered over the couple.

''She lives here, *man,*'' Poldy said, and pronounced the

word "man" with a dollop of sarcasm. This, of course, made a mildly tense situation worse.

"You're walking the line, Poldy. You're walking the goddamn line. You shoulda sent her out for coffee. I don't like no one knowing my business."

Poldy was talking loud, wildly using his arms. "Look Erno, Gina don't speak no English. She's Puerto Rican. Only Español." He said this last word with a heavy Spanish accent.

"Oh yeah? Get her to talk."

Poldy turned to Gina, paused for a hard swallow, and said something in Spanish. Gina said, "Sí." After a few seconds Poldy urged her on by making circular motions in the air with his right hand. Spanish charades. Soon Gina began babbling away.

"See, Erno. She's talking Spanish."

"Big fucking deal. She speaks Spanish. How the fuck do I know she don't speak English?"

"I told you, man, she don't!"

"You've gotten sloppy. No way your old lady should be hanging around. She goddamn better not understand English!"

"No way, man. I told you. She only speaks Spanish."

"We'll see. You don't mind if I give Gina a little test, do you?"

Poldy shook his head. "Do what you want, man. She only speaks Spanish."

"If you're lying, Poldy, you gotta share your little enchilada here. I mean I'm gonna do her right now, in front of you. Rip her fuckin' clothes off, then screw her and see if your baby'll give me a blow job."

"Jesus Christ, Erno, what the hell is wrong with you? Don't you have no respect? Man!" Poldy started to stand until Erno waved the Browning at him.

Gina didn't say a word. Poldy put his arm around his woman. He thought about grabbing a gun, but he knew that Erno knew they were all empty.

The next move would have to come from Erno, and he didn't disappoint. He slipped the clip into the grip of the pistol, and smacked it into position, hard, with the palm of his hand. The loud click made Gina jump.

"Okay, so she don't speak no English. That don't matter no more. I don't trust you, you doper." The Browning was in Erno's hand, aimed nowhere in particular. What he did next, however, scared Poldy more than looking down the barrel of a loaded semiautomatic. Erno turned up the TV. Loud. Loud so the plastic box surrounding the picture tube vibrated with the voices. Loud so that Regis was now screaming at Kathy Lee, something about Gelman's garden.

Without a silencer on the gun Poldy knew there was only one reason Erno wanted the volume so loud.

Poldy swallowed hard. "Hey, man, we go back. What's the big deal? You *know* me, Erno."

"That's right—I know you, but I don't know her. And I don't like other people knowing my business, *and you know that.* The only reason we go back is you always been a loner! Why the hell'd you get involved with *her.*" Erno was furious. Spittle flew out of his mouth as he yelled and landed on Gina's knee. His voice had the tone of a schoolyard bully about to throw a punch.

It was working. Gina was trembling, starting to cry, and clutching Poldy.

"Don't shoot her, Erno. Don't do it. She's got my baby. Please, I forgot you were coming. I'd never cross you, Erno. We go way back. You know I'd never—"

Erno leaned over the coffee table and his eyes grabbed Poldy's. "Now it's my turn to talk, so shut the fuck up, you pothead." Not even Regis, volume turned all the way up, could compete with Erno.

He was getting the feeling. The one he'd had so many times before. Auto-drive. First the confusion. Then the breathing, harder and harder. *Stop it. Stop it.* He could hear the pulse in his neck. *I can't trust her. A fuckin' loose end.* He didn't want to do it. *Pop. Pop. Pop.* He was fighting to keep himself under control. It was easy to flash back to his childhood and see Poldy. A big head. Poldy always seemed to have a big head. *What the fuck is going on?*

A voice was screaming in his car. Not Regis, but a dark voice that said, "Kill them. Kill them." *Pop. Pop. Pop.*

Erno never walked away from a situation, and this was a situation. But it was Poldy. *I grew up with the guy, for Chrissakes.* He had to get control. *Talk to them. Say something.*

"You listen to me, Poldy, and you listen good. You keep talking about how you'n me go back, well if you'n me *didn't* go back, I'da pulled the trigger already. I'm gonna give your baby a little present. I'm gonna walk outta here. That's right, no one gets hurt. But if you or your little mama here talks, I'm comin' back. And I won't touch either of you. But I'll kill your kid. And I'll do it right in front of you. Let you both watch."

Gina let out a little gasp and placed both hands on her belly. "Get the hell away from us, you . . . you . . ." she screamed between sobs.

"You lying bastard." Erno brought the pistol up and aimed it directly at Poldy's big head. As he squeezed the trigger he jerked to the left and put a bullet into the sofa, right over Gina's shoulder. She screamed and ran from the room.

Erno aimed the gun again at Poldy. "You're way over the line. Can you see the white light? It's coming to get you."

Poldy spoke in a hoarse whisper, "I promise you, she won't talk." Then he buried his face in his hands and started to cry.

Erno reached behind his back, slipped the gun up under his leather jacket and tucked it inside his pants. He turned the TV down, watched for a second, then flicked it off. "Fuckin' crap. Regis Philbin."

Erno walked to the door, opened it, and turned back to Poldy. He hesitated, controlled the tone of his voice, and said, "Hey, Poldy, congratulations."

After he left, after he slammed the door, after he scared the living hell out of Gina and Poldy, Gina's water broke.

She would not know the joy of motherhood for another two years.

Twenty-eight

September 26, 1996

Erno walked out of the Medical Center parking garage—
the parking garage—around ten after seven. Not yet dark,
but with the buildings blocking most of the sky the cars
had on their headlights. It was early, too early to go up
to the ninth floor, so Erno took a seat in the coffee shop—
the coffee shop—the one with the view of the truncated
maple sapling. When the coffee and sandwich came Erno
didn't try any bullshit with the waitress, even though she
had that teased-up-hair look. He was thinking about Satch
and whether he could trust Einstein. *Einstein. Stupid
sonavabitch.*

His leather jacket wasn't sitting right. He was starting
to smell like a potato. And pulling the right side of his
lopsided coat forward every couple of minutes was driving
him crazy.

Erno had stopped by the Giant Eagle supermarket mid-
afternoon to buy a potato. One Baking Potato. In his black
leather jacket, shiny polyester pants, and cheap Italian
boots Erno caught more than a few glances as he passed
by the new potatoes and the red potatoes, touching some
of them as he walked. The produce boy watched as Erno
handled more than a dozen Idahoes until he seemed satisfied. It was a huge one, almost perfect in shape, at least
six inches long. He paid for it with a buck, refused the
small bag the checkout girl offered, and slipped it into the

side pocket of his jacket as she pocketed a thirty-seven cent tip. He might not be traveling light, but he'd make damn sure no loose change would be rattling in his pocket. More than one person watched as Erno walked out of the store sporting a ridiculous bulge in the leather, the potato bouncing off his right hip, keeping cadence as he headed to his car.

While he drove to meet Einstein, the potato, still in his pocket but resting on the seat, pulled his jacket open, exposing his gut. Keeping his right elbow flush on his ribs made him look like a stroke victim, but it was better than having the jacket flop open every time he made a turn.

Twenty minutes later he was checking out the dummy. And Einstein was really pissing him off.

"All right, Einstein. Listen up." Erno and Einstein were working together, alone, in a garage Antony rented on the South Side, far away from Mr. Bevel's Strip district office. The panel truck with the PITTSBURGH UNIVERSITY MEDICAL CENTER magnetic lettering that could be removed in two seconds was parked off to one side. Under the shelves, holding an impressive array of stolen license plates, the stretcher waited. Erno was restuffing some old bluejeans with newspaper while Einstein readied a button-down plaid shirt. It looked like the preparations for a Halloween party. "Here's what you gotta do. Ya gotta think. Everything matters. Like the labels, it all matters. Okay, now at ten o'clock you drive the truck where I showed you. Back it in, take it slow. Don't be in no rush. When you get to the loading dock, turn the lights off. Roll the stretcher onto the dock. There's a light."

Einstein was turning his head back and forth focusing his attention between Erno's instructions and pushing balled up sections of a local newspaper into the shirt-sleeves. Finally Erno assembled the lopsided man in the open body bag and zipped it up. Then, straightening the bag on the stretcher, he fastened the safety strap securely but not so tight as to squash the scarecrow.

"You've got to remember the code: 5-7-3-4," Erno continued.

Einstein looked at him, genuinely confused. "What code?"

"For the elevator, you idiot. I got an idea. Why don't *you* go in the fuckin' bag. I think you're already brain dead."

Einstein nodded. "Funny, real funny."

Erno fished in his pocket and pulled out a ballpoint pen. "Here, write it on your hand. 5-7-3-4." Erno watched as Einstein started to write on his palm, but the ink didn't flow. He scribbled a series of circles and lines on his skin until a thick blue smear of ink flowed onto his hand, giving him that preschool look. "Five. Seven. Three. Four," Erno spoke slowly and made certain the numbers were written clearly.

They stowed the stretcher in the panel truck and slammed the double doors. The garage was musty—smelled more like a basement—and had stacks and stacks of old newspapers and magazines tied up in bundles. A sprinkling of confetti—those little rectangular mailing labels—littered the floor. Erno brushed several under the truck with his foot. He'd given Einstein one simple assignment, and he'd blown it.

Everything had to be redone.

Satch would've taken off the stupid mailing labels.

"Anyway, take the elevator up to nine. That's the only other floor it stops at, so you don't have to write it down. When you get to nine roll off our stretcher and pull the one that'll be waiting onto the elevator. Go back to the truck but—hey, are you listening or going to sleep?—*Don't take the fucking stretcher off the elevator*. Leave it, get in the truck, and come back here. Okay? Drop off *our* stretcher, roll the one waiting *onto* the elevator, but *don't take it off and load it onto the truck*. And Einstein, drive around, make sure you're not followed or nuttin'. You got it?" Erno shoved his hands, filthy with newsprint, into his pockets and pulled out the Idaho and a switchblade. A push of the button, the swish of the blade, and Erno proceeded to carve out a sizable plug from one end of the potato.

"What the hell are you doing?" Einstein asked.

"Breaking the law. You don't want to know." Erno used the blade as a lever, popping the cone-shaped piece of potato up into the air. Both men watched it fall silently to the floor.

"Ooooh. Call the police. Someone's carving a chunk a potato. Arrest this man. What are you gonna do next, deep fry it?" Einstein laughed.

"Well, Carmine, that's a good example of why you're running errands for Mr. Bevel and screwing up stuffing the dummy. You haven't learned jack shit. Now, you got the plan, or what?"

"Yeah. Yeah. I got it. I got it the last two times you told it to me, Erno. And I know how to use the cell phone, and if you call before ten I turn around and go back. I got it. I got it. I got it. Look Erno, you don't think I'm smart enough, get someone else. But Mr. Bevel told you I'm the man."

Erno held the spud in one hand and slowly burrowed the knife into the conical cavity with a spiral, drilling motion. Small bits of potato worked their way out of the deepening shaft like wood shavings around a drill bit. When the six-inch blade was buried halfway into the potato Erno stopped and slipped his thumb inside to size it. As he wiped the knife clean on an old rag, he said, "It's my ass in that hospital, Einstein. I'm the one with the gun."

Einstein pulled the cellular phone out of the pocket of his deliveryman's jacket. "How 'bout I call Mr. Bevel and you tell him you want somebody else?"

"How 'bout you shut the fuck up, *Carmine*," Erno said and gave his partner-for-a-night a shove on the chest before walking out of the garage.

*   *   *

Erno was still pissed at Einstein when his second cup of coffee arrived, along with a piece of pie. That's all he could think about. He couldn't even remember what kind of sandwich he'd just eaten. The coffee shop was packed with students, but Erno was alone, running the plan over and over again. Always a man of action, these quiet moments before a job were difficult.

Not having Satch to talk to was killing him.

An hour in a coffee shop tested the capacity of anyone's bladder, and before leaving he spent one totally peaceful minute at the urinal. On the way out, paying his tab, telling the girl to keep the change, he said, "Toothpick?"

She slid a heavily fingerprinted stainless-steel dispenser across the counter; he grabbed one and popped it in his mouth. By the time he was on the street, trekking up the hill to the Medical Center, his heart was beating hard. The walk would do him good, maybe clear Einstein from his brain.

Going through the hospital was programmed. Twice the route had been rehearsed. It took Erno, wearing his lumpy leather jacket, past the information booth, past the gift shop, to the main bank of elevators. Erno knew he'd stick out more in the medical school and so chose to wind his way through the hospital as much as possible. Up to the ninth floor, a right past the med-surg nursing station, and a long walk past patient rooms lining both sides of the long corridor. The smell was awful. Chemotherapy and urine.

Finally he went around a corner, where it started to get darker, past the solarium. At the end of a second long hallway waited the heavy metal fire door that separated the hospital from the medical school. While he caught his breath and made certain no one had followed him, Erno thought through each step of his plan one more time.

He pushed on the metal bar of the door with gradually increasing pressure until the mechanism clicked softly. As the door eased open, his fingers found the spring latch, that little wedge of metal that pokes out the edge of the door like a mouse in a cubby. It pushed back easily into its housing, and after plucking the toothpick from his mouth, Erno forced the wooden sliver into the small crack of space surrounding the metal latch. It jammed in half an inch, freezing the movement of the spring latch. The mouse's head was gone. Erno snapped off the rest of the toothpick, entered the medical school, and closed the door silently.

New to old. The hospital was constantly being refurbished, what with keeping up with Allegheny General and Mercy. The Pittsburgh University Hospital, known by all as the Medical Center, looked like any modern facility, but the transition to the medical school was a different story. It was gloomy: thick layers of paint—no peeling, just thick layers—on plaster walls, brown linoleum floors, and ceilings with yellowed water stains. Every other globed light was dark.

The corridor looked right, the same way it always did when he made a delivery. Shadows everywhere. File cabinets. Boxes. An old stretcher, noticeably empty. Erno slipped into the shadows and stood absolutely still for several minutes. He rotated his senses and asked himself, "Hear anything? See anything?" Down the hall, thirty or forty feet, on the right, was *the* elevator. Directly across the hall from it, set in about a dozen feet, were the doors to the anatomy labs. No light shone on the floor between the elevator and the lab. Everything was right.

The watch on Erno's wrist read 8:39. An hour and twenty minutes until Einstein would arrive at the loading dock. Erno figured Dr. Antony would show no later than ten of the hour. Erno would wait; it was better to be early. He never wanted to arrive second. To walk in on a situation. Maybe tip someone off. When Erno did someone, he did it right.

All of a sudden it hit him. Dr. Antony would have to arrive *before* ten to get the stretcher ready. *Why the hell is Einstein delivering the dummy?* Dr. Antony had never been late with a delivery. He was reliable. The stretcher was always waiting, positioned at the same angle every time, making it easy to get one stretcher off and another on. Never a wait. Never a problem.

As far as he could tell, Dr. Antony would be by in the next hour or so, and everything would be over by the time the elevator doors opened with Einstein and the stuffed clothes. *Einstein'll panic, he'll fuckin' panic!* Erno's mind raced as he saw the scenario play out: Einstein, both hands frozen to the stretcher, gawking at the body, standing there like an idiot when the police arrived. He'd talk, talk his guts out. Name names—not Mr. Bevel, of course—but Erno would be the man. Wanted.

He flipped his cellular phone open; the keypad lighted automatically. His fat fingers punched at the numbers, hitting two or three at a time. Twice he dialed before he got it right. It rang more than a dozen times. Finally Einstein's voice, talking loud over the street noises, "Hello. Is that you, Erno?"

"Forget it, go home," Erno said in a quiet, controlled voice. No cute stuff.

"Why? What's wrong?"

Asshole. "Go home, Einstein. Go home." Still the quiet, controlled voice. He snapped the phone shut and ended the possibility of a series of stupid questions. Ended the possibility he'd blow his cool. Later, maybe, in the morning, he'd say to Einstein, "Why? What's wrong? You dumb fuck." And pop him one in the mouth. Erno smiled.

A men's room, on the near side of the elevator, was the best spot. Erno had stopped there to relieve himself during one of his dry runs, checked out the view, and planned to wait in the darkness of the doorway. It wasn't perfect. Standing a step into the bathroom would constrict his view so he wouldn't actually see the elevator doors or the anatomy labs directly, but he'd know when Dr. Antony arrived.

Erno, the potato in his right pocket, the Browning Hi-Power in a holster tucked inside the back of his pants, walked among the shadows and quickly pushed open the door marked MEN. It smelled good, like pine trees.

There was no squeaky hinge; Erno had made sure of that. He pulled out a small square of cardboard, wadded it up in a crude wedge, and stuffed it under the door. The makeshift stop worked, and Erno stood in near-total darkness looking out into the lonely corridor.

Dr. Antony could approach from a variety of directions. Erno carefully reviewed the possibilities. The fire door to the left, although now equipped with a silenced spring latch, would make more than enough noise when the push bar was depressed. The elevator to the right had that distinctive whine of the motor, and if Dr. Antony entered from the medical school elevators at the other end of the corridor he would momentarily have to cross Erno's field of vision to get to the anatomy labs.

He was set.

Sweet Loretta's was becoming their place. At least that's what each of them thought as Merlin and Tory walked into the bar for the third time in four days and almost bumped into Martin Wheeler. Always well dressed, jacket and rep tie, he was leaving alone. "Hey, what're you two doing here?" Wheeler said as he stepped aside.

"We came to spy on your conversation, but as usual I see you dined solo, so . . . maybe we'll just get a bite to eat," Merlin answered. Tory already had her fill of Dr. Martin Wheeler and chose only to nod hello.

"What about the big sting?"

"What are you talking about?" Merlin said, looking at Tory, surprised that the word was out.

"Look, I know. Catching Dr. Antony and the guy who delivers the bodies," Wheeler said in a hushed tone.

"Dr. Wheeler, how do you know about it?"

"Banks told me," he said proudly. "I've got my

sources. Anyway, isn't tonight your big night?'' Wheeler said, looking at his Rolex, ''In about an hour?''

''No it's *tomorrow* night, so please be discreet,'' Tory requested.

''You'd better inform the rest of your team.''

''Wait a second, Wheeler. What the hell's going on? What do you know?'' Merlin asked.

''All I know is I just ate dinner with Mark Peters and that reporter—''

''How do you know Mark Peters?'' Tory wanted to know.

''He didn't tell you?''

''Tell me what?''

''The H-Y-P Club,'' Wheeler said using the same tone of voice he used when answering the not-often-enough-asked question, ''What clubs does your family belong to?'' ''We're both Princeton. You didn't know?''

''I don't believe this. What a setup.'' Tory hit herself in the forehead. ''Oh God, I'm such a jerk. Are you absolutely certain Peters said *tonight*?''

''Hey, don't cross-examine me, Counselor. It's *tonight*.''

Tory looked at Merlin. ''I'd like to kill him.''

Merlin checked his watch. ''It's after nine. Let's get up there.''

As the two crossed the street toward the Medical Center, Wheeler took a few moments to repack his pipe.

Erno's eyes had grown accustomed to the dark. He stood back on his heels, let his gut hang out, and bent his neck slightly to the left. The stance. Cops use it on parade duty, at ease. Long ago he'd gotten good at the stance. He could wait forever if he had to.

The Browning Hi-Power slid smoothly from the small leather holster, but the potato wanted to stay in the leather jacket and had to be wiggled free of the silky material in the pocket. He'd gauged the diameter of the short barrel accurately, and it easily slid several inches into the homemade silencer. The gun no longer was balanced; Erno would have to steady the spud with his left hand like he was holding a medium-sized automatic. The pistol was held chest high, elbows flexed, and he practiced pivoting his body from side to side, taking aim at a variety of objects in the hallway. Not very accurate. Erno would have to work in real close.

The feeling was starting. Good. The pounding in his head, the faster breathing. No indecision, no confusion this time. The lighting was fine. There was no reason to see his victim; he wouldn't recognize him anyway. *Pop. Pop. Pop.* He heard the words in his mind louder and louder. It was impossible to turn them off.

Footsteps. Definitely. Hard leather-soled footsteps. Erno stopped breathing. Then he saw the figure, a dark silhouette of a man coming *out* of the anatomy labs. The dark anatomy labs. He was sure of that. He hadn't considered Dr. Antony might have beaten him. The figure stopped momentarily, looked about. His hands were empty. No doubt about it, this was the guy. Dr. Antony looked about, looked toward the bathroom doorway, *and started to walk toward Erno.* Not menacingly, like "I know you're there and I'm still coming," but regular walking. Like he needed to take a piss. The guy was headed for the bathroom, and as he approached, Erno got his first glimpse of the man. He was wearing a suit and tie. Glasses. All dolled up.

When Dr. Antony was a dozen feet from the men's room he stopped in midstep, as if he noticed Erno standing in the doorway, holding something. He just stood there for a second and was starting to turn around when the first bullet caught him in the shoulder. The bang from the weapon was muted, sounding like a champagne bottle being opened under a cloth napkin. Erno pulled the trigger three more times as Dr. Antony was spun around, hitting him in the chest and neck. None of the 9mm bullets missed their mark. Two of the hits were through-and-through, smacking the wall and splintering a hole in the paint, leaving a white pockmark of plaster. It was too dark to see the spray of blood trailing the bullets, but Erno knew what he was missing. Each squeeze of the trigger was accompanied by a louder and louder report as an expanding hole was ripped through the potato. The four casings ejected to the right, bounced off the wooden bathroom door, and clicked noisily off the floor. The man went down, never made a sound.

Erno put a fifth and a sixth bullet in the filing cabinets and rattled them wildly. The metallic clanging somehow sounded right after the gunshots. Then he dropped the silencer, wiped down the Browning, and made his exit. He flipped the gun in a trash bin half a block from the Medical Center and never even heard the girl scream. In fact, he was in his car and driving out of Oakland before he realized the sirens hadn't even started.

But the police were *already* in the building, patiently waiting for Erno. Tightly sequestered on the eighth floor, just as Tory and Peters had planned, but a full twenty-four hours early. Half a dozen of them, waiting in a small office for the walkie-talkie signal, drinking coffee and doughnuts that Peters bought. This was a simple sting and Mark Peters had been blinded by the glare of the spotlights he could see in his future. *Tory, where the hell were you? I said THURSDAY night. You weren't listening. The boss isn't gonna like this.* That would work.

He wanted to surprise them, catch them exchanging the bodies, put a gun on them and use the walkie-talkie. And doing it in front of Sandy Keller bordered on the— well—sexual.

Once he secured his pistol in the shoulder holster he felt invincible. The .38 Smith and Wesson snub-nose—the Chief's Special—had only been fired once. The guy at the gun store showed him two versions of the gun, stainless steel and blued steel, and told him the stainless steel required less maintenance. Then the guy said blued steel was more discreet in a Bond—James Bond—sort of way and Peters didn't really have much of a decision to make. That night he even put on his tux, stood in front of the mirror, and said, "My name is Peters. Mark Peters."

Any cop would have marked him for a funzie; the blued-steel barrel was way too clean, no fingerprints or tarnish, like it just came out of the box. If you meant business when you carried the .38 caliber S&W, you chose the stainless-steel model. It looked better with less work. The blued steel was nothing more than a designer color to Mark Peters.

That night he and Sandy ate at Sweet Loretta's with Wheeler. Peters had one celebratory beer and about three Diet Cokes. In the excitement he'd put off the urge for a while. After they had been sitting around the gross anatomy lab for about an hour, whispering in the dark, Peters finally had to go to the restroom.

When Sandy heard the popping noise in the hall she fumbled with the buttons on the walkie-talkie. "Help, I hear gunshots. Come up now!" she screamed. Her manicured fingers pressed the wrong button, and she changed channels four times, screaming desperately for help. Sandy waited another minute, more than enough time for six overweight cops to lumber up the stairs, ventured out of the dark anatomy lab, saw Mark Peters on the floor, and fainted.

Tory and Merlin never noticed Jake Barnhouse watching them from across the street, or the man in the leather jacket who held the door for them as they dashed into the hospital.

Then they raced through the first-floor corridor and up the elevator, and crossed into the medical school on the eighth floor, mindful not to disrupt the sting in progress. Out of breath and talking way too fast, Tory and Merlin arrived as the cops finally got the mayday call from Sandy Keller and tore up the stairs.

By the time Jake Barnhouse sauntered halfway around the hospital, he had a good idea what was happening. He had an excellent view of the ninth floor of the medical school. And it was just a matter of minutes before all the lights went on.

Something had been wrong with the whole setup, he thought. The idea of a delivery when the labs were under surveillance was ridiculous, and then there was the peculiar way the phone call had been routed through the operator.

He breathed a sigh of relief, lit a cigarette, and went home.

The puddle of blood had grown. Wall-to-wall blood, almost black against the dark floor, reflected little pinpoints of light off the shiny surface like stars in the night sky. Mark Peters seemed to be floating in the middle, about six feet from Sandy Keller, who had also become enveloped by an amoebae-like pseudopod of dark blood. For several frantic seconds it appeared that both were dead, but Sandy suddenly started to move and soon was hysterically flopping about in the blood, a huge fish caught in low tide.

When he heard who he'd killed—on the news at eleven—he didn't bother packing. Erno Pantuzzi was on the turnpike headed for Philly before midnight.

Twenty-nine

September 29, 1996

Tory was almost a regular in the fourteenth-floor residents' lounge. For three days, as the aftermath of the Mark Peters's tragedy ripped everyone's emotions to shreds, she'd caught up on paperwork in her office. Her nights were spent with Merlin, either in his apartment or his on-call room on fourteen. And the Medical Center buttoned itself up tightly, totally restricting access *from* the medical school back to the hospital except on the first floor.

Tory was wearing a gray pleated skirt and a dark blue ribbed cotton turtleneck under a light cotton tailored jacket when she arrived on fourteen carrying two brown paper bags. Merlin greeted her with a different look. In addition to the usual white pants and light blue scrub shirt, he wore a midlength white coat and looked impishly professorial. Merlin kissed her and mumbled something about how great she dressed and how he needed to class up a bit, which was why he wore the white jacket. And Tory thought it odd because Merlin couldn't care less how he looked.

The two sat at a round Formica table eating spicy General Tso's chicken brought from town and talked about everything but Kevin Hoover and Mark Peters. There was never a meeting of the minds *not* to talk about the murders, but each avoided the subject and instead enjoyed the glow in which new lovers find themselves.

The TV played in the background, tuned to KDKA in anticipation of Sandy Keller's next emotional update. It was getting close to the late news, and if three days constituted a ritual, then it had become a ritual for Merlin and Tory to watch the news together, silently, and retire to an hour or two of creative lovemaking.

"I'll do the dishes tonight," Merlin said, and in a smooth gesture swept the empty white cardboard cartons and paper plates into a large trash can. "You've got to-morrow night."

"That's fair," Tory said with sarcasm. "We alternate nights for dishes and you coordinate it with your on-call schedule so you get all the paper-plate nights."

"Then your problem is with Martin Wheeler, not me. He makes the on-call schedule. You vant I should call him?" Merlin said with a whiny Brooklyn Jewish accent that made Tory laugh.

The table was empty, except for their water glasses, and Merlin drained his in three final gulps before setting his eight-ounce tumbler back on the table. Then he cracked his knuckles and reached in the deep side pockets of his white jacket with both hands, fumbled around a bit, and finally pulled a purple silk the size of a man's handkerchief out of his right pocket.

"You ready to be dazzled?"

Tory smiled. The white jacket *was* worn for her, but only as a prop.

Merlin began to stuff the purple silk into his closed-fisted left hand. He moved woodenly, much less graceful than usual, and Tory wondered if this was a new trick he was practicing. For an instant, Merlin spread his fingers slightly, shifting his grip on the disappearing silk, exposing something white inside.

Tory's mouth curled up in a grin. She'd caught him—for the first time—and politely said nothing. But Merlin looked up at her, saw her eyes smile, and knew. He went on bravely, tightened up the fingers on his left hand, and the purple silk vanished completely into his balled-up fist.

"And now, I offer you . . ." Merlin opened his left hand showing, in place of the purple silk, a medium sized egg, ". . . breakfast."

"That's nice," Tory said, without much enthusiasm.

"Now you probably think the silk *turned* into the egg. Of course not. The egg appeared, magically—whatcha expect?—and the silk has returned, safely, to my pocket," Merlin said, and again reached into his right pocket, this time slowly—and a bit melodramatically—retrieving a purple silk. "Ta daa!"

"Very good," Tory said a bit flatly. She was disappointed and showed it in her tone, a bit more than she intended.

Merlin looked hurt and pushed the purple silk back into his pocket. "Want to see how it's done?"

"Since when do you tell?"

"Since I disappointed you; I can see it in your face. I don't perform this one usually; it's terrible," Merlin said earnestly.

Tory leaned forward, elbows on the table, her chin resting on her palms. "This is going to be good. Like going behind the scenes at Disneyland."

"First of all, the white coat's not mine. The ceramic egg makes my pants pocket bulge way too much."

"And I thought it was my tight sweater."

"*That* bulge is more midline," Merlin said, and slowly spun the egg in his left hand, showing a large oval hole in the back of the egg with a wisp of purple silk hanging out. "The egg is fake; maybe you guessed," Merlin continued, and banged the egg on the table loudly without cracking it. Then he pulled the silk out of the egg, held it also in his left hand, and revealed the hollow inside. "In my right pocket," Merlin continued, and reached back into his right pocket, this time pulling a matching purple silk out in a crumpled heap, "is a second silk. What do you think?'' Merlin asked and transferred the ceramic egg to his right hand before he restuffed the purple silk into the hole in back.

"I see why you don't like this one. It's not . . . I don't know . . . dazzling,'' Tory said, gently.

Tory watched as Merlin swept up the crumpled silk with his left hand and stuffed it into his left pocket so that only the egg, crammed tight with the original square of purple silk, remained in his hand.

"So let me ask you, Miss Welch, what would be dazzling? What does it take to dazzle you?''

Tory gave Merlin a long stare. A Mona Lisa smile slid across his face and vanished. She'd been had. The transformation, of course, had been imperceptible. A trick within a trick, like those Chinese dolls that fit inside one another. First he was a bumbling magician, blowing an easy illusion. Now he was in control, poised and graceful. It was suddenly hard to concentrate on the ceramic egg.

Tory smiled. "I can't even begin to guess what you have in store for me.''

"Well, if I could take a boring ol' ceramic egg and turn it into a real egg, how would that be? I mean what if I take this hole in the egg,'' Merlin said and peeled off a dark purple oval-shaped sticker on the egg, and stuck it on the table, "and removed it.''

Merlin then took the egg with one hand and gently cracked it on the edge of the table. Finally he emptied the gooey albumin and perfect yolk into the water glass. The trick had come full circle. "Would that dazzle you?'' Merlin asked and smiled broadly at Tory.

"Oh yeah, yes, *that* is a dazzler.'' Tory smiled so hard her eyes started to tear.

The bouncy theme from the eleven o'clock news filled the room.

It had been easy for Tory to forget what Mark Peters was really about. The newspapers lionized him, each trying to outdo the accolades of the others. If a reporter could track down his junior high school track coach for an interview, it became an exclusive.

At 11:04 Tory and Merlin settled on the plaid sofa and watched Sandy Keller do her penultimate tribute to the man. As she recounted Mark Peters's heroism for the last time, Sandy tearfully admitted that theirs had become a relationship that "transcended the depths of their professional boundaries."

Merlin summed things up succinctly. "Now there's a euphemism for you," he said with a chuckle, then going into a faux Walter Cronkite voice he continued, "And as hundreds of sailors left the confines of the all-male submarine, finally back in port after almost four months at sea, each hoped to meet a girl in a local tavern and transcend the depths of their professional boundaries."

"So that's why he was so desperate for any crumb of information. The whole thing was foreplay. What an asshole," Tory said, frowning.

The Medical Center, and more specifically the ninth floor of the medical school, had been scoured by the police. The Browning Hi-Power was recovered less than an hour after the hit on Mark Peters, but no fingerprints were recovered. Two of the bullet casings, however, had prints that were identified as belonging to Leopold Escobar. Less than twenty-four hours after Mark Peters was murdered, Poldy Escobar was arrested coming out of the Giant Eagle—the same Giant Eagle where Erno bought the potato—and he sat in jail, refusing to tell even his public defender who he sold the gun to.

More people in Pittsburgh knew Poldy's name than Mark Peters's.

Poldy was going down for the premeditated murder of a district attorney. He was more terrified than when Erno shot a bullet through his couch and caused Gina's water to break. The cell he occupied was set off from the others.

Poldy sat on the edge of his cot holding his stomach, rocking back and forth like a mental patient.

He went over his options. There were only two.

The second day one of the guards told Poldy he'd be very popular in prison, and Poldy thought the guard meant he'd get prison respect for killing a DA. Then the guard thrust his pelvis back and forth a couple of times and made a series of loud kissing sounds with his big lips and burst out laughing.

Doing time for killing a DA was hard to weigh against going back on the street. Erno would come looking for him. Fuckin' Erno. Every time the phone rang or there was a knock on the door it would be Erno. He'd never sleep all the way through to morning. And if not Erno, then someone else.

Poldy was so scared he became incontinent and wet his drawstring pants again and again until his cell smelled like the urinals at the bus station. Not about getting killed. That was part of it when you dealt in guns and drugs. What scared Poldy was that Erno would do unimaginable things to him that would make a bullet in the head something to beg for.

After a sleepless twenty-four hours, after hushed conversations with his court-appointed lawyer in case the room was bugged, the public defender finally approached the district attorney's office asking about the witness protection program. Word filtered down to Tory pretty quickly that organized crime was somehow involved.

And everyone forgot that even if organized crime had everything to do with the hit on Mark Peters, there still had to be someone on the inside. Someone working somewhere in the Medical Center.

Nothing more was ever made of her prints on the hood of the BMW, the police focusing their attention elsewhere in the Medical Center, and her connection with Satch Pantuzzi was never pursued.

Over and over Tory reviewed what she knew about Jake

Barnhouse and Dr. Olsen. Something was there, like in one of those computer-generated Magic Eye drawings, but Tory couldn't get it in focus.

The subject of police escort hadn't even come up within her department. And Merlin never mentioned it, either, Tory assumed, because the case had been commandeered by the police, and for the last three days the Medical Center looked like the police academy.

Beep-beep-beep. Beep-beep-beep. Beep-beep-beep. Merlin's beeper interrupted Tory's thoughts and brought her back to reality. Merlin's barrage of calls to scut duty continued and she was getting used to the frequent interruptions, but as a senior resident he also had to be involved in the more complicated problems of the hospital. "Dr. Merlin STAT to ER. Merlin STAT to ER. *Merlin!*" A female voice, with a sense of urgency, came through the micro-speaker in Merlin's beeper. The way she said "Merlin" the third time, Tory noticed, was different from the usual pages.

Merlin bolted for the door, grabbing Tory's hand, pulling her behind him. "Come on, walk down there with me. If it's nothing we'll come back and I'll reexamine your appendix scar. If it's a goodie you'll page Big John to walk you to your car."

As they waited for the elevator, Tory said, "I've got to finish this case."

"No, you don't. The police are handling it."

"The police are handling the Mark Peters murder investigation. Kevin Hoover's forgotten."

"The police can't offer you protection twenty-four hours a day. What if this thing was a mob hit? Suppose Kevin was involved. So what? Maybe I don't really want to know. At this point, is it worth it?"

"It's worth it," Tory said softly, sensing his uneasiness discussing the case.

His face tightened, and he looked away from her.

They stepped on the elevator and Merlin quickly retreated to safer subject matter. "You know that trick I did for you tonight? It's all in the patter. That's what makes it. Not just what I say, but the body language, making you think I blew it. Once you have a great patter—I mean a real grabber—you can get away with anything. It's almost like hypnosis."

"Really," Tory said absently, thinking both about what Merlin had said about Kevin as well as her recent visit to the coroner's office.

"I betcha you could do surgery on someone if you told the right story. I sew up lacerations on kids all the time, spinning some ridiculous tall tale. They lie absolutely still."

The ER was unusually quiet. A few stretchers with patients wrapped up tight, like mummies in white cotton blankets, waited for an escort to take them either to X-ray or one of the inpatient floors. A couple of uniformed cops were just walking out the automatic doors. And in the center of the big room, right out in the open, no curtains or drapes to offer privacy, a flurry of activity buzzed around a single stretcher. Doctors and nurses, working in an obstacle course of red crash carts and IV poles, fluttered around a completely naked woman, her protuberant pregnant belly cresting at the umbilicus, a volcano about to burst. She lay motionless, looking for all the world like she was dead, her skin the color of a slate roof. Her head was turned hard to the side, parade right, awkwardly like she would wake up with a stiff neck. A heavy plastic tube ran into her mouth, was taped to her lips, and a nurse stood at the head of the stretcher methodically forcing oxygen into her lungs by squeezing a clear plastic bag attached to the tubing.

Someone in a long white coat, a stethoscope dangling from his ears, shouted orders to no one in particular.

Merlin's arrival had been anxiously anticipated. A nurse

immediately broke from the crowd and hustled over to Merlin and Tory.

"Merlin," she said breathlessly. "Got a twenty-three-year-old Hispanic girl, beginning of her third trimester. Baby's dead. Started hemorrhaging three, four days ago. Sat at home with a towel stuffed between her legs. BP is fifty over thirty. Thready pulse, can't get a line in her. Anesthesia tried a sub-clavian. She's so shut down we need a cut-down. Tray's ready for you."

Normally when a patient needed an IV, a tourniquet was applied to one of the extremities, causing the veins to plump up from back pressure and allowing a needle to be inserted through the skin and into the bulging vein. With a patient in shock from severe blood loss, however, there might not be enough blood in the system to allow a vein to be palpated. That's when a surgeon was consulted. A small incision was made in the general vicinity where a vein was supposed to be so that a collapsed vessel could be visualized, and a thin plastic catheter could be threaded inside.

"Tory, I gotta go, this is gonna take some time," Merlin said. Then turning toward the ER secretary, called, "Hey Rosa, page Big John, will ya? Have him walk Tory out." Then he gave Tory a little lover's punch in the arm. "I'll call you," he said, and as he walked toward the pregnant girl who had been bleeding at home for days, he donned sterile gloves.

Tory sat in the waiting room, the same chair she'd occupied eight days earlier, but this time she was alone, except for an old woman sitting in the corner asleep. If she leaned to the right and looked around Rosa, who was now devoting her full attention to filing her nails and blowing the dust into the waiting room, she could watch Merlin bending over the girl, accepting various instruments from the nurse. Tory lost track of time. Watching Merlin work was fascinating, even if it was from a distance.

As she waited for Big John and glanced at her watch

now and then, Tory held her keys, fingering one in particular, a heavy brass one with "Unlawful To Duplicate This Key" stamped into one side of the metal. The flip side of the key said "Md. Sch. Master." Tory's plan to have Julian Plesser examine the cadavers in the gross anatomy lab hadn't been scrapped the night Mark Peters was murdered.

Looking at the key, wondering if Big John even got the message to walk her to her car, Tory remembered how she had resurrected the idea the very next morning. Eleven hours after the murder, Tory had found Julian Plesser working the middle autopsy table, alone in the room, hunched over Assistant District Attorney Mark Peters, examining the bullet wounds. A Bach cantata played quietly in the background, not quite drowning out the tinkling sound of the water as it washed away the liquified clots of the deceased.

Peters was naked, which somehow surprised Tory. As Jules stood to his full height she spotted three of the bulletholes, two in the chest and a third in the neck. They were smaller than Tory expected, black holes, almost slit-like, barely big enough to fit one of her fingers, and the blood must have been wiped away.

The entrance wounds were always tame compared to the exit wounds. In fact, the bullet that entered Mark Peters's neck had come out the base of his head, removing a chunk of skull the size of a silver dollar.

Plesser seemed puzzled to see Tory. "You sure you want to see this?"

"I'm not staying, Jules. I need to check something." Tory spotted Peters's clothing, scissored to shreds, piled in a dark maroon mess on an adjoining table.

"What's up?"

"Can I go through his personals? Wallet, electronic organizer?"

"Over there, behind the clothes," Julian said. "Put on gloves."

Tory fumbled with a pair of surgical gloves, two sizes too big, while Julian chatted briefly about Mark Peters, saying the usual how-much-the-department-will-miss-him things that have to be said, even if through clenched teeth.

"Believe it or not, I owe him my life, Jules. He was an SOB, but I'm standing in front of you because of him."

Jules put his scalpel down, slipped his gloved hands into his armpits and leaned back against the autopsy table, crossing his legs to get comfortable. "Do me a favor—don't give me the short version."

Tory picked up Peters's thick brown wallet and removed the credit cards, money, and a few scraps of paper. Each one was briefly examined as it was replaced back in the wallet. "We intercepted a phone call—actually Mark did. He listened in and found out about a delivery, a body, including a payment of fifteen grand. It was set up for tonight."

"Tonight?"

"Yeah, that's what Peters told me, *Friday*. Sounded too good to be true, almost like they were giving themselves up." Tory, finished with the wallet, picked up a Sharp Wizard electronic organizer, clicked it on, and began perusing Peters's schedule. "Anyway, Peters sets up this sting operation, *for me,* he says—he specifically told me it was my case and he was helping me set it up—which, of course, *I* think is going down on Friday, but was actually set up for last night. So I'm out of the loop.

"Apparently everything was in place last night to grab these guys, whoever they are. And Peters really dots his *i*'s and crosses his *t*'s. *Sandy Keller* was there for on-the-spot coverage. And he had a gun," Tory said and picked up the blued snub-nosed Smith and Wesson in the leather holster, crusted with reddish-brown blood. "He also secreted some cops one floor below, the cavalry if he needed them. But from the beginning the plan was Mark Peters making the bust."

"And where were you?"

"About to have dinner with one of the surgical residents, someone helping me with the case," Tory said, her cheeks blushing.

"You holding back on me?"

"What?"

"You blushed. A definite crimson color in your cheeks when you mentioned the surgical resident. You a betting woman, Tory?"

"Oh no, not again. I've heard this routine before." Tory said, picking up Peters's soft leather keycase, unsnapping it, flipping the keys out of the case one by one as she talked.

"Five bucks says this resident is . . . how should I put it—"

"Oh, I'm sure you'll find a way," Tory said with a little laugh, looking at Jules, then back down to the keys, knowing all the while exactly what Jules had surmised. "I'm not one of your poker buddies, Jules."

"Never knew a DA wouldn't take a bet."

"That's why I like you. You're so perceptive. His name's Jack Merlin."

"Aha!" Julian said clapping his hands together and laughing.

Tory beamed at him. "Of course you'll be invited to the wedding, the birthday parties for our three children, and our golden anniversary. Is that what you want to hear? Of shall I continue?"

"I'm listening," Jules said, slipping his hands back into his stained armpits.

"They found a homemade silencer—a potato. Ever hear of that? So it sounded like a setup. The delivery was probably bogus, just an excuse to take out the inside person at the hospital." Tory replaced the key case on the autopsy table, and picked up a small notebook, no bigger than the palm of her hand, and flipped through each page. "Peters must've surprised him, and if he hadn't been a greedy, back-stabbing bastard, you'd be mumbling about me into your microphone right now."

"So you owe him. You gonna name your first son Mark or Peter?"

"I think I like Peter," Tory said, and became more serious. "Jules, I feel like I'm living on borrowed time."

"Don't get mushy on me, Tory. Peters didn't save your life. He doesn't deserve credit for being anything more than an opportunist. I wouldn't wish him this, but I wouldn't lose any sleep about it, either."

Tory gave the small pile of personal items a final once-over, touching each one with her gloved fingers. "Well, nothing here."

"What were you expecting to find?"

"Maybe he had other information he withheld. I don't know—a shot in the dark, I guess."

Tory looked over at Rosa sitting at the ER registration booth and admired her remarkable powers of concentration, her ability to block out a young girl dying twenty feet behind her while she finished her nails.

Rosa admired her work, then checked her watch. "Miss, you want me to page him again?"

"That's okay, I'll give him a few more minutes." Tory read the stamped inscription on the key again. Some dark material, probably dried blood, filled up some of the letters.

When she thought about Merlin's musings on the importance of patter she had to smile. Her timing with Jules had been perfect, she told herself. She'd waited for the right moment, casually choosing the keys after examining the wallet and the electronic organizer, not rushing or looking repeatedly at Jules. When it felt right, while he went on about her love life, she unclipped the bloodstained brass key and dropped it into the patch pocket of her blazer. It was sticky and Tory had to wiggle her fingers to loosen it from her gloves, but it disappeared neatly out of sight, and Julian Plesser was none the wiser. Later, when she got home, Tory slipped her hand into a Glad sandwich bag, using it as a makeshift glove, and carefully removed the key from her pocket and plunked it into a boiling pot of Chlorox for ten minutes. Then she put her blazer in the pile for the dry cleaners.

The sterilized key had been waiting on her own key ring for several days.

Tory couldn't wait to tell Merlin how she'd pulled the wool over Julian Plesser's eyes, practically telling a shaggy-dog story while she fiddled with Peters's things and then slipped the key off the little brass latch with such finesse. Misdirection and patter. Merlin would be proud.

And Merlin would flip out if he knew what she was about to do.

The medical school would be empty. And the key had been sitting in her pocket for two days. Rosa was on the phone now, talking softly and smiling like she was schmoozing a lover, cradling the phone against her shoulder and untangling a knot of gold chains around her neck. As Tory walked out of the waiting room she whispered to Rosa, "Thanks, anyway. I'll be okay."

Tory took the same route Merlin had shown her, winding through the first floor of the Medical Center to the elevators of the medical school. Every other light was dark and huge shadows sprawled across the floor.

With the building empty, the high-pitched whine of the elevator seemed annoyingly loud as it sped Tory to the ninth floor. She pursed her lips and blew cool air into her sweaty hands to dry the keys. The last time she'd taken a solo elevator ride late at night she met up with that man. Satch. It was easy to bring his hideous face into her mind's eye, his pockmarked skin and decaying teeth. She remembered the way he ground his pelvis into hers, then hissed and screamed when she Maced him. Knowing he was dead didn't change things. There would always be monsters in the night, hanging in the shadows, catching a smoke

around back, puffing up their egos while they tore someone apart.

"Cut it out," she said to herself firmly. This was no
time to let her thoughts run wild. Tory pushed herself to
think about Kevin Hoover, review the facts, get logical
and technical. The more she thought about things the more
she convinced herself Jake Barnhouse would figure into
the case before it was over. He was either a great liar or
an unaware simpleton haplessly working for Olsen.

The ninth floor was empty and quiet except for an occasional creak of the ventilation system or Rayma's voice
crackling from the overhead speakers. Tory walked slowly
toward Dr. Olsen's office, stopping several times to turn
around, checking every shadow and doorway. Olsen's door
was closed. The rectangular panel of glass set in the wood
was dark; the slit of space at the bottom of the door was
black.

Her hand was shaking like an old Parkinsonian's as she
tried to fit the master key into the lock. As she leaned in
closer for a better view, her shoulders eclipsed what little
light shone on the door. Now she was threading the needle
in the dark. She leaned back. The key kept missing the
cylinder and sliding off the brass plate. Tory was breathing
hard. Finally she grabbed her right wrist, steadied it, and
slid the key into the lock. The mechanism was well lubri-
cated and the key turned effortlessly on the first attempt.
The door pushed open silently.

Tory stepped inside and blinked several times. It was
pitch black except for the orange glow of a digital clock
on the secretary's desk. Tory slid her hands up and down
the wall next to the doorway and found the light switch.
Keeping her hand on the switch, she quietly closed the
door behind her before clicking on the lights.

The outer office was incredibly tidy. The secretary's
desktop had the usual coffee mug full of pens and pencils,
a computer terminal, and Dr. Olsen's appointment book.
Tory flipped through a few pages of schedules and perused

the catalogue of conferences and meetings he attended on a daily basis, putting off her invasion of Dr. Olsen's inner office as long as possible.

His door was closed but not locked. A turn of the knob produced a metallic clicking noise as the latch snapped out of the strike plate and Tory jumped back, startled, letting the door swing open by itself. Olsen's office had a small window and a perfect view of the moon. Tory found the light switch, and instead of the unnatural light from fluorescent bulbs on the ceiling, a small desk lamp—brass with a green ceramic shade—lighted the desk brightly and left the remainder of the small book-lined office in a soft green glow.

This was a working office, not a showplace to impress visitors and arrange golf games. The desk was a mess. Piles of papers and notebooks covered most of it as well as a nearby credenza. Neat little stacks of slides and an empty plastic carousel sat on a large leather blotter. Timidly at first, Tory picked her way through the papers and notebooks looking for the clipboard with the information about each of the cadavers Jake said had been confiscated by Olsen. With that in hand she'd be able to have Julian examine the cadavers and determine if the paperwork matched up. As she leaned over the desk her hair dangled in front of her face, and every minute or so her hand flicked at her hair, tucking it temporarily behind her ear. She looked anxiously at the opened door from time to time, whispering to herself, "Calm down, calm down." It wasn't helping.

The process was slow; everything was so unfamiliar. Tory had seen Jake read from Eugene Fletcher's sheet and had a general idea what she was looking for, but she was reading upside-down, craning her neck rather than take the walk around the massive desk. Most of the paperwork was correspondence and journal articles, and in ten minutes Tory had gone through the entire desktop. Then she tried the pencil drawer. It was filled with paper clips and dozens of yellow Post-it note pads.

The side drawers were all locked. Tory searched for the key, first looking in the pencil drawer and then under the blotter. "Where do you hide your key, Dr. Olsen?" Tory sang to herself softly. Hearing her own voice felt good, like she wasn't completely alone.

Then the first ring cut through the silence. Tory froze. A short break before it went again. The phone in the secretary's office was ringing, and the phone on Olsen's desk was blinking in silent rhythm. She was terrified, as if she'd been caught. It was after 11:30 P.M. *Did someone expect Olsen to answer?*

The ringing went on for half a minute and Tory stood there, one hand on the desktop, the other covering her mouth.

Tory knew this fear well. Every woman living alone knew this particular brand of fear, whenever she was awakened by a noise in the middle of the night and was too scared to do anything more than pull up the covers and pray. But then in the morning, coming down the stairs, seeing the sunlight play with the lace curtains dressing up those long, narrow windows on either side of her front door, she always felt a little bit foolish, letting her imagination take control of her like that.

Now Tory tried to imagine herself in her car, the doors locked, driving home and feeling ridiculous for being so scared. But those bulletholes in Mark Peters came into her mind—two in the chest, one in the neck—and she wondered what it must have been like that night. The noise of the gun and the smell of the blood.

It seemed more terrifying to her now than when she saw his naked body on that metal table.

Finally the ringing stopped and Tory sat on the edge of Olsen's chair and steadied her nerves. She wanted to run, let the police handle it, and live happily ever after. Forget it, just like Merlin said. But the Kevin Hoover case had wrapped itself around her, a passion that she could not let go. Kevin Hoover was imprinted in her mind—even if no one else gave a damn anymore—and she would pursue it with the intensity of a lost child looking for her mother.

If she walked away now she'd always wonder if she could've handled it and gone the distance.

The credenza was piled high with files and papers, each stack supporting the next, a house of cards waiting to fall. Tory walked to one end of the credenza and gently began to examine the documents. She'd picked her way halfway down a series of manuscripts when the delicate balance came undone, and a landslide of correspondence flopped loudly to the carpeted floor.

Tory got on her hands and knees, her skirt riding up several inches, and hurriedly put them in a semblance of order. A brown hospital chart was among the mess, and as Tory gathered it up she noticed the name typed on the label: MARGARET EMONT.

"Oh, God." It was suddenly an emotional moment and Tory thought she might cry. She clutched the chart to her chest, almost hugging it. And she was frightened for her life.

The final piece of the puzzle had slipped into place. The picture was whole. It all made sense. Tory saw the various elements of the case in a vivid clarity. Nothing to question; this was it. Jake's wild, desperate rantings about Olsen were true. And Olsen's behavior toward her—a madman on the verge—suddenly seemed logical. *OLSEN. Oh, my God.* It was there all along. Tory felt weak; the room started to spin. *Of course it was him,* as if he wore a sign around his neck.

Once you knew someone was guilty it was easy to spot something in their eyes to confirm the look was indeed there all along.

For a second she glanced toward the phone. She wanted to call the police, scream for help. The back of her neck was sweaty and she saw her hands shake as she heaped the mess of papers back on the credenza. In less than a minute she'd turned off the lights and locked the outer door.

She strode to the elevator and looked up at the small monitor. Both elevators were on the ground floor. *The ground floor?* Why wasn't the elevator waiting for her? Maybe they automatically returned to the ground floor. Before she reached for the "Down" button she heard the familiar sound of the elevator motor whine, and the numbers on the monitor started to change. 2 . . . 3 . . . 4 . . . 5 . . .

Oh, my God. It's Olsen. There was no doubt in Tory's mind; Olsen was in the elevator. Coming up to nine. Late for his phone call. Maybe waiting for another delivery. And if he saw Tory standing there, holding the chart, he would know. And he'd fly into a murderous rage.

Tory ran down the gloomy hall with its dark walls, away from Olsen's office, past the anatomy labs and to the heavy metal fire door leading to the Medical Center. She grabbed the handle and pushed down on the thumbplate. It moved without resistance, up and down three or four times, never engaging the latch. Locked. *Locked!*

A second later, just as the elevator announced its arrival with a friendly *ding,* Tory slipped into the small dark alcove leading to the anatomy labs. That made sense. Olsen would walk away from her, go into his office, and Tory could take the elevator down. Her plan seemed logical. The elevator would still be on nine, waiting for her. She'd linger in the alcove until Olsen disappeared into his office, then wait a little more, giving him time to get on the phone, or whatever he came to do, and then make her getaway. It was hard, impossible, to quiet her breathing, and her stream of consciousness created a scenario that was as full of holes as it was hopeful.

Footsteps clicking off the floor, echoing off the walls. Getting louder. The footsteps were getting louder and CLOSER. Olsen was walking toward the gross anatomy laboratory! *What the hell is going on?* No time to retrieve her Mace. She was trapped.

Tory crept backward and realized she still had her keys in her hand. Fortunately the master key was the longest one and it was easy to identify. There would only be time for one attempt at the lock. She clutched the Emont chart in one hand as she slipped the key into the lock and turned it. There was an audible click that sounded as loud as a gunshot to Tory. *Forget it.* A furtive glance over her shoulder, a quick pull on the handle, and the door opened.

Tory turned sideways, slipping in silently, leaving the door to close by itself. She dashed to the middle of the room. All she could see in the moonlight were the tables, not covered in bright taxi-cab yellow, but shrouds of black, like fresh graves in the night. It was a matter of seconds before Tory was squatting behind an autopsy table, the tarp hanging down from the body like a curtain, leaving her in near total darkness.

The lights went on and she heard voices.

"I'm sure I locked it."

"Jake, get your stuff and let's go," a woman's voice said. The voice was familiar.

"Relax, goddamnit, will you? Someone's been in here. Probably Olsen," Jake said.

Tory could look through the table legs and see Jake and a woman, waist-down, standing in front of the office. It had to be Rita. Jake disappeared inside the dark office and his words were muffled.

"I don't like this, Jake," the woman said and started to pace. She dropped her keys and bent over to pick them up. She paced some more. "Jake, c'mon," she said in an angry voice.

Tory watched as Jake stepped out of the shadows and hissed, "Shut the fuck up, will you?" Jake disappeared back in his office.

Tory was an uncomfortable statue, squatting in a forest of table legs like a giant mushroom. Lactic acid filled her quads and her thighs burned. Her calves were starting to twitch in a precramp warning. She needed to change position, get the blood flowing, maybe kneel down.

The woman quieted and walked over toward the wall next to Jake's office and seemed to be reading something. Tory tried to remember if there was a bulletin board on the wall.

"I'm gonna get that clipboard and we're outta here," Jake said, walking toward the cadaver storage room. The woman followed him. Tory heard a key slide into the lock, then a squeak as the door opened.

Tory had a great view into the room as Jake walked inside. It was empty. Two dissection tables, with their skinny metal legs and yellow tarps, were all that separated Tory from the woman. Less than twenty feet.

She crouched lower, her bag hanging off one shoulder resting on the floor, Margaret Emont's chart clutched tightly to her chest. In an effort to disappear, Tory squeezed herself into a tight ball, tucking her head between her knees. And her pulse was so loud she never heard the footsteps walking around the tables, approaching her without so much as a word, sneaking up on her, relishing the element of surprise.

"Jake, get out of here, fast! We've got company," the woman shouted.

Out of her crouch, as stiff as the twenty-eight denizens of the room, Tory pushed up to her feet to make a dash for the door. The woman—Rita!—latched onto her shoulder for a moment and slowed her down just enough for Jake to come running out of the storage area and grab her.

Jake spun Tory around by the shoulders, his fingers digging into her flesh through her jacket, her black hair flying about, getting in Jake's face. Margaret Emont's chart flew across the room.

With her back toward him, feeling her shoulder blades in his chest, he enveloped her in a powerful bear hug, pinning both arms to her sides, locking his hands together across her breasts, squeezing so hard Tory thought he was going to suffocate her.

"*Help! Help!*" Tory screamed.

Jake slid one hand up to Tory's face and roughly clamped it over her mouth. The soft flesh on the side of his hand was forced into Tory's mouth like a cork, and she bit him hard.

Jake screamed and pulled his hand away, a flap of skin hanging like a broken shingle and blood running down his wrist. Tory tried to wriggle free, screaming all the while like a cornered animal. Controlling Tory was his first priority. He ignored the bleeding and locked his hands again in a cruel bear hug. "Rita, go into the embalming room. On the shelf is a goddamn can of ether. Bring it and some rags."

Instead Rita picked up the chart from the floor and read the name on it. MARGARET EMONT. She scrunched up her face. Rita knew she should have thrown the damn chart away the night she took it from Medical Records. Now her breathing quickened and she began to cry.

"Rita, you hear me? Get the ether and get some rags."

Rita walked slowly toward the embalming room, taking the time to flip Margaret Emont's chart in a trash can.

Tory struggled and screamed.

"You shut up or I'll kill you right now," Jake said in a cruel voice. Again Jake slid his bloodied hand up toward Tory's neck and this time pulled his forearm up under her chin in a choke hold that extended her neck, forcing her face-up toward the ceiling.

Tory all but abandoned the idea of escaping. She wanted to say, "No, please, I'll be good, just don't kill me. Please, please, let go." But the choke hold was crushing. Each breath became a small victory. Tiny sips of air were all she could manage, in and out, sucking noisily. She concentrated very hard. In, out, in, out.

Tory stopped her struggle, concentrating on breathing, and Jake eased the pressure on her windpipe.

"You couldn't leave well enough alone. No, all those questions. Pushing, pushing. I never lied to you. *Never.* I didn't kill that kid, never even met him. Why the hell couldn't you leave it alone? That's all you needed to know. I didn't kill the kid. They had me by the balls, had me switching bodies. One stiff for another. That's all. They were already dead, for Chrissake. I ain't going down for this one." Jake pulled up on Tory's neck, hard, for emphasis.

Rita returned from the embalming room. "I can't get the can open."

"Open the fucking can, Rita!"

Rita banged the can against the corner of the metal autopsy table like she would a stuck cap on a ketchup bottle and struggled with it loudly.

"Jesus Christ, push the cap down, like a medicine bottle, you imbecile!"

"Okay, okay." Rita worked the cap.

Tory strained to watch, her eyes all the way down in their sockets, looking over Jake's forearm.

"Now spill some onto the rags." Rita sprinkled the rags. "More!"

When the rags were saturated, sopping with ether, a puddle on the floor, and the air reeking, Jake released his choke hold, grabbed the dripping rags, screamed "Shit! Jesus Christ, Rita!" as the ether ran into his open wound, and slapped the wet rags over Tory's mouth and nose.

Again Tory struggled. And the more she struggled the harder she breathed in the horrible ether. Jake held firm, turned his head to breathe clean air, and let her struggle.

The ether dripped down her throat and burned her mouth. She started to vomit, and as she retched, the woozy feeling started in her legs, and spread like a warm blanket being pulled up to her neck. As the muscles in her body went limp, her breathing slowed, relaxed, and became almost imperceptible. Her eyes were slits, the world getting darker, and Rita's shrill voice was amplified like a child screaming in her ear.

She was unconscious before Jake said, "Get the car and back it up to the loading dock. Leave the keys. Then you walk away, you understand me? Walk away. Take a cab to your mother's. Maybe your sister's. Just don't be there."

"You gonna kill her, Jake?"

"Get the fuckin' car, Rita! I don't want to see you when I get down there," he screamed and let Tory slump to the floor, taking care not to let her head crash too hard and even checking to make sure she was still breathing.

Thirty

The OB resident in charge of the pregnant Hispanic woman, a lanky third-year fellow who kept his tie cinched tight to his neck even in the middle of the night, kept changing his mind how to manage the bleeding. Each time someone offered an opinion he raked his fingers through his short hair and immediately barked out a new set of orders, scurrying the nurses about the ER, drawing up syringes with different medications, hanging different IV solutions, all in anticipation of a successful cutdown. He desperately wanted to call the attending physician, tell him to get the hell down there STAT, but was afraid to break away from the ER crowd and risk having them talk about him while he was on the phone. Finally, Merlin—threading the long plastic catheter into a vein in the leg—convinced him that the patient needed to go to the OR for a possible emergency hysterectomy to stop the bleeding. The OB resident agreed and trotted off to call the OR and have a surgical team readied.

A half hour later Merlin was first-assisting in surgery. The bleeding, it turned out, was easily controlled once the placenta and fetus were removed and the woman's uterus was saved.

Merlin saw the woman in the ICU and, as she was waking up, listened as the OB whispered to her that they couldn't save the baby but they saved her uterus, so not to worry because she could still have more babies. It wasn't until almost four A.M. that Merlin hit the fourteenth floor. He stretched out on his bed in his scrubs, pulled off his socks, and threw the smelly things across the room. His thoughts drifted to Tory. For a moment he tried to smell her, remembering how long it had been since he'd slept alone. Either four or five nights, he decided, but Merlin was too tired to reconstruct the last several days. A normalcy of sorts had been restored, and not having Tory with him made him feel lonely.

The wobbly bedside table held a phone and two empty Diet Coke cans. Merlin rolled to the phone, his beeper digging in his side, dialed 9, and waited for an outside line, then dialed Tory's number over and over, each time letting it ring fifteen or twenty times. By the fourth call he was sitting up, exchanging the phone from hand to hand while he jammed his toes into his running shoes, using his index fingers as shoehorns to avoid the hassle of untying and tying. There was no answer.

In ten minutes he'd dashed through the ER, yelling to Rosa that he'd be on his beeper, and he was in his Audi, driving hard up Fifth Avenue toward Aspinwall, a ten-minute trip with no traffic. He'd been to Tory's once before, waiting for her in the car—and falling asleep—while she ran inside to pick up some things. When he arrived on Ninth Street, with its modest homes and tidy yards, he found a parking space under a streetlight and walked up to her house, a small two-story with green aluminum siding and a nice wooden front porch decorated with heavy ceramic flowerpots and a porch swing off to one side. None of the houses had porch lights burning or lights on inside. Everyone on Ninth Street was asleep.

It was windy and a few leaves whipped down the street in the moonlight. A dog began to bark, yipping at first like it needed to go out. Merlin walked up the several steps to the porch, hearing them creak under his feet. Then the barking became louder, challenging. The animal knew something was outside and wanted at it. Merlin's mouth went dry. He shifted his weight and drew in his breath.

Even though the barking was coming from next door, the house remained dark. He figured the dog went crazy every time a squirrel ran across the yard.

Merlin rang the bell and knocked on the door, rattling it loudly. He peaked through the small window at eye level, but no interior lights came on. He tried the knob.

The barking got louder and in the distance a door slammed shut. Pepper was outside, racing all out across the short span of grass that separated the two houses, barking and exposing white teeth in black gums, thick saliva spraying here and there.

It happened so quickly Merlin barely had time to turn around. His hand was still on the knob, playing with it, when Pepper hit the porch, jumping up the steps, his nails clicking off the wood as it skidded to an angry halt, growling with a deep throaty noise that reminded Merlin of the worst day of his life.

Merlin turned around, saw the teeth and eyes barely two feet from his groin, and he ground himself into the door hoping it would burst open, raising his hands to his chest and trying to stand motionless, avoiding any sudden movements. "Hey, boy. Calm down. Everything's cool."

Click. A bright light from a powerful flashlight shot directly in his eyes, completely blinding him. He squinted hard, forgetting the dog for a moment. The voice he heard was gravelly. "What the hell you doing here?" she yelled at him.

Pepper paced back and forth, growling, showing teeth, rippling his snout, waiting for the signal to attack. Merlin looked down and saw how big the ugly dog was.

Whichever way Merlin turned the light followed. He held his right forearm in front of his eyes to shield them. "Get the dog away from—"

"I said, Whatcha doing here, four-twenty three in the A.M.?"

"Looking for Tory."

"I can see damn well you're looking for Tory. Now,

you listen to me son. State your business, NOW, real slow, real clear. Otherwise I give Pepper a nod and she'll take your leg off.''

"Look. I'm a friend of Tory's," Merlin said, talking quickly, nervously. "My name's Jack Merlin, I'm a surgeon from the Medical—''

"Merlin?'' The woman's voice softened. Pepper continued to pace but stopped his growling, relaxing a little at the change of tone. Mrs. Kincaid took a couple of steps closer, aiming the light a little lower.

"Yes,'' Merlin said, hoping there was some name recognition, as if Tory had mentioned his name to this old woman. "Tory's been investigating a case—''

"That's right. You don't like dogs, do you, Merlin?''

"How'd you know that?''

"You told me. Doc, it's me, Claire Kincaid. Don't you remember?'' Mrs. Kincaid shined the light on her own face so Merlin could see who she was.

"Oh, hi,'' Merlin said, having absolutely no idea who the old woman was.

"You got bit on your bum playing football or something.'' Mrs. Kincaid was wearing a short housecoat that looked pink in the glow from the flashlight, the little lacy collar turned up. With one hand she undid a couple of big plastic buttons in the middle and exposed her midriff and a six-inch long purple scar. "You took out my gallbladder back in June.''

"Mrs. Kincaid, the dog,'' Merlin said with a sense of urgency to his voice.

"Oh, my, almost forgot. Wouldn't bite a burglar anyway, probably just lick him to death. She just wants to play. C'mon, Pepper,'' she said and made a clicking noise with her tongue until Pepper retreated to a corner of the porch and sat down. "I had a picture of Pepper on my nightstand, and whenever I invited you to come for homemade pierogies you told me you hated dogs and wanted take-out instead. You were so funny.''

"Not hated. Terrified. And it was baseball, Mrs. Kincaid." Merlin smiled and relaxed a bit.

"Whatever. You got bit as a kid and *you're nervous around dogs.* That better? Anyway, you said to come back for follow-up; guess I forgot." Mrs. Kincaid buttoned up her housecoat and Merlin stepped away from the door.

"Do you know where Tory is? It's urgent I find her."

"She hasn't been here in several days, but she warned me someone might be after her. Me'n Pepper have been keeping a watch. I'm her landlady," Mrs. Kincaid said proudly as she shuffled over to the porch swing in her slippers that at one time must have been fuzzy. Merlin watched her wiggle onto the swing, her thick ankles swaying several inches from the ground, "Tory called me to tell me she wouldn't be around for a while, so I wouldn't worry or anything. You her sweetie or something?"

"Sort of. She call you today?"

"Uh-unh—couple days ago. You're really worried, aren't you?"

"Look, she left the hospital before midnight; where else could she be?"

"Step aside, Doc. I got a passkey."

Mrs. Kincaid wiggled off the swing and shuffled past Merlin, her slippers never leaving the porch completely. As the door pushed open Mrs. Kincaid actually said, "Pepper, go find Tory!" as if it were an episode of *Lassie.*

Instead Pepper accompanied them into Tory's house, walked right through the pile of mail on the floor beneath the slot, sniffed at Tory's Reeboks by the front door, and generally stayed close to Mrs. Kincaid. While the flashlight was shined around the living room, Merlin found the light switch.

It was to be an experience Merlin couldn't easily categorize. Exploring Tory's world was something he'd looked forward to, discovering her secrets, getting to know her, seeing the private world she'd created. But all he could think about was Mark Peters in that pool of blood, lying in that awful position with his right arm bent back under him. The living room furnishings looked like hand-me-downs from her house in Philadelphia: a plaid sofa and a green leather chair with brass-head tacks piping the front of the armrests. Merlin guessed the glass coffee table with wrought iron legs was Tory's contribution, cluttered with a copy of *Time,* several rolled-up still-in-the-cellophane *Post-Gazettes* stacked up like logs in a fireplace, and a box of Ritz crackers. Merlin examined the photos on the mantel. A formal black and white of a young police officer in his dress uniform looking proud. Her dad. Another of Tory and an older man, her father years later, standing on a beach, arms around each other, hair wild from the breeze, beaming into the camera. And one of a woman, set off from the others, a formal pose, gaunt features, hair pulled back tightly, the single strand of pearls. Tory's mom. Merlin held the photo and looked for Tory in the face. Maybe in the eyes, possibly the nose.

Tory should have been there, taking the photos down one-by-one, making the introductions.

They went room by room, calling her name from time to time, as if it were a routine part of a house search.

The kitchen was small and neat. The drying rack next to the sink had a ceramic mug and a single plate. A box of English muffins, twist-tied in a clear-plastic bag, sat on the counter. The back door was locked from the inside.

Merlin hesitated before going upstairs. Two paperback books, a Patricia Cornwell and a Dominick Dunne, tight in their bindings, were neatly stacked on the third step. Merlin smiled and imagined Tory bolting up the stairs, knowing he was waiting for her, maybe taking them two at a time, in such a hurry to get her toothbrush and nightie that her bedside reading never made the trip upstairs.

Merlin kept flashing back to Mark Peters in that dark pool of blood and immediately looked down at the floor as he entered her bedroom. A double bed, white comforter with thin blue lines, white pillowcases, everything neat, matching bedside tables stacked with books and journals, and a small TV on the dresser. Mrs. Kincaid had a few comments in each room like, "Not much here," or "Pepper, what is it, girl?" but after awhile they became background noise and Merlin almost stopped hearing them.

There was nothing out of place, no drawers dumped on the floor. Mrs. Kincaid finally concluded, "Not here."

"What the hell's going on?"

"Maybe we should call the police."

"Tory never made it home. She wouldn't have walked over the pile of mail. You know what? I bet something happened when she left the hospital. She never *made* it out of Oakland. We want city cops. I know where the Squirrel Hill Station is."

Merlin left after exchanging phone numbers with Mrs. Kincaid—just in case—and drove to Northumberland Street, a couple of miles from the Medical Center. There he found a beefy desk sergeant, alone, eating a thick sandwich, wiping his ravenous mouth with a tiny, bunched-up wad of napkin after each bite.

"Officer, I need to report a missing person." Merlin looked around. Safety posters, a few obligatory wanted posters, and the big desk sitting up a step, setting it off so that it felt a little like you were in a courtroom addressing a judge.

The sergeant nodded slowly, then finished chewing his mouthful, took a swig of grape soda from a bottle, and worked his tongue between several teeth in lieu of dental floss. After the doughy pieces of bread were worked out of his teeth, he made Merlin wait a bit longer as he made several loud clicking noises with his lips. Then he surveyed Merlin, wearing scrubs and running shoes—no socks—and hair that went in every direction. "Second one this week. Usually get one or two a month—not in person, though, over the phone."

"This one's different," Merlin said emphatically.

The sergeant made a face, raised his eyebrows, bugged out his eyes, and puckered his lips. "Oooooh. Haven't heard *that* one before. Different, huh? Okay, I gotta fill out a yellow form, maybe a light blue one, too—cause *this* one's different. Then I gotta file it, discuss it with the captain—I wonder if I should wake him?—follow up on it. I can make a career running this thing down. Yeah, yeah, yeah. Okay, whatcha got, Doc?"

"A woman—actually, she's an assistant DA named Tory Welch—left the Medical Center about 11:30, twelve o'clock at the latest. She's disappeared."

The sergeant looked at his watch. "Last night?"

"Right."

"What's it now, 5:50? Five hours ago."

"Closer to six," Merlin said, expecting the policeman to somehow swing into action.

"She's not a missing person, Doc. Can't be a missing person after five hours. Christ, some people can be on the can that long."

"Look," Merlin said, raising his voice and pointing his finger at the officer, "We don't have a lot of time to play games. Something's happened. I'm telling you, *Something's happened, goddamnit, listen to me!!* You gonna give me a hard time, or what, Sergeant"—Merlin leaned forward and squinted his eyes to read the nametag— "Steckman?"

Sergeant Steckman rolled his eyes and slowly took a yellow sheet of paper from a drawer and placed it in front of him. He prepared himself to take notes, wiping his hands on the greasy napkin and picking up a ballpoint pen. "Okay hotshot. What happened? You see someone kidnap her? Any ba-lood stains?" Steckman said, exaggerating the way he said "blood" into something with two syllables.

"No, if I did, I would have come in here and said 'I want to report a kidnapping.' Right? She's missing, that's all I know."

Steckman leaned forward, the edge of his desk indenting his massive gut. "You're a doctor, right?"

"Yes," Merlin said with a new tone of hope in his voice, as if being a professional would make his allegations believable, "My name's Jack Merlin; I'm at the Medical Center."

"And how do you know something's happened to her?"

"Look, Tory Welch's been investigating that body found in the anatomy labs."

"You mean that DA got shot couple of days ago?" Steckman asked. He looked interested for the first time, sat up in his chair, and leaned forward on his thick forearms just slightly.

"No. No. You're thinking of Mark Peters. He was working *with* Tory on the investigation of that doctor that was embalmed a year ago. The police are handling the Peters murder."

"Oh, that," Steckman sounded disappointed. He thought a minute, leaning back. "So you're tight with this—what's her name?"

"Tory Welch."

"How long you know her?"

"A couple of weeks," Merlin lied.

"Right. So you're tight with this *Tory* and she left the Med Center—what, five hours ago?—and you can't find her. That it?"

Steckman was working it, trying to make Merlin feel like a jerk, and it was clicking. Talking about being "tight" with her, like he *knew* they were having sex. Making him feel like some goofy guy, no socks and hair every which way, lost his girlfriend and had to come running to the cops. Big deal! The boy who cried wolf.

Merlin felt his cheeks burn. "That's it. She's not home, her landlady hasn't seen her. *She's . . . not! . . . home!* She's gone."

"How long you know this girl?" Steckman said again, driving the point home.

"I told you. Two weeks."

"Two weeks. So now I gotta play adviser. Okay, let me solve the mystery for you. You met this Tory couple a weeks ago. Hit it off. Had a couple of drinks. Maybe you hopped between the sheets, I don't know—and I sure as shit don't care—but she's got another guy, and when she left you last night she didn't go home. I betcha her Castro's been smokin' some guy's cigar, if you know what I mean." Steckman laughed to himself and drained the bottle of soda, enjoying the moment.

Merlin was losing control. He stepped forward, reached up, and put his hands on Steckman's desk. As he began to crumple a stack of papers Steckman slammed his fist down and bellowed, "Now I know who the fuck you are. You're the guy went nuts on TV with that Sandy Keller. Don't make me arrest you."

"*Goddamn you,*" Merlin shouted, flinging the stack of papers toward Steckman's gut, "*That's enough. That's enough. Shit!* You sonavabitch. You gonna help me or not?"

"Not!" Steckman stood, looking down at Merlin. "Why don't you get some sleep, Doc? Maybe call her in the morning," Steckman said and picked up his sandwich.

"Okay, porkchop. Go back to your sandwich. But so help me God, if anything happens to her, I'll make goddamn sure you never see the inside of a jelly doughnut again."

Steckman pointed a fat index finger at Merlin. "Hey, why don't you call the DA, get him out of bed, give him some shit 'bout how you voted for him and you want to report your girlfriend's missing for five fuckin' hours. Go ahead, big shot. There's the door, Doc. Don't let it fuckin' hit you."

Merlin glared at Steckman for several seconds, memorizing his face, the short red hair and matching mustache, the gut hanging over the leather belt, letting the asshole know he meant business. Steckman chewed the last bite of his sandwich.

At last Merlin turned and left. The cool morning air should have felt good on his face. If he'd been closer to the Medical Center a brisk walk might have been refreshing. Instead he drove back to Oakland, parking near the driveway leading to the ER, but was too keyed up to go inside. Merlin needed to let off some steam; he was that close to exploding. As much as he wanted to smack Steckman in his fat face, Merlin knew the police officer was right. No one would believe him. The DA's office wouldn't be as obnoxious, but they'd probably ask the same questions Steckman did and dismiss him with a thank-you-very-much-we'll-check-into it. Never mind that Mark Peters was murdered, Tory hadn't been missing long enough for anyone to take him seriously. *Jesus Christ, I'll sound like Chicken Little.*

He felt helplessly out of control. While his fists were balled up so tight his nails dug into his palms, he began to kick a brick wall, harder and harder. Not until his feet throbbed did he finally limp into the ER, tears drying on his cheeks, through the automatic doors, and to a phone in the nurse's station. This was the only peaceful time of the day in the ER, when the remains of yesterday had been cleaned up and the ruins of today hadn't yet got off the bus. First he tried Tory at home again. Then he left a message on her office voice mail.

Martin Wheeler slipped into the chair next to Merlin, unnoticed, pleased with his stealth. Now he was ready for Merlin to notice him. *Where've you been, bucco?* Some loud toe-tapping and a couple of quick glances at his watch, and Martin Wheeler felt ignored. Finally he said, "Where the hell have you been?"

Merlin looked up. "Wheeler, you little sneak. You greased up? At one of your Mazola parties last night?"

"Merlin, I want to know what happened last night."

"I had a personal emergency."

"Personal emergency. If you need to leave the hospital at night there's a protocol to follow. You're supposed to call me and then find someone to sign out to."

"I couldn't reach you, Martin. I didn't know the number of any of the strip clubs on Liberty." Merlin got up to leave.

"Not so fast. What you did potentially put every surgical patient in jeopardy."

"I wore my beeper. It never went off."

"So that justifies everything."

Merlin sat back down and rolled his chair right up to Wheeler's. "Listen to me, Martin. Something happened to Tory last night. I had to leave," Merlin said through clenched teeth.

Wheeler was clean shaven and looked splendid in his neatly pressed white coat, light blue shirt, and yellow silk tie with the perfect knot. Two gold Cross pens peeked out of his pocket. He *looked* like a doctor, and he waited a few seconds to collect his thoughts so he could sound like one. "Let's get this straight, Jack. I'm the chief resident. You pull another stunt like last night and you won't finish your training in Pittsburgh." He stood and walked to a wall-mounted chart rack and pulled out the lone chart in the bin marked "Surgical." "Here, why don't you see what"—he read the name on the chart—"Robin Winters has going on. I'm sure it's a fascinating case." He didn't wait for Merlin to take the chart, but rather flipped it on the desk behind Merlin and walked purposefully out of the ER.

"I need a shower." Merlin couldn't think of a single comeback line.

In several minutes he had calmed down and found Robin Winters, a nineteen-year-old with abdominal pain, on a stretcher in the ER, almost completely surrounded by a white curtain.

"Hello, Robin, I'm Dr. Merlin." Merlin pulled the curtain open a bit wider than he had to. As Robin craned her neck to see how much of her privacy she'd just sacrificed, Merlin sat on the edge of the stretcher, just below Robin's hips, reading her chart.

"Hi," she said in a tiny voice.

"You go to Pitt?"

"Yes. I'm a sophomore."

"Your belly hurt?" Merlin shifted his weight, tried to get comfortable.

"A lot," Robin said and started to cry.

Merlin smoothed her hair down as he waited for her to stop crying. A stream of hospital employees started to come in through the ER. Someone was laughing. An excellent view of the parade was afforded Merlin if he looked over Robin's shoulder.

"Hey, it's gonna be okay. When did it start?" Down the hall it looked like Wheeler was holding court, but Merlin couldn't quite make out who he was talking to.

"Yesterday. I had to miss class," Robin said.

Tory walked by. Merlin spotted her. As if by instinct he looked up, past Robin's shoulder, and caught a glimpse of Tory walking into the hospital. Absolutely. Her shiny black hair, parted on the side. The springy walk and tailored suit. Merlin was energized, the weight of the world was off his shoulders. He smiled, and gave out a little yelp.

Merlin blurted out, "Tory!" But she was gone.

Robin tried to look over her shoulder but ended up grabbing her belly.

Merlin hopped off the stretcher, causing it to roll several feet. It banged quietly into the wall as he whipped the curtain out of the way. "Sorry, I'll be right back," he said over his shoulder and trotted off. "Tory! Wait."

She kept going, walking quickly through the crowd, heading for the elevators.

Merlin weaved through the crowd, occasionally zipping around people so quickly that he momentarily had to hold their shoulders, giving them a friendly squeeze to steady them as he happily blurted, "Coming through, hot soup," and everyone smiled back at him. Finally he reached her, grabbed her arm and enthusiastically spun her around. "I've been so worried about you."

It wasn't Tory. Of course it wasn't Tory. She looked nothing at all like Tory. Dull features, a hideous brooch of a cat on her lapel, and buck teeth. She gave him a startled look. Merlin released her arm, rubbed his eyes as he made his unenthusiastic apology, mumbled something about from the back she looked exactly like someone he knew. Slowly he wandered back to the ER, ready to cry.

He was going crazy.

Again Martin Wheeler came out of nowhere and was walking next to Merlin, keeping a cadence, before he said, "How's our friend?"

Merlin stopped. "What're you, following me? I told you I don't know where she is."

"I mean the girl, Robin Williams, or whatever her name is. You haven't finished with her."

"You've got nothing better to do than spy on me to see if I've finished with some coed who probably ate too much pizza. Aren't you embarrassed?"

"Let's finish up with her. Okay, Jack?"

Merlin nodded and trudged back into the ER, through the generous crack in the curtains surrounding Robin, and sat down.

"I'm sorry, Robin. Uhhh, where were we. Any fever?"

"I think I want another doctor. Someone else. You seem . . . too busy."

He looked at her for the first time. She was attractive, auburn hair pulled back with a widow's peak, sad eyes. He found her hand and held it. Then he spoke softly, never taking his eyes off her face. "Ohhhh, God. Look Robin, I'm sorry. You deserve better than what I've given you. I know you're scared and in a lot of pain, and you're right, my mind was elsewhere. If you really want someone else,

I'll find another doctor, but I'd really like to help you get better."

Robin was quiet for a while. "Okay."

"Great. Let's start over. First of all, everyone calls me Merlin." He squeezed Robin's hand and she smiled. "Robin, have you had any fever?"

"I haven't felt warm or anything."

"Diarrhea or vomiting?"

"No."

"I'm gonna check your belly while we talk. Is that okay?" Robin nodded and Merlin lifted up her hospital gown to her ribs and pulled down the sheet so that only the top of her underwear was exposed.

Robin wore very sexy bikini underwear, pink lace. She flexed her neck to look down at her panties, as if she was surprised she had worn that particular pair, and as her stomach muscles tightened, gave out a little cry of pain. "I thought I would get a female doctor. I'm so embarrassed."

"Hey, don't be." And Merlin gently lifted up the sheet to cover her pink underwear. "Not a big deal." Merlin gently palpated her abdomen, asking several times whether this or that hurt. Robin answered yes, *everything* hurt. "Robin, when was your last period?"

"I don't know. A few weeks ago, I guess."

"Any chance you could be pregnant?"

"Uhhh. I don't know. I mean, no, I'm not. At least, I don't think so." Robin was crying again.

"Tell you what. I know it hurts an awful lot. I want to run a few tests on you, maybe get an X-ray and keep you twenty-four hours. Just to make sure. Okay?"

Robin sobbed softly.

"Where do your parents live?"

"Scranton."

"Let me get a phone. You can talk to them, then I'll talk to them. You'll feel better after. We'll get through this together."

Thirty-one

The morning shower after a night on call was a way to mark time. It meant the beginning of a new day and signaled that one more night of call was history. And when the body's own circadian rhythms were thrown out of whack by a total lack of sleep, ten minutes under a hot spray seemed to reset the clock. As Merlin wrote admission orders on Robin Winters all he could think about was his morning shower, but Martin Wheeler was waiting for him as he left the ER and dragged him along to surgical ICU rounds, lecturing him about responsibility as they rode a crowded elevator.

Wheeler all but ignored the interns and medical students on rounds, peppering Merlin, who by now looked like a homeless person who stumbled into a medical convention, with a ridiculous barrage of trivial questions about patients he had never seen. The chief resident seemed to enjoy the experience. Every time Merlin said, "I'll have to check on that," Wheeler's mouth curled up in a slight grin. "Why don't you check on that after rounds?" he responded, putting a heavy emphasis on the word "don't."

By the time rounds were over, Merlin had a scut list that included dressing changes, a wound debridement, running down two lost X-rays, and tapping fluid off the chest of an old woman with a tumor in her lung. As rounds broke up and Wheeler strode off to another meeting, Merlin mimed a child writing at a blackboard, saying "I will not play hooky, I will not play hooky . . ."

The fourteenth floor was empty when Merlin finally stepped off the elevator. Before he made it to the shower room his shirt was off and his pants unzipped. It was almost four P.M. The shower was wonderfully relaxing, and after a few minutes a sad smile crossed his lips as he thought about Tory and how nervous she was showering with him their first morning together, worried that Martin Wheeler would see her dashing about in a pair of scrubs and know exactly what they had been up to.

But then he thought about the conversation that led to their first night together, how dreamy it seemed, and Merlin remembered—vividly, as though it were being played back on a tape recorder—how Tory had questioned whether a second cadaver wasn't who he was supposed to be. Had she unwittingly stumbled onto more than she realized? He wondered if she had ever talked with Julian Plesser and decided to call him.

After the shower, he put on clean white pants topped with a fresh blue scrub shirt and sat on his bed, deciding who to call first.

Mrs. Kincaid answered the phone on the first ring, dutifully reported she'd sat in her kitchen all day watching Tory's house, and that there'd been no sign of her. Then he called the district attorney's office and got Tory's secretary, but was instantly put on hold as soon as he started asking too many questions. After a minute of waiting he had to lie down, put his feet up, let his head sink into the pillow and enjoy that crinkly sound of the plastic mattress beneath him. Any surgical resident could do a thirty-six hour stretch without sleep, but the stress of chasing around the city had left him exhausted.

The uncomfortable bed felt wonderful. His eyes were closed long before the secretary came back on the line, the phone cradled in the crook of his neck, the bland on-hold music hypnotically lulling him to sleep.

He slept fitfully, awakening for the first time when his call was disconnected and the phone company blasted an awful beeping noise to warn him the phone was not properly hung up. Then he rolled over, releasing the receiver. It popped back toward the phone, and he jumped when he heard it bounce off the floor. Finally the beeping stopped and it was quiet. Sleep came quickly; deeper and deeper he descended through the various stages. He began to dream when he entered REM sleep for the first time, his eyes darting about, checking out the action on the silver screen of the mind.

A crowded street. Heavy traffic. Horns beeping incessantly.

Merlin was standing at an intersection, a gridlock, nothing moving, frozen in time, the cars—no, they were taxis—lined up, waiting to go, but standing still. When he tried to see who was riding in the taxis, the passengers were hidden, impossible to see, the door panels going right up to the roof. Merlin looked hard, leaned in real close, but he couldn't see the passengers. He tried over and over, racing between the cars, but the fumes spewed thick, burning his eyes, making him cough. He banged on the windows, but there weren't any.

Then he became aware of people talking, joking, and laughing, their voices echoing loudly in his ears, and Merlin spun around, looking for the party, but couldn't find it. A lone taxi rumbled up next to him. It had a window and he could see inside, but the car started to move away from him, slowly at first, leaving him in a black cloud of smoke. Merlin saw a hand come up inside, waving to him in slow motion. He started to walk alongside the car, keeping up with it, bent over at the hips, walking faster and faster, trying to see the face. The taxi accelerated, rumbling as the engine picked up speed, and the face turned toward him, a Mona Lisa smile, hard to read. BUT THE FACE WAS KEVIN'S.

Merlin screamed, but his voice was silent, and his legs were thick and sluggish, like he was standing in cement, and he slowed down as the taxi sped off.

But he kept walking, following his friend.

The voices changed. Deep guttural noises; no laughing. The taxis weren't taxis! That's why he couldn't see into them! They weren't cars. They were cows. Moo-cows, all lined up, neat little rows of cows, walking together, slowly, a head lifted here and there, mooing sadly. And one man on a horse, wearing a long tan cowboy coat, came trotting up to the cows, talking to them, whistling at them, urging them faster.

Merlin knew the cowboy. He looked so familiar, but he couldn't think of a name to call him.

Merlin thought to himself, My God, I know what he's doing. I know where those cows are going. "STOP, COWS. STOP." The cows clomped up the ramp, noisy, one turning sideways, being straightened out by the man on the horse, and on into the house.

Then Merlin saw the room, the cold room, behind the house, stood there looking into the room like a helpless child, his hands clasped behind his back. Always looking in from the outside. The room was dark inside, but he could see the cows after they'd been through the house, hanging there, floating in space, red and raw, and Tory was with them—just like that—floating, too, but translucent, her feet ending in a disappearing wispy trail. Floating.

Merlin woke up. The sheet was crumpled up underneath him, moist with perspiration. He peeled his wet cheek from the plastic mattress and he was breathing hard, sweating, like he needed another shower. He sat up and checked his watch: 8:25 P.M.

He had the sickest feeling in his stomach that he knew where Tory was and he felt like vomiting. The muscles in his neck were so tight he had to go through range of motion exercises to loosen up. The revelation hit him hard, shocked him that he hadn't even considered it before. Tory had laid it out for him to consider, practically spelled it out, but then Mark Peters got murdered and everything seemed to go into suspended animation.

The one that was *supposed* to have died of liver disease wasn't jaundiced. Bodies were coming and going *all* the time.

He ran to the elevator and punched the button over and over, pacing back and forth like a hungry animal.

The heavy metal door from the hospital to the ninth floor of the medical school banged loudly as Merlin hit the push-bar and marched into the dark corridor. But then he stopped for a second, did a double-take, and looked down at the floor, shiny even in the dim light, wondering who had cleaned up all that blood. Absently his hand went to his mouth. Then he walked over to the wall and examined the two pockmarks, white against the brown wall, where the slugs were dug out of the plaster. This was the first time he'd been back.

Since he'd awakened from his horrible dream, it felt as if his emotions were dragging him around the hospital, an angry dog pulling its helpless master. And when he stepped into the small alcove of the anatomy lab he realized he wasn't thinking things through logically: The doors would be locked. *Goddamnit, of course the doors are locked.*

But he rattled them anyway, hard, making some noise, not caring if he broke the locking mechanism. When he finally felt ridiculous fighting the locked doors he retreated to the hallway and found a wall mounted house phone and paged security.

"Security." It sounded like Big John, and made him think, reminded him that Big John might have seen Tory in the ER that night.

"Big John, Merlin."

"Yeah, whaddya want?" he sounded in a hurry.

"Hey John, last night did you walk Tory, you know the DA lady, out to valet to get her car?"

"That's what you called about?" Now he sounded mad.

"Did you?"

"No, man, and I ain't got time for this, Merlin," he said. "If you must know, I was off Tuesday, Now I pulled a double. Carlos is sick, man, so I gotta go."

"Wait, John. I called to ask you a favor. Would you come up to anatomy and let me in?"

A pause. "Olsen know you're going in?"

"I'm the lab assistant; you know that."

The elevator bell dinged and a cleaning cart—mop, bucket, portable vacuum—rolled out, pushed by a young woman wearing too many earrings and grooving to tunes on a Walkman. She turned and walked toward Olsen's office, moving slowly, stopping every so often to do a slow motion dance step, like she had all the time in the world.

"Listen Merlin, you'd better talk with—"

"Never mind, John, it'll keep 'til morning," Merlin said, and hung up the phone, trotting after the young woman from housekeeping, who shrugged and said "Hell, I don't care" when he asked her to unlock the doors to anatomy.

She hung around for a few seconds, making sure Merlin found the lights, changing tapes and adjusting her headphones, eventually trucked down the hall toward Olsen's office.

Merlin zigzagged his way to the cadaver storage room, through the yellow-covered dissection tables, slapping his fist on some of the covered bodies as he cornered around them, and grabbed the knob of the door, intending to whip it open like a man about to catch his wife sleeping with a neighbor.

Locked. "Jesus Fucking Christ," he said in desperation. A new door, probably oak, prehung, solid, no play in the lock.

Merlin looked around at the cadavers, twenty-eight of them, covered with their bright yellow plastic tarps. Neat little rows. Like being in a dream.

He played with the door forcefully, shaking it violently, screaming, "Shit" loud enough to draw attention from anyone in earshot, but he couldn't even rattle it.

This was not a time for finesse. His anger was exploding

inside his head and he had tunnel vision. *The door. Get through the fucking door.* He stepped back a few feet, stood between two of the long dissection tables, looked around a final time, and flung himself at the door, hitting it hard with his shoulder, feeling the dull thud as he hit the wood. The door remained closed, unfazed by the attack. He grabbed the knob again and tried desperately to shake the door. Nothing—no wiggle, no play to the lock, as if it weren't a door at all, but part of a massive wall.

Again he stepped back, farther this time, enough to run half a dozen steps before hitting the wood, and took three deep breaths before he hurled himself forward. He smashed his weight against the door, bouncing off, stumbling backward, banging into one of the dissection tables before he caught his balance.

"What the hell are you doing to my door, Dr. Merlin?"

Merlin stopped rubbing his shoulder and spun around, stunned to hear a voice. "Dr. Olsen," Merlin said breathlessly. That's who it was. The cowboy.

The chairman of anatomy was standing directly behind him, less than the seven-foot length of a dissection table, wearing a white lab coat with an apron tied loosely over it, holding his familiar pipe chest high, elbow cocked, very professorial. Olsen stood straight, the heels of his wingtips almost touching, his toes six inches apart, like he was addressing a class, clarifying some anatomical detail, except he was holding a scalpel in his left hand, down at his side, subtly out of the way. At first glance Merlin didn't notice the knife, but Olsen's hand moved and the blade caught the light and advertised itself.

Merlin's first thought was to run, weave through the tables—Olsen was pushing sixty—run the portly bastard out of breath and then make a break for the door. But then he thought of Tory. "Where is she?" Merlin said forcefully as he slowly back around the dissection table. It seemed safer with the buffer zone of a cadaver between them.

They stood opposite one another, Olsen pivoting slightly to face Merlin. "Who are you looking for?"

"You know goddamn well who I'm looking for. Tory. What have you done with her?" Merlin's voice rose louder each time he spoke.

"What have *I* done with her?" Olsen said incredulously. "Merlin, I have absolutely no idea what you're talking about."

"Then what're you doing here at night? What about the knife?"

Olsen raised the scalpel and regarded it as if he were holding a confusing puzzle. "What?"

"Stay the hell away from me, Olsen."

"Olsen." He reared back at the sound of his name. He hadn't been called "Olsen" since he was a kid, and he hated it then. It was "Dr. Olsen" to residents and staff, "Jonathan" to senior attendings. No middle ground. No fooling around. No pat-on-the-ass nicknames to get in good with the house staff. And absolutely no impudence. Ever. Now he was angry. "Have you gone mad? You think I'm going to use this on you?"

"Then put it down!"

Olsen looked confused. "*Now,* I have absolutely no idea what's going on. Let me guess. You're the one who broke into my office last night. You made quite a mess, Merlin." He carefully placed the scalpel on the yellow tarp, balancing it on what must have been a belly. "So let's talk. First of all, don't you ever—and I mean as long as you live— don't you ever call me 'Olsen' again. As if you have the right. All of you have put me through the worst hell of my life, but I will not tolerate rudeness. It's *Doctor* Olsen to you," Olsen said firmly, then paused for a few seconds, looking around the large room, making certain they were indeed alone. "Now, Merlin, would you mind telling me what's going on? And why in the world do you think I did something to Ms. Welch?"

"Open the door to the storage room. Please."

Olsen thought Merlin sounded like a desperate child, pleading for assistance. "The answer isn't in there, Merlin. I've looked. You're in the wrong room," Olsen said, unlocking the door with a key he produced from his side pocket. He pushed it open. "Go ahead, see for yourself." Olsen stepped back, held his pipe out, inviting Merlin to examine the storage room.

The room was dark. Merlin walked in, did a full three-sixty. "Thank God," he said with a feeling of relief, and looked up at three dozen head braces suspended from their tracks on the ceiling, every one of them empty.

Olsen said, "Was it you last night?"

"No, of course not." Merlin looked around. "What about the embalming room?"

"Let me get this straight. You think the district attorney is in there. You're way off. Take a look." Olsen led the way toward the front of the room to the door marked EMBALMING ROOM. He unlocked the door using the same key and flipped the lights on. Without entering the room it was obvious that it was a male cadaver lying supinely on the table.

Merlin exhaled loudly. "Then she's alive. I know it."

Olsen looked at him strangely. "Maybe we're both here for the same reason, Merlin. Different motivation, perhaps, but the same reason." Olsen felt as if they were having an important conversation, two adversaries finally meeting on common ground, forming a bond. As if they were at a crossroads and might work together or even walk away friends.

"You're wrong about me, Dr. Olsen. I'm not here about Kevin. I know it sounds trite, but Kevin's gone, and the police can have their little investigation. Tory's missing, almost twenty-four hours now. The cops don't care, and I'm thrashing about in the dark. You know something. Please," Merlin said, waiting a few seconds, "Tell me what you know."

"I've had a complete career. Textbooks, monographs.

Lectured all over the world. You know I was there for the post on Kennedy? I've done it all. And to have that body show up in my lab, right under my nose.'' He touched his face, traced a heavy wrinkle around his jowl, as if to remind himself how old he was, that his career could not go on forever. ''They remember you for the one mistake you make, and what's mine? It happened on my watch. That's all. This has got to be mine.''

Merlin was confused. ''*What* has got to be yours?''

''The mystery. I've got to unravel it.''

''Do you know anything about where Tory is?''

''I do not.''

''But you've already unraveled it, haven't you? You said, '*Now* I have no idea what is going on.' You emphasized the word 'now,' as if you thought you *did* understand things, but seeing me here somehow confused you. So I ask you: What do you know? Look, Tory's missing. Help me find her.''

''I'm sorry to hear that. I am,'' he said sincerely, shaking his head, considering his options. ''I'll go to the police in the morning, not tonight. I've got to be sure. I'll not be blindsided ever again. I won't have a swarm of news reporters pointing out what's in my own lab. I'm checking everything myself. A couple of hours should do it. Give me to morning.''

''Share it. We can go to the police tonight. I'm not looking for credit. It's yours. What are you sitting on?''

''In the morning,'' he said quietly, sounding tired.

''*We don't have 'til morning.* It's Jake, isn't it? How long have you known?'' Merlin blurted out, fishing for a reaction. It was a gamble, but the odds suddenly seemed good.

Merlin studied Olsen's face carefully, searching for a silent confirmation. He watched his eyes, the corners of his mouth, the bushy eyebrows. But Olsen maintained his composure, nodded his head gently, saying nothing but telling Merlin everything. ''I've got to go now. I want to be home before midnight,'' Olsen said quietly, walking back to retrieve his scalpel, and slowly again past Merlin on his way into the embalming room.

''You've got to do more than nod your head. What if he's got her?'' Merlin said when Olsen was practically next to him, his voice raised. ''That matter to you, Dr. Olsen? You said we're here for the same reason. Not really. There's one big difference. You think this whole thing is about *you*. I thought you were a bigger man than that. Stop worrying about a little tarnish. *I'm trying to save a life.* Please help.''

Olsen ignored him. He stood next to Eugene Fletcher, keeping his back to Merlin.

Merlin felt desperate. Time was running out and he needed a plan. Gathering information while time slipped away was unacceptable. The more he ran the facts the less doubt he had.

Jake Barnhouse. Mark Peters was right. It had to be.

In the end it was the expanding-circle theory. Jake Barnhouse was closest to everything. A wave of confidence captured Merlin.

And besides, why else would Olsen show up at night?

Because Jake had free access to the lab during the day.

Olsen knows something's wrong with the cadavers, otherwise he wouldn't be ready to cut. Maybe he saw the one in the embalming room—the one Tory spotted—and knew it wasn't the one he'd signed for.

Merlin wanted to run to the police station, grab Steckman by the shirt, and say, ''Listen to me, asshole, I know who's got her, now get off your goddamn butt and *do your job!*'' But all he had was a hunch. Sergeant Steckman would throw him out on his ass and laugh at him.

In the short time it took to walk back to the elevators Merlin formed his plan.

He went to the lobby of the hospital, found a phone book in a public booth, and looked up Jake's number. The street name was unfamiliar to him and he had no idea what community it was in, so he dialed Directory Assistance and said to the operator, "Could you give me the number of Jake Barnhouse, 618 Sterling Road?" The operator recited the same number listed in the phone book and Merlin asked, "Where is that, Swissvale?" The operator replied that it was in Cheswick.

Cheswick. Up the Allegheny River, north of and across the river from Oakmont, up river from where the first body was found.

Then Merlin dialed the number and let it ring. No one answered. Merlin had gotten lucky; his plan didn't have a contingency if Jake were home.

He was out of Oakland, across the Highland Park Bridge, and in the small middle-class community of Cheswick before 10:15. It was a cool night with a sky full of stars, the moon lighting the Allegheny River with a white light that twinkled in the water.

He got directions for Sterling Road at a Sunoco station and drove down the long road pockmarked with holes and ruts. Houses lined the left; thick woods the right. Then there was a nursery and some small frame homes. He followed the numbers to a wooden post with twin mailboxes, 616–618, the last house before the road came to a dead end. But he kept driving, fifty yards further down, parked the car on the wooded side of Sterling Road, and sat for five minutes, never once taking his eyes off the house. It was a two-family dwelling with side-by-side front doors, white in the moonlight, set back further than the other houses. The numbers were rising, going left to right, so he knew 616 would be on the left, 618 on the right. A large wrap-around porch, empty of furniture or bikes, needed some maintenance. No lights were on anywhere in the house. The driveway off to the right was empty and there were no street lamps. Merlin decided the road didn't get much traffic. It was practically an invitation.

He fished through his glove box and found a small penlight with advertising for an antibiotic written in large yellow letters.

Merlin walked up the steps to the front porch, scanning each of the windows, looking up and down the street, and checked the number, 618. The bell rang for a full minute. If a single light went on Merlin was ready to bolt to the car and go to the police.

A large picture window, off to the right, caught his attention. He wandered over to it, leaned close to the window, cupping his hands around his eyes to block the moonlight filtering in through the trees, and saw it immediately: a tiny dot of red light—a burning cigarette—the only light in the room.

Jake! All he could think about was Jake, sitting in the dark room—maybe it was the living room—smoking, waiting for him, knowing he was coming. He felt like such a fool and ducked down, crouching below the window, feeling desperate, waiting to hear footsteps coming around the porch. Jake with a gun. Jake with a scalpel. Merlin's imagination was flying.

His legs began to cramp so he duck-waddled back toward the front door, then slid up the wall next to the window, safely out of Jake's view. Far away a dog barked, and the wind picked up and rustled the leaves still on the trees. Merlin reminded himself he hadn't actually seen Jake, just a dot of light, and he felt a little embarrassed breaking a sweat over a dot of light.

Until he made certain it was Jake, he wasn't going back to his car.

A second look was in order, but this time his eyes were adjusted to the dark. He leaned in from the side, peering around the side casing and spotted the dot of light immediately, off to the right. This time the angle was different and a splash of moonlight illuminated the room just enough to see the TV with its shiny screen and the VCR with its glowing LED on the power switch.

It's the stupid VCR button, Merlin thought, feeling every

bit the fool. He swallowed hard, trying to get his confidence back, then tried the front door, an old wooden one with a large rectangular pane of glass set in it, like it was a kitchen door. It was locked, a dead bolt, offering no hope of busting in quietly.

Then he went around back, walking silently on dead grass, looking into the dark woods for any sign of activity. The backyard was a mess: an old car on cinder blocks, some building materials, and a couple of industrial-size trash cans overflowing with newspapers were easy to identify in the moonlight. Each of the families had its own tiny back porch, just big enough for a single lawn chair. Merlin climbed the three steps to Jake's and tried the kitchen door, the twin of the one in front, and Merlin decided they must have been bought at a two-for-one sale at Busy Beaver.

This door was poorly hung, the latch fitting loosely in the strike plate, giving a quarter-inch of play.

Merlin jiggled the door quietly and tried to force it open. A single kick above the handle would splinter the cheap pine. It also would shatter the glass and summon the neighbors.

He sized up the doorway, examining it carefully, looking for any sign of weakness. Then he turned sideways, scrunching himself into the doorway, his right shoulder up against the door, his shoulder blade tight against the hinge-side jamb. Lifting his right foot he pushed mightily against the opposite jamb, trying to push the wood apart, stretching the frame and allowing the latch to have more and more play. But the doorway was too narrow, and his leg was bent at such an awkward angle he couldn't generate any force.

Merlin stood in front of the door and tried to think like Harry Houdini, devising an elaborate escape, knowing he could beat it. In a creative burst of inspiration he gathered some cinder blocks and bricks from the yard and fashioned a small wall in the doorway, flush against the door and the hinge-side jamb. When completed it was about three feet high and there was eight inches of space between the stacked-up cinder blocks and the latch-size jamb. Then he went back to his car and got his jack out of the trunk.

It was to be a Rube Goldberg setup for sure. The jack was turned sideways and placed in the eight-inch gap. Slowly it was opened until it wedged tightly between one edge of the masonry wall and the door jamb just below the lock. It grabbed the soft pine and cut into it with a crunching noise. Merlin kept working the lever, opening the jack wider and wider, the wood creaking as it gradually bowed out.

Finally the door came loose and squeaked opened several inches. Merlin whispered, "Ta daa!" to himself as he dismantled the masonry wall, flipping the bricks and blocks silently to the soft ground below, leaving the jack on the top step so it would not be forgotten.

He entered the kitchen and before he snapped on his flashlight he could smell the coffee from dinner. An oval table sat to one side of the tiny room, and dishes were stacked in the sink.

This felt entirely different from exploring Tory's house with Mrs. Kincaid. No tour guide came with this one, familiar with everything, walking into each room saying, "Here's the bedroom." This was enemy territory, and for all he knew Jake was waiting for him in a shadow, smoking a cigarette.

The kitchen opened into a dining room. Thick curtains draped the windows, making it almost pitch black; Merlin had to use his penlight. There wasn't much to see—a heavily lacquered table with seating for four, sideboard, and prints on the wall. Merlin quickly opened and closed the empty drawers on the sideboard.

There was a narrow hallway with a long, skinny rug leading to the living room. Merlin started slowly down the hallway, stopping and holding his breath every time the floorboards creaked beneath his feet or the furnace made a noise.

The living room felt crowded. It was a good-sized room, but too much was haphazardly thrown into it. Thin wall-to-wall carpeting, light green walls filled with cheap artwork, and a seven-foot ceiling with a large four-blade fan hanging down over the couch completed the decor. He shone the flashlight about, first on the couch with the throw pillows and the loosely knitted afghan draped over the back, then the big TV and VCR across the room on a flimsy metal stand, a couple of easy chairs, and a wooden coffee table layered thick with newspapers, magazines, and paperback books.

Merlin came closer to the table. One book looked familiar, and he picked it up. As soon as he touched it, felt the smooth leather, he could feel his heart booming in his throat and he felt light-headed. It was Tory's. His hands began to tremble and suddenly he felt so weak that holding the small notebook became an effort. He fumbled with the pages, clumsily thumbing through it, drooling over the flashlight held tight in his mouth, biting down hard on the little metal pocket clasp that was also the on–off switch. He found a page with his name on it, read it over and over, then ran the tip of his index finger over her precise handwriting, feeling the page like a blind man until his horrible emptiness exploded in anger. Furiously he ripped the page from the metal rings and crumpled it in a tiny ball before throwing the scrap across the room. He wiped his nose on the back of his hand and slipped the small notebook in the back pocket of his pants. ''Fuckin' asshole,'' he hissed under his breath.

Suddenly he saw the stairs, leading up from the front door. He had the evidence he needed, proof that Jake had Tory. Now he could go to the police, shove the book in Steckman's face and demand they arrest Jake Barnhouse. But Jake was secondary, now. He called out, ''Tory, you up there?'' and waited a few seconds before starting up the stairs.

Creak. The stairs were old and made awful noises that echoed in Merlin's stomach. Eleven steps in all, a sweaty half minute of one step, wait, another step, wait.

When Merlin reached the top step he heard the dog. Loud barking, right in his ear, caught him off guard. He stumbled backward, losing his balance, and fell down the stairs, screaming as he bounced, bounced, bounced and spun backward off the landing, finally coming to rest next to the front door. Protectively he held his hands over his face and rolled up into a ball waiting for the attack. The dog was still barking wildly, desperate to get at him, but the sound was coming from upstairs. The dog was either tethered or locked in a room.

Merlin groped for his flashlight, fumbling like a blind man until he found it and mounted the stairs for the second time. This time he was angry, not one step at a time, not worried about making noise, but racing up the stairs two at a time, using the rail to pull himself faster to the second floor. The dog was quiet for a moment. This time Merlin was prepared for the barrage of barking that started as soon as he hit the second floor. But the sound was coming, Merlin finally realized, from *next door,* in 616. The walls were paper thin, and he gave the wall a powerful smack with his hand and the dog stopped.

The danger in what he was doing hit him full force. He looked about frantically, feeling out of control, screamed Tory's name twice sending the dog into a wild frenzy that would not abate.

Now he moved quickly, desperate to locate Tory and get the hell out of there. There were two bedrooms on the second floor; one used as a den, with a couch, TV and desk. The other was the master bedroom. An old four-poster bed, queen-size, sat in the middle of the room, clothes slung over the two posts at the foot of the bed with two suitcases opened and filled with a tangle of clothing. Merlin dumped the suitcases and rolled them off the other side of the bed, knelt down and took a quick look under the bed with the tiny flashlight. He completed his search, wildly rummaging through the small closet full of clothes on hangers. When he was finished the room looked professionally ransacked. He almost forgot the bathroom, and before charging back down the stairs, slapped the shower curtain open, ripping it off the plastic rings.

The basement. *What about the basement?* Merlin suddenly realized he hadn't seen a door to the basement. Back through the living room, taking time to kick the coffee table over when he saw it, making a quick search of the first floor until he found a narrow door off the kitchen.

A string dangled in front of him, and he tugged on it, lighting a single sixty-watt bulb somewhere near the back of the musty basement. Merlin took the stairs slowly. Boxes and suitcases were scattered about, an old dining room table and chairs sat abandoned in the corner, and two rolled-up rugs were against one wall. Everything was covered with a powdery grime. Merlin knelt down and saw he was leaving Big Foot prints in the smooth layer of dust on the floor.

No one had been below the Barnhouse home in a while.

Now he was ready to face Steckman. Never mind that Cheswick was clearly out of the Pittsburgh Police jurisdiction. At least Steckman knew the story, and Merlin reminded himself the abduction no doubt took place at the Medical Center and the report should be filed there. Besides, Merlin was mad, pissed off at the world, and wouldn't mind getting in a fight.

Merlin drove like a crazy man, whipping around slower cars, making them swerve to get out of the way, taking the Highland Park Bridge at seventy, screeching to a halt *and* double parking right in front of the Squirrel Hill Police station.

"You again," Steckman greeted him. "Hey, Doc, don't

they have enough sick patients for you to take care of?''
He laughed at his own joke.

"You're not gonna be so cocky when you see I went
out and did your fuckin' work for you,'' Merlin said, and
slapped the small brown leather notebook on the desk.

Steckman stood up and pointed a finger at Merlin.
"Slow down, pal. Where do you come off busting in here
talking to me like that?''

"As long as you sit on your butt, Steckman. *Listen to
me!* I told you Tory Welch was missing. You didn't give
a fuck!'' Merlin screamed. "I tracked her to a house in
Cheswick. You got some paper?''

Steckman stared at Merlin, picked up a bottle of orange
soda, and took a long swig, tipping his head back so the
air bubbles exploded through the syrupy beverage. He
wiped the back of his hand across his mouth. "Look, Doc,
if you got a problem up in Cheswick, why don't you drop
in on the boys in blue up there?''

" 'Cause you know the goddamn story. And she was
probably abducted in Oakland. That's her notebook. I
found it in a house that belongs to a man who works in
the department of anatomy. She wasn't there. His name is
Jake Barnhouse.''

"Whoa! Whoa! Whoa! How the hell d'you *find* it?''

"I broke into the house, for chrissake.''

Steckman lurched forward, slamming his fists on his
desk, spilling the orange soda. "Oh shit, see what you
made me do.'' Steckman disappeared into a washroom
somewhere behind the desk and came back with some
paper towels. As he mopped up the spill, picking up sheets
of colored paper and patting them dry, he growled, "You
know what you did is a crime . . . I should fuckin' throw
your ass in jail. Shut you up. You go breaking into somebody's house—what are you, stupid?''

"Last chance, porkchop. You either get things popping
or I got public and tell KDKA how you ignored this.''

Steckman hesitated, thought things through. He was

breathing hard, almost wheezing. "Gimme the address," he said and slapped a wet piece of paper out for Merlin to write on. "What's your name again?"

"Merlin."

"Like the magician, huh? Why don't you make yourself disappear," Steckman said and laughed. Then he got serious, and his voice took on a meanness. "Let me do my work. I see you around here again I'm gonna kick your ass."

Merlin started to walk out, but turned around before reaching the door. "I mean it, porkchop. Pick up the phone."

Steckman stared Merlin down, refusing to pick up the phone until the door had closed completely.

Thirty-two

Merlin sat in his car a good long while, double parked in front of the police station, deciding what to do. Though he needed rest—at home with his own pillow—he felt drawn back to the Medical Center in a way he didn't understand. It was as if his only link to Tory were somehow through the hospital, that if Tory wanted to reach him she would first try him there. He didn't trust the police and decided to spend the night in his on-call room. Parking places were plentiful in the early-morning hours and Merlin found one less than a block from the automatic doors of the emergency room.

There were only two patients in the ER waiting room when Merlin came through the double doors. The air was stale and had that peculiar smell of blood and antiseptic, but the only thing he noticed was Big John taking a rest, parking his butt in one of the red molded plastic chairs, stretching his long legs way out in the middle of the room, like a fallen tree jutting halfway across the burnt orange carpet. Rosa, the unit secretary, chatted quietly with Big John, enjoying the hospital gossip, and looked up from her magnificent nails as Merlin burst in.

"Hey, Merlin, what are *you* doing here?" she asked, looking at her watch, careful of her wet nails.

"Just going to sleep. Seems like I live here," he said, and kept on walking toward the hallway that would take him to the elevators.

"You see that, John? That Merlin is so rude, see him

jus' keep on walking past us," Rosa said loud enough that Merlin could not help but hear.

Merlin stopped walking and smiled. "Okay, I can take a hint," he said, succumbing to the need to change subjects, relax a little. "I could use some talk. You got any pizza?" Merlin sat down next to Big John.

"It's coming," Big John answered. "By the way, what the hell were you up to before? Want me to lose my job?"

"A long story. You don't want to hear it."

Big John uncrossed his legs and recrossed them the other way. "I got all night."

"Look, it's no big deal. I was just looking for Tory," Merlin said, minimizing the situation. "I ran into Olsen; he let me in."

"You find her?"

"Not yet."

"What the hell's going on up there? People coming and going. First you call me, then I see Olsen leaving. *Then* I'm making my rounds in the medical school and I see that guy from up there, you know, dude does all the shit to the bodies."

Marlin sat up straight, putting his hands on the sides of the chair, ready to spring himself out. "Who? You mean Jake?"

"Yeah, that's the guy."

"You sure it was Jake?"

"No, it was your mother. How long I been working here? Longer than you, that's how long," Big John said.

"Where'd you see him?"

"Outside. I walked some nurses to the parking garage and I stopped for a smoke. He was backing his car down to the loading dock."

"The loading dock. He see you?"

"Nah. I was on the sidewalk."

"How long ago?"

Big John looked at his watch. "How long I been talking with you, Rosa?"

"I dunno, maybe ten minutes," Rosa said, looking at her watch again.

Merlin grabbed Big John's arm. "This is it! He's still here! John, you've got to help me." Merlin started to talk quickly, little choppy phrases, his mind racing three sentences in front of his mouth. "Tory's been kidnapped. She must've found something. And—look, you just gotta believe me—I tracked her to Jake's house, and then I broke in, and I found some of her stuff there. He's got her someplace, man. We've got to go up there. Now, before he leaves."

Rosa sat quietly, ignoring her nails for the first time. Big John sat up. "This for real, Merlin?"

"Of course it's for real. John, please believe me. If I'm bullshitting you, you can kick my butt across Fifth Avenue."

"Don't be fucking with me, Merlin," Big John said, lumbering to his feet. Not for a second did he even consider telling Rosa to call the cops. This was his turf and he was the law.

Merlin ran out of the ER, his running shoes squeaking off the polished floor as he raced down the hall toward the elevators. Big John did his big-man trot, holding his gun down to his side with one hand to keep it from flapping, and by the time he stepped into the cab, Merlin was holding the door, telling him to hurry up.

The ride seemed to take forever. Merlin gave Big John a quick review of the last few days, and by the time the doors opened on nine, Big John had his service revolver drawn. Merlin noticed how puny it looked in Big John's huge mitts.

The hallway looked pretty much the same as Merlin had left it earlier. It was quiet—no sign of Jake Barnhouse. The doors to the anatomy lab were closed but the slit of space between the doors was bright with light. Merlin put his index finger to his pursed lips as he pulled one of the doors open just wide enough to scan the large room. The rows of tables, each with its yellow tarp, were exactly the way Merlin had last seen them, but the lights were on in Jake's office. Voices could be heard, a conversation off in the distance, maybe from Jake's office, but too far away to be understood. One of the voices was female, Merlin was sure of that, and with it came a rush of disappointment as Merlin quickly realized it wasn't Tory's. "He's with someone," Merlin whispered. "Did you see anyone else?"

Big John shook his head.

After several seconds of listening Merlin changed plans. In the elevator Merlin had every intention of rushing into the anatomy lab, catching Jake by surprise, maybe pinning him to the wall, and forcing him to tell where Tory was. But Jake wasn't alone, and everything seemed different. Merlin pulled the door open wide enough for the two of them to slip through, and they silently made their way into the room, walking all crouched over, zigzagging a path to a spot some thirty feet from Jake's office where they'd have a good view from behind one of the dissection tables. With simple hand signals, Merlin motioned to Big John to get down low, and they ended up kneeling on the floor, peering through all the long, skinny table legs, getting a limited view of Jake's office, while listening to the voices.

". . . that kid's body shoulda been carved up beyond recognition by now."

"That's great, Jake. You're just a woulda, coulda, shoulda kind of guy. Face it, you blew it," a woman's voice said with a tone of disgust.

"Forget it, will ya? We got enough stashed away we can go someplace—anyplace—disappear forever."

"You sure Antony is the only one who knew you're the guy?"

"I'm not answering that stupid question again, Rita. Ask it again and I'll give you the back of my hand."

"Rita," Merlin mouthed the name. "Holy shit," he whispered and exchanged glances with Big John.

"You better hope so, Jake. If that girl could find us,

another one of Bevel's guys will be back. Then we'll really disappear forever."

"We gotta get going," Jake said.

"How many times you call Antony?"

"I called enough."

"Doesn't it scare you Antony disappeared?" Rita asked.

"Forget it!" Jake said, his voice raised.

"Maybe before they killed him he talked. Told 'em who you are."

"Shut up, Rita! Couple of suitcases and we're outta here."

"What about the girl?"

"I told you, I'll take care of it."

Beep-beep-beep. Beep-beep-beep. Beep-beep-beep. Merlin grabbed at his beeper, clamping his hand over the small speaker, frantic to quiet it, but the damage was done.

"Jake! Someone's out there!"

Jake and Rita ran from the office, saw Merlin and Big John coming at them from behind the table in the middle of the room, and dashed out of the anatomy lab. It took Merlin only two or three seconds to reach the door, just as it closed completely, and he hit it hard, trying to run right through it, bouncing it off the wall so it snapped back in Big John's face. Big John stumbled, and as he regained his balance, Merlin hesitated momentarily in the hallway. First he looked to the right toward the locked door to the hospital and then to the left, only to see Jake and Rita disappear into a stairwell near Olsen's office.

"C'mon," Merlin yelled as he took off down the hallway and gave chase to Jake and Rita, racing down two flights of stairs and out onto the seventh floor. Jake was now at the opposite end of a long hallway, past the amphitheaters and classrooms, desperately trying to open the metal fire door to get back in the hospital. Rita stood behind Jake, shaking her hands in front of her, looking back at Merlin and Big John as they ran toward them, screaming at Jake to open the door.

"They're all locked. Forget it." Big John gasped between breaths, slowing down. "Stop what you're doing. I wanna be able to see your hands."

Jake turned around to face Merlin, his face a mask of anger.

Merlin walked right up to Jake and grabbed him in a choke hold, screaming in his face, "Where is she? Where the hell is Tory?"

Jake's face was red, and his eyes bugged out as he tried to peel Merlin's hands from his neck, but the death grip was too tight.

"Merlin, let him go, he can't tell us anything if you kill him," Big John said forcefully, yanking Merlin away from Jake, leaving him leaning against the door, sucking air noisily.

"I'm gonna kill him."

"Cool down, Merlin," Big John said angrily and looked around for someplace to stow his prisoners and protect them from Merlin. "All right, you two, in there," Big John said, motioning Jake and Rita with his gun into the surgical amphitheater, a small twelve-seat viewing area atop the only operating room not physically located in the Medical Center. This OR actually jutted into the medical school from the contiguous hospital, allowing interesting surgical procedures to be scheduled for viewing and teaching purposes.

"Cuff 'em, John! Goddamnit, put the cuffs on 'em!" Merlin screamed, following Big John through the door. "Where is she, Jake? I heard you. You got her."

The room felt tight. Twelve movie-theater type seats were arranged in a semicircle around a glass bubble looking down into a dark operating room. A curved wooden banister ran the perimeter of the glass, permitting those excited spectators something to grab onto when things below really got going. Big John took out a pair of police-issue handcuffs and first cuffed Jake's left hand, then slipped them around the banister before clamping the other bracelet to Rita's right hand.

"I don't know what the hell you're talking about," Jake said, breathing hard.

"Don't play dumb with us. I heard you in there. We both did. I've been to your house on Sterling Road, and the police have Tory's notebook. *I know you've got her.*"

Jake looked at Merlin with angry eyes. "The only thing in my house is your fingerprints, Merlin."

Merlin stepped forward and punched Jake in the stomach, then stayed right in his face, "I'll dig out your eyes with my fingers if you hurt her."

Jake spit right in Merlin's face, then pushed him away with his free hand. "Fuck you. You've got nothing."

Big John inserted himself between Jake and Merlin.

"I've got you and your lady, and right now I'm happy to mess you both up." Then, turning to Rita, "So you're in this, too. It's all making sense. Did he hurt Tory?"

"She don't know anything. Keep your yap shut, Rita."

Rita said nothing.

"Answer me. Did he hurt her?"

Big John said, "Merlin, now we gotta call the cops."

"No," Merlin shouted. "You heard him up there. He said he's taking care of Tory. We don't have the time for the cops. This is you'n me."

Beep-beep-beep. Beep-beep-beep. Beep-beep-beep. Merlin's beeper went off for the second time. "Dr. Merlin, call extension four-three-one-one. Call four-three-one-one."

"Shit, *shit, shit*!! How the hell do they know I'm even here?"

"Merlin, make the call. They're not going anywhere. Cool down, man," Big John said.

Big John holstered his gun and sat down in a seat not far from where he'd cuffed Jake and Rita.

Merlin went to a wall-mounted house phone and dialed the extension. He looked back at Jake as he waited for an answer. "Yeah, it's Merlin . . . no haven't had a chance . . . yeah, I know . . . where's the pain? . . . I was just on my way up . . . right away."

Merlin hung up and came back and sat next to Big John. "I'll be gone ten minutes. Fifteen, max."

"Where you going, Merlin?" Big John asked.

"I need to clear my head, check on something. Look, do me a favor. Check the anatomy lab, see what's in the office. I'll meet you back there. And please, man, don't call the cops."

"I don't know, Merlin," Big John said, getting to his feet. "You're scaring me a little."

Merlin smiled, the first happy moment since Tory had been missing, and as far as he was concerned the momentum had shifted.

Merlin didn't get back to the anatomy lab for almost a half hour and found Big John looking through some boxes on the desk in Jake's office. On their way back down to the seventh floor he and Big John talked, went over everything, and Merlin convinced him that letting Jake and Rita stew for a while was the healthiest thing for them.

When Merlin and Big John walked back into the surgical amphitheater Jake stopped his whispering.

"Let's talk turkey," Merlin said with a cocky tone.

"You're the turkey, Merlin. I don't know what you want from me, but as far as I'm concerned you can piss down Big John's throat for all I care. *Call the fuckin' cops.* I'm done talking to you."

"Jake, how's this sound? You're not leaving this room until you tell me. That's final."

"Then you better order takeout."

Merlin walked up to Jake, close enough to smell his breath, and said, "I'm a desperate fucker right now. If I have to kill you, I'll do it."

"You don't scare me, Merlin. You just can't do it. And if you had the balls, it wouldn't help you a lick."

"I kill you, Jake, and Rita's a babbling idiot. I'll have Tory in twenty minutes."

"Borrow his gun, Merlin. Go ahead, put it in my mouth and pull the trigger. Put up or shut up. But when your friend here calls the *real* cops, Rita'll be on her way home and you'll be wearing the cuffs."

"Let's call the cops. Things are gonna get out of hand," Big John said.

Jake said, "Kill me. Shoot me. Do it, Merlin. Do it. She doesn't know crap, Merlin."

"So it's a puzzle. I can't kill you, but I gotta find a way to loosen your tongue." Merlin stared hard at Jake for almost a minute. "All right. No more chances. You stay here. I'm taking Rita downstairs," Merlin said pointing to the glass viewing bubble. "And I'm gonna operate on her. See if she's as pretty on the inside as she is on the outside."

Rita let out a little gasp. "Oh, my God. Jake, maybe—"

"Shut up, Rita. You really think Merlin's gonna operate on you? You nuts? He's a bluffing pile of shit."

Merlin spoke calmly, in a voice as smooth as single malt Scotch going down. "No, I'm not. I'll keep it simple, something I can cover. Maybe pop out her gallbladder. Or her appendix. Yeah," Merlin said, smiling, pleased with his sudden inspiration. "I'll do her appendix."

"Bullshit. You'll be in jail when the path report comes back," Jake countered.

"No, it's too easy. Before I lop it off, I'll roll it between my fingers for a couple of minutes," Merlin said, making a pill-rolling motion with his thumb and fingers. "That sucker'll be so angry it'll plump up all red and swollen, like one of those little cocktail weenies. Not even your buddy Olsen will be able to tell it's not infected. And as soon as I'm done with her, I do you."

"Big deal," Jake said, sounding unimpressed.

"One more thing, Jake. And you listen, too, Rita. This is the show stopper, maybe give you a case of the runs

when you hear it. It'll be *one*-drug anesthesia. Forget the
Pentothal to put Rita to sleep. And screw the fentanyl to
numb the pain. One fucking drug. And you know what
that is, Jake: pancuronium bromide. The good stuff. Same
shit you tried to peddle to Tory. Tell Rita all about it.
Payback's a bitch, isn't it?''

"Fuck you!" Jake said, his voice quiet for the first time,
confused what Merlin was talking about.

Merlin turned to Rita. "What's your worst fear, Rita?
What really scares you? Death? Blindness? Huh? What
makes your sphincters tighten up? Let me tell you about
something you didn't learn in secretary school. Pancuronium bromide's one powerful little drug. It'll paralyze
every muscle in your body.'' Merlin spoke slowly, drawing out the words. "You won't be able to move anything.
Blinking your eyes, moving your fingers, screaming . . .
all impossible. But you're gonna feel everything. Nothing
to block the pain. Every cut of the scalpel. The electric
jolt of the Bovie. Imagine the pain.''

A look of terror crossed Rita's face. Her mouth hung
open and her eyes didn't seem to focus. As the blood
drained from her face she started to look like one of
Jake's cadavers.

Merlin was getting to her. "Cold, sharp steel, sliding
across your belly, cutting down deep, through the skin and
the muscles, opening you up as easily as pulling a zipper.
Imagine what that will feel like without anesthesia. What
do you think, Rita, what does a scream sound like in
your mind?''

"Jake, tell him," Rita pleaded, grabbing Jake's shirt,
clawing at him.

"He's bluffing.''

Big John put his hand on Merlin's shoulder. "Hey, Merlin, no way, man! I can't let you do this.''

"You talk to Jake, then. Go ahead, John. Tell *him* you
can't let him do what he's done to Tory. Time's running

out. You want to have a tea party with these assholes, or you got some better idea?"

"I don't know, man."

"I know, John. *I know.* This is it. Our last chance. Let's not kick ourselves the rest of our lives while the criminal justice system makes celebrities out of them!"

Rita screamed, "Jake, it's over! Tell him, please, Jake. Ohhhh, baby, you gotta know it's over. I don't care. Don't let him do it to me. Jake. *Jake!!!!*"

"Uncuff her, John."

"No, Merlin!" Big John said firmly.

"Listen to me, John," Merlin said, facing Big John, going chest to chest with him, grabbing as much of one of Big John's massive biceps as he could. "I'm giving you an order. *Undo her and bring her downstairs. Now!*" Merlin said as he stepped back, several feet from Big John, and pointed the pistol at him.

Rita gasped.

Big John did a double take, then slapped his hand at his empty holster. "Gimme my gun, Merlin."

Jake's jaw dropped open and he felt faint.

"Merlin! Don't do this. This is wrong," Big John said.

Merlin said, "Screw what's right or wrong. There can only be one person in charge. This is gonna happen."

Big John shook his head violently. "Okay, Merlin, goddamnit. You win. But, shit man, *you* shoulder the responsibility."

"That's why I took your gun. You're free and clear. All you gotta do is follow orders. Now take her cuff off."

"*No.* Jake, please, Jake. Help me. *Help me.* Tell him where she is."

As Big John uncuffed Rita and snapped the cuff around Jake's other hand, leaving him shackled to the banister, Merlin said, "Relax for a while, Jake, old boy. It'll be about a half hour. I gotta get an OR team, fill out the paperwork, make it look good. I'll let you know before I make the first cut."

Merlin hustled Rita toward the door. Big John took her by the arm and began to pull her out of the room. Rita was out of control, kicking and clawing at Big John, screaming at Jake, yelling obscenities. Then she managed to grab onto one of the seats, digging her nails into the back of the chair like a frightened cat. Big John kept pulling. Finally, as her grip slipped, one of her nails caught on something and pulled away from her finger and she howled in pain.

Merlin stood by the door, about to let it close, and looked back at Jake. Rita's screams could be heard as she was dragged down the hallway.

"You know if she's got real insurance? Or some HMO crap that's not gonna pay me without prior authorization."

"Fuck you, Merlin."

"Don't forget, you're next."

When the lights in the operating room finally went on, Jake was leaning against the observation bubble, sitting awkwardly on the hand railing, lost in thought. He jumped, startled by the bright lights. Then he looked down and saw Merlin looking up at him, glaring at him over his mask. *He's crazy. He's going through with it.*

The OR was alive with activity. Rita was wheeled in on a stretcher, her naked body covered by a white sheet, her hair up in a paper cap that looked like something she might wear in the shower. Merlin waved to Jake, acting silly, making rabbit ears on the anesthesiologist as he orchestrated transferring Rita to the narrow operating table. Then things happened quickly. Small green tables, covered with neat rows of instruments were swiftly wheeled around Rita while the anesthesiologist intubated her.

Jake watched intently.

"Can you hear me, Jake?"

Jake looked around, surprised to hear Merlin's voice.

"The speaker behind you, Jake. See it?" Merlin asked. "We're all ready down here. I want to make sure you've got a good view. If anyone gets in the way, you bang your head on the glass and let me know. Rita's been paralyzed, too bad we can't get you down here, you could slip her a quick six. Christ, you could do anything you want to her. You ever tickle her uvula?''

"She's ready, Merlin,'' the anesthesiologist said.

"Enough sex talk. I gotta get to work, Jake. Nurse, please adjust the light so Mr. Barnhouse can see.'' Merlin waited. "Good. I'm going to make the incision at McBurney's point,'' Merlin said, and placed the scalpel against Rita's skin, just above her right hip. He drew the blade in a straight line, almost three inches long, opening the white skin, tiny dots of blood appearing behind the blade.

Rita did not move.

"Watch this, Jake. Bovie, please.'' Merlin accepted the electric wand from the scrub nurse and zapped each of the bleeding arteries and cauterized them.

Jake was sweating profusely, white-knuckling the banister, trying to rip it from the wall, but not for a second taking his eyes off the Emerald City below. At times he screamed and pulled at the handcuffs until they cut into him and his wrists began to bleed, but Merlin never noticed.

As the surgery proceeded, Merlin paid close attention to his work, his head down, watching as his fingers spread the abdominal muscles, occasionally using the Bovie. At last he exposed the peritoneum, the thin, Saran Wrap-like membrane that tightly enclosed the various organs of the abdominal cavity. After the skin, fat, and muscle layers, the peritoneum was the final barrier, like tissue paper inside a gift wrapped box.

"Well, what do you know! Jake!! This appendix is normal. I was wrong, there *is* nothing the matter with it. What a terrible misdiagnosis. Oh, well. Let me just . . . Hey Jake, where the hell are you. You still with me, or what? *Jaaaaaake,*'' Merlin yelled, like a mother calling her kid to dinner. "There you are—thought I lost you. Look. Here it is."

Merlin held up the appendix, three inches long, thick as his thumb, red as cherry Jell-O.

Merlin began the process of sewing Rita back together, again going layer by layer, starting with the peritoneum and finishing ten minutes later with the skin.

As the anesthesiologist extubated Rita, and the green tables with the bloody instruments were whisked away, Merlin asked one final time, "Okay, Jake, you're next unless you tell me where she is."

Jake heard a clicking noise above his head and looked up to see a microphone. "Next door," he said in a thick voice, "You were there. On the other side of my house. I didn't touch her."

By now Merlin was standing next to Rita, removing the multilayered green drapes. When he was down to the final one he said, "Now for the big finish," and reached across his body with his right hand and pulled the drape off with a magician's touch. The bright lights lit up the young girl's body brilliantly, showing off her pert young breasts and her sexy pair of lacy underwear.

It was Robin Winters.

"Ta-daa," Merlin said triumphantly, taking a bow as Jake became dizzy and lost consciousness, sliding down the bubble, smearing a trail of saliva on the glass like a slug. Jake was left dangling from the wooden banister by his bloody wrists.

Merlin was out the door in an instant, running past the lounge where Big John was holding Rita under house arrest, and raced to his car, which was still parked close to the ER.

Thirty-three

While Merlin was driving his car out of Oakland, Eddie and Mike, a couple of cops, drank coffee out in front of Jake's house on Sterling Road and got their fingers sticky from eating chocolate doughnuts. They passed the hours talking about hunting.

It had been a good long while since they walked around Jake's house and found the busted back door. They had even ventured inside—after ringing the bell for almost a minute—and found the house exactly the way Steckman had described it to their sergeant. Ransacked. But without anyone home Eddie and Mike eventually returned to the car and their supply of doughnuts. They knew to stay put, and check in every couple of hours. Mike put his seat back as far as it would go and leaned back, closing his eyes, trying to get some rest as he listened to Eddie ramble on. Eddie could go on about this or that for hours and Mike could pretend he was listening just as long.

Merlin ran every light he could, blasting his horn and flying through the intersections, pushing the speed. Driving like a cabby, he was either stepping on the gas to go faster or hitting the brake hard to avoid an accident. There was no in-between. His car flew up the ramp to the Highland Park Bridge way too fast, scraping paint off his door on the Jersey wall in a shower of sparks, not slowing down but going all out across the Allegheny River. He drove north up Route 28 toward Cheswick, checking his rearview mirror, looking at the speedometer, trying to push it past a hundred.

By the time he thundered onto Sterling Road he'd cut his speed in half, but this was the most difficult driving. His car bounced violently in the potholes, and he had to grip the steering wheel tightly to maintain control.

Now Eddie and Mike were both leaning back, resting their eyes just a little as they watched out for Jake Barnhouse. Suddenly Merlin drove right up on the lawn, slammed on the brakes and did a little fishtail. He was running up toward the house before Eddie realized what was happening.

"Holy shit, here's the guy," Eddie said, giving Mike an elbow to the ribs.

Mike sat up, spilled the lukewarm coffee he was balancing on his thigh and seemed more concerned with grabbing a handful of napkins than watching the house.

Eddie watched Merlin go not to 618, but to 616.

Mike looked up and saw Merlin at the wrong door. "Oh great, that's the neighbor. See what you did?" Mike said, turning his attention back to his pants.

Merlin tried the doorknob to 616, shaking the door hard, and when it didn't open immediately, he took one step back—not giving a damn if he woke the whole world—and kicked it, right above the knob, splintering the jamb. The door swung open violently shattering the single pane of glass into a thousand shards.

"Tory!" Merlin yelled as he stepped inside, making a crunching noise on the broken glass. Merlin was without his little flashlight, and he fumbled in the dark rather than go back to the car for it. There were two light switches at the bottom of the stairs and he flicked at both of them. A light above his head and another at the top of the stairs went on. Then the dog started to bark upstairs. He'd completely forgotten about the dog and it startled him, sending him backward a few steps into a wall. The barking was loud, and Merlin watched the stairs as his eyes adjusted, but the dog remained out of sight.

There should have been no doubt where Tory was and why the barking canine stayed upstairs, but when it came to dogs Merlin's thinking was shaped by a deep fear that ran like ice water through his body. First he decided to search the downstairs. The living room was empty, so was the dining room, and his feet echoed off the hardwood floor as he raced back to the kitchen, found the light switch, and saw it, too, had been cleaned out.

Then he had no choice but to go upstairs and face the dog. He walked back through the several rooms slowly, thinking about the dog, swallowing hard, his legs all rubbery, looking for some kind of weapon. Then he spotted one. A broom, leaning against the banister. Not a big heavy broom but a cheap one with short shiny plastic bristles attached to a skinny yellow handle. The kind of broom his grandmother used for sweeping up crumbs from the kitchen floor. But that was all Merlin could find, and he took it with him as he started up the stairs, holding it down near the bristles, the skinny handle sticking up in the air like a wimpy club.

He took the steps one by one, creating huge shadows as he blocked the light from below. The air reeked of urine. Each step he took drove the dog crazy; the barking became ferocious.

While Eddie got his shotgun from the trunk, Mike talked to his sergeant. "Sarge, listen to me. It can't be Barnhouse. He went into the wrong house *and* he kicked in the door. It don't seem like no burglary either, the way he just went up to the door and kicked it in. You want us to go in?"

The sergeant asked him a few more questions, finally instructing Mike to take up positions in front and back and wait for backup before going inside.

Merlin saw the dog for the first time when he got to the top of the stairs and he grabbed the rail to keep from falling. All he could see was the head, the long black ugly snout bouncing around, pulling against something, trying to get loose. Every few seconds it poked out of the doorway from what would be the second bedroom if the layout was anything like its twin next door. It looked big, maybe a Doberman, foaming and dripping a puddle of goo, and Merlin silently prayed whatever was holding it back wouldn't let go. The noise was deafening, bouncing around the narrow hallway, no carpet on the floor. Merlin pressed up to the wall dividing the two halves of the house and looked into the first bedroom—the master bedroom. It was empty; that was obvious even with the dim wash of light from the hall. He moved slowly toward the second bedroom. Merlin held the broom with two hands out in front of him like a Samurai, sliding his back along the wall.

The dog was much bigger than he thought—no loose skin, just a tight package of muscle straining violently against a heavy rope clipped to a thick chain around its neck. Merlin looked into the room, past the dog, and followed the rope to a radiator in front of the window. And then Merlin could see her sitting in a heavy wooden chair, off to the side, facing away from him, ropes binding her to the chair, a gag tied around her head. "Tory, is that you?" When she turned her head to profile, nodding her head quickly, he could tell. "You okay?" Again she nodded.

There was no way to get past the dog. It pulled at the rope, scratching its claws on the floor, going up on its hind legs, barking wildly, then dropping back on all fours for a second, back again on its hind legs, the length of rope holding tight.

Merlin had seen the results of dog attacks in the ER. The sight was worse than a burn victim. The head and neck always seemed to be involved. He debated leaving, calling the police and letting them shoot the dog, but that might upset the balance. As terrified as he was of this animal he was more frightened that it would turn on Tory.

Merlin watched the dog going up and down on its hind legs and saw a rhythm developing. As the dog went down on all fours Merlin went up on the balls of his feet, getting ready. Then the dog went back up on its hind legs. Merlin timed it right. At exactly the moment when the rope became taut, limiting any forward movement of the animal, Merlin kicked his right foot up at the dog like a place kicker, getting it good on the side of the neck, making it stumble backward for a second. It recovered quickly and went into a vicious frenzy. This dog wasn't going down. It was coming back, getting madder.

Tory was so close, not a dozen feet away, wearing the same blazer as she had on the last time he'd seen her, but Merlin dared not look away from the dog.

Merlin flipped the broom around, the bristles behind him now, toward the wall, his hands wide apart for control, a soldier brandishing a gun with a bayonet. There was no way to do it without getting closer. It was all timing. He stood like a statue, fixing the tip of the handle an inch from the dog's snout. Again and again the dog came at him, up on his hind legs, shaking his head. Merlin waited. The barking was deafening. Saliva sprayed from the dog's mouth as it gnashed and growled and showed off its back teeth. Each time the dog went up on its hind legs there was a moment when the rope seemed to tug the neck back and the animal was off balance. Merlin watched the rhythm, up and down, up and down. Then he too began to sway, forward and back, just slightly, getting into the rhythm, coming forward at the hips, imperceptibly, as the dog went up and the rope tugged. Carefully, Merlin kept the tip of the broom handle as close to the dog's snout as possible.

Up and down.

Forward and back.

Merlin was a coiled spring, waiting to release. Again, he timed it perfectly. NOW!! He thrust the end of the broom directly at the open mouth, the handle hitting its mark squarely, meeting no resistance, pushing past the pharynx and down the esophagus in one swift, forceful motion. The broom went straight down, like a sword in its sheath, and the dog made a horrible gagging noise, turning its head sharply to the left. The straight-line course was interrupted and the tip of the handle went ripping throught the wall of his esophagus just at the point where it connected with the stomach.

Merlin let go. The dog went down, making desperate noises, rolling on its side, using both front paws to scratch at the long broom handle. It did not budge. Blood leaked out of the dog's mouth and puddled on the floor.

It was finally quiet.

Merlin stepped over the animal, still wary of it, watching it take its last few breaths.

"You okay?" he asked and hugged Tory from behind.

He untied the gag. "Oh Merlin, I knew you would come," Tory said and began to cry.

Merlin came around and kissed her and began to loosen the ropes.

"Hold it right there, goddamnit!" Eddie yelled as he jumped into the room and aimed his shotgun at Merlin.

Merlin stood up, stepped away from Tory and put his hands in the air.

"Don't shoot!" Tory screamed. "Just listen to me!" Tory wriggled free of her bonds and stood up, a little wobbly, and reached out for Merlin. "Put your gun away. This isn't Barnhouse."

Tory then rolled into Merlin's arms and hugged him until the two of them seemed like one, swaying gently with each other, until finally Eddie put his gun down. The other officers arrived and they stood there watching Merlin and Tory hold each other like there was no tomorrow.

Epilogue

October 2, 1996

"How're you feeling, Robin?" Merlin asked, walking into Robin Winters's room. She was watching late-afternoon television.

"It only hurts under the bandage," Robin said, looking at Merlin but checking the TV frequently.

"Let me take a look. Maybe we'll get you home later today. Where's your mom?"

"She stayed in my dorm room. I'm going home for a few days."

"That's a good idea."

"One of the nurses said you got my appendix just in time. That it almost burst."

"I'm glad it's over with for you." Merlin sat on the bed.

"So I guess you're sorta famous now."

Just then Sandy Keller appeared on the TV. Sandy sat at a news desk and talked quickly. "Another busy day in what has been dubbed the 'Gross Anatomy Murders.'

"Multiple indictments were handed down today for the murdres of Kevin Hoover and Michael Demasi. Among those indicated were Frank Bevel and his nephew Anthony Bevelini.

"Also in the news was Tory Welch, who returned to work at the DA's office for the first time since her kidnapping. In a stunning move, the district attorney announced that Ms. Welch would serve on the team that will prosecute Jake Barnhouse. This shocked many court watchers because Ms. Welch has been with the DA's office only a year, and she was held captive by the very man she will help prosecute.

"But our top story tonight is Jake Barnhouse—back at the Medical Center, but this time as a patient. Mr. Barnhouse has apparently developed an infection on his right wrist. He sustained a cut from a pair of handcuffs put on too tightly the night of his arrest. Earlier today guards at the jail noted pus draining from his wrist.

"Almost an hour ago Mr. Barnhouse arrived at the Medical Center for antibiotic treatment and has already been discharged from the emergency room.

"Later in the broadcast we'll go live to the Pittsburgh University Medical Center for an update on Mr. Barnhouse's condition with Chief Resident Martin Wheeler . . ."

Sandy put her usual twist on the news, but somehow it seemed reassuring. The Pittsburgh mob was out of commission but a minor wound infection was what Sandy wanted us to care about.

Merlin listened to Sandy as he changed Robin's bandages, smiled, and shook his head. For the first time in several days Merlin's name didn't make the five o'clock lead-in. Things were getting back to normal.